Hang On

by Nell Gavin

Edited by Lynn O'Dell
ISBN-13:
978-1475023213

ISBN-10:
1475023219

Acknowledgments

Many thanks to Ian Thorpe for coaching me in British-isms, to Karl Kuenning and Dave B. at http://www.roadie.net, who graciously answered questions, Sandy Sandifer who was my "roadie on call," and Klaus Weiland, who prodded me (between verbal sparring and musical riffs) to keep writing. Thanks to Kristen Stappenbeck-Baker and Amy Pointer for being my beta readers, Sugar Blue for being my Best Top Friend, Dona Carter for being ceaselessly wonderful, Peg McCarthy for being a great sister, and to my husband and sons.

Chapter 1

February, 1958

On bad days, Mommy stretched out on the sofa, wrapped herself in blankets and didn't speak. Her eyes were strange and unfocused, and her voice was distant whenever I prodded her to respond to a question. Her answers sometimes didn't make any sense, or she let them drift off and fade away, unfinished. Sometimes she told me to leave her alone and go find something to do. I would obediently turn on the television, and watch it for hours. Mommy listened to the radio or slept, and let me play by myself, find food for myself, fend for myself. It had always been like that, with her intermittent "bad days."

Since I couldn't read yet, and Mommy didn't like to read to me on bad days, I would tell her stories, making them up to go along with the pictures in my Golden Books, which I held in my lap while sitting in the crook of Mommy's limp arm. I always pulled her arm around me in a kind of a hug. Sometimes I made her tea with cold tap water and a tea bag. When I would offer her the cup, she would take a sip and smile, then place it on the table and forget about it.

I would try other things to entice Mommy to notice me on bad days. I played my red 78 rpm record, "Tina the Ballerina," and twirled and danced to it in front of her. I sang the songs I'd learned from children's programs on television. Or I drew her pictures, which I would tape to the refrigerator myself after Mommy absently told me they were "good."

1

Mommy would occasionally lift herself up to go to the bathroom, then would patter barefoot into the kitchen and open the refrigerator. She might grab a piece of fruit or a few slices of bread, or merely shut the refrigerator door again, seemingly preferring hunger to the effort involved in food preparation, or even in making a decision on what to eat. Then she would get herself a glass of water from the faucet before settling back on the sofa.

Sometimes the effort of getting up for fresh water was too much, and Mommy would drink my stale tea, still waiting for her on the table. Whenever she did, I was very proud.

Mommy had had one bad day after another for a long time before she went away. Just before she left, she'd stopped changing her clothing or combing her hair. She stopped giving me baths as well. When I would speak to her, she'd stare back as if she didn't know who I was. Other times, she'd run her fingers down my cheek, then let them fall as if it all required too much strength.

I lived on grape jelly sandwiches and water on most bad days. I made the sandwiches myself, leaving trails of sticky jelly that eventually hardened into a kind of cement on the countertop, the table or the floor, creating a feast for the cockroaches. For a treat, I would pull a kitchen chair over to the counter, climb up, and help myself to handfuls of sugar from the canister on the shelf. Mommy never said anything about that. Sometimes I'd pull a carrot from the refrigerator—they had long white hairs growing from them the last time I got one, and were kind of floppy and limp—or I would find an orange and saw it in half with a steak knife, then suck on it.

The last summer I spent with Mommy, she had a friend, Jack, who came to see us. He took us to the movies and the beach, and took Mommy out to eat and dance while I stayed with the babysitter, Trudy.

Mommy had lots of good days that summer when she sang, lifted me up in the air, or tickled me. She took me to the park where she pushed me on the swing. She told me stories and fussed over my hair, twisting it into curls and setting it with bobby pins after my evening bath so I could look like Shirley Temple in the morning. I liked Shirley Temple movies a lot back then. Mommy talked and talked, sometimes about things I didn't understand that involved my Daddy, whom I didn't remember ever meeting. Sometimes she talked about Jack. She told me about the places the three of us would visit someday, and the house we would live in with a swing set in the yard. Mommy and I went shopping for pretty clothes so we could look our best for Jack. We made Rice Krispies treats together, and

Mommy cooked for us, day after day, one wonderful dinner after another, with vegetables and dessert. Sometimes Jack ate with us and later read me bedtime stories.

On warm sunny days, Mommy often threw open the windows. The two of us stuck our hands into buckets of soapy water and scrubbed down the kitchen and appliances, then polished all the furniture. Mommy swept and mopped and vacuumed, humming the whole time. She did the laundry in the basement and hung it out to dry on the clothesline in the tiny yard behind the apartment building. My sheets smelled like sunlight in summer. As if nothing made her tired, Mommy cleaned and folded laundry long after I went to bed.

That summer, Mommy wore lipstick and dresses and took me to restaurants or on a bus to the zoo. We went downtown on the El train and got rock candy at Carson's, then visited the Field Museum to see the Egyptian mummies. We went to lots of places that summer and did lots of things together.

That summer was nice, but as soon as it got cold outside, and the days got shorter, Mommy's friend stopped coming to see us. She got quiet more and more. It seemed as though winter was longer than summer.

Then Mommy was gone. I could still recall what she was like on the last day we were together, and how she had told me to "always be a good girl" before sending me off to bed. She'd had tears rolling down her cheeks, but she had had more energy than usual that day. She had also seemed more decisive than usual. Looking back, I knew that she had made her choice and roused herself to an action she could not have taken in her usual lethargic state.

I had offered her my doll that night, asking her if she needed it to feel better. Mommy had shaken her head. She had hugged me especially hard, and for a long time, before letting me go. I didn't wonder what Mommy had meant when she'd said, "I'm really sorry, Pumpkin. Please don't hate me." She'd often say that to me. Years later, I would merely wonder where Mommy had gotten the gun.

I clearly remember being roused from sleep by hands lifting me. I heard sirens and unfamiliar noises, but managed to blend them into my dream for a little longer.

"Johnson. Hey. Would you grab that doll for me?" The voice was gruff and authoritative, but somehow very pleasant. It didn't register in my mind as familiar. "Yeah, yeah, that's it. And it's freezing out. Get me that

3

blanket off the bed and cover her up real good for me, okay? I can't do it with one hand."

It was a man's voice—a stranger's—and it broke me free of my dream. I opened my eyes to find a policeman holding me close to his chest. Johnson was pressing a blanket around me and tucking my doll into my arms. The rotating blue lights of two police cars parked in front of the building swirled around my room, which was otherwise lit by one small lamp on my chest of drawers. I heard the police car radio down below, an approaching ambulance, and the loud, anxious voices of our neighbors in the street.

"Mommy!" I screamed, twisting in the policeman's arms. "Mommy!"

The man held me tightly and said, "Shhh. I'm not gonna hurt you." I saw him look around the room, sparsely furnished with a little bed, the chest of drawers and a rocking horse. He would have seen that my room was messy and covered with dust. The entire apartment was filthy. Leaning away, I saw the grim look on his face, but didn't understand enough to be embarrassed or ashamed of the way we lived. I didn't understand any of the expressions that crossed his face, or why it softened and was angry, sad, and sorry all at once when he looked down at me.

The frosted windows were smeared with little fingerprints and months of grime. Red Kool-Aid had spilled on my bed sheets weeks ago. The pillow had no pillowcase and was badly in need of a washing. My dinner for the last two nights, an open bag of stale potato chips, was spilled on the bedroom floor. A cup of milk was on the windowsill from last week and was now a yogurt-like solid floating on clear yellowish liquid. In the kitchen there were cockroaches and a mess of dirty dishes in the sink and on the countertops, but there was very little food in the pantry or refrigerator.

I was wearing street clothes instead of pajamas, and probably smelled as though I hadn't taken a bath or changed clothes in a week or longer, because I had not.

"I couldn't find a suitcase," Johnson said.

"Use a paper bag then. Try under the sink in the kitchen."

"I want my *Mommy*!" I insisted, sticking out my lower lip in a frightened pout. I squirmed and pushed against the policeman's chest. "Mom-meee!" I screamed. Then I lapsed into hysterical tears, arching my back and wailing.

Someone in the hallway called out, "McNulty!" and my policemen answered, "In here!" Then he looked at me and cooed, "Shh, Baby. Shh." He did *not* say, "It will be all right." As a third policeman came into my room, McNulty absently patted my back and asked, "How old would you say she is?"

"Four, I guess."

"That's what I was thinking, too. My Chrissie's about the same age."

The other policeman—McNulty called him "Costello"—leaned over to study me. I stopped crying and looked back at him warily, sticking my thumb in my mouth and glaring. I pressed my shoulder and cheek into McNulty's chest to edge away. I reached my other hand out of the blanket and anxiously twirled a lock of hair. Then I couldn't endure his examination any longer and pushed my face into McNulty's chest to hide.

"Natalie Wood in *Miracle on 34th Street*," Costello said. "That's who she kind of looks like. Maybe even prettier."

"Yeah, she's a real cutie, that's for sure," McNulty said. "Aren't you?" he asked, bouncing me slightly, but it wasn't really a question, so I didn't answer.

I peeked out at Costello, who was still looking at me, but now he seemed angry and upset. Costello looked mean, and he scared me. I didn't like him.

"Son of a bitch, I hate this kind of shit," he muttered. He turned abruptly and left the room.

Johnson returned with some paper bags. He opened my dresser drawers and quickly stuffed the bags with handfuls of my pants, shirts, underwear and socks. He then moved to the closet and pulled down my dresses and my winter coat, dropping the hangers onto the floor in a messy pile. He came over to me, pushed the blanket aside, and slipped a pair of socks and shoes onto my dangling feet.

Outside the bedroom, a rush of footsteps pounded up the staircase and into the apartment. "Where is she?" I heard someone call from the hallway. I caught sight of two men carrying a stretcher. "Is she alive?"

Johnson shook his head. "She called the station to say she was gonna shoot herself, and to come get her kid. We got here, and she was already gone." He pointed to the door across the hall. The men disappeared into the other room. Johnson glanced at me and quickly closed the door behind them.

"Let's get the kid out of here."

5

I stiffened. McNulty shifted me to his hip in the confident and practiced manner of a daddy who had done it countless times before. He gently stroked my cheek with one long, thick finger. I didn't pull away because I was too afraid.

Johnson continued, "The suicide note has a phone number for the grandmother. We'll bring the kid to the station and call her from there."

McNulty look down at me. I was sniffling, sucking my thumb, and hugging my doll.

"What's your name, sweetie?" he asked gently.

I responded around my thumb with a sound like a low grunt.

"Say it again, sweetie. What's your name?"

"*No!*" I said more clearly, pulling my thumb out of my mouth. Having heard that they were taking me somewhere, maybe jail, I was starting to panic. "I *want* my *Mommy!*" I demanded.

"Her name's Holly." Costello had come back from another room. "It's in the note."

"Holly, little darlin', you're going for a ride."

Chapter 2

I went to live with Grandma Hazel and took over my mother's childhood bedroom. I waited for my mother to come and take me home because I didn't like it at Grandma's, and I missed her.

Months passed and she never came back. I eventually stopped waiting for her.

I sometimes thought about the policemen waking me up in my old bedroom and the ride to the station, and Grandma Hazel coming with Aunt Lily to pick me up after what seemed like hours and hours of thinking I was in jail for being bad. No one sat with me or spoke to me. I had fallen asleep on a hard wooden bench in the middle of the station where it was very noisy, and people milled around me. When they finally came and got me, Aunt Lily was crying, and Grandma was chain-smoking. Grandma had looked angry, stunned, and betrayed.

I saw Mommy one more time after that. She was sleeping out in the open, where anyone could see her, in a bed that was shiny metal and had puffy, white satin sheets. She was wearing her best dress and had her hands folded across her chest. I wanted to wake her up, but Grandma wouldn't let me.

The funeral parlor held a visitation for three nights, but nobody came except family: Grandma, the aunts, Dahlia, Lily, Violet and Iris, two uncles, one cousin, and me. Uncle Gregory, Mommy's younger brother, had moved away to California and called Lily to tell her he couldn't afford to come. Lily passed the news along to Grandma—Gregory never called Grandma. Nobody else besides our neighbors who had stood out on the sidewalk at home, and whom Mommy had never really met, knew she was dead.

Grandma wanted the ordeal behind her and her tracks covered, so she announced to the world in a vague Chicago Daily News obituary that Rose had died in an "accident" and had been laid to rest in an unnamed cemetery after a "private" funeral service. She placed it in the Chicago Daily News because my father Nick's family took the Sun Times. She couldn't prevent someone from telling the Salvinos that Rose was dead, but she wanted to increase the likelihood that they wouldn't find out, and then come looking for me and raise me God-knows-how in a family full of garlic-eating Dagos. She also liked to think that Nick might never know he was free to marry again.

She permitted the funeral home to conduct the pointless visitations because that's what you did, and because she didn't want the funeral director to think she was a bad mother who wouldn't even allow her daughter to have a wake.

I remember Mommy's lovely face in the open casket at the funeral parlor. Her light brown hair flowed around it in perfect waves, and covered the wound. I remember sitting for three evenings in a row staring at Mommy who, in death, was not very different from the Mommy I had known on her bad days, except that Grandma wouldn't let me touch her or make her tea.

The simple gravestone read: *Rose Salvino, Born 1934, Died 1958*. I couldn't read it, so I didn't know what it said, or what it meant. There was just family at the frozen, wind-whipped graveside when we put Mommy's new bed into the hole in the ground. Nobody was speaking to anyone else for some reason—they were like that a lot. If they did speak, it was usually to bark orders. All of them liked to bark orders, and none of them liked to receive orders, so there were very few instances when I could recall them all getting along. On this occasion they all stood stiffly and didn't look at each other. I hadn't figured anything out yet, and nobody was telling me where Mommy had gone, or why they were burying her bed.

The news didn't travel, just as Grandma had hoped. Rose had long ago lost touch with her high school friends, who never called to inquire about her. She never made new friends after high school, except for Jack, and Grandma didn't know about him. Nick didn't learn that Rose was dead until their tenth-year high school reunion, where they held a brief tribute to her and another classmate who had died the previous year. The reunion organizers learned about Rose's death after sending her invitation to Grandma's house. Grandma had written "Deceased" on the envelope and returned it so they wouldn't pester her again.

Still, Nick didn't call or try to find me for another four years. His mother and the rest of his family never claimed me.

As years went by, my memories of Mommy became tied to the framed black-and-white photograph on Grandma's mantelpiece. In that photo, Mommy was younger than I could have remembered and standing in a doorway wearing a long taffeta gown with spaghetti straps, which Grandma told me was pink when I asked. She looked hopeful and beautiful for her prom. Other prom photos that included my daddy, who had worn a tuxedo for the occasion, were around somewhere, but Grandma had put them away and claimed she didn't remember where they were. I didn't know what Daddy looked like until years later.

When I was twelve, Daddy finally contacted us. He was as handsome as I'd imagined when I'd pictured him coming for me and taking me away. He was tall and had dark hair, dark eyes, arched brows, and a strong jaw. His features were even, and his body was trim and muscular. His face and hair looked just like mine.

I was polite and smiled. I wore my best dress and tried to be as appealing as I could so that he would want to take me home with him. He looked nervous and uncomfortable as he sat across from me in the restaurant. I sipped my Coke through a straw and looked at him adoringly, expectantly.

Would I come live with him? I finally asked. It was hard living with Grandma, and I didn't mind changing schools—

"No," he answered, looking trapped. He seemed a little indignant that I had made him feel trapped that way and shot me an affronted, accusing look. Then he smiled as if he was sharing a secret and told me that he'd remarried, and his wife wasn't ready for a teenager.

"But I'm twelve," I assured him. "I won't be a teenager for another year."

"We have a little baby boy," he countered, "and my wife has her hands full."

I had a brother! I was thrilled and wanted to meet him. I loved babies! I started to say something about how I'd baby-sit whenever he wanted, but he cut me off. He knew I'd understand, he told me. It just wasn't possible for me to come with him.

"You're fine with your grandmother," he said. "Think of how lonely she'd be if I took you away."

"But could I please at least meet my brother?" I asked. I was almost going to cry, but I couldn't in front of my daddy.

9

"When I have the time," Daddy said. "Maybe in the summer." Then he smiled, looked at his watch, asked for the check, and drove me home.

I wondered why he had come to see me if he didn't want me. Then I realized he'd changed his mind about wanting me after meeting me. I had failed some sort of test.

"I *told* you your father didn't want you," Grandma sniffed when I ran into the house in tears and slammed the door to my room. "I *told* you I'm the only one who'll have you," she said through the door.

That was when the tears stopped. I couldn't ever get them back.

The following Christmas, my father sent me a card pre-printed with *Merry Christmas from the family of Nick Salvino*. It didn't mention my birthday on Christmas Eve or include a gift. After that, Grandma and I moved. He didn't try to find me, and I never attempted to find him, so we permanently lost touch. I never met my half-brother. I never even learned his name.

Grandma fed me well and kept me clean and warm. She rarely hit me; she found other ways to beat and humiliate me. Over the years, I learned of my limitless shortcomings from a series of questions to which Grandma never seemed to really want an answer: Why was I such a pest, always talking and getting underfoot? Why was I always so secretive, and what was I hiding, closing the door to my room? Why did I always have my nose in a book when I should be outside playing? Why was I always outside playing when I should be cleaning my room? Why didn't I ever do something with my messy hair? Why was I always fussing with my hair? Why did I eat so much? Why was I such a picky eater who didn't like anything? Why was I always so dirty? Why was I always using up so much water taking so many baths? Why didn't I make my bed without being told? Why did I ask for new clothes when she, Grandma, hadn't ever had new clothes during her entire childhood, and had to wear hand-me-downs that at least two, and sometimes four older sisters had worn first? Who did I think I was, living on her charity and asking for things? I should be grateful she had taken me in. Nobody else would have had me, she liked to say to bolster any argument. Who did I think I was?

She screamed and called me names. Grandma also punctuated any situation with observations of my personal failings. If I came home crying, I was "just being dramatic," and she would mimic me in a sneering singsong, "Crybaby! Always looking for attention. Holly, Holly, Holly. Look at *me*! I'm *Holly*!" If I brought home drawings or papers from school, they were never as good as Uncle Gregory's had been. My efforts to cook or sew were declared failures. My efforts to clean or iron fell short. When I got older and kept a diary, she sometimes tore my room apart until she found it, then triumphantly read passages aloud to me, criticizing my private thoughts and laughing, while I screamed in agony and lunged for it.

She complained about my mother and father. My mother was a whore, she said—she pronounced it "hoor" to rhyme with "lure"—because she'd become pregnant before she was married. My father, Nick, was a "hoodlum"—she pronounced it "hude-lum" to rhyme with "rude-lum"—because he was Italian, married my pregnant mother in City Hall instead of a church, and then left us just before my first birthday. I would grow up to be just as worthless as they were, just as selfish as my father, and just as crazy as my mother, whom she should have had put away. I was just as much a thorn in her side as my mother had been; Rose couldn't keep her man, couldn't keep a job, and kept sticking Grandma with the bills, which cost a fortune.

Grandma hated Italians, and often announced this while looking at me. She also hated blacks, Polacks, Jews, Mexicans, Germans—though she admitted Germans were "clean"—and anyone who wasn't like her.

When I was out of the house, she periodically purged my room of my favorite keepsakes and possessions. When I returned, she would defend herself by stating, "Nothing is yours. Everything in this house is mine, including you, and I can do with it as I please." I was terrified to leave the house for fear of what I would find missing when I returned, but I couldn't stay in it because of her constant attacks. There was no safe place for me.

My system was constantly bathed in adrenaline because I lived in a perpetual state of *fight or flight*, always either feeling under attack or on guard, never feeling safe or at peace. If things weren't bad at that moment, they would be very shortly, so I was always braced for it. I was always fearful, ashamed, or outraged, frequently all at the same time. I ground my teeth in my sleep and had stomach pains after eating.

As the years passed, I would never hear from Grandma any version of my life story that did not make me largely responsible for my father's disappearance, my mother's suicide, and my grandmother's burdened unhappiness. It would all eventually wear me down as the guilt and the anger ate away at my core like acid. I rebelled, pulled away, and then finally left when I was still far too young.

11

However, I did have my Aunt Lily throughout my childhood. She came for me every weekend and spirited me off to one adventure after another. She was a teacher, and helped me with my schoolwork. She talked to me about the books I loved and the boys I had crushes on. She told me what a wonderful girl I was, how smart and beautiful, and that I could be anything I wanted to be when I grew up. She came to all of my school events and showered me with presents on my birthday and Christmas, which were a day apart. She even started a tradition of celebrating my half-birthday on June 24th so I'd have a special day all my own, far away from the holidays. She always made me half of a two-layer chocolate cake.

I loved to stay overnight with Aunt Lily and hear all of the Mommy stories until way past my bedtime. But, that only happened when Grandma was still speaking to her and permitted me to go away. Lily also knew my father and described his parents and the rest of his family to me in order to give me a more balanced picture of them than the one Grandma painted.

The Mommy Grandma always described was different from the one Aunt Lily recalled. Aunt Lily's face would light up, and she would talk about how funny Rose was, and how she loved to draw, paint, and take pictures.

"You love to draw and paint just like your mother," she always marveled. "You get your talent from her."

She sometimes pulled old school paintings out of a box she kept in a drawer of her buffet and showed me my mother's artwork from when she was a child.

"I think you may be even *more* talented," she always said.

When I was thirteen, Aunt Dahlia died. Before the visitors arrived for the wake, Lily and Grandma got into an argument while standing in the visitation room in front of the casket.

"You're always putting on airs," Grandma accused. "Lily Lily Lily! It's always about Lily!" she shouted. "Look at *me*! I'm *Lily*!"

Aunt Lily responded by angrily shoving Grandma's shoulder. Grandma flailed back, grabbing Lily's hair and pulling her down. They rolled on the floor in front of the casket and their sister's corpse, two old ladies pulling handfuls of each other's hair, grunting and screaming, while I looked up from my book and watched. I knew there was no point in trying to stop them. Grandma would haul me into it. So I sat there silently until they finally let go, stood up, brushed themselves off, and left the room. Then I went back to my book.

When the visitors arrived, Lily and Hazel each took their places at opposite sides of the room and received their condolences separately. They never spoke again.

Afterward, Grandma severed ties with Lily altogether. Lily didn't call, and she didn't press to see me. She was angry enough to let me go.

I still called her sometimes, and she sounded the same as ever, but she never offered to come get me. She stopped coming to my school events and never initiated a phone call. The half-birthday celebrations stopped, and she mailed me a card instead, for a few years at least. I presumed she'd changed her mind about me like my father had and didn't love me anymore, so I called her less and less, and then finally stopped altogether.

It was just me and Grandma, after that.

Chapter 3

February, 1973

The Skokie Swift was an express train. Hell began when the doors shut, and I was trapped on that train for twenty minutes and unable to scream aloud, though in my mind, my scream had the same pitch and cadence as the squeal of the wheels on the tracks when we rounded a curve. As the train barreled out the northern tip of Chicago and into the suburbs with no stops in between, I was subject to the kind of anxiety that keeps some people from ever boarding a plane or an elevator in their lives—rising panic, choking fear. My heart palpitated. I heard it in my ears so loudly that I heard little else.

Other passengers looked out the windows or read their newspapers. Some closed their eyes and dozed. I stiffened as the train built up speed on its tracks. My personal roller coaster—the one in my mind—inched toward the peak of its incline, then pushed itself over the crest and swept downward, out of control. *No escape!* The Skokie Swift moved steadily, purposefully forward toward the northwest. It moved as swiftly as its name.

I did a freefall into a full-blown anxiety attack, and no one was waiting to catch me.

I looked ahead, not seeing. I clasped my hands together tightly, and I concentrated on not screaming. I never screamed. I never gave in to the temptation to run wildly down the aisle past shocked or indifferent passengers and hurl myself out of the back door and onto the tracks. There was a deadly third rail on the tracks, and it would have ended my life swiftly. I often considered the irony of ending *swiftly* out the back of the *swiftly* moving Skokie *Swift*, then waded through the panic and groped for more alliteration to distract myself. *Peter Piper picked a peck of pickled peppers. One. Two. Three. Four. Five. Six. Breathe in. Breathe out. Breathe in. Breathe out. Don't scream. Ten. Twenty. Thirty. Forty. She sells seashells by the seashore. Don't scream. Don't scream. Don't scream...*

This was my morning routine, like brushing my teeth. I always looked calm and self-possessed because I did this every morning. I would do it again in the evening, when I boarded the Skokie Swift to return home.

And when the train stopped and the panic receded, I took my place in the impatient, pressing crowd at the doors, which opened and through which we all spilled like spreading liquid onto the platform at the end of the deadly third rail. Once it was empty, the two-car Skokie Swift moved to the very end of the track, reversed direction, and scooted forward to receive a crowd from the other side of the platform. It then began its hellish ride back toward the city.

I walked the half-mile to work, which was my life. The train-induced panic was parenthetical, morning and evening, with my life in between.

Dr. Silverman never helped with the panic attacks. I considered getting another job, and I considered not taking the train. However, if I had done either, the panic would have won, and I would have lost. I could have made my life smaller by avoiding the things that triggered panic, but then where would it have ended? I had panic attacks without warning. I had them on the train, and I had them when I wasn't on it. If I thought for a moment about panic—if I merely thought, "What if I were to have a panic attack *right now*?"—I got one. Panic attacks were like a genie I could summon with a thought. So, if I had made my life smaller by eliminating the things that caused panic, or equated a place or a situation with panic and avoided it, I would have ended up in my apartment, crippled, unable to leave, and unable to pay the rent because I couldn't work. If I panicked at home, then where would I have gone?

Panic was a badge of courage and freedom to me. It represented the imprisonment to which I could have succumbed had I chosen, or had I weakened. So I didn't let it hinder me, and I never would. I simply gritted my teeth and didn't scream while I waited for it to pass. I never died, I never exploded, and my health was intact. It was just terror, and I faced it because not facing it was not an option. Death was my only option, and I toyed with it, but I somehow kept forcing myself awake each day and onto the train, out of which I never, ever jumped.

I would not go the way my mother did, I vowed to myself. I would live to the end of my natural life, no matter what. My mother had always been held up to me as an object of contempt and scorn. I would not—*will not*—let whatever plagued her win over me as well. I would not be sneered at and trivialized in death as she was, and be dismissed as self-pitying or weak.

I was very familiar with the issues that plagued my mother. I inherited the gene, the brain chemistry, and the home life that triggered her depression. The difference is, I was made of sturdier stuff and was angry enough to live. Anger forced me out of bed and off to work when I otherwise would not have felt able to lift my head. It allowed me to shudder in mental and emotional agony, year after year, wanting nothing more than to die, but not taking my own life as she did.

So I did not stay in bed, and I did not gain possession of a gun. I woke up each day and went through hell to arrive at work. On the way, I did not scream. Then later I went home.

I did the best I could.

Chapter 4

My job was my life. It wasn't much of a life because it wasn't much of a job, but it comprised my entire social life, and it was what I did. I was a customer service rep for an insurance company. Each month I earned three hundred and fifty-five dollars, sometimes with a little extra for overtime, minus taxes, split between paychecks I received on the fifteenth and the thirty-first. It covered my rent, phone bill, and transportation, as well as the other sundry things one needs to survive, but it was still tricky, getting from one paycheck to the next. I already had learned the fine arts of fasting and floating checks.

I didn't have discretionary income for things like movies or restaurants. I didn't own a car and couldn't foresee a time when I would ever be able to afford one. I never bought new clothing, but I had the foresight to go through a *black period* two years earlier when I was still living with Grandma, so all of my clothes could be mixed and matched for variety, of a sort. It didn't matter that I was mightily sick of black.

I did, however, save five or ten dollars from every paycheck no matter what. I had a little over a hundred and fifty dollars in the bank. I had that.

The only budget categories I could squeeze emergency funds from were savings and groceries. Rent must always be paid on the first of the month, or I had no place to live. The phone bill must be paid, or I had no phone. When I needed money, I took it from the grocery fund first because I would never save anything if I permitted myself to view that five or ten dollars of savings as accessible. It was not accessible because savings were sacred.

I seemed to always have an emergency that left me with just a half-loaf of bread, a box of crackers, or a box of pancake mix—I mixed it with water, no egg, and I used no syrup—to see me through until the next paycheck. Emergencies included my grandmother's birthday, Christmas, and Mother's Day (for my grandmother), and those maddening, seemingly voluntary, but really mandatory, collections at work for everyone's wedding gift or baby shower; I never got married or had babies, so the sacrifice was wholly one-sided. I also viewed books as emergencies. Sometimes I simply couldn't find what I wanted to read in the public library.

When I made the decision to move out on my own and leave school at the beginning of my senior year of high school, I deliberately took the twelfth-grade reading list home and read every book on it after work, while my former classmates read the same thing in class. I dutifully moved through Victor Hugo and the Brontë sisters, read Jane Austen with pure elation, shifted to Shakespeare with surprised delight, and then wrapped up the year with Thomas Hardy and George Eliot. After school let out for the others, and they graduated without me and moved on to college, I expanded on my own. I read books from the library that were labeled classics, and had now been working my way through them for two years.

I read other things as well, including contemporary novels, college textbooks, magazines, and newspapers. I read while I ate, before bed, on the bus whenever I had a seat, and on my days off. I always had a paperback in my purse in case a moment presented itself during the day. I could never make up for missing out on a high school diploma and college, but I could stave off total ignorance, I hoped. It was worth a shot. More importantly, I did it because I liked it.

Art and literature were cheap. There were museums and libraries in Chicago—I was born in an excellent city—and both were within my weak financial grasp. In addition, the Loyola University Bookstore sold used textbooks that I browsed through and selected with great care, pretending I was a student. I posed like one, wondering if people mistook me for one, imagining what it felt like to go to college and have conversations with people who liked the same things I did. I tuned into TV college classes on Saturday morning, if I woke up in time, and typically watched Public Television in the evenings.

Textbooks, even used, were expensive, so occasionally, as a treat for myself, I brought home something fun and interesting and therefore frivolous, like Art History, Anthropology or Sociology. Typically, though, I stocked up on Abnormal Psychology books I thought might conclusively shed some light on what was wrong with me. I was convinced that the secret was in the diagnosis. If I knew what was wrong with me, and had been wrong with my mother long ago, I could figure out what to do to cure myself.

Primarily, I wanted to find out what Dr. Silverman saw when he looked at me. He was keeping secrets, he had to be, because he never told me what my illness was or what I could do to get better. Thus far, I hadn't found the answer either. I found pieces of me in a number of abnormal mental conditions, but I did not hear voices, get violent, or have lapses from reality, at least not that I knew of, nor did I constantly wash my hands. There were no lengthy periods of time I couldn't account for, and no one ever addressed me by someone else's name, so I was confident I did not have multiple personalities.

I'd been compiling an "Is/Is Not" list and comparing my symptoms to every condition in every book. My "Is" list never closely matched any condition I ever found. The only thing apparent to both my shrink and me was how I got this way.

I also kept a "My Fault/Their Fault" list to isolate the things I'd done that I should be accountable for and things about myself that I should try to change, versus the situations when Grandma or someone else was at fault. Then I picked apart and explored these items in a detailed journal, examining every aspect of a situation until I fully understood who was responsible for what, and which of everyone's actions were good or bad. Since Grandma always told me everything was my fault, the exercise was freeing. Only sometimes was I to blame. Without frequent My Fault/Their Fault reality checks, it was too tempting to believe I should put everything in one column or the other, depending on whether I was depressed and feeling futile, or angry and feeling accusatory. It helped maintain my sanity, even more than visits to my shrink.

I had had a sustained diet of light-to-moderate hunger for two years, now, and was used to deprivation. I hardly noticed it and typically crawled into bed and slept when the hunger bothered me too much. I sometimes slept twelve to sixteen hours per day, not only to escape hunger, but because hunger made me physically tired. So did depression.

I had learned from my books and my shrink that there are different types of depressed people. We either ate too much of all the wrong things, or we ate too little. We either sat up all night because we couldn't sleep, or we slept all day because we couldn't wake up. We were slobs, all of us, because depression sapped our energy, and everything, including housekeeping, was completely overwhelming and simply not worth it. I was a no-eater—though not by choice—all-day/all-night sleeper, and of course, my apartment was always an area of devastation.

However, I could work. I had the strength to do that, and when I did not, I forced myself to find that strength. My entire life was tied to my job because the important thing was that I live independently. Everything depended on that.

But depression was just a part of my problem. I had no tidy diagnosis that encompassed the panic attacks, the mood swings, the hostility, and the periodic rages.

Dr. Silverman charged fifty dollars an hour, and I saw him twice a month. Insurance paid twenty dollars of that after a hundred-dollar deductible, maximum fifty-two sessions per year, not to exceed five hundred dollars, *whichever comes first*—I called that "insurance humor." The rest I paid monthly, sometimes thirty, sometimes twenty dollars. I owed him over six hundred dollars. I was indebted to him for not helping me, and from his standpoint, the failure was mine.

I had an illness that didn't have a name yet. It would have a name one day, but not quite yet. On my insurance forms, my diagnosis was merely "Depression and Anxiety," which was like responding to a request for directions with, "It's that way." It was certainly true enough, and thank you very much, but please tell me more. I suspected Dr. Silverman didn't tell me because he didn't know. It was disconcerting to think that I might be paying money to someone who had no idea how to help me, and that he accepted it from me nonetheless.

I pored over abnormal psychology textbooks and medical magazines during those short hours before I crawled into bed to escape the illness I was trying to identify. One day, when there were finally research studies, medical papers and the validation of names, I would learn that I had at least two separate conditions, and I would know what it was that I was fighting.

In the meantime, there was no help for it but to pay a psychiatrist to listen to me speak, and watch him furrow his brow, take notes, and ask questions, then schedule another appointment in two weeks so I could speak and speak again. In speaking, I could report what I saw, or tell him how I felt about the things that happened in my life. I could not, however, describe what I experienced when an inelegant mood gripped me and took over, or explain why I did the things I did. He never connected with me anyway and often replied in a way that seemed off-target, as if I had spoken but he didn't quite hear. Or, it was as if he heard a voice from his textbooks speaking to him about an illness he could define and medicate, and he was responding to that voice instead of to me. Perhaps he was responding to his hourly fee and thinking about the Cubs.

I didn't want medication. Lithium, he insisted, would bring relief. I tried it for two months, and nothing changed. I apparently didn't have whatever it was he first thought I had, so he didn't argue when I told him I wouldn't renew the prescription. Anti-depressants didn't work either, except to make me more depressed. I eventually stopped offering myself up to him as a pharmacological guinea pig while he groped to appear in control and knowledgeable about my situation.

Primarily, I couldn't afford to pay for drugs, even with insurance. I also couldn't afford to pay for Dr. Silverman and would no doubt be paying his ever-growing bill for the rest of my life. I was left with the alternative of making myself well by sheer force of will. I didn't necessarily need a shrink for that.

I saw more immediate value in buying groceries, but I continued with the sessions anyway. I liked having someone to talk to. I was also aware of the degree to which I was at risk. Dr. Silverman was more than a sympathetic ear; he was a necessary precaution. It would have been reckless of me to give him up. I had no one else.

I had been living on my own for two years, since I was seventeen. I left school and moved out because there are some places you just need to leave, right that minute, no matter what else is waiting for you on the outside. Home was one of those places. School was collateral damage. I had to work to pay my bills, and didn't drop out by choice. Since then, I succeeded in always paying my rent and bills on time. I always had a job and always went to work. I never moved back home, never applied for welfare, and was never institutionalized. I never committed suicide.

These are larger, more impressive achievements, than they may at first appear to be.

21

Chapter 5

"Are you a model? No? I'd like to see about getting some shots of you sometime for the agency. Can we…?"

A man handed me his business card, which displayed his name and the logo for a modeling agency. I took the card without slowing, thanked him, and dropped it into the next trash bin. It was very flattering, of course. Perhaps some of these men were serious and not just approaching me with a sleazy pickup line and a fistful of bogus business cards. They appeared whenever I went downtown, usually sidling up to me as I walked, proclaiming their credentials and my modeling potential in broken breaths as I outpaced them.

I had my own "signature runway walk" already. I walked rapidly and boldly and swung my hands in fists. I made no eye contact and looked at nothing by the wayside. I slowed for no one and glared straight ahead. I shot off sparks and arrows of hostility. Since assuming this walk after a frightening incident in the subway, I had not been attacked, assaulted, or mugged by anyone, not even once. I had learned that even a harmless, unarmed, beautiful young woman can be scarier than muggers and rapists. My walk alone made them seek an easier target.

I also had other strategies to survive the city. I could stare without moving or blinking for unnaturally long periods of time, far longer than even a cat. This typically unnerved the men who approached or leered at me on the bus or El train. If they were not scared off by my stare, I could turn my eyes crazy and grin. If I took one step toward them looking like that, they ran.

And so I made my way safely through the transit system and walked the city streets, traveling through the poorer, rougher neighborhoods on buses and El trains, living in a poorer, rougher neighborhood alone, fearless and in control. Nobody worried about me. But then, nobody would.

Slowing my walk and shortening the swing of my arms, I breezed up the steps between the great green lions and eased through the entrance of the Art Institute. I checked my old hooded ski jacket with the coatroom and adjusted my mental attitude to *hushed and reverent*. I was here to pay homage to Renoir.

The Art Institute was perhaps my only luxury, aside from books. I paid admission to most of the special exhibits, and even paid the extra two dollars for the tape recording that guided me through. Sometimes during the summer I purchased lunch and sat by the fountain in the courtyard outside, slowly picking at my very expensive fruit and cheese plate to extend my pleasure as I sat alone at a little table beneath an umbrella amid the wealthy matrons and art patrons. It was indeed a bank-breaking event each time I went, but I would not sacrifice it.

Should I go straight to the exhibit? Or warm up with a visit to my beloved Impressionists? I chose the exhibit, paid for the recording, and experienced that gasping thrill of "It's all so beautiful!" the instant I walked into the room. I didn't know why it was beautiful. I hated not understanding the technicalities of beauty, why one piece was good and a similar one was not, so I checked out an artist's biography from the library every two weeks, studied it, then made my way to the Art Institute as often as I could to see a few of the paintings up close. I sometimes tried to replicate them in pencil sketches on cheap notebook paper.

I passionately loved Toulouse Lautrec, Gauguin, Picasso, Monet, and Manet. Of course, there were Escher and Mary Cassatt and Cezanne, and so forth... my list of favorites was a long one. I was less fond of Van Gogh and Degas, again, without knowing why. I promised myself that one day I would learn enough to find out. Or, perhaps I would learn enough to appreciate them. One day I would actually study art in a classroom.

Art was my first love. I stood in the midst of Renoir and breathed, turning the tape machine on and off as I moved from one painting to the next.

"Renoir is nice, but I prefer Gauguin," a gentleman commented. He was in his late thirties, wearing a suit and black-framed glasses. He looked affluent and well-bred. He was pondering a painting as if he barely noticed me.

I looked at him through narrowed eyes, assessing him suspiciously. He looked respectable, older, and detached, clearly focused on the art. I relaxed and smiled.

"I love Gauguin too! But they're totally different, don't you think? I don't think you can compare them." I answered, warming toward someone who shared my taste in art and wanted to discuss it with me. Maybe this man could explain to me why I preferred Gauguin to Chagall, even though they used a similar color palette.

"What do you think of Chagall? If you were to compare him to Gauguin, which would you choose?"

"Are you a student here?" he asked, ignoring my question.

"At the Art Institute? No."

"Where do you go to school?"

"Nowhere at the moment." There was no good way to answer that question.

"Ah." He nodded, sinking deeply into ponderously intelligent, musing and well-bred, affluent thoughts about the painting he was studying. I hated to disturb him.

"I prefer Gauguin because of the way he painted breasts," he said abruptly, and turned to stare over at my chest. "You've got nice tits, maybe as good as Gauguin's. So what are you doing after this?" He moved toward me, pretending to be jostled from behind by a man who had barely brushed against him, grabbed my shoulders as if to catch his balance, then let a hand graze my breast as if by accident. I could tell by the focus and concentration in his eyes that it was no accident. Next, he pressed his groin into my hip. He had an erection.

"You stinking turd," I said under my breath, but loudly enough for him to hear. Then I sighed and shook my head in disgust.

I was furious with myself. I should have known. Why would a man in his late thirties want to have a conversation with a nineteen-year-old girl about art? Men never wanted to have a conversation with me. Nobody wanted my opinion or cared what I thought about anything, unless the conversation was a prelude to sexual advances.

This episode was a lapse and a failure on my part. I had been fending them off since I was fifteen years old, and I typically could spot them, no matter how respectable they looked, how cleverly they masked their true intentions, or how improbable a situation seemed for a man to express or demonstrate his prurient inclinations. God help me, the next one wouldn't catch me off guard. I was so tired of this.

I had looked forward to this exhibit for weeks, so I walked away. I tried to forget about the man and concentrate on a different painting. He didn't follow me, but I was no longer in the mood to worship Renoir. That man had killed the joy. I was barely into the exhibit for which I had sacrificed a meal to pay the entrance fee, but was too angry and sad to think about art anymore. So I left the exhibit, handing my tape player to one of the attendants as I went. I checked my jacket out of the cloakroom and walked slowly down the steps between the great green lions, then north on Michigan Avenue to the bus stop. Head down and hands in my pockets, I stood and waited for the bus home.

A man winked flirtatiously as he stopped to hand me a flier. He paused to strike up a conversation believing that, "Hey, Foxy. Nice bootie," was an appropriately charming lead in, presumably thinking that I should respond by opening my coat in mid-winter and exposing my breasts to him in gratitude.

I calmly told him to go to hell and let his flyer flutter to the ground. I turned away so he couldn't see me press the tears out of my eyes with my fingers. They dried on their own as the bus pulled into sight.

"Bitch!" he snarled.

"Why does it keep happening to me?" I asked Dr. Silverman. "I wear high necklines, and my clothes are all really plain. I don't wear perfume or jewelry, my shoes are ugly, and everything I own is old. I don't do my nails. I have split ends and a pimple right here." I lifted my chin and pointed. "I act like a bitch, and *still* they come at me."

"It's easy to objectify someone in your position. You're a very pretty girl with no socio-economic cushioning."

Dr. Silverman shrugged to convey there was nothing either he or I could do.

"If you had money, that would be a cushion. You wouldn't be taking buses, and you'd live in a secure building. If you wore newer, more expensive clothes, you'd send men a message that you're pampered and worthy of more respect than they're giving you now."

"Thank you for your advice. I will go out and do that now." I stared at him.

"I'm simply explaining why this is happening. They can see you're struggling; you display a level of vulnerability and defenselessness that signals to a segment of the population that you're fair game for them to punish or exploit, for whatever reasons they might have to punish or exploit a beautiful woman. Sad but true. It also makes you appear to be more accessible to men in a wider socioeconomic range. Men feel you're approachable in spite of your beauty, which normally would scare most of them off. Your relative poverty makes you less intimidating to insecure males." He nodded and summarized, "Therefore they approach you."

He'd called my circumstances *poverty*. I looked down, ashamed and embarrassed.

"Surely you know this, don't you? That your looks are intimidating?"

Yes, I knew that. I looked up at him warily.

"The thing is," I said, "I can't even talk to people about this. I can't ask people for advice or help. I can't even admit to them that I *know* I'm beautiful or they get indignant, and then they're mean to me."

I looked down quickly. I'd said I was *beautiful*. Would he react? Would he say no, I *wasn't* beautiful, just to put me in my place? Would he accuse me of being vain and self-centered? I was paying him (more or less, in small spurts), so he couldn't really do any of that, but talking about this made me uncomfortable, anyway.

Nevertheless, I looked up again and continued, "If I know I'm pretty, I'm conceited. If I pretend I don't know I'm pretty, they roll their eyes and get angry. It's like complaining that you have too much money. What am I supposed to say to people? It creates all kinds of problems, but I can't go to anyone for help, and I can't complain about it. I have to just take it and keep my mouth shut."

I hung my head. I was so tired of it all. I'd never really spoken about my looks to anyone before. I didn't know how he would react. I waited for the blows to fall.

"I imagine people project negative things onto you, too."

"Yeah. I'm either dumb or evil. Beautiful women are always dumb or evil."

Dr. Silverman shook his head sympathetically. "You are *not* evil, and you are most definitely not dumb."

"Oh, and you're always a bitch. You're either a dumb bitch or an evil bitch." I was warming up to the topic now. I had plenty to say. "They can be as malicious as they want. Nobody defends you when someone insults you because everyone wants you to rot in hell. And they all still get to think of themselves as *nice* because nobody thinks there's anything wrong with being mean to the pretty girl. People love it when anyone strikes a hit." I punched my fist in the air. "Score! They think it's funny. And if anything good happens to you, they begrudge you. Sometimes they punish you. And that doesn't even include the sabotage they do behind your back that you never find out about."

"And if you tell them what you just told me, they get angry and defensive." He said that as a statement, not a question. "They probably also list all the reasons why they were within their rights to be cruel to you, and why you deserved it."

"What I don't understand is why everyone wants to be beautiful. They'd just be on the receiving end of the same crap they dish out." I sighed. "But it really doesn't matter how nice they think they are, or how nice people are to other people. They don't give the pretty girl any sympathy because looks are supposed to compensate for everything, no matter what happens to you or who dies. If something bad happens to you, they win."

I picked at my cuticles. "I get some perks from my looks, but mainly it's just getting compliments and getting into places. I get away with things, like when I act crazy. Nobody cares if I'm crazy as long as I'm pretty, but I'd rather not be crazy, you know? And I get all the men I want, but that's like drinking from a fire hose. How many men do you really need? One. So it doesn't compensate you for the things you lose. Not me, anyway."

I supposed I could get more if I exploited my looks, used them as a weapon against other girls, got a sugar daddy, bilked men out of expensive presents, or married for money, but I wanted everything I got to be something I'd earned and deserved. I wanted to achieve things with my own efforts. I didn't need to win over other women, and I got no satisfaction from it. I just wanted to be loved and liked for *me*. I wanted to love and like someone for *him*. I wanted girlfriends.

Dr. Silverman was taking notes, and then he quickly glanced at his watch. "You might actually be better off in a place where your looks aren't so extreme. Seriously. You may just require a more rarified atmosphere, like modeling. You might fit in better if you'd just go into modeling. You always have the opportunity, am I right? Then you'd be around girls like yourself, and you'd just be one of them, instead of always asking for trouble by being the most beautiful girl on the El train. The money situation would take care of itself."

"I can't go into modeling."

"Why not?"

I gave him a look. We had had this conversation before, several times.

27

I didn't want to be a model at all, much less enough to fight for it against cutthroat competition. I couldn't deal with the stress and uncertainty of potentially going for weeks without work, with no one else to fall back on financially. They also comment on your failings right in front of you, and criticize you as if you were a slab of meat, or so I'd heard. I was hypersensitive to criticism and rejection; either one would send me into a depressive tailspin, whereas both together made me suicidal. I typically didn't go out of my way to invite situations that drove me to suicide.

Most importantly, I didn't function well in unstructured work situations. I required boundaries. I required security. I needed something that forced me out of bed at the same time every day. I needed to know I had a job and health insurance. I needed my job to be my parent. Even if the pay was one sixtieth of what I could make as a model, my job was crucial to my survival.

"I don't want it. I would suck at it. They would eat me alive, and I would hate them."

"I see."

"So give it up."

"I will."

"You and the jerks on Michigan Avenue with the business cards."

"I can only speak for myself."

Chapter 6

I didn't have girlfriends. There were girls I went to parties with sometimes, and girls from work who went out as a group on weekends and included me, but I had no best friend I could call on the phone and talk to for hours or confide in. I only had Angie, my lunch partner and party companion, and she was my lifeline.

Angie sat at the desk behind me, joined me for breaks every day, and planned my weekends. I was, for some inexplicable reason, her first choice as a drinking buddy. She forced me out of bed when I otherwise might have been content to read and sleep through the weekend, and told me where to be and when to arrive. I merely had to obey.

I had no input into where we went, ever, because Angie cheerfully only did what Angie wanted to do. She took me to back-alley dives, neighborhood taverns for darts or foosball, meat-market bars where people went to find sex and little else, noisy rock-band bars, or to all of these in succession depending upon her changing mood, not mine. If I occasionally suggested something, she rarely wanted to do it and couldn't be coaxed. She led; I followed. Not always, but sometimes, I had fun. Other times, depending upon my mood and her choices, it was excruciating. Sometimes it was far worse than being alone.

An evening with Angie was much like attending a progressive dinner party, with each course served in a different location. It never ended where it began. Her bar of choice was usually crowded, noisy and filled with friendly men who were looking for friendly women like Angie.

There were several areas to choose from within the city, and each had its own bar atmosphere and type of crowd. Rush Street was *the* meat market—upscale, deliberate, judgmental and heartless. You only entered the bars in

29

designer clothing or business suits, or you entered at your peril. Entering was perilous for me, in my old black garb. Men approached, then either evaluated me contemptuously and jabbed me with superior, scathing remarks, or presumed I was cheap and easy because my clothing was worn and moved in for the kill while I backed away. I preferred to keep my distance, hating Rush Street nights.

The Lincoln Avenue blues bars were perhaps the most civilized. People sat at tables and decorously sipped foreign beers and Chablis while they listened to blues performed by blues greats, like Luther Allison and Koko Taylor. Lincoln Avenue people were respectful and dignified, and only rarely staggered or fell off of their bar stools.

Angie usually preferred the New Town neighborhood at Broadway and Diversey. The New Town crowd was matter-of-factly promiscuous, open to offers, and was there strictly to party. In contrast to Lincoln Avenue people, New Town people pressed up against the bar in a jostling crowd, performed bar tricks with saltshakers, pelted each other with lime slices, and packed back shots of tequila, then slammed down the glass with a loud "Yow!" A jukebox provided background noise over the loud conversation and laughter.

No matter where we'd spent our time earlier, if I held up and didn't fall asleep in a corner booth before midnight, we ended up at the Oxford Pub, which was one of the larger bars open until four in the morning.

To walk into the Oxford Pub at two in the morning, and past the ever-hopeful-yet-never-lucky receiving line of dateless men was an admission of tangible defeat for hundreds of people. It felt that way too, to me, but Angie was always oblivious to disappointment and lowered expectations. All she noticed were the men, and by then she wasn't that particular.

When even the Oxford Pub would have us no longer, we ended the night at the local Denny's for a bleary-eyed, sober-me-up breakfast of coffee, omelets and hash browns amid a largely failed and silent post-Oxford crowd.

On any night, one drink was all Angie needed before she felt the urge to investigate another bar with the people to her left and to her right. We traveled in a pack at all times with at least five other people, often more, most of whom we had just met and would never see again. Off we went under Angie's direction, walking up and down the street, bursting into bars in a mostly-laughing, high-spirited cluster.

Angie made friends everywhere she went, women as well as men. She always gathered them up and took them along with her, losing a few here or there, replacing them with others. I was the only constant in her crowd and her plans.

Sometimes I followed sullenly behind Angie and the others, head down, gripped by a mood I couldn't shake, hating her and finding fault with everything about her, even down to her choice in jewelry or the color of her eye shadow. In that mood, I also hated everyone else wholly and indiscriminately, and snapped at anyone who dared to approach me.

Sometimes I was the life of the party, linking arms with people and laughing while we skipped down the street. Sometimes I would start out that way, then shift without warning into a mean mood, or else dissolve into tears. I could never predict at the beginning of any evening with alcohol how I would feel by the end of it, but Angie was always good-naturedly accepting, no matter what mood I presented. She was the only person who was.

Angie was ceaselessly positive, slow to anger, fiercely loyal, cheerful, generous, kind-hearted, forgiving, open-minded, and quick to laugh, even at herself. She had inexhaustible levels of tolerance and genuinely liked everyone she met. These, coincidentally, were precisely the character markings that lead to severely impaired judgment in one's friendships and personal relationships. This worked to my advantage, because Angie suffered through my mood swings, irritations, sarcasm, and passive-aggressive jabs with charity and patience when no one else would. She even forgave my appearance.

"Holly has a Gemini rising, so she's two people," Angie would say and shrug when anyone wondered aloud why she stayed friends with me. "I just ignore *that* Holly until the other one comes back."

When anyone asked how she tolerated my looks, she crossed her arms over her chest as if she were offended, and said, "Hey! Excuse me, but *I'm* the pretty one. Ask Holly how she handles hanging out with *me*."

She buffered my relationships with the other women in the office by making friends with them first and then easing me into the corporate social arena, or at least to a manageable position on its periphery, as her official drinking buddy. We didn't bare our souls to each other or confide things the entire office didn't already know. We were *pals* more than friends. But work, and even life, would have been even more difficult without her.

Angie came to my desk one Monday morning with snow still sticking to her coat. She leaned over and grabbed my sleeve.

"Coffee," she said, tugging my arm. "Now."

I was turning my boots partially inside out, and stuffing them with paper towels from the bathroom to sop up the wet. I had already slipped on a pair of shoes I kept in my desk drawer and was waiting for my toes to thaw. I rose, followed her into the break room, and poured myself some black coffee. Angie measured four teaspoons of sugar and then liberally poured

31

powdered coffee creamer into her Styrofoam cup. She added coffee last, as the snow on her coat melted before my eyes into glittering dewdrops.

It was about her friend Karen, Angie announced dramatically, loosening her coat buttons with one hand. She ran her cup under her nose before taking a sip.

"Karen called last night," Angie said, looking at me meaningfully. "I am *really* serious. This is a major, major, *super*-big deal." She sipped.

Karen was a groupie who had fallen into the groupie lifestyle because she was an Anglophile. For her, this meant she could only have sex with men who were English—she wasn't sure why that was. Her Englishmen didn't have to be rock stars. They could be mechanics or accountants or Anglican vicars, provided they had the accent and retained their British citizenship. However, there was a serious dearth of Englishmen in Chicago, so Karen headed for the concert halls whenever English bands came through on tour.

Karen's objective was to meet an Englishman who would marry her and take her to England, where she vehemently insisted she belonged, and where she planned to live out her remaining days. Her life's sole focus was saving the money to move there. Meanwhile, she haunted rock concerts where she sought out Englishmen who might be so taken with her that they would feel compelled to ante up part, or all, of the cost to move her there. Thus far, none had. She had successfully accumulated the funds she needed twice before on her own. However, each time she had arrived and settled in, England had sadly sent her home again when her visa ran out before she'd found that husband. She was back in Chicago once again, and had been for several months, living with her parents and saving for her third attempt.

Angie recapped all of this at our table in the break room, as she slithered out of her coat and threw it on the back of a chair. She sat down, cupped her hands around her coffee and breathed it in, shuddering as the cold left her.

There was an unofficial Groupie Network, Angie explained, and Karen was plugged into it. These girls all kept in touch with each other and shared information about which bands were coming through town, what hotels they were staying at, and where they were headed for drinks after their concerts.

The band Torc was arriving tomorrow, and Karen had learned they would be coming to the Rush Up for drinks between ten and eleven that night. That, Angie informed me, punctuating the statement with raised eyebrows and her meaningful look, was where we must be. Our objective was to plant ourselves in their path and be irresistible. If we met the right person, we could get backstage passes for the concert the following night.

She told me when to be ready and what to wear: her clothes, not mine.

"But what if they change their minds before tomorrow and go somewhere else?" I asked, not quite convinced of the magnitude of the event, but edging closer to anticipation despite myself. "What if Karen is wrong?"

"Then we have a Rush Street night," Angie answered evenly over the rim of her cup. "But we can't not go." She gave me her deepest, most solemn and utterly meaningful look. "Right?"

"Okay..." I groaned with resigned displeasure over the prospect of another Rush Street night. Then I thought about what it would be like, if everything actually happened as planned, and grew increasingly excited. My excitement and anticipation grew throughout that day and the next.

The following evening, preparation took me two hours. Angie had brought to work the blouse that she wanted me to wear. I had taken it home and changed into it. After I was showered, shampooed, dried, curled, combed, dressed and booted, but not wearing any makeup, I rushed out the door and headed for the bus stop. It was just starting to snow a little, so I tucked my hair under my scarf to keep the curls from getting wet.

A car pulled up to the curb alongside me. The driver leaned across the front seat and rolled down the passenger window.

"Hey, doll, need a lift?"

"No, thank you." I said it nicely, looking ahead, still walking. Even in a heavy coat, with a scarf covering my hair, and no makeup, I thought. What is it with men?

"Fucking cunt!" He took off with his tires churning snow and slipping somewhat before they gained traction. If it were summer, they would have squealed. This was the third time it had happened today, that a car had pulled alongside me and a man invited me to get into it. I barely flinched, it happened so frequently.

This gentleman had fallen into a cruder, more hateful minority, and ranked below his more elegant and respectful colleagues who shouted the milder, "Bitch!" Out of curiosity, I thought I might keep a little notebook and pencil in my coat pocket and put tic marks beside the insults to calculate their scores. Usually men just shouted, "Bitch!" or "Fucking bitch!" Those two easily accounted for approximately eighty-five percent of the shouts I received as I walked city streets or stood at bus stops. The other fifteen percent included random, over-reactive shouts like, "Fucking cunt!" or "Suck my dick!" or "Slut!" I wasn't certain of the figures, of course, just as I wasn't certain why declining rides from strangers made me a slut, and wouldn't be until I approached it all scientifically with my little notebook, which I thought I might share with my shrink. But I would rather be a bitch than be raped. I would rather be a 'fucking cunt' as well. Viewing things that way, I took the shouts in stride.

So, what do you say to rock stars? I wondered, stopping at the corner beside the bus stop sign. Hoping my wool scarf wasn't crushing the curls, I nervously touched my hair. I hoped I wouldn't sound too young and silly; they were all older, famous, exotic and worldly, after all. They were British! Would they like me? I hoped they didn't ask me if I liked their music, though, because I did not, and I had always had a difficult time telling lies, even to be polite. Torc was similar to Alice Cooper in that their music appealed primarily to eighteen-year-old males and was heavy on screeching vocals, drums, and bass. I was more a fan of Jethro Tull, Joni Mitchell, and the Moody Blues. I shouldn't tell them that. Maybe I shouldn't say anything at all and just smile.

This was all very exciting and glamorous. I looked at my watch. It was eight forty.

Another car pulled to the curb, and another man offered me a ride. This one was older, gray-haired, and obviously wealthy, driving a new black Lincoln Continental. He was the fourth one today. It was a slow day because it was winter; in summer this happened more frequently. Nevertheless, the day wasn't over yet.

"No, thank you," I said.

"No, thank you" really set a man off, I'd learned. In a way, it was satisfying to prod a man into fury with simple good manners. It was a kind of power. With three polite words—I always spoke them very pleasantly, as if I were declining a mint—I unequivocally declared myself superior.

"Bitch!" Tires churned snow. Men did not leave the scene of a rejection, even one they surely had to know was self-inflicted, without hurling an insult and burning tread, including older, wealthy men in Lincolns. It meant I won.

A car filled with young men sped past. One of them rolled down the window and screamed something that I couldn't make out, but the car didn't slow. I would need a category in my little notebook for drive-bys as well, I thought to myself.

I hated that buses came less frequently after eight o'clock. That was when I was usually dressed to go out, looked very nice, and thus drew attention for long, unendurable stretches of time while I waited and waited under a street lamp for the bus. That was also the time when men who couldn't get dates and couldn't afford prostitutes began cruising the bus stops to deliberately court rejection and fling retaliatory insults at strangers. Or else they actually thought they'd get lucky with this approach because they were just that stupid. Here came another one…

Finally the bus arrived. The bus doors slammed open, and light spilled onto the dark pavement. I climbed the steps, threw my fare into the box, and surveyed the passengers to look for a safe place to sit.

I ignored the sly, sidelong glance of a young, mustached Latino who had an arm slung carelessly across the back of his seat. As I passed him, I briefly noticed a street gang insignia crudely tattooed across his knuckles, but was momentarily distracted by a drunk who reached out to grab my leg. A heavyset old woman with a babushka knotted under her chin peered at me with hugely distorted eyes through thick cataract glasses. She saw the Latino turn to watch me. She saw me whack the drunk's hand. She glared at me meaningfully and disapprovingly and drew her shopping bag closer to her chest as she lifted her chin in the air, turning away as if to make the point that *good* women, herself, for example, didn't attract unwelcome attention from men.

I preferred not sitting next to anyone, but I couldn't find a seat until I reached the last row of the bus—the "hoodlum row," Grandma Hazel called it. "All the hoodlums sit in the back row of the bus," she said. I chose to sit in the middle of the last row so no one boarding later could corner me against a window.

The Latino thug turned around to give me a lazy, suggestive, appreciative stare. He puckered his lips in a kiss.

I stared back at him calmly, steadily, unblinkingly, as if I were watching television. He returned my gaze, but his eyes flickered slightly. Then he blinked, indicating I had unnerved him within the first few seconds. That meant I had already won. Still, I pressed my advantage because it amused me. I slightly lifted one eyebrow in a haughty challenge, narrowed my eyes, and leaned forward slowly as if to suggest I might be about to pull a knife or pounce like a cat.

He turned to face the front of the bus and didn't look at me or anyone else again.

"Don't you ever worry that that sort of thing is going to backfire?" Dr. Silverman once asked.

"They don't scare me," I'd replied. "I'm a depressed person."

I disembarked at Belmont Avenue and walked to Angie's house on Sheffield without further incident.

Angie's tiny attic apartment smelled of cat urine. It didn't matter how often she changed the litter box, which wasn't often, because her two cats were male and unfixed, and created a more suffocating, musky urine stench than seven female cats would have. The odor also permeated the drapes and furniture, which both cats routinely sprayed. Total fumigation following a replacement of her furnishings, new paint, gallons of bleach, and removal of the cats would have been her only solution, had she been inclined to seek one.

Angie had obviously just gotten out of the shower because she answered the door wearing nothing but a towel.

"Hurry up! Hurry up!" I cried. "Why aren't you ready?"

"You're early. What time is it?" She dropped her towel and tossed it onto the bed, then walked over to her closet and stood naked in front of it, pushing the hangers back and forth.

"I am *not* early! It's almost nine-thirty!" I said, exasperated. "You always do this! You're always still buck-naked when I get here! Get dressed! Hurry!" I went into the bathroom to put on my makeup. I had worked myself into a state of irritable excitement, and now simply wanted to commence with the evening as quickly as possible.

A few minutes later a clothed Angie joined me, and we stood talking nonstop and over each other, fighting for mirror space while we brushed on our eye shadow or used the curling iron. We babbled about meeting rock stars and speculated on the likelihood of being invited back to their hotel for a party. If that happened, would we all trash the room? Would we have champagne fights? Would it make the newspapers? Would someone fall in love with us and make us rich and pampered rock star wives?

We had no experience with this sort of thing and presumed that knowing one groupie opened the door to meeting every famous rock star who came through town. Additionally, men tended to gravitate toward both of us. Meeting the band was more likely than not, if we were in a room with them, so our speculation was actually more realistic than one might have thought.

Angie wanted to marry a rock star. Or sleep with one. She arched her back and looked at herself sideways in the mirror.

"Foxy bitch," she declared, flipping her long blond hair and provocatively protruding her lips. "I'm a stone fox, and I'm going to get me a rock star tonight."

She looked at me critically, and said with a warning tone, "I have dibs on Angus Adkins."

"I think he's married," I responded. "I think they all are except for John Collier." The Tribune had published their bios in the entertainment section of today's paper, which we'd perused together at lunch. "Do you not remember *any* of this?"

"I was looking at the pictures," she explained defensively. She sniffed and pouted. "He's not the cute one, though. Angus is the cute one."

"I'm sorry."

"I have dibs on John Collier."

"Fine. He's yours." I was using a safety pin to separate my eyelashes, which were crusty with two coats of mascara. I slapped Angie's arm when she leaned into me. She never seemed to respect my eighteen inches of space and always pressed in too close. "Please! Stop bumping into me, or you'll blind me!"

A rock star boyfriend or husband was admittedly tempting, and it was certainly fun to speculate with Angie about getting one, but I wasn't seriously interested.

"They make the news," I would later explain to Dr. Silverman. "I feel no compelling urge to be crazy for a wider audience."

I could also predict my anxiety over having a boyfriend who was a rock star, always knowing he could have any woman he wanted, always worrying that he would leave me for someone else until I finally drove him away with jealous paranoia. One of the more complicated issues I was addressing in therapy was my intense fear of abandonment, and it would certainly surface in that situation. I'd have a psychological meltdown. I wouldn't survive it. It truly wasn't worth it. So, I had no problem with Angie calling dibs on every celebrity in the world.

The fitted blouse Angie had let me—demanded that I—borrow was fire engine red with a low-cut neckline. Pleased, I stared at myself in the mirror. Red was definitely my color, and it was a shame I owned nothing like this.

Angie wore a tight, too-small, midriff-and-cleavage-revealing, pale green sweater with jeans and no bra. Underneath the jeans, she wore low-cut, black lace bikini panties in anticipation of a successful evening. Before pulling on her jeans, she had posed in them and demanded my compliments.

She loaned me her red lipstick and a pair of gold hoop earrings from Avon, and offered me a splash of cologne. I borrowed her eyelash curler, while she applied the final deep violet touches to her eyelids. Then we posed for a moment in front of the bathroom mirror as we imagined rock star girlfriends would pose, one beautiful blond and one beautiful brunette, slender, braless, curled and perfumed, with dark-lidded, heavily made-up, 1970s whore eyes. We adjusted our poses to study the effect, then high-fived each other and prepared to leave.

The cab was a grand extravagance in keeping with our very grand plans, and it enabled us to make an entrance in front of the nightclub. We split the cost of it, and then each telescopically exited the cab one long leg at a time while gauging the effect on the men outside the club. Aware of the impact we were making, we walked to the entrance, test-driving the attention of these lesser men in preparation for our real targets: rock stars. A number of men followed us with their eyes. Some of them walked behind us, up the long flight of stairs, and into the club. Success.

Because I was nineteen, I could only drink beer and wine. The bouncer glanced at my birth certificate without displaying any real interest in my date of birth, although he would have adamantly refused entry to a male with only a birth certificate for identification. He stamped my hand with a large BW—for "beer and wine"—and waved me in. Angie received the over-twenty-one stamp and followed me.

The band was loud but good. The crowd was happy and hopping, and fairly large for a Tuesday. I liked this place. I was excited and in a pleasant mood. I was having a remarkably good day, in fact. It might be a good night, I thought to myself, even if no rock stars appeared.

"Great band, isn't it? I'm really loving this!" Angie screamed in my ear while bouncing up and down and dancing in place to the music. "I call dibs on the lead singer." She pointed toward the stage.

Angie always called dibs on everyone. She meant it, too. If she had dibs on someone and he approached me instead of her, Angie made her sad face and pouted. Sometimes she pinched me. She never had reason to be angry. I took the Girlfriend Code seriously, and would never have returned the interest of a man a girlfriend was dating, married to, or even just had dibs on. I routinely turned all those men away out of deference to the Code because men were easy to come by. It was girlfriends who were difficult to find. Plus, it was only right and fair.

While all is theoretically fair in love and war, the Girlfriend Code clarified rules and responsibilities girlfriends enforced on themselves and each other as they engaged in battle against men. The Code was unconditional and not void toward girlfriends one disliked or envied. Since it was not in writing and was discussed only when someone broke it or was pondering breaking it, different women understood the Code to varying degrees. They adhered to it in varying degrees as well, based on their personal thresholds of empathy and affection versus vanity, selfishness, desire, and ability to rationalize hurtful actions.

As for me, my interpretation was demanding, stringent and inflexible. I took it all very seriously. It was my only way of insinuating myself into the private Girl Club and feeling as if I belonged to it.

I understood that girlfriends do not, under any circumstances, initiate advances toward, or accept advances from, a man another girlfriend has any sort of past, present or potential relationship with, including "dibs" in a club situation. Girlfriends were required to ask permission if they were interested in someone with whom another girlfriend had ever had any kind of emotional attachment. If the request was declined, or accepted with obvious distress, a girlfriend could proceed no further.

Things got a little complicated when a man cheated. The offended girlfriend was obliged to shift anger toward the man and presume the other girlfriend was as much a victim as she. If two girlfriends were seeing the same man at the same time and learned this, both girlfriends were obligated to conclude that the man was a total jerk and a cheat who was lying to both of them, and be too proud to want him any longer.

They could, at their own discretion, convene at a bar and get drunk together with arms slung over each other's shoulders, buy each other drinks, and giggle and chortle over the man's penis, bald spot, bodily hair, farting habits, or idiosyncrasies in bed. This was best served with the offending man helplessly watching from the other end of the bar. In this instance, both girls won.

On the other hand, if one girlfriend still wanted him and made placating gestures toward him out of panic or regret, she automatically defaulted to a pathetic loser with no self-respect, and the other girl won.

Girlfriends addressed other issues on a case-by-case basis. They were to choose an acceptable course of action only from those rooted in empathy, kindness, sensitivity and respect toward their fellow girlfriends, with a sincere desire to cause no pain or embarrassment, except toward grievously offending men who deserved it. Girlfriends who broke the Girlfriend Code were entirely at fault no matter what the situation, and were officially at the mercy of the offended girlfriend and her other supportive, Code-adhering girlfriends.

If personal sacrifice or heartbreak was called for in order to adhere to the Code, so be it.

Women who had no Girlfriend Code seemed to be at war with men and women alike. To me, they were traitorous, selfish and untrustworthy, fighting over men at the expense of other women, viciously competing against the rest of us for dubious 'prizes' without regard for the damage they caused. At the same time, they were working against themselves. They had no trust of other women and no sisterhood for support whenever men won battles at their expense, and they received no compensating accolades for their favoritism toward men, who were just as dismissive toward them as they were toward the rest of us. They betrayed loyal and well-intentioned girlfriends, and trivialized, or even celebrated, the pain they caused on both sides, often mistaking losses for wins.

I tried to never do this. My loyalty was always with the women... who would not have me because of my looks. I pondered this at times: Perhaps it made me a pathetic loser with no self-respect, just of a different flavor. Nevertheless, a sense of sisterhood braced me, even if it was misplaced. It was *something* at least, wasn't it? In lieu of a family and real friends? Even if it wasn't entirely reciprocated?

Dr. Silverman called it the "Objectification War" between the sexes, where both sides viewed the other as objects. At its worst, he went on to explain, woman were headless, big-breasted bodies in porn magazines, and men were wallets that paid for the whims and demands of grasping, unfeeling, self-serving women. We each viewed the other side as the enemy, heartlessly used each other, and deliberately hurled missiles, not really believing the other side felt them much, or that their pain mattered. We each stole a little of the other side's dignity and humanity, and demeaned it.

When I was under siege, for instance, I certainly didn't care about any pain I might inflict on a man I rejected, just as he didn't care how I felt about being leered at, spoken to inappropriately, or grabbed, and then called a "bitch," or worse, for not going off with him. Men weren't entirely human to me—not really, not after years of insulting assaults—just as I, like any beautiful woman, was not entirely human to men. We were mere objects on opposite sides of a fence, rifles raised, at war.

Women were also guilty of objectifying each other, making victims of the overweight ones, for example. I knew about that firsthand because of a painful, transitional plump and acne-riddled period I'd experienced from the ages of twelve to fourteen; I was still as sensitive to and indignant about their rejection of girls with beauty challenges as I was to their rejection of me. Women on either end of the spectrum were objects to both sexes, so I had gone straight from receiving adolescent contempt and mockery to receiving jealous resentment and crude overtures without really enjoying any respite in between. Being objectified by both men and women made it difficult, and often impossible, for me to form friendships with either gender.

Someone grabbed Angie's hand, and she followed him through the crowd onto the dance floor leaving me with her coat and purse. I asked the waitress for a glass of wine and gratefully thanked the man who reached around me to pay her for it. He then asked if I would like to dance.

Unwritten bar etiquette dictated that I owed him, at minimum, five minutes of conversation or a dance in exchange for the drink—if a girl wasn't willing to spend five minutes with a man, she was morally obliged to decline the drink. With that drink, a man bought five minutes to sell himself to the girl with his dance moves or conversation. If it was *no sale*, neither was obliged to remain in the company of the other beyond the five minutes or that one dance. Everyone, male and female, except for the very drunk or very dense ones, understood this.

I couldn't resist. I was already bouncing to the music, so I smiled and nodded, set my wine on the bar, folded the coats and placed them under my bar stool, tucked our purses beneath them, and followed him onto the dance floor.

Angie had moved to the front of the crowd by the stage platform and was now dancing with her back to her partner. Facing the band's lead singer, she arched her back so her braless breasts bounced in his direction. He didn't appear to notice, though several men on the dance floor did. He was singing with his eyes closed.

When the song ended, I thanked my partner, and without looking back at him returned to the bar, where I had left my drink. Correctly taking his cue, the man slipped back into the crowd in search of a more willing female.

As I reached for my drink, a clean-cut young man in a rumpled business suit and loosened tie leaned over and grabbed my breast.

I turned to him, angry and exasperated.

"*Please* do *not* grab my breast!" I snapped, glaring at him with my death stare and pushing his hand away.

The young man dropped his jaw and lifted his hands into the air with exaggerated affront, as if he were well within his rights, and I was unreasonable and wrong to not cooperate. I had been to Rush Street enough times to be able to sort men into career categories. I guessed this one was employed in some field that rewarded arrogance, such as stockbroker or investment banker. From his sense of entitlement, and condescending-yet-crude demeanor, I guessed he had had a very expensive private education that involved fraternities.

He gasped in indignation.

"Well, excu-use me! Who the *fuck* do you think *you* are? Eh? Huh?" He continued in a mincing falsetto, sneering, "A precious little princess?" Then he snarled, "*Wrong*! You're just a sad little loser bitch. Fuck you."

He turned to his friends, all still dressed for work and disheveled, which meant they had been drinking for several hours. They all looked at me and laughed, then moved away into the crowd.

I'd never hit anyone before, but I edged closer each time something like this happened. I hated men. I hated bars.

Then suddenly, they came. I marveled at the accuracy of the Groupie Network, which somehow knew they would.

There was no question when Torc arrived that they had arrived. They coincidentally timed their arrival just as the band wrapped up a song, after the screaming cheers and whistles had died down. The Torc band members had all run up the flight of stairs before bursting into the room, and were looking around themselves with a proprietary air of, "My public! My fans!"

Apparently you had an air about you, when you were a rock star. These guys had that. They also had women with them, and men who did not quite exude that rock star aura walking a few paces behind. The band had come with a sizable entourage, which was filling the club with loud English accents we could hear from where we stood near the stage.

Lead singer Angus Adkins had swoon-inducing good looks. It was surreal, seeing a live version of a rock idol, someone I had only seen in magazines, and on television and album covers, but had never once ever dreamt I'd see in person. He was tall, with long, curly blond hair that fell over his shoulders and down his back, a broad chest bursting out of a too-small t-shirt and leather jacket, with small hips poured into a pair of skintight custom-made blue jeans. He had piercing blue eyes, heavy brows, a thick mustache, a strong jaw and a cleft in his chin. He had a smile with the impact of a stun gun. He looked like the hero on the cover of the cheesiest of romance novels, except that he was real.

Angie pulled me off the dance floor and floated, with me in tow, toward the shimmering glow of Angus Adkins's unearthly aura.

"I'll just kill his wife," she said, staring. "Is that her?" She gestured toward a tall, thin, and impressively-fashionable brunette who was leaning over, apparently checking her hose for tears. She stood upright, linked her arm through Angus Adkins's, and looked around with a bored expression.

"I can take that skinny bitch, easy."

"There's the one you have dibs on." I answered, pointing.

Bass guitarist John Collier was smaller and darker than Angus, with long, straight brown hair, sideburns and a mustache. He had a nice face, but emitted no unearthly, godlike shimmer. Beside Angus, he might have appeared almost gnome-like had he not had an engaging, good-natured smile, a rock star's air of self-confidence, and an eye-catching custom-made black leather jacket with studs.

"Yeah, he's okay," Angie answered.

Drummer Lucas Stanton was thin, small, and wiry, with a quick grin. His expression was one of perpetual pleasure and surprise, and he appeared to be interested in, and curious about, everything. He walked over to John Collier and Geoffrey Ames, the tall, dark-haired guitarist, and spoke a few words into John's ear. They wandered off toward the stage to watch the band. Geoffrey strolled over to Angus.

Angus Adkins moved straight to the bar.

Angie saw something that distracted her attention from Angus. She pulled me over to a table in the back where a noisy group of Englishmen were accepting their first drinks from the waitress. Angie stopped in front of a pretty, brown-eyed woman with short, pixie-ish dark hair, then leaned over and hugged her.

"This is Karen!" she yelled over the noise from the music and the screaming crowd. She touched Karen's sleeve and pointed to me. "Holly!" she shouted.

Karen nodded vigorously, and then tugged at the sleeve of a small blond woman who was standing with her arm around the waist of an Englishman, whose back was to us. She screamed the introduction: "Amy!"

Amy smiled and turned to join us. The Englishman she was with turned around to see where she had gone. When he looked up at me, his eyes stopped.

This was not unusual. Men's eyes stopped on me wherever I went. I was always being studied, observed, and staked out. I barely noticed except to ignore it, or to hunch over, avert my eyes, assess the area for viable escape routes, and react with varying levels of annoyance.

He had smallish eyes, unevenly set and brown, with nothing remarkable to commend them. They were not beautiful eyes, nor were they positioned in a beautiful face. I saw a beaked nose, a receding chin, and thin brown hair with wispy cowlicks. I saw huge protruding ears and thin lips. When he smiled, his teeth were crooked. It was a face and eyes to pass over when one looked for a potential boyfriend. It was a face that would compel a girl to refuse that drink or that dance, or to say, "I'm sorry. I just want to be friends."

What was unusual was my reaction to that particular set of eyes, and that particular face. I felt as though my electric current had shorted out, as if everything had gone black for an instant before starting up again. I caught my breath and looked back at him, then blushed and looked down for a moment. Then I looked back up again. I had never felt this kind of insane attraction toward anyone. Not ever.

"Trevor!" Amy hollered, pointing to him, pulling him into our conversation. She linked her arm through his possessively while Trevor studied me, seeming almost transfixed.

"Nice to meet you!" I screamed. He was studying, calculating, measuring, and approving me. Then, he was inviting me. I saw the invitation; an invitation was usually there when I looked into men's eyes. But this time, it was as arousing as a soft tickle at the nape of my neck. This time I was attracted in return, only it was more than attraction. I couldn't say what this was.

"Nice to meet you as well!" He shouted back. "What did you say your name was?"

"Holly!"

"Holly! Good to meet you, Holly! Very good indeed!"

Karen introduced Angie, and Trevor looked away to nod and deliver pleasantries to her. Then, as if he'd left his finger on a passage in a book so as not to lose his place, he returned to me. He didn't smile; he just looked at me intently.

I sipped my wine and glanced at him over the rim of my glass. Then I looked away. Then I looked back. Each time I glanced his way, he was studying me.

A few minutes passed. During that time, the invitation had, by degree, morphed into a beckoning, which then became—what? A yearning? After half an hour, he looked impatient, even tortured, like a tomcat pacing back and forth behind a window while a cat in heat cried and wailed for him down below.

I was the cat in heat, looking up at that window. And now I was looking away again.

He had Amy. He glanced down and edged away from her imperceptibly. He extricated his arm from hers under the pretext of reaching for his beer, and then did not link arms with her again. He shifted his weight to add inches to the space between them, and turned so that his back was slightly toward her. He looked at me, trying to read my face, trying to decide what to do on the basis of what he saw there.

I self-consciously looked back at him for a moment. How my eyes may have appeared to him, I did not know. I knew what I felt, and I tried to cover it up; I thought I had. I knew what I saw in his eyes, and I tried not to send any signals in response; I thought I had not. But I realized I'd failed because the look in his eyes was gaining strength and confidence. It had grown brazen with expectation. I had accepted his invitation against my best efforts, and he knew it.

We had not said a word to each other beyond our introductions, yet I was already feeling guilt and shame over the blow this was going to be to Amy. I had never once broken the Girlfriend Code, and didn't care that she was not my girlfriend, or that Trevor was merely passing through and not her boyfriend. The Girlfriend Code was a pact of decency and trust between women in general, *good* women, anyway, at least as I defined them, and I was about to steal another woman's man for the first time in my life. I mentally apologized to Amy, and to women everywhere in the world.

Backing out, though, was not an option. Trevor and I crackled when we looked at each other. It went beyond chemistry or mere sexual attraction. It transcended even lust. This was scary voodoo. Soon it would be desperate. Soon, so would I.

I excused myself and went to the bathroom, where I studied myself in the mirror. I wasn't happy with my hair and tried to arrange it two or three different ways with a decorative hair comb Angie had leant me. I wanted to look as pretty as I could for Trevor.

Two girls stood beside me, retouching their makeup, both dipping into an open makeup bag for eye shadow and mascara. I smiled at them and grimaced.

"I have such a hard time with this hair," I said in a self-deprecating tone, trying to apologize for taking up mirror space for as long as I was. I worried that I looked vain. "I wish I could trade mine for yours," I said to the girl with the red waves. I smiled.

The girl with the red hair stared at me. She exchanged looks with the other girl, and then gave me a stiff smile. She closed the makeup bag and shoved it into her purse. The two of them left, indignant.

"Do you believe her? Who the hell is she to complain about anything?" the redhead asked, loud enough for me to hear.

"Girls like that are just fishing for compliments. They're so shallow," the other one observed disdainfully. "What a bitch." She pushed the door open, and their giggles faded into the crowd noises.

I stood for several moments staring at my hands, while tears welled up in my eyes. Then the tears withdrew to join the hardened lump in my chest. I looked up, sighed, and shook myself a little, then returned to our table. Trevor visibly perked up and smiled as I approached. I smiled back.

A half-hour passed, and then an hour. The larger group of Englishmen dispersed into the nightclub, leaving just a few of them with us, including Trevor, two of his *mates*, as he called them, and Angie, Karen and Amy. While we all made small talk and laughed as a group, polite interaction between Trevor and me had become a situation. I tried not to look at him, but kept stealing peeks nevertheless.

Each time I glanced his way, he was looking at me. Between musical sets when it was quiet enough to speak, his focus was on me, even though he primarily spoke to everyone else. His face had gone beyond brazen expectation to the impatient question, "How?" He didn't even ask, "When?" because the obvious answer was, "The first opportunity."

A seemingly oblivious Amy shouted and communicated with her hands to Karen and Angie, or exchanged laughing comments when it was quiet enough. She didn't spend much time trying to speak with me, and she gave me no eye contact, but women rarely did. Trevor responded when she addressed him, but if I said anything to anyone in the group, he immediately turned and gave me his full attention, seemingly catching every word.

So this is love at first sight, I thought. Amazing. It was like getting sucked into quicksand, or being pulled into a planet's orbit. I would never have believed it.

I also would never have believed that I'd experience it with a man who was… not handsome. But then, I had never found any man more attractive.

I pulled back sharply. Where had that thought just come from, that he was mine? But it was a stubborn one. He was mine, and I knew it. He knew it, too and was merely trying to decide the speed with which he would succumb and admit it.

This may be the man I'm going to marry, I thought, looking over at him. He returned my glance with a wink and a smile. I smiled back and changed my mind. I reworded the thought to *I've just met the man I'm going to marry*. I wanted to giggle a little from the shock of it.

The song concluded, and the cheering died down. The band took another break, and a Pink Floyd tape began pumping through speakers at a much lower volume, enabling us to merely talk loudly, instead of scream.

"Let's all go back to the hotel," Trevor addressed the group but looked at me, "where we can talk."

Everyone agreed and made motions to locate coats and finish drinks.

"Come now, hurry." Trevor slipped on his coat and helped Amy into hers. He glanced at me as I pulled on my coat unassisted, then quickly looked away.

Trevor took charge, flagged a cab, and directed us into it in such a way that everyone was seated before he was, except for me. He sat in the back on the passenger's side and looked out at me standing on the curb.

"You'll have to sit on my lap, love," he said with an innocent smile. "Come now." I squeezed in and sat on his lap, sideways, with my feet toward the center of the car, head pressed against the ceiling, as Angie settled onto Charles's lap beside us. Thanks to Trevor's maneuverings, Amy was in the front seat by the window, so I couldn't read her face, and she couldn't easily see mine.

I sat stiffly, trying to process what was happening and explore the sense I had about Trevor. It felt monumental. We hadn't really spoken yet, but I had already identified this man as the great love of my life. It was crazy.

Or was it just lust? If it was, it was certainly packing a punch. I turned my head to glance at him and saw that he was still looking at me. He reached up, wrapped one of my curls around his finger, and mouthed, "You're lovely." Then he pressed the curl to his lips and kissed it. He obviously found me attractive. If I was in lust, I wasn't alone.

My hair was long, and Trevor lightly fingered the ends of it behind my back, where no one could see. Then I felt him push my hair aside and press his lips to the nape of my neck. My hair was thick and spilled over to hide his face. It was dark, except for the headlights and streetlights shining into the windows. But still, could anyone see what he was doing? Could anyone tell that I liked it?

Apparently not. Everyone else was engaged in an animated discussion about the backup band's guitarist, who had broken his arm in a fall and was being temporarily replaced on the tour with someone who was a much better musician than he. What would the band ultimately do? Keep the good guitarist? Or invite the original one back when his arm healed?

On every level, this was a bad situation. I created a *Pro/Con* list in my head: This man was with another woman. He was doing this to me with the other woman only inches away, suggesting disrespect and a serious deficit of class and conscience. He could be a total jerk and a cheat. I could be a pathetic loser with no self-respect. He was leaving town in two days, probably never to return. He had formed his attitude toward women through a long association with groupies, so he would love me and leave me without even considering or caring what that might do to me. I would be used and discarded. Amy would be discarded as well. Could I have Amy on my conscience while I was feeling used and discarded? I already felt bad because I was about to break the Girlfriend Code. I was already sorry.

This was only my first night of Rock and Roll, and I was in over my head.

On the *Pro* side of the list was my sense that a list was completely beside the point. He was mine and was merely stepping forward, declaring himself. How else could he have done it, with the time constraints we'd been dealt? Under ordinary circumstances, we might have danced around our attraction for weeks or months. During that time Trevor could have ended his relationship with Amy, with whom I would have carefully avoided any sort of friendship so I would not be forced to betray it. Then we might have proceeded in a proper and mannerly fashion.

The reality of the situation was that we had no time. The courting process was accelerated out of necessity, and delving into territory that was squeamishly cheap and trashy.

His lips moved to my earlobe, and his tongue teased it just a little. I shuddered, thinking that there had never been a time in my life when I had met a man I was more willing to make love to than right now. I turned and looked at him. He looked back. The lust was there, but it felt like love.

I turned my head away again. It had come on too suddenly, so it had to be only lust. Love takes time. Love is preceded by conversation.

The cab pulled up in front of the hotel, and we shifted and prepared to disembark. Charles paid the driver, while I climbed out first. Trevor and Amy got out at the same time. I stood and watched Trevor look down at me, wondering what I should do.

Then Trevor turned away from me and pulled Amy aside. Her face fell. She shot him a hurt look, then nodded and accepted a twenty dollar bill from him. She climbed back into the cab without looking at me and was gone.

He walked over to me and stopped.

"Let's talk," he said, taking my arm. He led me into the hotel.

Angie looked at me with an exaggeratedly shocked grin and whispered something to Karen, who was frowning at the disappearing cab. Then Karen shrugged, and everyone turned to go through the revolving door.

Inside the hotel, Trevor led the group to the lounge. He waved everyone away and resolutely steered me to a corner booth in the back. He sat next to me, shifting sideways to face me. When the waitress came, he asked me what I wanted to drink, and then ordered my white wine and a Guinness for himself.

"Tell me about yourself," he said. "How old are you?"

"I'm nineteen."

"Your whole name, including middle name."

"Holly Noelle Salvino."

He listened to my answers intently with his head cocked, nodding and watching my face while lightly playing with my fingers under the table. I felt his fingers as if they were lightening bolts.

"Your birthday and your favorite color," he prompted.

"December twenty-fourth, yellow."

"Were you named for the Christmas holiday?"

"Yeah." Tradition in my family demanded that baby girls be named after flowers or herbs. The plant my mother had chosen for me was a beautiful, shiny shrub with knife-sharp leaves and toxic berries. While she had only been thinking of the season when she named me, I found her choice to be fitting and insightful.

"Very festive! What do you do in your spare time?"

"Read. Study." Sleep? It was an honest answer, but I didn't mention that.

"Are you in school?"

"No, I just buy the textbooks if I can't find what I want in the library."

He seemed surprised and looked at me with a different kind of interest.

"What kind of textbooks?"

"Psychology, mostly. Anthropology. English literature. Art history. Whatever I feel like reading and whatever books I can find used and really cheap." I made a face. "No Algebra, though. I draw the line at that." I sighed. "Though someday I'll probably have to break down and do it because I really should, you know? I should really learn math."

"Why don't you enroll?"

"I don't know." I shrugged and looked away. "I will someday."

I didn't tell him I was afraid I couldn't succeed at school because, unless I was pumped up with excitement, as I was tonight, I usually crawled into bed at seven thirty each evening, exhausted. Night classes were out of the question because I worked during the day. My energy didn't extend to a second job or to a scholastic effort in the evening. Oftentimes, it was brutal just forcing myself to last through the workday when I was going through one of my depressions and only wanted to sleep. Forcing myself to push through exhaustion frayed my nerves and sometimes triggered episodes of rage or violent tears. I lived in a precarious physical and emotional balance that allowed for no additional sustained effort.

Furthermore, I absolutely could not afford to go to school, and was completely overwhelmed by the forms you had to complete to apply for financial assistance, just as I was overwhelmed by housework. I had no one to ask for advice or help, and wasn't motivated to wade through the application process on my own. I would simply sneak into classes if I could, rather than go through the hassle of applying, because I didn't need the degree. But I was afraid I'd be caught sneaking into class and would get into trouble.

Mostly, though, I had simply given up because it was all so hopeless. College, like the prom and a big wedding, was something I had grown up knowing was for other girls, and out of my reach.

"What religion?"

"Catholic."

"I am as well. Are you lapsed? Or practicing?"

"Lapsed."

"I am as well. Though I'll probably rethink that when I have children. Do you have any pets?"

"A dog. Pansy."

"Ah!" he said, nodding. "I like dogs. What kind?"

"Cockapoo."

He laughed. "Silly name. And what do your parents do?"

I stiffened. I shot him a frozen smile and shook my head. I edged away.

He leaned closer.

"What happened to your parents?" he whispered gently. "You don't have to tell me," he added reassuringly.

I hadn't planned on telling him, but I did: Suicide. Abandonment. He looked away, pulled my hand to his lips and kissed it, and then laced his fingers through mine. He pulled my hand into his lap and held it in both of his. He said nothing.

"What about you?" I asked.

"Well then. I am Trevor Anthony Vincent Wyatt. Vincent is my father's name, and therefore I took it as my confirmation name. Anthony is my mother's father. Trevor is my very own."

"My confirmation name is Christina," I offered.

"Ah! Very nice." He continued, "Birthday, April twenty-sixth. I'll be twenty-four years old this year. Favorite color, blue. No pets. Two sisters, a great deal older than me, no brothers. Aunts, but no living uncles. Three nieces, but no nephews. And six female cousins. Except for my father, I am the only male in my family for years and years, miles and miles. I was kissed and fussed over and spoilt by the females in my family, and taught all manner of household tasks. You'll find I'm quite a handy bloke. Favorite food, roast beef with Yorkshire pudding. And I like custard."

"What's Yorkshire pudding?"

"It's a delightful English delicacy." He paused to ask, "Do you cook?"

I shook my head.

"Then I shall make it for you, and we'll have a feast."

"*You* cook?" I asked incredulously.

"Absolutely. I'm quite good, in fact." Trevor squeezed my hand. "You'll see."

He drifted off into somewhat nervous introspection, still holding my hand. He glanced over at the table where the others were seated, but didn't appear interested in them. The red-headed Daz was nuzzling Karen's neck, while Charles was turned toward, and speaking to, the newly-arrived band member, John Collier. Angie was leaning over and flirtatiously laughing with a man at the table next to theirs, either forgetting she had dibs on John, or changing her mind about it, or shifting her focus because John had rebuffed and ignored her.

Trevor glanced back at me, and then looked down. He was silent, tense, and even brooding for a moment or two. He took a long swallow of beer and wiped his mouth. He played with the bottle and looked at it thoughtfully. Then he looked up.

"It's quite clear that I'm going to come to love you, Holly Noelle Christina Salvino," he said softly, looking straight into my eyes with a serious, somewhat pensive expression. His admission took me completely off-guard. "What do we do about it?"

51

His words had almost the same effect I'd experienced when I first saw him. My electrical current shorted out for an instant into black, and then started up again, this time at a higher voltage.

I had heard this sort of declaration before. I had already received three first-date marriage proposals, and one no-date marriage proposal from a boy in the neighborhood. "If you ever get pregnant and need a husband," he'd offered, "I'll marry you." There were other men— mostly drunk—who had told me they loved me within minutes of meeting me. Trevor was mostly drunk. This was not new.

But yes, it was. This time, the man spoke to me over crackling, scary voodoo, and his inviting looks had gone beyond desperation to something even more intense. He was articulating what I felt toward him. He was confirming that he sensed as well as I did that we were supposed to be together. Love or lust? He said *love*, and I was inclined to believe it.

I couldn't show my fear, so I turned to him and smiled teasingly.

"How many girls have you said that to?" I quipped somewhat lamely, at a loss for a witticism. I shrugged and made a face, somehow knowing quite well that he did not take this lightly.

Trevor shook his head. "I've said that to no one," he answered earnestly. "But I have said it to you." He looked at me steadily and waited for an answer.

"Okay." I nodded and looked down. I swallowed down the anxiety. I had never been in a serious relationship before, and I knew this was going to be my first. I wasn't sure if I could manage it, but I couldn't not try.

"Will you have a roadie instead of a rock star?"

I looked up at him wide-eyed with surprise and laughed. I nodded.

He smiled. "Will you come with me on the tour?"

I shook my head. "I have a dog and a job."

"Can you find someone to keep the dog? Will they give you a holiday? I'd like you to come with me." He reached up and ran his fingers through my hair. "Two weeks? Three? Longer?"

"We just met!" I was being sensible. We hadn't even kissed, and he was inviting me to live with him on the road. It seemed that common sense was missing from this discussion. I was summoning it back.

"We have just got thoroughly familiarized, haven't we? We know everything about each other. Please come with me." His voice was a caress. He leaned closer.

"How can you possibly know that you want to be with someone you met less than two hours ago?" I asked. A better question: *How could I?*

Trevor raised his hands in a careless, swooping gesture then lowered them. "I don't know. I just do."

We were marked people. It was as clear to me as it was to Trevor. Marveling at it and acknowledging it, I had no choice but to follow him and accept it.

"Will you come, then?" He stood and reached for my hand.

"On the tour? Or to your room?"

"Both."

"Yes."

Chapter 7

In the morning I awakened not quite hung over, but feeling enough of the effects of alcohol to press my temples and wonder how ashamed I should be for whatever I'd done, naked with a stranger, the previous night. I took stock of the situation and knew where I was. I knew who Trevor was and why I was there. I remembered everything quite clearly.

We had barely made it into the room. In fact, the door was still closing when Trevor began tearing at my blouse, and I at his zipper. We sank to the floor, only pausing momentarily for, "Are you on birth control?" "Yes."

We had no time to be coy and no time for foreplay. We came together like animals, only partially undressed, still three feet from the bed.

"It wasn't really the best way to start a relationship, I suppose," I would later tell Dr. Silverman. "I honestly don't know what got into us. It was all really sleazy in retrospect. Kind of."

"Did you feel sleazy?"

"That's the weird thing. No. It's like it was meaningful and meant to be."

Dr. Silverman didn't appear to be convinced.

I looked over at Trevor, who was still sleeping, and had a moment of chest-squealing excitement. I was feeling the same way in daylight as I had the previous evening, even with that strange, frightening desperation for him sated. Well, not quite sated. I wrapped my legs around him and kissed his eyelids to wake him up. *Quietly, quietly. Don't wake Charles. Yes, that. Yes. Sshh. Oh! Sshh. Oh my darling. Sshh. Yes.*

Love or lust? Love? Really? Yes. Yes, it was. It was. Amazing.

Ever practical, even in the midst of throwing myself headlong into wildly risky stunts and behaviors, I carefully took note of everything I still felt toward him, and concluded that my attraction had not been from alcohol. Therefore, I could not allow him to leave without me. I didn't want him to leave, but it was also apparent that we had to stay together so I could pursue this and see where it led.

I concluded that I had made the right decision and pressed forward with it. I climbed out of bed and showered, then dressed myself in last night's clothes. I dug through my purse for a safety pin to close the tear in Angie's blouse.

I made arrangements to meet him later. Then I kissed and reluctantly left him, still naked in the hotel bed. I slid out the door blowing kisses he pretended to catch in his fist. Charles snored, then shifted in his sleep and was quiet.

I went to work and arranged for a quick vacation. I got grudging approval for it and presented Angie with the earthshaking news that I was going on tour. She made her pouty face because she wasn't going, but cheered up immediately when she thought about the evening's concert. She asked if I could get her a backstage pass, and I promised to try.

After work, I stopped at home to pack my things. I then called a cab and took Pansy to my grandmother's.

"You ought to be committed," my grandmother said. "Who is he anyway? Crazy and on drugs. They're all crazy and on drugs. You don't know anything about him."

There was that aspect of it, potentially, but I didn't care. I knew Trevor was safe, and I knew he was mine. Even if it didn't work out, I was still going to have an adventure!

Despite her obvious misgivings, Grandma took Pansy's leash and a sack of dry dog food. I left them standing in her doorway with Grandma shouting dire warnings that I would be murdered and left by the side of the road.

I took a bus back to the hotel, where I met Trevor for dinner before the concert. We talked over our meal about the logistics of traveling together, then of me flying home in a week. In less than twenty-four hours, we had gone from being complete strangers to a couple planning our short-term future, with a mind toward the long-term.

"We can toss Charles out during the early afternoons, before work," Trevor said cheerfully over dinner. "The room is ours in the afternoon.

And we'll always have the room to ourselves until one in the morning because Charles likes to end the day with a pint or two. That isn't long because work doesn't end until nearly midnight. Then we'll have to get dressed and let him in. It's his room as well, after all."

I couldn't help but feel sorry for poor Charles.

I watched Trevor press his food onto the back of his fork, holding his utensils almost entirely differently from the way I'd been taught. I stared, feeling a little too fascinated. Then I felt a small stab of fear because my fascination with other people's personal habits usually led to uncontrollable, obsessive irritation and insurmountable problems.

"You hold your fork in your left hand," I observed. "You schmoosh your food into it." I had found that I could sometimes quell the irritation by emulating the behavior and finding forgiveness for it through shared guilt, so I tried to hold my utensils and eat the way he did, but I found I was as clumsy doing that as I was with chopsticks. It was a desperate effort.

"This is the only proper way to eat," he replied. Then he held his hands out and demonstrated. He leaned over and held my hands, helping me to schmoosh my food correctly. "Like this."

"But my way is more efficient. Food doesn't get stuck between the prongs." There was a hint of affront in my voice.

The irritation was creeping up on me. If I didn't do something quickly, it would grow into indignation, and then finally outrage. I would have to leave him because I would hate him, all because of the way he held his fork. I focused on schmooshing food into the back of my fork to make it all recede somewhat.

Irritation was another thing about myself that I could never confess to anyone. Whenever I asked people to stop doing something that pushed my nerves to the edge, they laughed and did the irritating thing even more, just to punish me for finding it unendurable. They would never think of laughing at, or persecuting someone who was in physical pain, but mental torment was always fodder for a joke.

"It's the only proper way." Trevor pointed his fork at me in response to my challenge. Then he nodded in agreement with himself.

"I beg to differ. My way is equally proper. Perhaps it's even *more* proper."

"*My* way is the *English* way." He sniffed, turned his head, and looked down at me condescendingly from the corner of a twinkling eye.

"I see," I sniffed back. And then I giggled.

Trevor knotted his eyebrows and squinted at me in a fierce frown to cover his grin, then leaned over and kissed my nose.

"We shall each eat in our own way," he said. "And that settles it."

I grinned back, but was inwardly hoping—I actually said a prayer—that his schmooshing wouldn't be a problem. The fact that it had come to my attention did not bode well for us.

Uncharacteristically, I decided in that instant to approach the matter a little differently. I simply wouldn't watch him eat. I would always look away. My inward reaction was a sense of unsteady relief at having identified a solution, combined with gnawing fear that it wouldn't be enough.

"I imagine there will still be some time for sightseeing, if we're in a city for two days," Trevor assured me, continuing our earlier conversation of time management. "Next week is St. Louis. They have a large arch I would like to climb. You don't mind if we take Charles along for that, do you?"

I didn't mind at all. In fact, that was one useful way to assuage my guilt over tossing Charles headlong out of his hotel room, and then banning him for hours and hours. It would be fun.

Trevor was happy to leave a pass for Angie. When I called her to let her know, she didn't answer her phone. I knew she would be devastated to learn that she'd missed her chance, but there would be other concerts... lots and lots. I somehow knew that as well.

I received my very first backstage pass, peeled it off its paper backing, and stuck it to my shirt.

We all rode in the tour bus on the short trip from the hotel to the concert hall. I counted twelve men. There were also three other girls about my age, whom I assumed were paired off with three of the roadies. One of these was Karen, who gave me a short wave as she walked past me to an empty seat in the back. It was a noisy ride, and I said very little, trying to memorize faces and attach names to them.

It was a thrill to see girls clustered at the backstage doors, staring at us, when we pulled up and spilled out of the bus. They were all standing in the snow and shivering in sexy footwear that was inappropriate for the weather, as they studied us and strained to get a glimpse. We filed past the security guards and into the backstage area. I had never before been a part of something so exclusive, or in a position so enviable to so many. I now understood how people could get addicted to the sensation. I was beginning to understand why those girls were shivering outside, hoping to get in.

Before the show Trevor led me onto one side of the stage and directed me to sit on top of one of the speakers, where I perched proudly but self-consciously, visible to the audience, only a few feet away from one of the microphones.

The houselights dimmed, and the footlights came on. The crowd screamed. Torc ran past me and onto the stage, so closely I could have touched them. The crowd roared as Geoffrey lifted his guitar into the air, and Angus screamed "Heeeee-yow!" into his microphone. The sound cranked up, and music became pure vibration as my speaker shook.

I considered my situation. Everyone in the audience, about forty thousand people, would have traded places with me, to have my spot on the speakers, to be close enough to these famous men to reach out and touch them as they walked past. The girls at the backstage door most certainly would.

I felt a heady rush and a surging excitement. I now understood why groupies chased rock bands! This little piece of knowledge was as valuable to me as anything I had read in my psychology books. I now had a bit of insight into human nature that I hadn't had before this evening, and considered this a rare opportunity to study rock-and-roll people closely, and analyze everything about this experience. Having unique and rare experiences like this one was like going to school, in a way. I didn't know what I would do with the information, but knowledge was never wasted. This particular lesson was definitely a thrill, and a seriously addictive one.

Trevor worked throughout the show, barely glancing at me when he passed by, never speaking to me, completely focused on his job, moving cables, props, lights and equipment.

I looked around and studied the women. Most of them were easy to identify as groupies, not because they looked hard, immoral and depraved, as I had imagined they would, but simply because they were there. There was a smattering of women who clearly were not groupies—one was a photographer, and two others wore press passes—but for the most part, the women I saw were carefully, stylishly coiffed and dressed, buffed and polished, squeaky-clean and heavily made up, their eyes darting about with interest and expectation.

The groupies seemed to be alone or in pairs, never in clusters, but they all seemed to know one another. During my trips to the bathroom, they were all friendly and talkative in front of the mirrors as they adjusted each other's skirts and loaned each other perfume or mascara, but outside, they retreated once again into a façade of reserve. Women I'd seen being friendly in the bathroom barely exchanged eye contact in the stage area. If a third girl approached a pair of them, one of the pair walked away so there were never more than two together. They fascinated me, and I watched them closely, trying to figure out the rules.

I noticed that most of the girls at the backstage door had made it in somehow. I was interested in learning exactly how they had done it.

Karen nudged me over and took a seat beside me on the speaker. She handed me a cold bottle of beer. I smiled and mouthed, "Thank you." Karen nodded and smiled back, looking squarely into my eyes before turning her attention to the band onstage. That was noteworthy: Most women didn't quite look me in the eye, even when they were speaking directly to me. Their eyes would slide over me as their faces closed and their body language told me to keep my distance, that I wasn't welcome.

I had a brief moment of joy, wondering if Karen wanted to be my friend. Then I reminded myself that she did not. Apart from Angie, women never did, and this little stab of hope always led to disappointment. I returned to studying the activity on the stage and behind it, happy in the moment with the company and the beer, not expecting a friendship, and thereby sparing myself the letdown.

The stage was awash in swirling red and blue lights as Angus, Geoffrey, and John tossed their long hair and pranced, paced, posed, and cavorted with their microphone stands, shrieking the lyrics to their songs. Lucas pounded the drums, shooting droplets of sweat that caught the lights like sparks. The audience screamed. The noise level was deafening, but not as horrific on a speaker as one might expect; I was above the sound, not in front of it. The primary issue was the vibration, and Karen and I might as well have been inside of John Collier's bass guitar.

Karen tugged my sleeve and pointed to the dressing rooms. She hopped down from the speaker and invited me to follow her. I went, grateful to have someone to talk to and be with while Trevor was working, because the stage performance wasn't necessarily interesting to me; I'd never been a fan of Torc.

"The beer and the food are this way," she said when we were far enough away from the stage to hear each other.

The backstage area was bleak and cold, and milling with people. It closely resembled a public garage. Doorways led to chilly, ill-tended rooms with dreary, battered walls and old, torn Salvation Army furnishings. None of the dressing rooms contained the lighted mirrors, carpeting, or plush couches you always saw in dressing rooms on TV, perhaps because the venue doubled as a sports arena.

"This is worse than a basement, isn't it?" I commented.

"You've never been backstage before?"

I shook my head.

"They're all like this. Sometimes they're worse. Wait until you see the Aragon. It's all pipes and really narrow walkways. You know, twenty-watt light bulbs hanging from cords. Damp walls and dripping ceilings. That sort of thing. It's like the catacombs or a horror movie." Karen was referring to the same Aragon Ballroom my grandmother and aunts had danced in decades earlier. It was now a rock-and-roll venue.

We moved to the food table and made ourselves some sandwiches. An occasional groupie briefly exchanged pleasant greetings with Karen, then drifted away. Karen seemed far less interested in them than in me.

"Trevor's taking you with him, right?" When I nodded, Karen didn't seem to be angry, despite the fact that Amy was her friend. "I'm hoping I'll go too. I'm working on it."

"With Daz?"

"Yeah." Karen put a pickle slice on her paper plate and smiled. "Trevor's a good guy," she said. "You're really lucky."

"I'm sorry about Amy." I said. I was still dealing with the guilt.

"Don't feel bad about it. You didn't throw yourself at him or do anything to be mean. It was his choice. That's the way it goes. Rock and roll." Karen tweaked my elbow. "Savoy Brown is coming to town in a few days, and she's already setting things up. She's not mad at you. Don't be so worried."

She took a bite of sliced roast beef on rye, washed it down with a swallow of beer, and then continued, "I saw what was going on with you and Trevor. Amy did too, by the way. Nobody's fault. *C'est la vie.*" She paused to smile at Daz, who darted past and disappeared. "I read an interview with Janet Planet, and she called it 'alchemical whammo.' It happened with her and Van Morrison when they met." She sighed. "I wish it would happen to me."

She was nice. Were groupies nice? They had a dicey reputation, but everything I was seeing suggested that I would probably like them. That was fortunate, since I was going to be with them for a week.

"He writes his love songs for her," Karen continued. "That's who the song "Brown Eyed Girl" is about."

"No kidding."

"When you—when *we*—get back, I'll take you with me to some concerts." Karen didn't appear to be making a hollow promise just to be polite. She appeared to be genuinely interested in making plans with me.

"Really?"

Karen nodded and looked at me appraisingly without any jealousy or resentment, then she dug through her purse and brought out a pen and address book. She handed them to me and had me write down my phone number.

"You're super gorgeous," she said. "They'll let you backstage in a heartbeat, no matter who's playing. Me too, if I'm with you." She tossed her paper plate into a trash bin and lit a cigarette. "We should pair up, you know? For concerts? I've got lots of connections, so I always know where they're staying and where they'll be hanging out after the show." She took a drag from her cigarette. "I'll drive us to the shows, and then you can talk to the security guards and get us in. Okay?"

I wrote my name, address and phone number on the second page under "S," after a dozen or more other names, and handed it back to her. I pulled out my own address book and had her write down her information, making hers the only name under "G." My address book only contained numbers for family, work, Angie, my shrink, and Pansy's vet. Two old boyfriends' numbers were also still there, illegible after I thoroughly scribbled through them to obliterate them.

The exchange of phone numbers absolutely sealed it. I had a new girlfriend! I had someplace to go that wasn't New Town or the Oxford Pub! I smiled, delighted, knowing I'd be too shy to be the first one to call and hoping she would call me soon. Then I nearly burst with gratitude when Karen squinted, reached over, and picked a piece of lint from my sleeve. I was touched to my heart. She really was a girlfriend.

Chapter 8

The bus was renovated with twelve short, shallow, curtain-enclosed bunk beds stacked in threes, one atop another in the back, a small refrigerator with beer, a stereo with eight-track tapes, and plenty of playing cards and ashtrays. There were two small RV tables with booth-style seating across from each other, and behind them, standard bus seats faced forward, providing seating for twelve.

I'd climbed onto the bus holding my small, round, white cardboard hatbox suitcase and was now awaiting instructions.

"This way, darling." Trevor had begun calling me *darling* during our first night in his hotel room, and it appeared to have stuck. I'd never envisioned myself as a "dah-ling," right out of a 1940s movie, but there I was, following my Cary Grant.

Trevor whipped open the curtain of the bottom bunk, furthest back on the starboard side of the bus. "This is ours."

He opened the foldout compartment beneath the bunks, rearranged three knapsacks, and then took my little suitcase and placed it in there beside them.

"The curtain is not soundproof so we must be good," he warned, holding a finger to his lips. Then he kissed my cheek.

I peeked past the curtain to a neatly-made bunk. In the corner of the bed was a small stack of books. *He reads!* I thought, delighted. The more I learned about him, the more perfect it seemed he was. I squinted to see what the books were. I saw classics! *Jude the Obscure* was on top. Thomas Wolfe was beneath that, with three by P. G. Wodehouse. And there was one about American Indians. He was so perfect...

"The loo is here." He opened the door to a cramped and tiny closet, and then quickly closed it. "Just the one silly toilet for two thousand

and three of us. Bloody nuisance, considering all the beer. But you'll adjust."

Frowning a warning, he said, "No bowel movements on the bus. *Ever.*"

"Seriously?"

"Seriously. We'd rather you rupture." He turned and moved back toward the front of the bus.

I followed him up the aisle and took a seat beside him in one of the booths.

They began filing in, running up the steps, jostling and insulting, one noisy roadie after another. They were shouting and hooting, laughing and shoving. Most of them walked past without giving me any eye contact. Two or three looked me over and smiled with prurient interest. One winked. Trevor took no note of any of it.

Karen climbed up the stairs followed by Daz, the red-headed roadie she'd met at Rush Up. She grinned and slid into the seat across from us. She raised and lowered her eyebrows to silently share with me her pleasure in successfully obtaining an invitation to come. Daz sat beside her.

"How far are you going?" she asked me.

"I was only able to get off work for a week." I turned to Trevor. "Where will we be in a week?"

Trevor jumped up and consulted a calendar taped to the side of the bus above the refrigerator across the aisle from us. "Knoxville," he said, and sat back down.

"How about you?" I hoped Karen would be going at least that far.

"I don't know." She shrugged. She lit a cigarette and crumpled up the empty pack, which she left on the table. "Is it too early for beer?" she asked of nobody in particular. Nobody answered her, but Daz leaned across the aisle and pulled one out of the refrigerator.

Another girl walked past and smiled at us. I remembered her from the previous night on the drive to the concert and backstage. She was blond, about my age and wearing an impractical pair of platform shoes that added three inches to her height, made her feet look over-large, and made her wobble when she walked. I couldn't tell which of the roadies she was with, but she seemed comfortable and at home on the bus. She took one of the seats further back.

Lucas Stanton and John Collier climbed the steps, sauntered past, and claimed the seats immediately behind our booth. Nobody seemed to find it particularly interesting that rock stars had just boarded the roadie bus. The two of them half-stood for a few moments, talking to the people sitting behind them, before settling in.

"I thought you said the band traveled in a Lear jet," I whispered to Trevor.

"They do. Lucas and John are just here to be sociable."

"Why?" One would think that a Lear jet was the preferable form of transportation, given a choice.

"We all traveled everywhere together in the early days. Lucas and I even shared a flat for three years. I was a groomsman at his wedding. They aren't always keen on being separate, so they sometimes come along with us. Partly nostalgia, I think. Partly, they like to hang out with their mates on occasion. That's us, really, more than Angus and Geoff. And the bus is more fun."

"And Angus?"

"He always goes by jet, and Geoff as well. They're keen on being separate."

A small, wiry, middle-aged man with graying hair and a Texas drawl climbed the steps.

"Ever'one accounted for?" He shouted. "If y'all ain't here, speak up now!" He chuckled at his own weak joke, took a hit off his cigarette, then scanned the group and counted on his fingers. He stopped at Lucas and John. "Y'all fuck me up, ever' time you ride with us," he said amiably. "I keep counting the two of you, and you don't count." He started again, skipping the girls and the rock stars. Satisfied with the tally, he shouted, "Twelve plus five! We're good." He slid behind the wheel, cranked the bus into gear, and then pulled away.

"Goodbye, Chicago!" he shouted. "Rock and roll!"

The roadies all responded with, "Rock and roll!" as if they were shouting "Amen!" to a preacher. Then they returned to their various conversations.

Charles was sifting through the eight-track tapes with a pained expression. "Rod Stewart or Cat Stevens?" he asked, receiving a few groans in response.

"I'm so bloody sick of Cat Stevens," Ritchie declared. "They've even added him to Muzak, so he's in every elevator. You can't escape him, you know. There he is. Everywhere. It's all you hear." He was dealing cards, slapping them down on the little table in the booth across the aisle.

"Blind Faith it is." Charles stuck the tape into the tape player and adjusted the volume.

"He's effing ubiquitous, Cat Stevens is," Paul said.

"Now *there's* a word. Ubiquitous. Is it from your bleeding word-of-the-day calendar? Is it today's word?" Bonzo crumpled a paper cup and hurled it at Paul's head. Paul ducked good-naturedly, and went back to his crossword puzzle. "Or is it just something southern wallies like to drop on people's toes?"

"Paul wants to be a writer one day," Trevor explained. "He carries a thesaurus and intends to write about his many adventures when he has enough words."

I giggled. "That's funny. 'Wallies'? I've never heard that before. Is it English?"

"I agree completely, mate," Cyril said. "Peace Train, my arse." He walked to the front and found the Cat Stevens tape. He threw it on the floor in the aisle and jumped on it until it broke, chanting, "Ubiquitous. Ubiquitous. Ubiquitous." He then stopped to take a bow to imaginary applause.

"Ah! 'Wally.' Yes indeed." Trevor leaned back, settling into storyteller mode. "It seems there was a group of hippies living on the Isle of Wight a few years back who ate only brown rice. They renounced their names and personal identities, and all called each other 'Wally.' Even the girls. That's where the term comes from, from the Wally Hippies."

"Hey! That was my fucking tape, you chuffing plonker!" Keith half-stood in his seat, but he was blocked by Ed, whose wide frame made it impossible for Keith to slide past him and grab Cyril's throat.

"Wally Hippies? You aren't serious," I said. I paused to ask, "Is there going to be a fight?"

"No," Trevor assured me. "They're cousins and best friends, so they go off on each other all day long. You'll adapt to it."

He cleared his throat.

"The Wally Hippies somehow knew to call each other 'Wally' naturally, by instinct," he continued. "Isn't that amazing? One might presume a group of wallies wouldn't have that depth of insight."

"Hit me." Butch scooped up his card, then tossed a dollar bill into the pot.

"I did you a favor, mate."

"It was my fucking tape."

"No, mate," Daz said. "It started at the Isle of Wight festival in nineteen-seventy. I was there, and I saw it. There was a group sitting nearby, and they saw someone they knew, so they called out, 'Wally! Over here.' Well, everyone picked up the chant and the next thing you know the whole bleeding crowd is shouting, 'Wally! Over here!'"

"I'll see that and raise you a quid," Ritchie said.

Keith's attention was torn between his poker hand and his ruined tape. He sat down, shot Cyril a deadly look, and muttered, "Arsewipe."

"It would have been mind-blowing to be Wally on LSD," Ed mused, looking over at us. "I wonder if Wally was on LSD? Or mescaline? Think about it, everyone in the world shouting your name: 'Wally! Over here!' And you're tripping on acid. What would you do, I wonder, with everyone calling your name from every direction, and you tripping?"

"Sorry, mate," Cyril picked up the tape and tossed it into the trash bin near the refrigerator. He slapped his hands together to brush off the imaginary dirt. "It had to be done for the good of all mankind. I'll buy you a new bleeding tape. I'll buy you two. Anything but Cat Stevens."

I was leaning against Trevor and looking around at everyone in the bus. I gazed out the window at an increasingly suburban, and then rural, Illinois, soaking it all in. It was a feeling I wasn't used to, and was akin to peace, hope, and elation. I languidly turned and looked up at Trevor, whose eyes met mine for a moment. He studied me and seemed pleased with what he saw. He leaned down and lightly kissed me on the lips, then gently rubbed his nose against mine. Not lust. Love, I thought. Love. I slid my arms around his waist and pressed my cheek into his shoulder. I was in love, and it was real. This was the happiest and most amazing day of my life.

"You heard him, didn't you?" Keith shouted. "Two tapes. Two tapes for the one he smashed. Fair enough, then. I was tired of it anyway."

"Now they do it at every festival, like holding up lighters at every concert as if we're all groovy and it's still fucking Woodstock." Ritchie sniffed, then added, "Even though it's not. Clearly."

"Not every festival. They did it at the Weeley Festival in seventy-one, though, the Wally chant. I was there, too. The same people went to that one," Daz said. "I haven't seen it since, though."

The aisle was narrow so that one had to step aside or turn sideways in order to allow anyone else to pass. When I stood to go to the bathroom, John Collier was blocking my way, talking to the card players in the booth across from ours. I smiled and said, "Excuse me," and he moved aside.

He then turned and grabbed my waistband as I passed. He pulled me back so I was up against him, face to face.

I looked over at Trevor in panic. He was watching closely with narrowed eyes that showed intense and expressive interest, but he made no move to intervene.

As for me, my reaction was anger and resentment that this rich and famous rock star—this rock *icon*—was no better than any of the drunken louts I met in bars. But it figured, I thought. A man was a man, and it was war.

"What's your name, love?"

"Holly." I'd stopped smiling and was looking down uneasily, avoiding his eyes.

I looked over at Trevor again, pleading. He looked back with a set jaw and that intense, watchful expression. He wasn't going to say or do anything to help me. But why, I wondered? Why wasn't he jumping in to stop this?

"I'm with Trevor." I tried to pull away, but John held tight. If we were in a bar, I would have simply lashed out with a rude remark, and then yanked myself out of his grasp, or screamed for the manager. I couldn't do anything here because the situation was tricky. I was a guest on this man's bus. He employed the man I was with. What was I supposed to do? I tried to think.

"Trevor, eh?" he asked. Then he exhaled through his nose derisively and grinned. "Come sit with me."

"Please let me go." I said in a low voice. I didn't like this man, but was afraid to say anything offensive lest he throw me off the tour. I didn't want to leave Trevor.

"Come sit with me for a bit, love. Come on, then, Holly. Just for a bit." He nodded his head toward his seat.

Trevor was not the only one watching. Everyone seemed interested in this little exchange. All conversation ceased. The bus had fallen silent except for the music, as people strained to hear.

"I'm with Trevor."

"You could be with me instead."

"But I don't *want* to be with you."

I was embarrassed and cornered, trying not to make a scene in front of everyone. I gave him my El train glare, but suppressed the words, "you arrogant bastard" just as I was about to blurt them out through gritted teeth.

"I want to be with Trevor."

I looked down at John's hand on my waistband, then decided to psychologically wrest myself away. I stiffened into my fisted, hostile posture. I slowly looked up and stared straight into his eyes without blinking, narrowing my eyes dangerously, thrusting my chin out, raising one eyebrow challengingly, daring him to *not* let go of me.

"Please let me go now." I still hadn't raised my voice above a whisper, but I slowly enunciated every syllable, and my expression was deadly.

John grinned, let me loose, and lifted his hands in gracious defeat. As I passed, he gave me a small sweeping bow, and said, "Milady." I heard him chuckle.

"Nor Elton John neither. He's another rotter." Cyril's voice was the first to break the silence. He returned to his earlier string of observations, turning his head to watch me as I walked to the back of the bus. "They rotate Elton John and Cat Stevens, first the one, and then the bloody other, over and over, all the dicking day."

When I returned from the bathroom, the roadies were all looking at me out of the corners of their eyes as they resumed their tangled conversations. I could feel the blush creeping up from my neck. I hadn't even been introduced to most of them yet, but already I was the bitch on the bus, and they hated me. I was ashamed and tried not to meet anyone's eyes.

"He's got a gift, Elton does, for writing songs that stick in your skull and make you daft." Cyril unapologetically watched me. His voice and his eyes followed me as I walked back to my seat. "Took me weeks to get *Tiny Dancer* out of my head. Then he releases *Madman Across the Water*. It's in my brain and won't leave. You're only safe from it if you never hear him at all. But that won't happen. He's got another album coming out. Head for shelter, I say, and cover your ears. It's fucking mind control."

One or two of the other roadies stared at me outright, and a few of them seemed to be suppressing smiles, but surprisingly not in a mean way. As I passed, John Collier grinned and winked as if we were sharing a joke. Lucas Stanton, still in his seat, raised his beer and smiled at me.

Ritchie, who had not yet given me any eye contact and had snubbed me to the point of rudeness when I'd tried to be nice at the concert the previous night, played host as I walked back up the aisle toward the front of the bus.

"Can I get you anything then, Holly? A beer?" He called it out in a very pleasant tone of voice, peering up at me over the cards in his hand.

I nodded and thanked him.

"I heard Wally was just a dog running loose at the festival," Paul said.

Ritchie pulled a bottle from the little refrigerator, popped it open with the bottle opener screwed to the refrigerator's side, then handed it to me. He poked Trevor in the shoulder from across the aisle.

"She's lovely. Congratulations." He smiled and went back to his card game.

"Doesn't matter, dog, human, or hippie. A wally is a wally. I believe we'd all agree on that," Daz said.

I sat down beside Trevor, who looked at me with a gentle expression and leaned over to kiss me.

I wasn't done with him. "What was all that about?" I snapped under my breath so no one else could hear.

"What do you mean?" Trevor appeared to be genuinely bewildered.

"He practically groped me right in front of you, and you didn't stop him." I was as hurt as I was angry. "Did you bring me here to pass me around? Is that what you people do? Is that what you think of me?"

"We've been friends since I was fourteen," Trevor whispered back. "Charles and I were the band's first roadies. He's the one who got me this job. He's my *friend*."

"Some friend." I was furious. "What a jerk! I told him I was with you. He's right there. It isn't like he can't see it. Why is he coming after me if he's your friend?"

Trevor laughed. "He won't ever touch you again, Holly. No one will. You passed the test."

I stared at him with an open mouth.

"He was looking out for me, is all. He's my friend."

"You had him *test* me? That's pretty insulting." I was less insulted knowing I had passed than I would have been, had I failed.

"I didn't ask him to test you. That would be absurd." He chuckled to himself. "I must look very daft and smitten over you, or he never would have done it."

I examined his face. I wondered how Trevor usually behaved around women, and why a friend felt compelled to find out if I was only using him, to possibly save him from me.

He ran a finger down my cheek and let it stop on my lips. I kissed it and smiled. I was daft and smitten, too.

"It's fine, really. You're safe with us. You're amongst friends here," he said reassuringly, as if he knew I needed to hear it. That was a novel concept to me—being among friends. I breathed it in with a satisfied sigh.

"Does anyone ever fail the test?"

69

"Most do. Maybe all."

I stared at him. "*All?*"

"They'd all rather have the rock star, given a choice."

"I'm the only one who's ever turned him down? You aren't serious."

Trevor shrugged, but he was looking inordinately pleased.

"What would you have done if I'd gone with him?" I asked.

"Nothing. You wouldn't be with me anymore, would you?" He said it without emotion, as if it didn't matter much, but his eyes indicated otherwise. "I can't stop you leaving. I would never hold onto you if you didn't want to be with me, or if you found someone else."

"So I'd be with John, then? Just like that? You wouldn't even try to get me back?"

"You wouldn't be with him either. He'd send you home."

"And there'd have been no going back to you, right?"

Trevor shrugged, but it was clearly a 'no.'

There was evidently a Guy Code too: Switch partners at your peril. It all seemed pretty dubious and underhanded to me, much as the Girlfriend Code must appear to men. It wasn't as though I planned on switching partners, but this kind of hostile attitude and premeditated ejection plan for women wasn't what I'd always envisioned when I thought of rock and roll.

Trevor leaned over to whisper, "John looks out for all of us. If Daz had been that way with Karen, he might have done it to her instead."

I looked over at the redheaded roadie. He seemed comfortable with, but not excessively attached to Karen, who was dozing with her head on his shoulder.

"What about that girl over there?"

"That's April. She's on her way to her sister's house in New York. Her boyfriend comes through there in May with the Deep Purple tour, and he apparently promised to take her with them to Japan."

"She's not with anyone?"

"She's with everyone. Cyril last night, someone else tomorrow. She's been with us since Phoenix," Trevor said matter-of-factly, without judgment, and with the expectation that I not pass judgment either. I got the sense that he'd turn very cold and scold me if I did. "She's lovely," he said simply.

"It's okay for April, though?" I asked. This was more like what I'd expected. But now I was thoroughly confused by these complicated rules. One set applied to me, and an entirely different set applied to April. I tried to get a good look at her.

"No one's invested anything into her. She isn't any trouble, and she doesn't hurt anyone. She's just getting a ride to New York."

I turned to look out the window and ponder. Then I turned back to Trevor. "Did you think I'd pass the test?"

"I had a feeling." He shrugged. "I'm amazed that I was right, given the odds." He smiled, then closed his eyes and leaned back to rest, squeezing my hand before dozing off.

We were on the same side. It was surprising to find someone with whom I could call a truce. I had been at war with men for years, and now two of us had stepped outside the fray and joined forces. There were two of us on the same side. I finally had someone on my side.

I watched him breathing in shallow sleep, and gently pulled his head to my shoulder. He sighed.

"I fold."

"Fold."

"What did you have?" asked Keith.

"Two pair, eights high," Ritchie answered.

"Bollocks! I folded on two pair, jacks high, you knacker."

"Ah! Thank you. Thank you. Your deal."

Chapter 9

"I want my tee shirt back, arsehole. Take it off." Cyril was upset to notice Keith wearing his tee shirt from the seventy-one Rolling Stones *Goodbye Britain* tour. Cyril was the only person on the bus to have worked that tour, so his ownership of the shirt was not in question. It was obviously a case of thievery.

Keith, who remembered the loss of his Cat Stevens tape and was still awaiting two tapes in exchange for it, pursed his lips at Cyril to suppress a smirk, then resumed his conversation with Paul.

"So you think Jim Morrison is still alive, then?"

We were traveling down a highway in Tennessee, through the Smoky Mountains past scenery so incredible it took my breath away. The word of the day should be *verdant* because this was the most beautiful place on earth. It had to be. Trevor and I were in the seat furthest back, holding hands, occasionally rubbing noses or pointing out the window and gasping.

"I heard it was a hoax. I heard he faked his death and went to Africa," Paul answered.

We had left for Clemson, South Carolina about four hours earlier, after a very early breakfast in the hotel restaurant. Since I'd first boarded the bus, we'd traveled through St. Louis and toured the Arch, gone on to Terre Haute, Indiana, where the girls cleaned and mopped the bus, and then went on to Louisville, Kentucky, where someone had broken into the bus during the show and stolen the eight-track stereo and all the tapes. It was an eerily quiet ride, except for conversation.

Cyril's position was that Keith's Cat Stevens tape would have been stolen anyway, so he, Cyril, was absolved of having to keep his promise to replace it. Keith disagreed.

"There were so many stories going around at the time, I don't know what's true. I think he's really dead."

"Look at me, Keith, you worthless tosser."

"I do not believe that I was speaking to you, Cyril. I was addressing Paul."

I was beginning to fall into the routine, days spent traveling, evenings spent sitting on speakers at the side of the stage with the other girls, watching tens of thousands of screaming fans and the backstage activity with local groupies. I was a little bored, watching the same performances while I nibbled the same cocktail rye sandwiches night after night, but I wasn't complaining. The backstage drama always changed, and there were dozens of people to study and watch. I still had new people to meet on the tour, particularly the people associated with the backup band, who traveled in another bus. Nothing about the experience was tiresome yet, even in the hours following the concert when the lights went on, the crowds filed out, and I waited sleepily in the front row for Trevor and the crew to finish taking down and packing the equipment.

Then we raced to the hotel. Our lovemaking had evolved from that first night on the floor into something that was only slightly less desperate, but which had considerably more thought, duration, and finesse. We were wonderful lovers. It was incredible, what being in love with someone could make you feel, both emotionally and physically, and I was determined to make this relationship last forever, whatever it took.

"I said give me back my t-shirt."

"I saw his grave when we were in Paris," Ritchie broke in. "He's dead."

"How do I know it's yours?" Keith raised an eyebrow provokingly. "Hmmm?"

Each evening, Charles dawdled in the hotel lounge before knocking tentatively after an hour or so and entering the room. He hadn't yet invited a girl to join him so we were becoming a solid threesome, eating our meals together and venturing out together when we went sightseeing. He would have sat with us on the bus, but he was taking a nap in his bunk.

"Because you have got on a bleedin' shirt you saw me wear for the last two years!" Cyril pointed out to Keith. "I don't need to defend myself. It's my fucking shirt! I should just kick your arse!"

"But did you see the *body?*" Paul persisted. "You simply won't find anyone who actually saw a body. He could be anywhere, really. Who'd know?"

"I saw his grave when we were in Paris," Ritchie replied. "That's how I know. Good enough for me, mate."

"I was just having a bit of fun with you, you fucking git! Kick my arse? Kick my arse? Over a t-shirt? Why? You'll get it back."

"You can buy a tombstone and pay someone to carve whatever you like on it. You don't have to be dead to buy a tombstone. You can be alive," Ed noted.

"Because you don't ever violate the sanctity of a man's *private bunk!* You don't go into a man's bunk and take his *things! That's* why! Give the bleeding t-shirt back!"

"Why would he pretend to be dead? He was a star. He was rolling in it," Keith spoke mildly and genially to Paul, then turned to Cyril and thrust out his middle finger.

"Worse than shitting on the bus, going through a man's bunk, stealing a man's t-shirt and wearing it right in front of him. You are a pud-sucking fuck-pig."

"There was no tombstone," Ritchie said. "Someone stole it."

"Aha!" Paul exclaimed. "No tombstone! You see? He's alive."

"Ooooohhhh!" Keith, feigning shock and affront, defiantly waggled his fingers in the air.

"I am sensing truculence on this bus. You two are behaving most truculently." Paul squinted genially at each of them. "Deep breaths, ladies. Deep breaths and see if you can't kiss and make up for the good of the rest of us."

"Excellent suggestion," Ritchie said. "Out of bounds, you two. Please give it a rest."

We didn't expect to find much to see or do in Clemson on our day off, the day after tomorrow; it was a college town rather than a big city. Trevor had been through it before, but couldn't recall anything about it. He had suggested we just locate a nice restaurant and spend our free time at the movies.

"I thought today's word was *untoward*. I saw it on the calendar. You should be saying their behavior is *untoward*." That was Trevor, who was gently fingering the nape of my neck.

There was laundry, though. Perhaps we should do that instead, Trevor had said, after mentioning that he was running low on things to wear. I enjoyed this, discussing laundry and mundane pleasures like the movies. I was feeling very "paired up," and very much one half of a solid couple. For the first time in my life, I felt as though I was capable of settling down with someone for the long term. I felt as if Trevor and I had been a couple forever, instead of just for a few days.

"Truculent was from January. You can still use words after they stop being the word of the day. No law says it's untoward," said Paul.

Charles awoke from his nap and crawled out of his bunk like a creature emerging from a hole. He walked up the aisle with sleepy eyes and messy hair, scratching, and took the seat beside Keith, which Liam had just vacated to head for the bathroom. He yawned.

"It was in my washing! *Jay*-sus. It came out of the fucking dryer with my clothes! I didn't go *near* your bunk! Here. *Here*, you bleedin' arsehole." Keith pulled the shirt over his head and hurled it at Cyril. "But when will I get the two tapes you owe me?"

Cyril didn't respond.

"Yeah? *Yeah?*" Keith blew a hard breath through his lips in disgust. "*Right*, you fucking nudger! Yeah, *that's* right."

"The pressure. He couldn't take the pressure of being a rock star," Liam said, heading back and looking for an alternate place to sit. He sat down beside April and grinned, then leaned over and stuck his tongue in her ear. She giggled. "He wanted to live his life as an anonymous wanker instead of a legend," he continued, looking up. "He used to tell people he was going to do it, run off and hide, and now he's done it. Can you blame him, really?" He pulled April onto his lap.

I had worried that Trevor might be vague about our future together, the way Daz was with Karen, or might avoid discussing it, the way men did when they didn't mind sleeping with a girl, but weren't interested in pursuing the relationship further. Trevor, however, had no such misgivings. He was already talking about the things he would show me the next time I came with him on tour and suggesting cities I might enjoy, so I could coordinate my vacation next year with Torc's touring schedule. He spoke about the future even beyond that, and didn't appear to be hiding anything from me about his feelings or his life.

"I knew Jim Morrison in sixty-eight," April said, shifting on Liam's lap to get comfortable. "San Francisco Summer of Love."

"Umph. Your pits smell." Cyril had gingerly lifted the shirt to his nose to survey the damage.

"The Summer of Love was sixty-seven," Butch corrected. "Summer of sixty-nine was Woodstock. Was the summer of sixty-eight anything at all?"

"Chicago Democratic Convention," Karen said. "Rioting in the streets."

Cyril waved his shirt over his head. "Have a whiff of this, everyone."

"Well, whatever," said April. "I was in San Francisco in sixty-eight."

"Did you just *know* Jim Morrison? Or do you mean you actually *knew* Jim Morrison like, you know, in the Biblical sense?" Karen was slouching against Daz, pausing to look up as she filed a nail.

"Why are you smelling the fucking pits of that tee shirt, you poofter? Eh? Why would you smell the fucking pits?"

"Is the 'Biblical sense' like when you do someone?" April reached up to brush her hair out of her eyes.

Karen and I nodded.

"Then, yeah. That."

"I didn't have to smell them. The odor came to *me*. It wafted up to my fucking nose of its own accord. And then I smelled the shirt to be certain there was no mistake. And there was none, I assure you."

"How old are you now, eighteen?" Karen gasped. "You were a *baby* in sixty-eight!"

"I was thirteen. I told him I was eighteen."

"Did he believe you?" Karen asked. "Lots of times they know you're underage, and they do you anyway. I'll bet he did you knowing all along you were still a baby."

"What Cyril is trying to say is, you have polluted his t-shirt with your rank effluvium." Paul had been flipping through his pocket Thesaurus and seemed very pleased with "effluvium." He circled it with a pen.

"They kept his death a secret for days. Do you remember? Something very suspicious about the whole thing," Bonzo said. "He either died under suspicious circumstances, or took off for Africa. We'll probably never know."

"Yeah! Whatever Paul just said to you, I mean it, you scrotty shower of shite," Cyril snapped.

"I wouldn't mind being a legend for a bit. I'd be Jim Morrison for a bit. I don't mind," Ed said thoughtfully.

"Would you like to smell me bicycle seat as well, then? Or me lacey little knickers? Eh? Pit sniffer." Keith was flapping his arms like a bird.

"Fuckwit. Sod off."

"I wore a lot of makeup, but I still looked really young. I guess he probably knew, but I'm not for sure about it. What's weird is really being eighteen. I been telling people I'm eighteen for practically my whole life. And I'm gonna stay eighteen for a few years, too. Don't tell nobody, okay? Nobody wants you unless you're eighteen."

"There. Go on. Do they really smell?"

"Or younger and lying about it," Karen noted ruefully.

"Pwah! Fuck off! Get your fucking hairy armpit out of my face!" Charles was waving his arms in self-defense.

"He used to say he was going to fake his death, then come back and call himself Mojo Risin. That's the letters in 'Jim Morrison' rearranged," Bonzo added.

Keith rose and walked to his bunk in the back of the bus.

"I'm nineteen. I'm already past it."

"God help me. I'm twenty-one," Karen said. "Completely over the hill. Hand me a beer, please."

"I don't mind that you're nineteen," said Trevor, hugging me. "I won't even mind when you're twenty."

What was clear to me, though, and what pleased me the most was the degree to which everyone held Trevor in high esteem. Not only the roadies, but the band members treated him with respect and affection. I was happy to be with him, not only because I was officially in love with him, but because he was a man I could be earnestly and uncompromisingly proud of.

"Wait a minute. That's bollocks." Keith had returned from his bunk and was pushing his arms through the sleeves of his shirt. He stopped and counted on his fingers, mouthing the letters in the name to himself. "Mojo Risin is missing an R. Morrison has two Rs. And it needs another M because there's also an M in Jim. That was really pretty careless of him, don't you think? Did he think we wouldn't notice?" He sat down next to Bonzo.

"If you call him *Mr.* Mojo Risin it takes care of the extra letters. Perhaps that's what he had in mind, for us to call him *Mr.* Mojo Risin when he comes back from the dead," Daz said.

"He is *not* coming back as Mr. Mojo Risin!" Ritchie shouted. "He's dead and buried in Paris. I've seen his fucking grave!"

"Why are we stopping?"

"What's here? Why are we stopping?"

"Where are we? There's nothing here. Why are we stopping here?"

"Hey Virgil! Why are we stopping?"

The bus had mechanical problems and required a part they had to order from Knoxville, some distance away. Virgil had pulled us off the highway, down a two-lane road, and into a service station at the edge of an isolated little Tennessee town, where the garage was a converted barn. It was the only garage in the area big enough to service a commercial band bus—Virgil knew everything, up and down every highway in the US, after driving a truck for twenty years—so we had made a detour that took us a little out of our way. A mechanic was now looking under the hood.

This was an emergency that required quick action. Clemson was still two or three hours away, and the crew needed to be there in five hours, at the absolute latest. Meanwhile, it would take at least two hours to get the part, and another three hours to work on the bus. We would not arrive until well past the time the concert was scheduled to begin.

"Anyone want to play gin rummy?" April, totally unperturbed, shuffled the cards and dealt the girls in while the roadies stood outside to listen to Ritchie describe his phone conversation with Rob, the road manager, who had flown with the band into Clemson.

Trevor came back and stuck his head in. "They're sending limos from Knoxville. They should be here within the hour. The girls and Wayne will stay with the bus and meet up with us later in Clemson." Wayne was the backup bus driver.

Virgil climbed back onto the bus, following the rest of the crew who had pushed in ahead of him.

"Ever'one, hey! Your attention, y'all. Ah mean it. Listen up!" He whistled through his fingers. When everyone was quiet and facing him, he continued, "Ah'm pulling it in so's they can have a closer look at it. Shouldn't take but a few minutes. Y'all can get back on in just a little bit. Then by the time they can work on the bus, most all y'all 'll be gone anyways in the limos."

"Will you ladies do my laundry while you're here?" Cyril held up a pillowcase filled with his dirty clothing. April nodded and held out her hand for laundry money, which Cyril pulled from his wallet and gave to her. The other roadies, thinking this was a very good idea indeed, gathered up their sacks of laundry as well and made a stack in one of the booths. They each handed us a few dollar bills, then filed off the bus one by one.

"We don't even know if there's a laundromat. I don't see one." Karen accepted money anyway. "But one can always hope, eh?" She made a face and stuck out her tongue. I laughed.

Karen, April and I grabbed our purses and followed the men off the bus, which Virgil started up and eased into the barn. We stood aimlessly in front of the garage while the roadies stood more or less silently in a huddle, smoking cigarettes and drinking orange or grape Shasta from the gas station soft drink machine.

Then Virgil pulled the bus back out and parked it. He waved us on and went to sit under a tree where he pulled his baseball cap—he called it a "gimmie" cap—over his eyes and went to sleep.

We all climbed back onto the bus and took our seats again. Karen, April, and I resumed our game of gin rummy, while the roadies grabbed beers.

"Think Connie will be in Little Rock next week?" Liam asked.

"I've always wanted to meet Connie." That was April.

"Of course she'll be there. She and Angus have a standing date," Bonzo said.

"Who's Connie?" I asked.

"Connie is a groupie in Little Rock," Trevor explained. "I heard Grand Funk are recording a song about her." He turned to Charles. "Did you hear about that? Amazing, isn't it? Connie is going to have her own song!"

"Yeah, but Angus has Petra this time," Ritchie said. "She won't let him." Petra was a girlfriend, not Angus' wife. Angus never took his wife, Terri, on tour. I wondered what Terri thought about that.

"Does Connie do roadies?" Butch asked. "Who here has ever had Connie?"

"Me. nineteen-seventy-one," Liam said. Then he snorted and laughed.

"Liar. This is your first tour," Cyril said.

"His too. He might have believed me."

"Did the Plaster Casters do Angus?" Butch asked.

"Everybody does Angus," Cyril said.

"*I* never did Angus," said Karen.

"The Plaster Casters don't do rock stars, giving head or otherwise. They just make plaster casts of their hard-ons. It's an entirely separate talent altogether," Ritchie clarified. "The rock stars are responsible for getting it up themselves."

"I've done Angus." That was April.

"You can't tell me they don't help it along a little, fluff it up for you before they cast it," Butch argued.

"Proudly, Angus is indeed in the Plaster Caster Hall of Fame," Trevor said. "They anointed and immortalized him last year. He is now part of history."

"From what I gather, it's strictly art," Ritchie said. "You have to wank your own. They're too busy mixing the plaster, and it sets too fast for them to stop and wank someone stiff who's perfectly capable of wanking his own self."

"One casts, and the other does the fluffing," Trevor said. "It takes two."

"I want to have them cast me. I should have asked them when we were in Chicago," Liam said.

"They don't cast roadies," Cyril said. "And you don't *ask* them. They *invite* you. It's an honor. That's why everyone always accepts."

"You're in Chicago," Daz said to Karen. "Have you ever met them? Nice girls."

"No. I'm pretty sure they'd never talk to me anyway because I'm not a rock star, and I don't have a penis."

"Here they are." Charles saw the limousines drive up and gathered his gear.

"That's them. Let's go." Paul set his book down on the seat and rose.

"Right then, rock and roll!" Trevor gave me a quick kiss and followed the others down the steps and out the door. "We left already!"

"You're always welcome to *my* penis, Karen, my dear," Keith called over his shoulder as he stood and then dashed up the aisle.

"We left already!" Cyril crumpled an empty Shasta can and dropped it into the trashcan.

"Thank you, Keith. I think I'll pass," Karen called back.

"Move it! Go on!"

"Come on! Rock and *roll*! Let's *go*! *Hurry*!"

The two limousines were parked in front of the garage. The roadies pushed their way into them, five in one and six in the other. The cars pulled away, leaving trails of dust, and us, behind.

Since the required engine part was still en route, we confronted the laundry.

"The gas station guy says there's a laundromat up the street." April pointed. "Do you want to do this stuff now?" She chewed her gum slowly, thoughtfully, and squish-ily with her mouth open, looking glumly down at the pile of laundry.

"Ugh. How far?"

It was a block and a half, the entire length of Main Street. April struggled in her platform shoes, wobbling uncomfortably and precariously the entire way, as we each hauled four bags the distance. We arrived at a dreary, brick-and-glass storefront with a faded sign that said, "Wash-a-teria." We pushed through the door and piled the sacks of laundry onto the worn laminated tables. Then we each tackled one sack at a time, dumping it into a washing machine before moving onto the next sack, filling as many washers as we could without bothering to sort whites from colors.

Two local women stared at us.

"Oh yuck. Ew." Karen held up a pair of white briefs with two fingers. "Skid marks. Doesn't Ed ever wipe?"

"Oh my God!" I exclaimed. "What size does he wear? Those are huge."

"Why would a guy let women do his laundry if he knows he has poop stains? What a slob. I'm never going to do him now," said April.

"I'm not looking closely at his dirty underpants to find the size. Sorry. Too gross." Karen dropped the briefs into the washer with pursed lips and gingerly shook the rest of the laundry in, straight from the bag, without touching it. Then she turned to April. "You were going to do Ed? Seriously?"

April shrugged.

"Well I guess there's something to be said for doing someone who'd be really grateful, huh?"

April nodded in noncommittal agreement.

The local woman grimly looked away with tight lips.

I fought with the change machine until I had enough quarters. Then I plugged them into the detergent machine and tossed little boxes of Tide to the other girls, who whooped and caught them in mid-air. They broke open the boxes systematically and poured one box into each washer. Then they pushed quarters into the slots and started the machines.

We sat and flipped through old *Look* and *Life* magazines that dated back to the sixties or gazed out the window until the washing cycle completed for one washer after another.

The local women departed and were replaced by others who carried on, staring where the original women had left off.

"Keep everybody's stuff separate in the dryers. You saw how pissed off Cyril was," I reminded. "We don't want to mix up the clothes."

April groaned.

"There aren't enough dryers. We'll be here for hours."

"We're going to be here for hours anyway."

I didn't mind, actually. Every minute of this tour, no matter what it entailed, was pure joy for me. I had sunk into a warm, insulated bath where women accepted me, included me, and allowed me to spend time with them, and where men treated me with friendly detachment, affection, and respect. And I was with Trevor. I wanted the entire rest of my life to be just this way. I wanted this tour to be the entire rest of my life, even if it meant doing someone's poop-stained laundry every day of it.

Since we hadn't kept track of who had given us how much money, we divvied up the leftover change amongst ourselves as payment for services rendered.

We hauled the sacks of unfolded laundry back to the garage and waited on the grass next to Wayne.

Virgil came over, smiling. "Fifteen minutes, and we'll be back on the road. Ah'm treating y'all to lunch."

When the bus was ready, and we had dragged and pulled the laundry onto it, Virgil steered us back on the highway and deeper into the Smoky Mountains. I turned to look and gasped at the scenery, wishing I had a camera and that Trevor was with me to share it.

"There's a stretch of road coming up where ever' establishment with a red light is a whorehouse," Virgil called back to us.

"No way!" This was an adventure indeed!

"Ever' trucker in the U S of A knows about this stretch of road coming up, right up here." He pointed with his cigarette. "There's one right there. And there. See them red lights? Whorehouses."

"No, they're restaurants!" I exclaimed.

"Yes, ma'am, they sure are. And upstairs in ever' last one of 'em is a whorehouse, big as life." He pulled into the parking lot of one of the restaurants with a bright red light. "Let's get us some lunch!"

We walked into the restaurant and were greeted by a waitress in sheer hip-length baby doll lingerie and high heels. Her breasts were somewhat blurred by the fabric, but mostly visible. She was wearing panties, which I was happy to see since she'd be serving our food. I looked at Karen and started to giggle. April buried her face in my shoulder and grabbed my arm.

"I just swallowed my gum!" April gasped and coughed.

We settled in and took our menus from the waitress, who looked at the girls with bored exasperation before smiling at the two men. She walked away, swishing her bottom.

"Ever done it with a whore?" Virgil poked Wayne in the arm. Wayne didn't respond. "How old are you?" Virgil persisted.

"Twenty."

"Done it with any girl at all?"

"Yes," Wayne snapped defensively.

"But never with a whore?"

Wayne looked away with feigned boredom and rolled his eyes.

"I'll pay for you."

We all giggled.

"Naw, man. I'm good." Wayne looked from one of us to the other, and then buried his face in the menu.

"Ah'm serious." Virgil pulled a twenty out of his wallet, snapped it, and then flipped it onto the table.

"Can I take the money and not go upstairs?" Wayne reached around the menu and fingered the bill, sliding it toward himself slightly.

Virgil shook his head and slapped his fingers down on the other end of the bill.

"It's only good for a whore, right here, right now."

Wayne looked at the money. He thought for a minute. He stood and picked up the twenty, then reached over and grabbed our waitress's hand as she walked past. They went over to a door that was crudely labeled, "Back Room." A black and chrome naked lady mud flap was nailed to the wall beside the doorway.

Wayne disappeared upstairs, and the door slammed shut.

As we chewed our burgers, we girls stared around, watching women clad in see-through nighties taking orders like other waitresses in harshly-lit burger joints everywhere in the world. We giggled with full mouths. Virgil sat back, tipped his chair, lit a cigarette, and relaxed as our benevolent host.

"Back so soon?" Karen eyed Wayne meaningfully as he sheepishly grinned and took his place at the table.

"What happened?" I leaned over and nodded encouragingly, grinning, waiting for him to tell us everything.

"What do you mean, 'What happened'? What do you *think* happened?" Wayne made a face at me.

"No," I said shaking my head. "I mean, what was she like? Did you talk? Is it all just beds up there, or what? Were the sheets clean? What did it look like?"

"First, there was a nurse who made me pull it out so she could check me." Wayne wouldn't look us in the eye.

"It's a clean whorehouse," Virgil said with a satisfied nod, taking a drag from his cigarette. He snubbed it out in the lettuce on his plate. "Ah wouldn't bring you to no cesspool of disease."

83

"Then she examined me. Then she told me I was okay, so I went into a room. Then we did it on a bed. The end."

"You and the nurse?" April put down her half-eaten pickle and noisily slurped her Coke through her straw.

"Me and the whore."

"But what was she like?" I really wanted to know. I'd never met a prostitute before. "What did you talk about?"

"Nice. I don't know. She was just a girl. We didn't talk. She was nice."

"That's *it*?" Surely he could have noticed more. This was my lifetime's great adventure, and I wanted to absorb everything, including everyone else's experiences.

Wayne shrugged and shook his head.

"Finish up." Virgil pointed toward Wayne's plate. Wayne blushed and wordlessly tackled his hamburger, while the rest of us watched him eat and giggled. "We're hellbound for Clemson! Rock and roll."

Chapter 10

"**I**t's Knoxville." I sadly looked up at the Hyatt as we filed out of the bus.

"You can stay," Trevor said. "You don't have to leave. We go to Atlanta after this. You'd like to see Atlanta, wouldn't you? It's just one more stop. Two more stops and you get to see Connie in Little Rock. Then Texas, then Florida."

"No, I have to go home." I sighed, switching my suitcase to my other hand as I climbed down the steps. "I have work tomorrow."

Daz had sent Karen home from Clemson when he spotted a girl backstage that he "fancied" more. Then he'd found he didn't fancy her quite as much as he'd thought and left without her, so April and I were now the only girls on the bus.

What if Trevor had sent me home like that, I wondered. It would have ended things, as far as I was concerned, even if I'd superficially carried on with the relationship for years. I could never, ever feel the same way about him. But Karen had left with a shrug and a hug.

"Your flight doesn't leave until three."

That meant one final roll in the room before I caught a cab to the airport, and Trevor headed for the concert hall. I would not be attending the concert, and it made me feel a slight, inexplicable sense of panic. I didn't want Trevor's world to carry on without me.

Trevor pulled Charles aside and took his bag. After looking at his watch and waving at us, Charles wandered into the restaurant. We went into the room and wordlessly undressed. I stopped and stood motionless for a moment, looking down. Then my face crumpled, and I was convulsed with sobs.

85

"I'm going to miss you," I cried. "I'm going to miss you so much."

Trevor immediately put his arms around me.

"What's this, Holly? What's all this?"

"I never cry!" I said defensively, rubbing my eyes furiously. "I haven't cried since I was twelve!" The last time I had cried was the day my father dropped me off at the house and drove away.

"It's all right, Holly. You can cry, darling." He sat on the side of the bed and held out his arms. I sat beside him and hugged him while he pulled me close and kissed the top of my head.

I sobbed and choked into Trevor's chest. I cried from my toes. I cried the blockage away while Trevor rocked me.

I was feeling embarrassed, wiping my eyes. At the same time, I felt as though I were living a miracle: I was crying for the first time in seven years! I felt as if I was being washed clean.

Trevor rocked me a few more moments, patting my back. I stopped sobbing and sniffled slightly, but I was fine for the moment. I felt quite good, in fact, except for being sad to leave. Then his hands found their way around and probed me rhythmically and deliberately. We refocused on our reason for being there, and made *goodbye* love on the bed until we were exhausted.

"Will I see you again after this?" I asked, lying on my back and staring at the ceiling.

Trevor laughed.

"What kind of a question is that? Of course." He propped himself up on one elbow and leaned down to kiss me. "This is just the very beginning."

"Do you want me to write?" My mouth was turned down in a sad frown, as if I hadn't heard what he'd just said and was expecting him to reject me. I couldn't quite believe that I could love someone, and it would be reciprocated. I couldn't quite believe that his leaving wasn't forever, even though I had his parents' address and had received earlier instructions to write to him as much as I could.

"Stop!" Trevor began to tickle me. "You're such a silly girl! I want you to write, and I demand that you do! I'll try and find some way to come back before the end of the year, and if not, I'll see you when the band comes through next year."

"Next *year*?" I stopped, frozen, then started to sob again.

"I'll do my best," He said, kissing my eyelids. "I'll think of something, my beautiful girl. I won't let it be long."

86

Before Karen caught her own flight back, she'd offered to pick me up at O'Hare Airport, and then confirmed the arrangements with me when I had called her from Knoxville. She was waiting for me when I arrived.

We hugged when I got off the plane. I looked around me to see if anyone noticed that I had a girlfriend who liked me enough to hug me, but nobody cared. They all took hugs for granted, whereas I walked through the terminal and toward the car with a bounce in my step, very proud. Even though I was parted from Trevor, I'd had a friend to come home to, and we'd shared the same adventures together!

Karen was full of plans and had a list of famous English bands we could choose from in the upcoming weeks. Angie wasn't like this, interested in the things I said and willing to take my preferences into account as we made plans. I couldn't talk to Angie this way. I was buoyant and excited because my whole life had shifted on one Tuesday night at the Rush Up. I could barely believe it! My whole life was different now! I was in love with Trevor, and I had a new girlfriend.

On the ride back, we talked about concerts, Trevor, and Daz. We also talked about the girl Daz had replaced Karen with, and how he'd left her behind after all.

Karen wasn't bitter.

"It happens," she said, pulling in front of my grandmother's building so I could pick up Pansy. "I got to go on tour for a while, I had fun, and he'll remember me next time. That's the important thing."

I took Pansy from my grandmother who, with the car waiting, only had a few short moments to shout at me. I nudged Pansy into the back seat and beamed at Karen, who pulled away from the curb to take my dog and me safely home.

Chapter 11

Trevor had no sense of real-world time. His day ended around midnight or one in the morning, and his wind-down time after work lasted another two or three hours. He climbed into bed at four o'clock, give or take an hour or two, and woke at noon, unless forced awake earlier to board the bus. He ordered his scrambled eggs and orange juice as the stragglers around him finished up their lunches. He ate a big dinner before the concert and ate a light snack after it ended, usually with a beer or two. He took no note of time zones, and rarely gave thought to how they compared with one other, or what time it might be for the person on the other end of the phone line. I would learn that when he picked up the phone to call at his own convenience and on his schedule.

About three weeks after I'd left Trevor in Knoxville, I stumbled out of bed and into the kitchen to answer the ringing phone. The backlit clock on the stove said three-twenty. I didn't turn on the light because it would hurt my eyes, and I was operating purely on reflex when I said, "Hello?"

"Hello, sweetness. How's my darling?" I would also learn that Trevor never, ever asked if he had awakened me.

"Trevor!" I slid down the wall and landed on the floor with my knees up. I cradled the phone against my ear with both hands. I hadn't expected a phone call. I knew the tour was over and had been trying to guess when I should start looking for a letter. My reaction was pure adrenaline. I was too excited to even know what questions to ask. "Where are you?" seemed logical, so I asked him that.

"The Bahamas. They're giving Charles and me a month-long holiday on the beach as a kind of a bonus. I've been here a week."

"That's so nice! Wow!" I turned coy. "Will you send me a postcard?" I was thinking of showing it off at work, tacking it to the wall beside my desk for everyone to see.

"There won't be time, and there would be no point. You're coming here next week."

There was a ticket waiting for me at the airport, he said. Althea, the bespectacled, sweet-natured secretary had made all the arrangements. I just needed to show up with a swimsuit and casual clothing. I'd be coming for a two-week rest, he told me. Kick back. Nothing fancy.

I squealed. Fully awake, I pushed myself up from the floor and hopped from one foot to the other. When I put the receiver back to my ear, Trevor was laughing.

"I really get to see you in a week?" I gasped. "I thought it wouldn't be until next year! Oh my God!"

The prospect of being with Trevor again had pushed the rest of it out of my head. It all came back now. "You mean I'm going to the Bahamas? Really? I've never been there." I'd never been anywhere, aside from the tour. "Oh my God…"

I started talking to myself, "I have to get my grandmother to keep the dog. Oh God, I don't have the clothes for a trip. What do I do?"

"It's nothing fancy. We all just lay around on the beach. Just bring jeans and a bathing suit. You're coming here to relax and be with me."

That day, the next day, and every day for the next week, I called the airline every few hours just to listen to them confirm my reservation.

I didn't know how my supervisor would react. I would get the time off, I decided, or I would quit. Finding another job seemed a fair price to pay for a trip to the Bahamas with Trevor.

I knew I wouldn't really quit, but I enjoyed toying with the thought. It made everything more daring and exciting.

I received permission. I still had a few vacation and personal days, so not all of my time off would be unpaid. I could have taken them in order to extend the tour with Torc, but had chosen to not to use them all because I always rationed things, just as I always saved my money. I worked doubly hard to clear my desk so my supervisor wouldn't object to my leaving for two weeks and find reason to fire me later.

On the morning of the phone call, I babbled to anyone who would listen. I noticed that no one was particularly happy for me, and that my coworkers all grew tightlipped around me. Denise wouldn't speak to me at all unless it was work-related and unavoidable. It had been bad enough that I had gone on tour with a rock band, and they'd had to listen to my stories about that. Now I was getting flown around like a jetsetter. They seemed to find that particularly irksome.

I stopped mentioning it by long before lunch. Only Angie sat with me at lunch and at breaks. Everyone else made excuses. I overheard one of the girls say the word "groupie" with contempt, quickly pressing her lips shut when she noticed I was in earshot. Then she rearranged her features into self-righteous indignation. She had just reminded herself that it didn't matter if I'd heard her, since I was only a groupie and didn't count. She let her eyes slide over me before she turned away.

I owned two pairs of blue jeans and two pairs of shorts. I packed them, just as Trevor had instructed, along with a bikini I'd had since high school. I had one long skirt I'd bought on sale at a discount store, so I threw it into my suitcase, just in case. I had some reasonably nice tops and some t-shirts that I packed, too, along with underwear and toiletries.

I went to the bank and withdrew half my savings. I took a very expensive cab to O'Hare Airport, which chiseled into the money I'd had left from my last paycheck. Then, when I reached the ticket counter at the airport, I found that the airfare had not been entirely paid. The airline wanted $75.00, which was nearly all the money I had with me. I pulled out my wallet and gave them half of my savings in exchange for my boarding pass.

I had never been on a plane in my life until my flight from Knoxville, and now I was flying on two more, all within a few weeks. The first was a jet. The second was a tiny prop plane out of Miami that was so small and flew so low I could see the waves down below. Then it circled the island and landed.

Following the other passengers, I disembarked and walked from the plane to the terminal. I grabbed my suitcase from the ramp and was directed to a holding area, where a customs agent had questions. Where was I staying? Who was I staying with? What was the phone number there?

Trevor and I had made arrangements with no contingency plans. I had no phone number because I had forgotten to ask for one, and Trevor hadn't thought to offer one. I knew only Trevor's name for certain because he hadn't mentioned who else was staying there, but he wasn't listed in a directory because he was just a guest. I had no address. I had no idea where I was going, even which island.

The agent asked how much money had I brought with me. I stepped backward, startled, as if he'd slapped me. Then I slipped my purse off my shoulder and opened it, hunched over, defeated. I hadn't expected that question and knew I was about to fail the exam.

I pulled out my wallet and wordlessly counted three dollars and twenty-one cents with shaking fingers, nervously glancing up at the agent. I placed the money on the counter and lowered my eyes, then clutched my purse close to my chest. He pushed the money back toward me impatiently, with obvious exasperation and disapproval. I scooped it up and hurriedly stuffed it back into the change compartment of my wallet.

I tried to explain that I had brought half of my savings, seventy-five dollars, but the airline had insisted the airfare wasn't paid in full, and requested most of my money before allowing me to board in Chicago. Did he understand? It wasn't my fault.

He wasn't interested. The agent looked at me with his mouth slightly skewed to one side and said nothing. He looked down at my "luggage" resting on the floor at my feet. My clothing was packed in my ancient, round, white cardboard hatbox suitcase, the same one I had taken with me to Grandma's fifteen years earlier, and the same one I had taken with me on tour. It eloquently communicated that I was not of the same socio-economic caliber as the tanned and bejeweled vacationers surrounding me, and was therefore highly suspect. I had no money. I had no phone number, name, address, hotel, or even *island* I could offer to him.

"I'm staying with a rock band," I said. "They're called Torc." Did they know about Torc in the Bahamas? Was this agent too old to have heard of them? "They flew me here as a guest."

I expected him to put me back on a plane and send me home. What else could this mean? My eyes started to tear up. Hoping to catch a glimpse of Trevor waiting for me, I strained to see into the terminal beyond. Maybe I could wave him over so he could talk to the agent and save me from this. But there was no Trevor.

It was possible that other girls had preceded me into this airport with cheap suitcases and no money, only to be whisked away by rock stars. Or, perhaps the agent gave me the benefit of the doubt because I had a return ticket. He may have determined that, while I was in somewhat tightened financial straits, I was obviously clean and groomed, and not derelict. Or perhaps the welling tears had an impact. He sighed and gruffly waved me through. I was free to go.

I had expected Trevor to be the first thing I saw when I emerged. He wasn't there. I stood paralyzed in the center of the milling airport crowd. Wide-eyed, I scanned the area around me, clutching the strap of my little round suitcase with perspiring hands. Had something happened? If something had happened, there was no way for him to reach me, and I had no idea who to call—

And then he was there, wearing shorts, sandals and a Hawaiian shirt, running toward me with outstretched arms. I flew into them and burst into tears. I had been so wound up for a week, had felt so stressed from the trip, had spent the last few minutes so frightened by the customs official, and was so happy to be there that seeing Trevor triggered hysterics. I choked and sobbed.

It was the second time I had cried in seven years.

Grinning, Trevor wiped the tears from my face with his fingers.

"I heard the plane fly over and hopped in the car to come fetch you," he explained. "I've been listening and waiting all morning." He took my suitcase and slipped his arm around my waist to lead me toward the exit.

I experienced a kind of culture shock on the way to the car as I tried to absorb the tropical climate, the tanned skin of departing tourists, the native Bahamian accents, and Trevor in sunglasses, shorts and sandals. I had left late-winter only hours earlier and had landed in a place where it was eighty degrees and sunny, with palm trees. And no chance of snow!

I stared around, lips parted, goggle-eyed, then turned to Trevor and squeezed him around the waist.

I remembered the customs ordeal and relayed the story to him.

"They almost didn't let me stay," I told him in conclusion.

"They thought you were coming here to live on the beach. They have a problem with that." He squinted at me in the sun. "You should really have brought more money." His voice was almost reproachful.

I told him about the seventy-five dollars, an enormous amount of money to me, scraped together painfully over a period of months and months. I didn't tell him that it was an enormous amount of money because that was self-evident. I didn't tell him about the effort it had taken me to save it, because it would have sounded like whining. I simply told him my airfare had not been paid in full, without pointing out that it was Trevor who had not paid it in full, and that I'd had to turn all my money over to the airline before boarding the plane at O'Hare.

"Still, you should have brought more for an emergency, don't you agree?" He then added quietly, almost to himself, "Everything here is impossibly expensive…" He suddenly looked a little fretful and worried, but I didn't really pay attention to that. What I did pay attention to was that he didn't appear interested in whether or not I agreed. I thought he sounded like a father. Stunned and offended, I said nothing.

"What if they hadn't allowed you to stay? What if you had had to go home after I'd paid for your ticket and waited ages to see you?" he scolded, steering us through the crowd. "But I'm glad it all worked out in the end."

What he was expressing was concern over his personal finances and how he would pay for the two of us for the duration of my visit. What I was reading was criticism and contempt. Had he not been listening? I reacted with an adrenaline rush of defensiveness, the white-hot danger signal that warned of trouble. I was bathed in the same defensive adrenaline that always preceded one of my outbursts or rages. I was choking on it.

Rage wasn't supposed to happen to me here. It was never supposed to happen with Trevor at all. He was my *one*. He was my happy-ever-after.

"I *did* bring money for an emergency," I said testily, but not showing my testiness to the degree that I felt it. "I *did* that. The emergency came up before I got here, so now I have no money. That's why they nearly sent me home."

I expected an apology. I expected him to pull out his wallet and force me to take seventy-five dollars while I protested and refused. In fact, my expectation was that I would have to console him for the dismay I was certain he would feel upon learning that his arrangements had been botched, and had cost me so much money and created so much anxiety. I had been poised to reassure him that everything was fine, and that I didn't mind. Just being with him anywhere was enough for me. Being with him in the Bahamas was beyond my imagination. I would have given up my entire savings to be with him, wherever he was.

I would have to do that anyway, I knew. My thoughts kept teasing and prodding me toward rage. Rent was still due at the end of the month. I had just handed an airline my emergency fund, so I would not be returning home with a few dollars, as I'd anticipated. I would have to withdraw the remaining balance from my bank account to make up for the nearly two week's salary I was losing by taking time off without sufficient vacation pay. I would no longer have a financial buffer and would have to begin again, five and ten dollars at a time, trying to rebuild my savings. It would be another year or longer before I replaced the money I had spent to be here, provided all went well, and I encountered no emergencies along the way.

Worst of all, I was now entirely beholden to Trevor and dependent upon him for everything for the next two weeks, like a charity case. If I needed something I would have to beg for it and hope he saw fit to provide it. I would have to feel guilty that I was asking for anything after he had spent so much to bring me here. I was three dollars and twenty-one cents away from being penniless, subject to this man's will and whim against my every effort not to be. I was now a burden. I was now at his mercy. I was now something for him to resent.

"I'm sure we'll make do," Trevor said. What he was trying to do was reassure me. What I was hearing was a displeased and patronizing dig for not having money.

My thoughts began to churn, stirring the adrenaline, reinforcing the anger. I could feel my outrage rising, manifesting itself as a lump in my throat and a tightness at the back of my neck. Then it broke loose and began coursing through me like carbonated black blood. It pumped with a throbbing rhythm I heard in my ears. My hands began to shake. My skin felt hot. Enraged that he had allowed this to happen to me, I looked at Trevor. He had subjected me to humiliation from that agent, had left me deeply frightened that I was abandoned, and had then compounded the injury by criticizing me. I hated him.

The shock of hating Trevor stopped me short.

A part of me far off in the distance, a whisper of me beyond the more immediate urgency of knee-jerk reaction and self-defense, said, "Quiet, now. You're exactly where you're supposed to be." That part of me would do anything to prevent me from pushing Trevor away and was working on me now, frantically trying to apply some sort of salve to the anger to calm me and move me past this.

That part of me also knew that I had just relinquished my last hope of an easy path to normalcy. Adolescent daydreams of an extraordinary man who would take me away had been partially realized. Trevor had come for me, and if Trevor was not the man I had waited for, nobody was. But with those daydreams came my promise to myself that I would live a normal life with him.

My rages and constant, simmering anger weren't normal. I had always known that. My feelings were always disproportionate and always out of my control. Our life together wouldn't be normal as long as I was like this. But what could I do? I had identified the problem and its cause. I knew that something in me had broken along the way. I knew every traumatic event and repeated abuse that had contributed to this in my childhood, but knowing didn't cure me. Therapy didn't cure me. Effort, shame, will power, and the chidings and disdain of other people didn't cure me. Worse, the problem was compounded by a sense of hopelessness, and exacerbated by depression that was sometimes so severe I had to struggle to lift my head and climb out of bed.

I had to fight all this when my will to live was so shaky that rage was perhaps the only thing that saved me. I was enraged by my father's desertion, my mother's suicide, and my grandmother's insensitivity. I was enraged at Lily for apparently deciding she didn't love me anymore. I was enraged by my father's family, who let go of me so meekly, and by my other relatives who rarely called or came to see me, and who never remembered much about me from one visit to the next. I was enraged by the women who wouldn't be friends with me, and by the men who all wanted to sleep with me.

I couldn't compromise with rage, nor could I temper it with patience and resignation. Rage sometimes woke me up at night. It followed me into public places where I was confrontational and rudely snapped at people if they spoke to me, or where I verbally attacked sales and customer service people if they didn't serve me quickly enough or give me the answers I wanted to hear. I started arguments with people who made the mistake of saying something I could take the wrong way. I glared challengingly at strangers for looking at me, even though they were probably only thinking, "What a pretty girl." However, it was only that toxic fury, and my vow that I would spitefully survive everything, that forced me through the bleak times.

Now I was enraged because of Trevor.

How does one become normal? I continually asked myself. I would eventually figure it out, I knew. I would *not* live my entire life this way because I simply would *not* permit my disjointed, dysfunctional, indifferent, and insensitive family to win. Maybe I would find sudden insight through meditation or prayer. Or, perhaps the answer was in a psychology textbook or magazine I hadn't yet brought home. If that were the case, I would continue to invest in them. I would keep searching for the reasons behind my behavior.

However, this problem was suddenly urgent and "eventually" had become "now." I had to fix it *now* when I had never before been able to make any real headway toward improvement. The best I had ever done was to repeatedly promise myself between episodes that I would be tougher next time, and I would beat it. Or I would beat it the time after that. I lived from one promise to the next. And when I failed, as I always did, I blamed the other person as much as I blamed myself. He was not the "right one," or he would understand me enough to not provoke me, and I would love him enough to not be angry.

But my emotions were tricky and slippery. When I was a child, I had had no problem sorting through my feelings. They had all been clear and distinct, and they always revealed themselves at the proper times. Then, at some point in my life, I lost the ability to distinguish between them, or to suppress and control them. I often mistook one emotion for another, or got confused about what I felt and reacted inappropriately. I interpreted every negative emotion as anger and reacted with affront, even when I was really experiencing frustration, exhaustion, disappointment, sadness, embarrassment, regret, or hurt. I was always angry, no matter the underlying cause. Then, if I was hurt or embarrassed because of one person, I felt anger toward *all* persons. I couldn't even properly set my sights when I aimed my anger, much less turn the switch to the proper emotion.

I was emotionally confused and unstable and had no control over any of it. I knew this, but nothing helped. Meanwhile, people didn't tolerate it. Angie was the rare exception, and Karen, with coaching from Angie, would come to be an exception as well.

Trevor, however, was still an unknown.

Trevor could have quickly ended this episode of the seventy-five dollars with an apology, but he didn't offer one. I now had to grapple with the emotional after-effects. Should I choose shame? Or anger? Anger? Or shame?

Whichever I chose, this was part of a pattern I had become accustomed to. This always followed swiftly after the Infatuation Phase, which in Trevor's case had carried me safely through the tour. I called this the Hate Phase. I could never date anyone for more than few weeks before it took hold and then took over. Something always triggered it; it could be large or small, but it invariably ripped open each relationship before it had a chance to develop properly. Even if I shifted from anger to shame, I couldn't continue the relationship. The Hate Phase always preceded the breakup, which I nearly always initiated because I never felt the same about the man again.

After breaking off a relationship at the first sign of trouble, I always let a period of time pass until I felt strong enough to deal with another relationship. Then I moved on to someone else, someone who was safe and who wouldn't abandon me or turn on me by doing the large or small thing that the last one, and the one before him, had done to me. I kept looking for someone who wouldn't trigger the hatred. I was only nineteen, but I had moved through this pattern so many times it felt as though I was looking into a mirror, with a mirror behind me, at a series of identical broken relationships continuing into infinity.

Here it was again, the Hate Phase, within minutes of our being reunited, and it was over money. Was this evidence that I was mistaken about him? Was Trevor *not* the man I should be with? Should I move on and keep looking until I found the man who was?

My gut argued down the question. It kept telling me, "You're exactly where you're supposed to be," yet nothing about me had changed. If I could feel one toward him, the adrenaline rages would never be far away. In the short minutes on the walk to the car, I understood with sharp clarity that no "right" man would cure me, and that the problem was with me, not the man. Except for really obvious transgressions, like a boyfriend's deceit, my relationships mostly belonged in the My Fault column of the My Fault/Their Fault list. There was nothing Trevor could ever do or be that would prevent this from happening to me.

That being the case, I might never escape the rages entirely. It might always be a question of will and self-control, a measure of how much I loved him, and a measure of how much rage I could withstand and restrain without erupting and saying something mean and hurtful that would injure him, and which he might never be able to forgive. If so, I would have to take each rage as it came, hoping I could hide it from Trevor, hoping I would never hurt him with it, or change his feelings toward me and make him want to leave me, until I could figure out how to stop them permanently.

I had to hope the anger wouldn't eventually corrupt my feelings toward him as well, as it had with other men in the past, and make me leave him. I would have to fight this, and the fight would be a constant one.

It was exhausting to think about. I would have to decide if that sustained and monumental effort, if Trevor, was worth it. Should I just let him go? Would it be easier on me, and kinder to him, to spend my life alone?

Shame was pushing itself to the forefront and shoving anger aside, so my emotional pendulum swung wildly back to guilt and sorrow. He was so good and so sweet and had done so much for me; the poor man was clearly overjoyed and bouncing with anticipation, while I was in the Bahamas at his expense, hating him because I was a bad, ungrateful person who didn't deserve him.

I hung my head, and my feet began to drag as I headed, once again, toward inevitable defeat. Trevor noticed and tilted my chin up with a finger as we walked. He hooked his hand through my arm to pull me along more purposefully, so I had no choice but to look ahead instead of down, and to match my walk to his brisk and cheerful one. Somehow, that lifted my spirits and made me feel hopeful, just a bit.

I didn't know what I felt or which emotion should take precedence, so I let the subject of my finances drop. I would come back to it again. I would have no choice but to come back to it. Often little, seemingly insignificant things found fertile soil in my mind. They always grew large beyond all good sense and proportion as I obsessed.

Consumed with the joy of the moment, Trevor was oblivious to my train of thought and didn't realize that our relationship had suddenly turned secretly shaky. He could never have fathomed how or why, even if I had tried to explain it to him.

He knew exactly where the car was and quickened his step as he led me there.

"When we first arrived, I saw a billboard that said, 'The Bahamas are for lovers.' I'll show it to you. I knew I had to bring you here straight away on account of that billboard."

He opened the trunk of the car and tossed in my suitcase. Then he opened the passenger door and kissed me on the nose as I slid past him and into the seat. With one hand on the car door and the other on the roof, he leaned in toward me.

He reached in to run his fingers down my cheek, and then tilted my chin up with a finger. "Because you are my lover." He kissed me, stepped backward and shut the car door, then walked around to the other side. He climbed into the driver's seat and started the car.

I was trapped with Trevor on an island for two weeks. Beneath this sudden anger toward him, which I knew I could suppress to a degree but could not entirely rein in or control, I was absolutely certain I loved him. And I owed him a great deal for this incredible vacation. Gratitude plus indebtedness minus seventy-five dollars held me captive. If I was angry or leaned toward hating him, I couldn't escape. I couldn't outrun my fear of abandonment and leave him before he left me. I would need to face this and work through it, maybe even past it, for the first time in my life. I had no idea how to do that, or what the outcome would be. I only knew there was no escaping it this time.

I wondered if there was a phase beyond the Hate Phase, if it had a name, and what that name should be.

As Trevor steered the car down the highway, I briefly marveled at the strangeness of riding down the left side of the road. Then I felt myself slipping into panic as I turned inward and considered my situation: No escape! I gritted my teeth and frantically maneuvered my way through an anxiety attack, staring ahead while Trevor chatted and patted my knee. I could hear him, but could only respond with nods and tight smiles. My heart raced, my head throbbed, and my chest silently screamed while I fell and fell and fell, and spiraled in circles through an emotional wind tunnel. No escape!

Finally, after a very long, almost unendurable few minutes, with my heart pulsing in my ears, the panic eased and passed. Smiling, I took a deep breath and turned to Trevor. "I missed you so much," I said, squeezing his knee. I had a banquet of emotions to choose from. I selected that one.

He looked at me and grinned, then turned back to the road. He whistled as he drove, slowing down once to point to the billboard that had brought me here.

The wrought iron sign spelled, "Harmony Acres," and spanned the entrance to a compound consisting of four little three-room cottages with plots of well-maintained grass, just off a private beach. Each cottage was nestled under palm trees and had a porch that looked out over the ocean. Stray coconuts littered the lawns.

Trevor pulled up at the end of the drive alongside three parked vehicles, all perpendicular to the edge of the lawn, and set the emergency brake. He gestured toward one of the houses.

"Our home for two weeks." He leaned over and kissed me. "Thank you for coming," he murmured. "And don't break anything, please," he warned in a suddenly stern voice. "This is Geoffrey's house, and his wife will sauté my entrails and serve them on toast points if anything goes missing. She's quite thorough about inventorying everything, and quite unforgiving." She was the "rock wife" I'd seen at the concerts. She and Geoffrey were vacationing elsewhere, making room for Trevor and Charles, who were the happy recipients of a bonus holiday for having worked so loyally for the band for so many years.

The view was stunning, and the beach was close enough that the cottages were within earshot of crashing surf. The ocean was a shade of blue I had only seen in magazine photographs that I had always thought were retouched because it couldn't be real… though it turned out it was. It was a deeper, richer blue than the sky and was framed by palm trees—I'd never seen a palm tree up close. I smelled the salt and the wonderful fishiness of the sea air and spotted sailboats in the distance. We were in paradise.

"We need to make love on that beach," Trevor said, as if he were reminding himself to buy milk. Then he led me toward one of the cottages. I noticed Angus Adkins in a lounge chair on the porch of the cottage across the way, lying still and silent in the sun with one arm thrown across his forehead, seemingly asleep. An open bottle of whiskey rested on the small metal patio table beside him.

"Only mad dogs and Englishmen go out in the midday sun," Trevor quoted Noel Coward—and more recently, Joe Cocker, who had an album, "Mad Dogs and Englishmen"—gesturing toward Angus. "He was there when I left. I should go over there and tell him to go inside."

"Is Angus the mad dog or the Englishman?"

"You're quite the witty one, you saucy little minx."

"It's a serious question."

"He is…" Trevor paused for effect, "… the Englishman. He is, in fact, my employer and has graciously invited us both to stay here on this lovely island. For which we are most grateful indeed." He raised his eyebrows as a warning. "Are we not?"

There would be no Angus jokes. I nodded, chastened. It was a travesty that I must be muzzled when Angus was so funny. I had learned this about him on tour. Close proximity to this famous legend had revealed him to be a pompous, self-absorbed and somewhat dimwitted fellow, whose looks and passable voice, not his highly evolved nature or intellect, had made his fortune. If it had ever occurred to me to be attracted to him, even briefly, that thought was entirely gone. If he were to confess he was in love with me, I would probably double over laughing until I choked.

The tour had had its moments when Angus had thoroughly lived up to his rock star billing. In Terre Haute he had passed out on a luggage cart in the hotel lobby and was unceremoniously wheeled, draped over the bags, to his room by a bellhop. In Louisville he'd entertained us in his dressing room before the concert by lighting farts. In St. Louis he'd vomited all the way from the elevator to his hotel room, leaving an unpleasant trail behind him. He was usually drunk at breakfast and seemed to be quite enamored of excess in all of its forms. I had often been tempted to make comments and observations, causing Trevor to frown, but which he had never contradicted. Now, however, the message was clear that I was to keep my thoughts to myself.

Angus was very fortunate to have Trevor and Charles, who had dutifully watched over him and kept him reasonably safe for the past six years. They mopped him up, dusted him off, tilted him toward upright when he listed, pointed him in the correct direction, and nudged him onto the stage. They did all of this without judgment, and with a good deal of affection and protectiveness. If Angus was appreciative, I couldn't tell, but neither Trevor nor Charles seemed to mind.

Our cottage was a modest little stucco building with tiled ceramic floors, a bedroom and bath on each end, and a large open living area with a full kitchen in between. Trevor led me to our bedroom as Charles emerged from his.

"Holly! Good to see you, girl!"

"Hey! Charles!" I greeted, only to be violently yanked into a bedroom and have the door slammed behind me.

"That was rude!" I scolded. "I wanted to say hello to Charles."

Trevor scooped me up, threw me over his shoulder, and carried me to the bed. He did not respond to my accusation. Neither did he walk over to the other cottage to wake Angus from his nap in the tropical sun.

"Where are all your necklaces?" We were just awakening from a short, but sweet and languid, nap, legs entwined, facing each other with our foreheads touching. My demons were quiet for the moment, and all I felt was love and affection. I was running a finger down his throat, which until now had always sported five or six gold chains and pendants. It looked very bare.

"I got rid of all that when I came to love you," Trevor explained.

"Got rid of all what?"

"All the gifts from other women. Jewelry, clothes. I haven't kept any. When I get home, I'll have more to clear out." He winked. "I need to make room for all the gifts I expect *you'll* be giving me."

"You love me?"

"As a matter of fact, I do." He gently brushed the back of his hand up my cheek. "I said it would happen, didn't I? The night we met? And that's why you're here, isn't it?"

"You've never once looked me in the eye and said 'I love you.'"

"My humblest apologies. I won't neglect it in the future."

Trevor pressed his nose against mine and stared at me so closely that his eyes merged together into one, like a Cyclops.

"I love you," he said while I giggled. "Do you love me?"

I nodded.

"Say it."

Still giggling, I shook my head.

"Say it!" He started to tickle me.

"I can't! I can't! Stop it!"

"Why can't you?" he asked, pausing.

"Because I've never said it before! It's too hard! I can't!" Squealing and laughing, I rolled off the bed and ran naked into the bathroom as if he were chasing me. I slammed and locked the door.

"Never once? Not even one time?" Trevor's mouth was on the keyhole. I didn't answer. "Say it, say it, say it, say it…" he chanted.

I opened the door. He was crouching, naked, with his mouth where the keyhole had been a second earlier. He stood up. "Say it," he ordered.

"Look away, then," I ordered. "Cover your eyes." He did. I cupped my hands, pressed my mouth to his ear, and whispered, "I love you."

Then giggling some more, I ran to the bed and threw myself on it. I bounced up and down.

"*Please* don't break the bed!" he barked sharply. "Belinda will stew my lungs and arse and serve them on toast points!" Trevor was genuinely concerned enough to spoil the moment; feeling a stab of intense fear and shame, just as I always did when I was reprimanded, I stopped bouncing.

Would he stop at this? Or would he keep going and going and going and going, ripping into me until I had no self-esteem left? I was used to that from my grandmother, and my reactions were a reflex. Sometimes when someone criticized or berated me, the adrenaline took over, as it had at the airport, and I either choked it down and fumed obsessively in secret, or exploded into a rage and fought back with disproportionate viciousness, accumulated over a period of many years, and overflowing.

At other times, I mentally threw my arms up across my face to protect myself and simply tried to live through it in shame, as I had always done when I was a child, mourning how bad, reprehensible and worthless I was. This time, I reacted as the child. I sat on my knees stiffly and looked down, terrified and ashamed, staring, frozen and still, braced and waiting for his attack. I waited without breathing.

He walked over to the bed, and lightly tossed himself onto it next to me. He gathered me into his arms. "I do love you, you know," he said seriously. "I really do."

I was immediately better. I relaxed and began to breathe again. I smiled.

"Am I the first one *you* ever said it to?"

Trevor pulled his mouth into a sheepish grimace and rolled his eyes to the ceiling. He shrugged.

"I'm not!" I gasped, pretending to be angry. He was over four years older than I was. I expected him to have had relationships. I teasingly slapped his chest then began tickling him under the arms. "Who is she? Who are *they*? How many are there?"

Trevor turned serious. I could see from his face that he had decided to tell me something he had kept from me previously. He grabbed my hands and held them tightly. He didn't want to play anymore.

"I've only said it to one." He said it casually, but with more underlying gravity than I would have expected, and he was watching me closely to gauge my reaction. I moved beside him to the edge of the bed.

"Okay," I said, a bit frightened.

Her name was Beth. She was Australian, he said, and had gone to college in England, where they had met shortly after she arrived. She was two years older than he—he'd always preferred older women, "until you," he added diplomatically. He reached for his wallet, which he'd left on the end table, and opened it. He wordlessly pulled out a picture and handed it to me while he continued to study my face.

So this was my competition. Typically when I had competition, I simply withdrew from the race because I wasn't equipped to compete, not really, not with my problems. I never got jealous, I simply offered my regrets and left. Oddly, I didn't feel inclined to do that now. This was the first time I had ever been willing to stay, even though I knew I could never measure up to another woman. This time, my problems seemed almost incidental, and our relationship more important than the relationship he'd had with this woman he had once, and possibly still, loved. This time, I was really going to beat my problems and be able to keep him.

Unlike previous competition, and despite the fact Trevor clearly loved her, Beth didn't feel like a threat. I didn't resent her, and I felt no twinges of panic. Trevor quieted my fear of abandonment, which was ironic considering his job, his distance, and his history with women that Karen had filled me in on. Nobody had ever done that before Trevor. I loved him, and for the first time, I felt completely safe and completely loved in return. He was the man I was going to marry and spend my life with. I knew this absolutely, even if Trevor might not know it just yet, and even if I continued to have times when I was angry enough to hate him, or felt as if I needed to run away from him. I would deal with that somehow because I had to. He was going to be my life. He already was.

I took the picture and looked up at Trevor. He was waiting for my reaction much as he might have waited for a coach to rank his athletic performance.

I was prettier than Beth. She had thin, straight, dark-blond hair and pale eyes, a round face and a gentle, rounded chin. Hers was a pleasant, comfortable face, but not a beautiful one. I considered her carefully, seeing eyes that seemed steady, kind and tolerant, and had intelligence and a kind of depth to them. I didn't have to ask Trevor to know that she was mature, very smart, and had done well in college. She was someone you might go to when you had a problem and wanted solid, fair, non-judgmental advice. She wasn't stylish and was a little overweight, but the curve of her mouth suggested a sense of humor and a ready laugh, and her dimples made her face very engaging. She was someone I would trust to not spill my secrets or betray me in any way, to be a good, loyal friend. I would look up to her, I thought. I would care what she thought of me.

"I like her," I said.

He seemed pleased, as if I'd said just exactly what he'd hoped I would say.

"What would have happened if she weren't so far away?" I returned the picture, which he glanced at, then tucked away in his wallet. I could see in his face when he looked at the photo that he still loved her. My heart fell, but I still felt no compulsion to run. He was *mine*. He *was*.

"We'd be married," he said matter-of-factly. He shrugged. "As it is, we just write." He stopped to correct himself. "*Wrote*. I stopped recently, about the time I got rid of the gold chains and all the rest."

They'd dated for the first two years she attended school in England, he told me, and lived together for the last two years before her graduation. Then she returned home to Australia for what was supposed to have been just a month-long visit to prepare for the wedding. But her mother took ill while she was there, so Beth stayed to care for her and her two younger brothers and told Trevor they'd have to wait. Then her mother died, and Beth didn't like to uproot the boys while they still had school to attend. She also didn't want to marry until her family no longer needed her, so they called off the wedding.

Trevor, meanwhile, had a job he loved and was seeing the world. He wasn't quite ready to give it up and move to Sydney just yet, so he'd agreed to whatever Beth suggested, even though it meant never seeing her unless the band toured Australia, which it had only done twice. They hadn't seen each other in two years.

"It was hard being apart," he confessed, taking my hand and squeezing it. "But I'm with you now."

I stared at our clasped hands and nodded. Something in his face conveyed that it was monumental from his perspective, like a sudden shifting of the Tectonic plates, that he was with me, telling me he loved me. I understood this in a flash. He was setting Beth aside because of me, at least for now, and that was something he had never expected to do for anyone.

For a moment I panicked, thinking I should leave because he was making the wrong choice, and it was my duty to save him. Another part of me told me again that I was exactly where I was supposed to be. I listened to that part. Again, I was going to stay.

What did he see in her, and what did he see in me, when we were so different? I had dark hair, complexion, and eyes; she was fair. I was bony-thin; she was a bit overweight. I was younger; she was older. Most men found me very attractive, whereas I knew just from looking at this picture that Beth had fewer options than I. We weren't even remotely the same type. I couldn't see, or even guess, a pattern in Trevor's choices.

Maybe it wasn't a question of "seeing" at all. Trevor felt like a puzzle piece that fit. He felt like family. I didn't have to examine or question it. It was enough to accept that he felt like "home." Perhaps I felt the same way to him.

"Is she the one who crocheted that sweater?" In lieu of a jacket, Trevor always wore a beautiful, white and brown, belted, crocheted sweater that I'd once complimented. He'd told me it was a gift from a friend, but the work and care involved in making it had made it clear to me that the gift was from a lover.

"Yes," Trevor answered.

I presumed he'd gotten rid of it along with the gold chains and the rest and felt a little sorry for Beth that she had worked so hard on it.

"And now for your lurid history." He nudged me with his elbow and raised an eyebrow.

"Nothing much to tell," I said. "Nobody I almost married. Nobody I ever loved. Nobody for you to be jealous of." There was no point in elaborating on my string of failures.

"So I'm the first you ever said it to? Really?"

"Yep."

"Good. That's very good." He nuzzled my ear. Then he slapped my bottom. "Let's get dressed and visit with Charles."

Charles was sitting on the couch strumming a guitar when we emerged from the bedroom.

"He's teaching himself," Trevor told me. "He knows three chords."

"That's all I need," Charles said. "Listen." He started playing a medley of rock song riffs with the same three chords. "One week into it and I can already play nearly everything. I may start a band."

He stood up with his legs spread in rock star fashion and waved his arm in large air-guitar circles, grimacing intensely and whipping his head down to flip his long dark hair into his face as he played one of his three chords.

"His talent is truly amazing, isn't it?" Trevor noted. "Particularly the way he poses."

"May I please play the tambourine in your band?"

A scream pierced the air. Charles shot to attention, put down his guitar, and bolted out the door. Trevor looked at me and hesitated, then followed Charles, running. I chased after them both, lightly, as I was barefoot.

A small group had gathered in front of Angus's cottage.

Angus was moaning, walking stiffly like Frankenstein, and darting frantic looks around with bloodshot eyes that appeared half-crazed. Petra, Angus's girlfriend, stood wringing her hands with an appalled expression, as if she knew she was supposed to do something but didn't want to go near him, while John Collier gingerly helped him through the door. Petra followed them.

Lucas's American wife Nancy turned to Trevor and Charles. "Sunburn," she said tersely.

Trevor wasn't meeting her eyes. He guiltily shifted from one foot to the other.

"Where was Petra all day? Anyone know?" Nancy lit a cigarette, and then angrily pushed her sunglasses onto her forehead, slipping the cigarette pack and lighter into the back pocket of hip-hugger cutoffs that were so short the front pockets dangled four inches past the frayed hems. I didn't know where to look—She was topless. She had no tan lines at all, anywhere.

"Visiting friends," said Lucas. "She's just got back and found him."

"Does anyone know how long he was out here?" She looked from one of us to the other.

"I saw him here about two hours ago," Trevor offered, looking down at his feet. I tried to decide if it was embarrassment over Nancy's breasts, or shame that he hadn't woken Angus and sent him indoors. It appeared to be shame.

My attention shifted back to the situation, but I couldn't help looking down at my chest while I listened, weighing my small breasts against my nerve. I decided... no. I would not be going topless.

Charles studied the angle of the sun and the shadows on the porch. "Most of the time he was in the shade," he said. "He was probably only in the sun for an hour, when it was directly overhead." He scratched his head. "I hope," he added under his breath.

"An hour in the afternoon is still way too long for his skin type. He's as blue-white as a fish belly." Nancy blew out a trail of smoke. "And he won't use any lotion. I've tried." You could tell she was thinking (although she did not say), "Idiot."

A shriek followed by sobs reached us as we stood there. Behind the door, Angus began making violent vomiting noises.

"Damn. He's got sun poisoning again," Nancy declared. "You'd think he'd learn." She turned to leave. "I'm going to see if I have anything that'll help. If not, I'll go to the store and get something. If he gets really bad, we'll need to find a doctor."

She started walking away, and then turned to her husband as an afterthought. "Tell Petra to stick him in the tub until I get back—tepid water, not warm or cold. It might soothe the pain. And tell her to keep an eye on him. I forbid her to go *anywhere*."

Lucas went inside to relay his wife's message. Nancy turned again and hurried away.

"And no more booze on the patio!" Nancy shouted from the porch of their cottage, and slapped the railing for emphasis before whirling around and going inside. Her breasts jiggled with the force of her earnest anger.

Angus vomited again. Trevor winced.

"Ew," I observed.

"Well..." Trevor took me by the arm. "There's nothing further for us to do here. Nancy has it sussed, and she'll take care of it. She and Petra." Charles nodded in relieved agreement.

We turned to leave. Behind us, Angus suffered. The sounds of his screams, vomiting, and piteous weeping would punctuate the air throughout my entire first romantic starlit night in the Bahamas.

Chapter 12

"**W**ow. First it's daylight, and then it's dark. What happened to dusk?"

We had gotten ready to go out for dinner during daylight and walked out onto the patio to find it pitch-black, with stars.

Angus was still moaning across the way. He screamed dramatically, much as a little girl or a bad actress might, and sobbed. We flinched and then ignored him.

"Something to do with latitude, I think," Trevor guessed. "Perhaps you lose dusk as you get closer to the equator."

We had our first dinner at the Travellers' Rest, a restaurant one or two miles up the road, to which we would return again and again. The atmosphere was casual, and the décor was nautical, with fishing nets hung on the walls, and seashells and starfish embedded in Lucite on the tables.

"Just beer, but something exotic," I told Trevor. Beer was cheapest. I was now tallying every dime Trevor had to spend on me in an attempt to minimize the degree to which I must feel burdensome and beholden, even knowing I'd contributed seventy-five dollars to this adventure. I still couldn't decide if I was more beholden or resentful. I was probably more beholden, I thought.

"Is Australia exotic?"

I nodded and agreed to an Australian beer even though Beth was Australian. Australia had suddenly appeared on my radar as it never had before in my life, and I briefly wondered if Trevor's suggestion had anything to do with her.

He ordered Foster's for all of us, and our beers arrived in the largest cans I had ever seen. I marveled at them, just as I had marveled at the ocean and the left-hand traffic. I would have to take some empty beer cans home with me in place of the souvenirs I'd planned to buy, but now could not. In fact, for the duration of my visit I would be examining everything around me and rifling through trashcans to identify items that were souvenir-worthy and free. *Could I steal a menu?*

I also marveled at the change Trevor received from the bartender; there were coins of every shape. I picked up a triangle. "Do vending machines take coins like this?" I asked. Trevor and Charles both shrugged.

"What are conches?" I was reading the menu. I'd never seen the word before.

"You say it, 'conks,'" Trevor corrected. "They're those little animals inside the shells you blow like horns—those big pink shells. They're called conch shells, and you eat the conches inside."

"Are they good?"

"Yes, indeed. Would you like to try them?"

The hamburger was cheaper, so I shook my head and ordered that.

After dinner we returned to the cottage and settled in for the evening. We all opted against sitting on the porch with Angus in the background, and instead opened a bottle of wine and lounged in the living room where Charles played three-chorded songs and posed rock-star style, while Trevor and I pounded rhythm on the coffee table and sang.

Trevor, Charles, and I devised a plan that equally divided all household chores between the three of us. Neither Charles nor I could cook, but we agreed to take our turns at it. On those nights when it wasn't our turn to cook, we would do the washing up. We would each cook a meal in rotation, beginning with me on my second night there.

Trevor supervised while I measured rice and cleaned broccoli. He showed me the vegetable steamer, how much of the broccoli stems to break off, and how much water to place in the pot with the rice. I set the pork chops in a pan, and looking up at him for his approval, slid them into the oven.

Trevor then told me when to remove them. He had magically timed preparation so that everything was ready to serve at the same time. And it was good! Both Trevor and Charles applauded me after dinner, while Trevor stood and gathered up the dishes to take his turn at cleaning up.

Charles poured wine into three of Belinda's wine glasses and handed one to each of us, then waved me out onto the porch while Trevor wiped down the counters. We paused, listening for audible signs of Angus, then hearing none, settled into the patio furniture. Sipping his wine, Charles sprawled comfortably in a lounge chair. I took a seat beside him in a rocking chair and looked through the palm trees reflected in the light from the patio door, and at the blackness beyond them, where waves crashed against the beach. I sighed happily.

Trevor pulled the radio over to the open window and came outside to join us. Van Morrison's *Brown-Eyed Girl* came on the radio. Trevor came up from behind me and kissed the top of my head. Then he reached down and took my hand.

"Dance with me," he ordered, pulling me to my feet and twirling me in a kind of a jitterbug while he sang the words. After the song stopped, he rocked me slowly and closely for a few moments.

"Van Morrison wrote that song for Janet Planet," I said.

"Hmmm."

"Karen said they had a chemical whammo thing happen, the first time they met."

"Did they?" he asked drowsily, kissing my ear. "Then it's our song, too, my brown-eyed girl," he whispered, lifting my hand to his lips and kissing it.

I had never had a song with anyone before.

Charles silently stood, saluted us, and moved indoors.

Angus moaned and whimpered from his cottage across the way, but the sounds had grown more angry and frustrated than extravagant and bloodcurdling. I heard no more retching, so Angus was far easier to bear on this second day. The waves crashed in the background. The air smelled like the sea. The palm trees swished in the warm night breeze, and Trevor and I continued to lean into each other, rocking and looking up at the stars.

A few days passed. Trevor, Charles, and I walked the beach, went sightseeing, visited the open-air market, and sat at the bar in the Travellers' Rest and drank Foster's. In the evenings we sat on the porch, sipped wine, and chatted. During our languid days, we tried snorkeling and body surfing, and spent our time relaxing under palm trees— until a coconut fell and hit Charles on the head, at which point, we moved back onto our porch and viewed the trees from a safe distance.

We made tea and carried it outside in civilized fashion on trays at Tea Time, which I learned was whenever someone happened to want tea, and rocked in the patio chairs while sipping from our mugs. I drank mine with milk and sugar and tried to handle my silverware as they did, consciously attempting to assimilate myself into the British culture in order to be closer to Trevor.

Most of our entertainment was free or very inexpensive. We went sightseeing but didn't go to clubs or expensive restaurants, and we didn't buy souvenirs. We spent most of our time at the cottage. We took turns cooking meals and washing up, went grocery shopping together, and sang songs, banging rhythm on the coffee table, while Charles played guitar.

Sometimes Charles took off by himself, and Trevor and I had the cottage to ourselves. When Charles was around, I was still happy. I was in love with Trevor, but I also thoroughly adored Charles. Four days into it, I hadn't thought much about the money issue at the airport. I hadn't hated Trevor again, and for some reason, Charles triggered no roiling irritation, the way most people did. I had never spent this much time in constant close proximity to other people without becoming crazed and enraged. Instead, I kept marveling over how very much I really loved and enjoyed both of them, feeling as though I had finally found the people I belonged to.

We came and went, having little to do with Angus, who demonstrated that he was recovering from his sunburn ordeal by entertaining guests. We observed these guests arriving in their amazingly expensive, sometimes chauffeured, automobiles from the distant vantage—in proximity, socio-economic, and philosophical stance—of our porch across the way. These guests all appeared to be excessively, even obscenely, well-heeled, and seemed delighted to be slumming with rock stars. However, I got the distinct impression that they would have little interest in Angus if he stopped being fashionable, or if his fame or fortune were ever to slip. But while he was still on top of the charts, they clapped and laughed at his comments and witticisms much as they might have applauded a favorite juggler or court jester. Or a monkey.

Angus understandably basked in the glow of their attention and seemed to have concluded that he was far more delightful than perhaps Trevor, Charles, or I may have thought. He turned on like a light switch whenever these people came around, greeted them in a jovial voice we could hear from our cottage, and cranked up Torc's newest album for their benefit, loudly enough so that we too could hear it across the compound and over the sound of the crashing surf. We too could feel the beat of the bass throbbing in our skulls… again and again, day after day. He was as smug and self-satisfied about the patronage of Bahamas' social elite as he was about the new album, and he foisted each upon the rest of us with tedious regularity.

"How does Angus find all these rich people?" I asked over a Foster's at the Travellers' Rest. We had just escaped a swirling bevy of social elite at the compound and were drinking slowly in hopes of returning only after they'd left, and the stereo was off again.

"It's a gift," Trevor offered. "The gift of being a famous rock star. Rich people simply find you when you have that gift. Amazing, really, how it all falls into place."

"Cocaine," Charles added, leaning past Trevor to address me at an angle. "They all share a passion for it. And a dealer."

"Angus does coke?" I'd always thought he only liked booze.

"No, Petra does," Charles replied. "She likes it very much indeed. That's where she goes when she's out and about, visiting friends."

This experience seemed more like a soap opera than real life. I was finding it educational to learn that some people actually lived their lives in mansions with nothing to do but snort cocaine and court rock stars or their girlfriends, instead of clawing their way through life chasing cockroaches with shoes and Black Flag, or wrestling themselves onto the Skokie Swift day after day. My eyes had been suddenly opened to life's cruel inequities, and my own social limitations. This was certainly an adventure and an education, but beauty didn't help me here.

Chapter 13

Trevor and I sauntered outside and settled into the patio rocking chairs to sip tea and watch the crashing surf for a while.

"What's Angus looking at?" I stood to get a better look, squinting across the way. I sat back down, but kept watching.

Angus was sitting on his porch with his head tilted back, holding what appeared to be a small piece of sheer cloth up to his eyes and looking through it. He placed it over his mouth. We could see him blowing it up and letting it fall back again. Up and back. Up and back. At one point, he evidently blew too hard because the object flew up sharply, then fell onto his chest.

"Is it a piece of tissue?"

"Hmm. I'm sure I don't know."

We stood up and unapologetically rearranged our chairs to face Angus instead of the beach, then sat back down and watched him as if he were the television set our cottage did not have.

Angus studied his shoulder intently, and then began to carefully peel away the skin. He said, "Bollocks!" when the piece tore sooner than he'd intended.

"Mystery solved," Trevor observed. The solving of this mystery made Angus no less fascinating to watch. He continued to stare.

"So *this* is glamour," I commented. "Ah!"

"There is no such thing as glamour close up," Trevor replied. "It requires great distance and proper lighting."

We both rocked and watched in silence for a few minutes as Angus peeled away little ribbons of skin from his shoulders, sides, and back. He did something different with each one, rolling it into a ball and flicking it, draping it over his knee and closely examining it, poking holes in it, or tearing it into tiny bits. He smelled one, then opened his mouth and placed it on his tongue, squinting thoughtfully. Once the strip was amply moistened, he pulled it out and stuck it on the tip his nose, where it dangled. Changing his mind, he rearranged it into a skin mustache, smoothing it under his nose with his fingers, popping it into his mouth again when it had dried too much to stick.

I finally spoke up.

"I haven't said anything about what Angus is doing with his skin. Did you happen to notice?" I tilted my head and smiled perkily, demanding praise.

Trevor nodded thoughtfully, not looking at me. "I did notice that."

"I know you don't like me to say things about Angus."

"Hmm."

"I thought things, though."

We both stared across at Angus and rocked in our chairs.

"I *could* have said the things I thought, but I didn't. Because I know how you don't like me to say things about Angus."

Trevor coughed, then nodded. "Hmm."

"If Angus were lighting farts again though, like he did that time in Louisville, I would probably have to say something. You probably couldn't stop me."

Trevor snorted, then recovered and attempted to remain expressionless. He glanced at me, frowned a warning, and then looked away again.

"Fortunately, he's not lighting farts so I don't have to say anything. I can still keep my thoughts to myself." I rocked.

"No, he most certainly is not lighting farts." Trevor rocked.

"Trevor?"

"Yes, Holly."

I held out a book of matches and gestured toward Angus.

"Angus asked for these. Would you mind?"

Trevor looked at the matches, and then fell off his chair and onto the porch, where he grabbed his stomach and rolled back and forth laughing. Angus heard him and glanced over. He squinted at us with mild interest before noticing a final flap of skin that needed pulling. He carefully attempted to remove the biggest slice he could before it tore.

Trevor, meanwhile, had partially pulled himself up and was leaning against the seat of his rocking chair.

"It is very wrong of you to do that," he scolded me, wagging his finger in my direction. "And you are a very, very wicked, naughty girl."

"I said nothing at all untoward." I sniffed and looked haughtily offended.

"I don't care what you do," he choked, still laughing. "You are *not* going to make me say anything about the man who pays my salary." He dropped backward and lay there with his head at my feet. He pressed the palms of his hands to his temples, shaking his head and chuckling.

What a good, loyal man, I thought fondly. I jabbed him gently in the ribs with my toes.

He looked up at me with a smile. "What was that for?"

"I just like you a whole lot." I ran my toes back and forth along his ribs in a caress.

"You do, do you?"

"Mm-hmm."

"Well, I like you, too."

Chapter 14

"**H**ey! Anyone home?" Nancy opened the door, poked her head in our doorway, and then pattered in barefoot without waiting for a response. She was wearing a blouse today.

I was at the kitchen sink washing the mugs and tea items and placing them in the drainer. I looked up, smiled, and invited her in, even though she was already there. Trevor poked his head out of the bedroom, where he had been reading.

"There's a party tonight on Paradise Island. One of Angus and Petra's friends invited all of us. You too! Be ready by seven, okay? We have to go there by boat, so we all need to leave together."

When Trevor had invited me, he didn't mention anything about parties on Paradise Island with friends of Angus and Petra. I had nothing to wear. I had only brought what he'd told me to bring—clothing to lounge around in. Thus far, I had been safely sequestered in the compound where it didn't matter how I dressed, or even if I *did* dress. When we ventured out, it was only to places where everyone was dressed informally, and I could fade into the crowd.

"Fantastic!" Trevor said. "We'll be there!"

I wordlessly left the room and went into the bedroom, where I sorted through my things. The only 'dressy' item I'd brought was a long black skirt. Perhaps I could work it out with a top of some kind…

I pulled on the skirt and tried on one top after another to see how they looked with it.

"Crumpet!" Trevor noted appreciatively, watching me try it with my bikini top. Then, seeing my expression, he asked what was wrong.

"I can't wear this," I said. "I don't have the right clothes. I can't go. I'm not going."

"Nonsense. It's lovely. And you *must* go."

He was the sort of man who wouldn't notice that my seven-dollar skirt was cheap polyester, or that it had pills and snags, or that the side seam was pulling apart near the waistband on one side. The seat of the skirt had stretched out unevenly from sitting. The hem dragged low in the front. It might have been fine for a darkened New Town bar amid the drunks, but it was not adequate for a party on Paradise Island where people arrived in obscenely expensive vehicles with chauffeurs. I couldn't wear it. I'd die of humiliation. I'd humiliate everyone else as well.

"You look lovely." Trevor said reassuringly. "Don't be silly. You're going, and that's final."

Trevor had obviously brought clothing that was suitable for an evening out, as he was dressed in a pair of slacks with a fashionable shirt and tie. He had just shaved and wet down his hair to fight back the cowlicks. He looked somewhat like Alfalfa from the Little Rascals.

"Hurry, Holly. We left already. They're outside waiting for us. Hurry."

I was still staring at myself in the mirror. The skirt was hideous. It was cheap and ragged—hideous. The word "poverty" crossed my mind. I did, indeed, look poor. The best I could do was look poor.

"I can't," I said decisively, and pulled off the skirt. "I have to do this as a 'rock chick,'" I explained to Trevor. "It's the lesser of the two evils. Nobody expects a rock chick to conform, right? It's the only thing I can do. I can't wear the damn skirt. Not here, not with these people."

I pulled on a pair of blue jeans and fluffed out my hair. I struck a defiant "rock chick" pose, hooking my thumbs in my front pockets, and lifting my chin.

"No!" Trevor said angrily. "You looked fine! You *can't* go in jeans. Put the skirt back on now!"

"I won't," I said, near tears. "I can't." If people were going to be contemptuous of me, let them be contemptuous of a defiant and rebellious rock chick, not a girl who was poor and out of place.

He stared at me, then abruptly turned and walked out the door without looking to see if I was following him.

Trevor fumed on the drive to the dock. John counted heads on our arrival, and we all climbed into a motorboat with a driver who was waiting to transport us to the other island. Nancy and Petra were heavily made up with their hair artfully arranged, wearing brightly-colored strapless dresses, jewelry—real gold and diamonds—and high-heeled Brazilian sandals they'd actually purchased in Brazil. They sparkled and shone, and emitted

117

whiffs of subtle, expensive scent, while I sat in my blue jeans trying to make myself small and invisible. The band members were wearing rock star regalia, gold chains, and expensive cologne. Everyone was dressed for a party but me.

I looked out at the water and the black horizon as we scooted and bounced over the waves in the darkness. Trevor looked out at the increasingly glowing lights of Paradise Island in the opposite direction.

A car with a driver was waiting to take us up to a mansion at the end of a long uphill winding road lit by Chinese lanterns. We climbed out of the car and stared appreciatively before walking up to the door.

The mansion looked like a public building, a museum, perhaps. It was huge, sprawling, and lit up, with a live Reggae band playing steel drums on a huge concrete veranda overlooking the ocean. Dozens of people sparkled and shone and wore real gold and diamond jewelry, emitting subtle expensive fragrances as they danced. I was in an Audrey Hepburn or Grace Kelly movie. I was Cinderella, but my Fairy Godmother had stood me up.

Trevor moved into the crowd, leaving me behind. He still hadn't spoken to me since our conversation in the bedroom.

I wasn't defiant enough to be a rock chick. I was just a poor, displaced working-class girl in blue jeans who had crashed an incredible party. Sadly, I knew it, and it showed.

A man walked over to me and tried to make conversation. "You're with Angus?" he asked. "Good friend, Angus. So, where are you from? Where did you go to school?"

He raised his eyebrows slightly at my answers, gave a tight smile, and charmingly excused himself. He felt no need to continue the conversation, even to be polite.

No one else approached me, though I noticed a few women speaking to each other sideways as they appraised me. They seemed to find me amusing. Trevor was keeping his distance, so I was clearly going to endure a humiliating evening alone.

I wandered off the veranda and into the house. Looking for an empty room where I could hide, I found the library. Of all the rooms in the building, I decided, this would be the one that suited me best. I tiptoed in and looked around. It contained a huge, ancient globe with a very oddly-shaped "America" that appeared to date back three hundred years. How old was that globe? I wondered. I squinted at it closely with my nose nearly grazing it. It was not a reproduction. I wanted to touch it, but didn't dare. What does a globe like that cost?

The room also contained a very large, mounted Chinese vase. Ming? I guessed it was Ming. I'd seen vases like that in my art history books. I was certain it was authentic, simply because it was in this room.

The fifteen-foot-high walls were lined floor to ceiling with shelf after shelf of leather-bound books, and in the middle of the room was a brown leather sofa. I sat on the leather sofa, folded my hands in my lap, stared at the shelves of books, and waited for the evening to end.

"There you are." Trevor was standing in the doorway. Apparently he was willing to speak to me if no one was watching. "I saw you wander off and wondered what you might be up to. John told me you were in here."

"I want to go home tomorrow," I told him without emotion. "When we get back, I'm packing my things."

"What are you talking about?"

"I'm done. I want to leave first thing tomorrow."

"Why?" He frowned.

I glared at him. My rage was back. "I don't fit in with you. I don't have the clothes, and I'm not right for you and your friends. I can't do this. I'm done."

He stared at me, dumbfounded.

I narrowed my eyes. "You weren't even *nice* about it," I snapped accusingly.

"Nice about what?"

"About my clothes."

"That's what this is about?" Trevor looked genuinely bewildered. "But *you* were the one who deliberately dressed all wrong for this party, knowing what I wanted you to wear, and knowing you always have to be your best in front of the boys because of my job! Because we're their guests! They didn't have to invite us, you know. We've discussed this! *You* were the one who didn't bring the right clothes!" He looked exasperated. "Why on earth didn't you bring the right clothes?"

"You told me to just bring blue jeans and a bathing suit."

"I did not!"

I dropped my jaw. He had, and now he was denying it.

"Why didn't you tell me in advance that I'd be invited to a party like this? How could you possibly expect me to bring clothes for..." I gestured angrily toward the priceless, gorgeous, museum-quality Ming vase "... *this* if you don't tell me?"

"You should plan for contingencies. You have to know that situations are likely to come up where you need to be presentable."

119

He was defending himself with an observation he seemed to feel was obvious. What I heard was a derisive commentary on my taste and suitability: I heard him tell me I had failed and wasn't good enough.

The rage spiked sharply higher. I began to shake. I couldn't hold my hands steady anymore. My skin felt as if it were rippling from fury. "I brought half my savings! I spent it all on airfare *you* told me was *paid*! And I don't *have* the 'right clothes,' okay? I told you that when you invited me. I don't *own* the 'right clothes' to bring them, and I can't afford to *buy* the 'right clothes.'" I sniffed in disgust. "Why didn't you offer to pay the money back?"

Trevor looked as if I'd slapped him.

"I couldn't have paid for your meals, could I?" He spoke it as a statement, rather than a question. "If I'd given you seventy-five dollars, I would have had to ask for it back to cover your expenses. I didn't arrive here expecting to bring a guest and pay for her airfare." He looked at me pleadingly. "You've seen the prices in the shops."

That made sense, but it didn't calm me down. It only made me shift toward shame. I pulled myself back to rage. "You made me come to this party," I continued. "I told you I didn't want to go. Thank you very much. It's been fun, and I'm really grateful for everything. Now it's time for me to go home." I turned away. I hated him. "You need another girl," I said after a few moments of silence. "Not me."

"I don't need another girl," he said softly.

I didn't answer. My pulse was still throbbing, my blood was still coursing, and my rage was edging toward a point beyond my control.

He reached over to squeeze the back of my neck in a caress. I whirled around. Don't touch me," I hissed, and pushed his hand away. "Get away from me! Leave me alone."

Trevor stepped away.

"I'm sorry," he said gently. "I shouldn't have made you come if you didn't want to."

I gritted my teeth and glared.

"Come get me when it's time to leave," I responded. "I'd like to be alone right now."

"Can I bring you a beer?"

"I wouldn't drink their beer," I snapped. "I wouldn't drink their water. They aren't nice either. I just want to be alone."

We didn't speak on the ride home from the party. Trevor tried, but I wasn't responsive. The band, Charles, Nancy, Petra all bantered back and forth while I silently rode in the boat, staring at the lights up ahead, then silently rode in the car, staring out the window.

When we got back to the cottage, Charles looked at me with concern from the bedroom doorway, and Trevor looked at me with helpless contrition as I pulled my clothes out of the dresser and folded them into my little white suitcase.

Charles backed out of the doorway and went to his room.

"I'm sorry," Trevor said finally. "I bollixed everything. I shouldn't have made you go if you didn't want to."

"You'll find someone who's right for you," I said dully. I fastened the suitcase clasps and turned to him. "Someone with pretty clothes," I sniped, glaring.

"I'll call the airline," he said, and walked out of the room.

I sat down on the bed and cried.

Trevor tiptoed back in a few minutes later. I hurriedly rubbed the heels of my hands over my eyes and turned away so he couldn't see that I'd been crying.

"The earliest they have a seat is next Friday. The flights are all full before then. It's the best they can do. Shall I tell them to change it?"

It was Saturday. *No escape! No escape!*

"That's only two more days to the end of your holiday. Why don't you just stay through the week, until Sunday?"

I didn't answer.

"May I tell them not to change the reservation?"

I sat motionless for a moment, then nodded and turned even further away from him. Two days didn't make any difference, and I knew I would probably never be back. I might as well stay in the Bahamas as long as I could.

He slipped out of the room, and then came back after hanging up the phone.

"It's all sorted," he said. "We are as we were," and then he slipped out again.

We slept that night without touching.

I had never had a fight with a boyfriend and made up. I always simply hated him and left. Again, I was trapped and forced into prolonging a relationship beyond its normal lifespan, which for me ended at the first fight or the first disappointment. I didn't know how one did a relationship, or what was expected, particularly now. I was still his guest. I was still beholden and dependent upon him for everything. Now I was going to have to feel my way through this blindly, stuck with a man I should realistically be broken up with, but whose bed I still shared.

In the morning, he awoke before I did and brought me breakfast in bed—pancakes with strawberries and whipped cream. On the tray he'd placed a tropical flower in a coconut shell filled with water.

His effort touched me, and even after a fitful sleep, I was calmer. Trevor managed to nudge me back into good humor, and even into grudgingly admitting to myself that I didn't, in fact, hate his guts. It was all conditional, though. I still might be broken up with him, I thought. I would have to wait and see.

Then, for the first time in my life, I stayed. As I fixed myself some tea, Trevor crept up from behind and hugged me. He nuzzled my neck and ear. Then he took me by the hand and led me back to the bedroom where we had makeup sex, something I had heard about, but had never experienced. I learned that hatred sometimes passes.

Later that morning, Trevor took a nap, and Charles drove into town. I wandered down to the beach and sat in the sand at the edge of the water, letting the waves lap at my feet and legs.

John Collier saw me and made his way over. He grinned and sat down beside me in the sand.

"I heard you might be leaving," he said, pulling a sad face. "Is it true?"

"Well, no. I'm still here until next Sunday." Who had told him I was leaving? I'd thought my conversations with Trevor were private. And why would John be interested? We operated in different worlds.

I looked over at him. Ah! He was attracted to me. It was there in his eyes: The Look.

"Wonderful! I'd be sorry to see you go." He leaned back on his elbows and looked out to sea. "I was the one who told Trevor to invite you. He saw a billboard and got very glum, poor chap. I told him, 'Bring her here! She's lovely!'"

I laughed because a rock star was attracted to me. I bit my lower lip happily and paddled my feet in the water, then pulled my knees to my chest and hugged them.

"Thank you," I said. I really meant it.

John pointed to a fish, and cried, "Look! A barracuda!"

I noticed something in the water slipping out of sight, but couldn't make out its shape.

"Amazing, isn't it?"

I nodded and smiled politely, still not sure what I'd seen.

Having opened up the conversation, John began to talk animatedly about himself, where he'd been born, his childhood, his school, what his family was like and all their names, including grandparents, aunts, uncles and cousins. He'd gone to art school, he said. Art school! He'd gone for just two years before Torc became successful, and he had to focus on his career, but he had actual training in art.

He spent the next half hour telling me random stories about himself and watching me for my reactions. I displayed rapt attention, not only because I had to, to be polite to my host, but because he was actually a very intelligent, funny, and interesting person; I enjoyed listening to him. In fact, under other circumstances, I would definitely find him extremely attractive. Under other circumstances, I would most definitely be having a debilitating meltdown over this incredible man. Fortunately, I knew I would not have to experience a meltdown. Going to him, and therefore having him reject or abandon me, was not an option.

When he was a child, he had wanted to be a photographer. He later had thought he might want to be an artist, but photography was his first love. Still, art school had taught him a lot about composition, and he used what he'd learned in his photographs. He had taken some really lovely pictures here, of the market and of the people and the children who hang out near the wharf. Whenever he left the compound, he said, that's where he went—to take photographs.

He seemed to be encouraging me to ask to see them, but I was too shy.

"Music is my career, and I do love it, of course. I couldn't live without music. But I need to capture moments. I need to own them because sometimes I can't quite let go of them, the people and the events. Do you ever feel that way? Do you know what I'm talking about?"

I nodded enthusiastically, grinning. I knew *exactly* what he meant.

"Music and photography… it's like a hunger." Again, I knew exactly what he meant. "In my opinion, if you don't find some form of creative expression, you exist in a kind of poverty. I couldn't live that way. I'd starve." He was reflective, making no attempt that I could see to impress me with his 'depth' or creative sincerity, the way other men had tried. He was simply talking to me and telling me about himself.

Trevor was only mildly, politely interested when I mentioned art, and then he changed the subject. I had once brought up my dream of being an artist, and he'd acted pleased in a detached sort of way, but didn't seem to entirely understand what was driving me to want it. Would he be supportive? Probably, but I wondered if he thought my dream was important, or if he would simply humor me as I pursued it, without really sharing it. I had no doubt, though, listening to him, that John would know. He would know exactly what art meant to me, and why I sketched on notebook paper in lieu of paintbrushes, canvas, and oils I couldn't afford, and why I tried so hard to learn.

I realized after listening to him for half an hour that if I weren't with Trevor, I would imagine that John was the man who was perfect for me, and my *one*. I pondered briefly what might have happened had I met him first, because something was clicking in me that made me take closer notice of John and how he was making me feel. He suddenly gave me butterflies, yet I felt safe and comfortable. I knew I was grinning goofily as I sat there and listened to him talk, but I couldn't help it. And I knew I was being a little flirtatious; he responded by flirting back. I realized I wanted to know everything that he thought and to listen to everything that he had to say. I was almost developing a crush on him, and he seemed to have one on me. He had completely overcome my first impression of him.

My attraction to him was not as sharply intense as the one I'd felt when I met Trevor, but it was surprisingly strong. I could have just as easily fallen in love with this man as that one. Within two months, I had felt a greater attraction than I ever had in my life—twice. It was turning out to be an interesting year.

"I try to capture moments when I write lyrics. I try to write like a painter, the way Joni Mitchell does. Do you like Joni Mitchell?"

I nodded vigorously and grinned. I covered my mouth with my hands. John liked *Joni Mitchell*? I found that fascinating. Her music was totally different from the music John wrote, but I would learn that true musicians appreciate good music in every form.

"She paints with words the way she paints with brush strokes. She's a really wonderful artist, you know. She's my hero, actually, because she's a triple threat with words, music, and images, all at once. She paints her own album cover art. Did you know that?"

I shook my head.

"I aspire to be like her. Her lyrics are very visual, the way I'd like mine to be. But I only really seem to succeed with a camera."

I didn't know how to respond. I understood that John was attracted to me, but this was not a typical prelude to sexual advances. John was treating me as his best friend and confidant, as if we shared something. For half an hour, he had been spilling his thoughts to me, almost breathlessly. Why would he do this with Trevor just a few hundred feet away?

"When I write songs, Angus takes them away from me, and they become his, or else I sell them to other bands. But my photographs are always mine to keep."

I couldn't imagine what had prompted this. He had never spoken to me alone before, or shown even the slightest interest in speaking to me. In fact, I had always found him somewhat cool and detached and presumed he didn't like me because he always looked away sharply if I happened to catch his eye.

Furthermore, Nancy had filled me in on the various quirks and personalities of the band members. John, she said, revealed very little about himself. He didn't talk much, except about weather, music, or business, and was the most reserved of the band members. He channeled everything into his songwriting and spent a good deal of time alone.

Yet he was eagerly telling me far more than I would ever expect from someone I scarcely knew, much less someone who spoke about himself to no one at all. If what Nancy said was true, I now knew more about John than she, and perhaps most of the others, did.

As Trevor's friend, he shouldn't be speaking to me this way. But, if I were to be honest, it didn't matter why I was sitting on a private beach in the Bahamas having a personal conversation with a rock legend. What mattered was that he was attracted to *me*! I was very pleased and flattered.

I nodded, dumbly but with enthusiasm, agreeing with whatever he said.

"What about you?" he asked.

"You want to know about me?" I was genuinely flummoxed and nearly asked, "Why?" before biting my tongue.

"What sorts of things do you like?"

"Art," I said. "The Impressionists are my favorite." I didn't tell him that I hoped to be an artist one day.

"Really?" He looked very pleased and beamed at me warmly. "Do you go to art school?"

I told him about the books I checked out of the library and the exhibits I attended at the Art Institute. "I don't go to school, but I'm trying to learn."

He looked at me a little intently, studying me, and seeming to approve of what he saw.

I asked him questions about art, and he was happy to explain things.

125

He seemed quite pleased that I was interested and drew diagrams in the sand to explain composition, pointing out colors and textures on the horizon as I listened, rapt and excited. He mentioned paintings I'd seen as examples of the things he was trying to explain. He grew more and more attractive to me. If it weren't for Trevor... if I had met John first...

Which is your favorite?" he asked, and then stopped. "No wait. I'll name two artists, and you tell me which you like best. Are you ready?"

I giggled and nodded.

"Matisse and Picasso."

"Picasso!"

"Picasso?" John blew air through his teeth while his eyes twinkled teasingly. "I'm a Matisse man, myself."

I persuaded myself not to ask him why I felt the way I did, and if it was wrong, deciding instead to leave the interaction as a game. I said, "Next!"

"Van Gogh and Monet."

"Monet! Monet! *Definitely* Monet."

"Oh, my darling girl. We shall never see eye to eye." He shook his head as if he were very disappointed in me.

"Next!" I said, giggling.

"Gauguin and Toulouse-Lautrec."

"Foul!" I cried, wagging my finger at John. "Unfair choices!" I tilted my head, and defiantly cried, "I pick both!"

John threw back his head and laughed.

"You're delightful," he said softly, smiling.

"Seriously, though. How could I possibly choose?"

"Wait here." John hopped up and walked briskly back to his cottage. He returned with a very expensive camera and pointed it at me.

"I'm not photogenic," I warned, covering my face with my hands. What I meant was, 'I'm not wearing any makeup.'

"Nonsense. You're utterly lovely, as always. Look at me, Holly." Click. Click. "Turn your head just a bit and look over there. That's right." Click.

John gave me further instructions. I started to giggle, and he grew playful. "Look over your shoulder and flirt with me. Beautiful! Give me a little leg, love. There you go."

"Can you stand on your head? Oooh! I'm so sorry! That looked like it hurt! Are you all right? Yes? Good!"

"Cartwheels. Can you give me a cartwheel? Bravo! You really are an excellent girl!"

I became more relaxed and less self-conscious as we joked and played. At one point I remembered Tina the Ballerina, my record from childhood, and pretended I could dance. I twirled with my arms over my head and sprang into a leap. I twirled again, then stopped and threw my head back with my arms outstretched and my leg lifted. I laughed.

John stood perfectly still and didn't say anything for a moment, just watching me. Then he roused himself. "Into the water with you, girl! And make a big splash!"

I giggled and obeyed, and he grinned and took pictures. I began making up my own silly poses, laughing until my eyes teared up. He laughed as well and continued to shoot.

Amazingly, I nearly forgot about Trevor for the entire hour.

"Bollocks! I'm out of film!" He wound the film back to the beginning of the roll and flopped down on the sand. "That was exceptional. I cannot wait to see the pictures." He promised to give me a print of each of them.

Completely content, I sat down beside John and looked at the surf. He was wonderful company, I was comfortable being with him, the scenery was beautiful, and the day had been spectacular.

I smiled. "You're just exactly like a regular person."

"Why thank you," he said. "But you, my dear, are most definitely *not* regular. You're quite different and special." He seemed a little too serious as he said that.

"No." I made a face in protest and shook my head. I knew I was different, but the things that made me different made me a little less than regular, and far less than special. I frowned, and then looked down at my lap and sighed. This conversation was beginning to make me uncomfortable.

He reached over and poked me gently in the arm with one finger.

"What? You don't realize that? You have no idea?" He smiled, stretched, and edged two inches closer.

I was very adept at handling men who were attracted to me. I ignored the fact that he had just moved closer and shifted the subject back to John. I stretched and yawned, then readjusted myself to recover those two inches of space without making it obvious that I was doing so.

"You have these preconceived notions about what someone famous should be like," I said. "And then you meet Angus—"

John hooted and laughed.

"So then your ideas about famous people go in this *other* direction." I laughed, too.

127

"But I...?" John tapped his chest with his index finger and nodded coyly. He surreptitiously stole an inch of space back.

"But you're just really nice."

John nodded thoughtfully, seeming pleased. Then he turned away from me, giving me back my stolen inch of space, plus an additional two.

"A pox on Trevor for finding you first," he said, smiling and looking out to the sea.

There was no mistaking his intent. He no longer tried to hide it with jokes or propriety and reserve.

I had hit a bump in the road with Trevor and had been thinking all morning that perhaps there was no hope for us, despite our having gotten past it for now.

John was so attractive, not compared to someone like Angus, I supposed, but John triggered a reaction in me that I'd never experienced before. I loved his mind, and it was turning into physical attraction. I was keenly aware of his nearness. My heart was pounding.

Still, I took issue with all this. I guessed John's momentary regret and reluctance, exhibited in those three inches of additional space, were his means of paying shallow homage to guilt, friendship, and obligation. I guessed the demonstration was only a formality—a solemn lowering of his head and a tip of the hat out of hollow respect toward Trevor as he stole his girl.

I had learned to analyze situations like this from making every effort to understand the My Fault/Their Fault list, which required purging all rationalizations or selfish, hurtful motives disguised as something else— mine or theirs—and examining people's actions in a form that was pure and unembellished. In this instance, I guessed that John was prepared to take me regardless of the impact it would have on Trevor, even as he protested and uttered his regrets. He might even be prepared to claim a powerful love that rendered him powerless. People often did that to justify heinous treatment of spouses, lovers, and friends. If so, I would be disappointed in him because I followed what was evidently a more rigid version of The Code. I wouldn't do this to Trevor, and neither should John.

John was very tempting. He was highly intelligent and exceptionally talented. We had a level of creative sympathy. He was fun! I had never before felt so drawn to someone's mind; I had never before felt so physically attracted to a man just from listening to him speak. I would have been thrilled to fall in love with him under other circumstances. In fact, I would have been helpless.

Under these circumstances, however, my attraction was of no consequence. I was used to deprivation and delayed gratification, and I accepted that most of the things I longed for were out of my reach. I was used to obediently following The Code without indecision or anguish, just as I was used to not stealing food when I was hungry, or not shoplifting pretty clothes I didn't have the money to buy. I never tormented myself with tantalizing rationalizations. There were just things you simply did, or did not, do.

I mentally bolstered myself with the "right" and "wrong" of things and fought down my wistful wanting by reminding myself of how John would recoil and reject me if he learned about my problems. I knew this man was fishing in a poisoned pond, and that I could only save him by declining him.

I didn't respond to his comment.

John, still smiling, looked out to sea. "If things ever don't work out between you and Trevor, please come find me. You'll do that, won't you?"

"Things are fine!" I said, surprised and a little defensive.

He ignored my remark and turned to me, quite seriously. "Feel free to come to me if you ever need anything. Anything at all. I am truly happy to provide it. I'm here for you. Truly."

He caught me up short. "Provide" things? Like clothing, perhaps? This *was* about last night. He must have cornered Trevor or Charles at the party at some point after I'd said I was going home and asked questions.

Yet I doubted Trevor had said anything. It wouldn't be like him. Frankly, it wouldn't be like Charles either. The band held them both in very high regard because they both had an impeccable sense of decorum, loyalty and honor. They didn't reveal secrets about the band, about each other, or I presumed, about me. Perhaps John was just drawing conclusions based on the tension he had perceived on the boat to and from the island and was just making a generalized statement about *being there* for me.

Or perhaps (and this was a disturbing thought) John had been hovering around us at the party, lurking, watching. Did he see me take off by myself with Trevor turning his angry back to me? Was he watching when I tiptoed into the library? Was he outside the library door at the party last night, listening? Surely not!

I had another thought. A man is a man, and it is war, I remembered. Was this another test? On the other hand, I thought, studying his face, it seemed more likely that he was just trying to step in when he suspected my relationship with Trevor was souring. There was a time factor involved, so he needed to make his intentions clear immediately and unequivocally, just as there had been a time factor when I first met Trevor.

The past hour hadn't felt like a test. It felt as though we were friends, and he sincerely wanted to get to know me better. Knowing about his friendship with Trevor and how far back it went, I doubted John would risk it on a casual fling. That meant he didn't want me as a one-night stand, but as a girlfriend. *He wanted me for his girlfriend!*

Seeming shy and uncertain, he looked at me as if I had the power to hurt or disappoint him. I was stunned. This had all come out of nowhere.

I had learned from my experiences on the tour that the Guy Code was much like the Girlfriend Code. John was clearly aware of The Code and honored it, but he was apparently prepared to break it for me, so I formed my words carefully.

"But even if things didn't work out for us, and I *did* come find you, you're Trevor's friend, so you would never, ever have me." I gave him a lopsided smile, half-chiding and half-questioning.

I watched his expression change slightly and grow thoughtful. I waited. He didn't respond, so I asked, "Right?"

John looked at me steadily with a guarded half-smile. He didn't say anything. He just studied me.

"Isn't that right?" I asked again, more softly and coaxingly.

"Milady," he said, lowering his eyes and bowing his head deferentially. "You are absolutely correct."

I smiled.

"He's a good man, our Trevor. One of the best." John looked at me mildly and distractedly. He turned to look back out to sea, squinting into the sun and frowning slightly. He no longer made attempts to breach the space between us on the sand and leaned the other way.

I nodded. "Yeah."

He continued staring out to sea. He cleared his throat.

"In this business, you see people every day who think only of themselves. You don't know who's lying and who isn't, who's true to you and who's not, and what their angle is—what they *really* want from you, and what they're *really* after. You only know that, whatever it is, it benefits them more than it does you, so you always seem to find yourself bleeding, particularly if your natural inclination is to be generous. You lose your trust in people and insulate yourself and shy away from them in self-defense. You buy expensive toys and find your solace in them. You cling to old friends, the ones who haven't changed, if you're smart, and if you still have them. Which fortunately, I do. That would be Trevor. I'm very grateful to him. I would never do anything to hurt him."

He glanced at me quickly, as if to make certain I didn't view him as a scoundrel for being attracted to me. I smiled and nodded for him to continue.

"The oldest of us is Angus, and he's only twenty-seven. I'm twenty-five. We've all been dealing with this craziness since I was nineteen, missing out on university and other things. Missing out on sweethearts and a normal sort of life. I'm not ungrateful," he added hurriedly. "I've been well-compensated for anything I may have had to sacrifice. I realize how fortunate I am. I cannot begin to describe how thankful I am for all my experiences and for everything that came to me.

"But so many drink, like Angus, or do drugs. It's to blunt the sense of imbalance, I suspect, because it's far too much, too fast, too young. Or we waste our time and money on hundreds of women in succession because they're there and willing, knowing they wouldn't look at us twice if we drove a taxi or worked as a shop clerk, wondering what they mean, exactly, when they say the word "love," and where they would be if this all went away." He gestured toward the sea and the cottages. "We think we're godlike because people tell us so, and that creates other problems, like ordering people about, or demanding things, or being childish or cruel. Such silliness, all that...

"But it doesn't last, does it? One can't get too comfortable and take it all for granted." He turned and asked somewhat forcefully, "Where are Gerry and the Pacemakers now? Paul Revere and the Raiders? Herman's Hermits? The screaming fans don't even remember them, except when radio stations play oldies. Their records aren't even in the clearance bin anymore."

"Where are the Monkees?" I added. "Remember when people said they were better than the Beatles?"

John threw back his head and laughed. As he did, he looked over at me with crinkling eyes and a delighted expression. That expression gradually morphed to thoughtful introspection, and he looked down.

"Then, some die untimely deaths, don't they? Jimi Hendrix, Janis Joplin, Brian Jones, Jim Morrison... I knew Hendrix very well indeed, when he first arrived in England, and we were just beginning to play the clubs. His death had quite an impact on me. It was quite sobering to lose a friend when I was still so young. One doesn't particularly like to admit it, but untimely death appears to be one of the risks of my job. It can be a treacherous career choice."

131

He was silent for a moment, then added, "Some lucky ones, like Lucas, find a lady like Nancy who's grounded and sane. She always keeps him well out of harm's way."

He shifted in the sand and scratched his ankle. Then he lay down on his back with his hands under his head.

"Nancy is the eldest of eleven children and was raised on a farm, you know. Kansas, like Dorothy from *The Wizard of Oz*. She does wardrobe for us. She sews, and she makes apple pies. Just throws things together, clothing, food. Everything she does is impossibly brilliant. She's a rare one."

He turned to me.

"Do you make pies? Like Nancy?"

I laughed. "I can't cook. I can't sew either." I shrugged apologetically.

He shrugged, too, and looked out to sea again. He became rueful and self-deprecating as he returned to his original train of thought. "Others of us get cloyingly romantic, and we write songs."

Those must be the songs he sold elsewhere, to other bands, I thought. Torc didn't record romantic songs.

"That's good, though. Being romantic and writing songs is better than the alternatives, don't you think? Dying and drugs?"

He looked over at me a little pleadingly and with some embarrassment. He apparently felt he'd revealed too much about himself. He sighed, shielded his eyes with one hand, and turned away.

I didn't reply, but I reached over and lightly patted his other hand. He seemed to need it, and I was happy to reassure him that his thoughts were safe with me. John looked down at my hand, and then looked up at me somewhat searchingly. I immediately pulled my hand back. He raised himself back up on his elbows, and continued in a lower, musing tone: "In America, hundreds of years ago, there were witch trials. Did you ever read about them?"

"Yeah." I couldn't imagine where his train of thought was going, or why it had shifted so abruptly.

"They would accuse someone of being a witch and then attempt to drown her. If she didn't drown, she was a witch. I suppose the reasoning was that a witch had special powers and could save herself—most people didn't swim, back then. Consequently, if she *did* drown, she was *not* a witch. However, all one could do after proving someone was not a witch was to bury her. Cold comfort, eh? All her accusers could do, really, was to say, 'So sorry. My mistake,' because the woman was dead and beyond their reach."

Where was he going with this?

132

"Do you see? If they accused her of being a witch, and they proved they were right about her—if she lived—they could have her but they didn't want her. They would find some other way to put her to death. Whereas, if she was proved innocent, they wanted her, but they couldn't have her back because the only way she could pass their test was to die. They could only be sorry for their loss. But at least they knew..." his voice drifted off until I could barely hear it, "... she was the one they might have trusted."

He turned to me. "You are not a witch."

"Excuse me?" I burst out laughing.

"Your priorities." He let that be his full explanation. He smiled. "It's humbling, but I certainly admire it."

I looked at him quizzically. "Which priorities? What do you mean?"

"It's complicated," he answered, chuckling. "Sadly for me, love, it's checkmate."

Still smiling, John looked around, noted the position of the sun in the sky and how late it was getting, sighed and slapped his thighs. He rose, gathered up his camera equipment, and started toward his cottage.

He looked back once and called, "He's a lucky man!" He waved and resumed his walk.

I wandered back up the beach and into the cottage where Trevor was still napping on the bed. I crawled in next to him, put my arms around him, and gently woke him up with kisses.

John Collier invited Trevor and me to dinner the following night. He told us to come by his cottage at seven and nonchalantly mentioned he had made reservations at a restaurant that permitted casual dress. He looked away from me as he said that, a little uncomfortably, confirming my suspicion that he had eavesdropped on us at the party, and knew precisely why I'd become upset.

Before we left, he smiled and snapped a picture of me kissing Trevor on the patio, then packed his camera away.

At the restaurant, I attempted to order the least expensive item on the menu, but John shook his head and insisted I order the steak and lobster, the most expensive entrée, instead. He ordered a side of conch chowder for me as well, so I could finally taste it, and selected a bottle of shockingly expensive wine. Against my protestations, he preordered a special chef's dessert when I mentioned I liked chocolate.

He toasted Trevor and me and affectionately wished us long lives, prosperity, and much love. Then conversation shifted to work as he and Trevor discussed the upcoming recording session for the new album.

While they spoke, I tried not to gobble down the lobster, which I had never tasted before but loved very much. I looked up when Trevor rose to go to the bathroom. I greedily licked the butter from my lips and glanced over at John, who caught my eye as my tongue slid over the corners of my mouth.

John winked and grinned naughtily. He tilted his head coyly, placed his hands over his heart, and sighed dramatically.

I stopped licking my lips, pressed them together tightly, put down my fork, and stared at my lap, waiting for Trevor to return.

"I'm sorry, Holly. I was only teasing. That was completely inappropriate. Forgive me." He reached over to touch my arm, then apparently decided against it, and pulled his hand back.

I glanced up warily. His voice sounded sorry and sincere.

"Friends? Never again. I promise." He crossed his heart. "Enjoy your lobster, sweet. I'm so sorry!" He laughed and pulled down one side of his mouth in an embarrassed grimace.

I smiled to show him all was forgiven.

Trevor returned and kissed the top of my head. "Were you good while I was gone?" he teased.

"As gold," John said. "As always, she was good as gold."

During the last few days, Trevor, Charles, and I congregated more frequently with the band, sitting with them on one of the patios and drinking beers, playing "coconut bowl" on the beach—which involved lining up the resulting beer bottles, and knocking them down with coconuts—gathering at a large table in the Travellers' Rest for dinner, joining them for tea, snorkeling, or sunbathing. I became so familiar with English accents I didn't notice them anymore, and I grew so used to being around the band members I barely thought of them as famous. They were just our friends.

On Trevor's and my last day, John Collier presented me with a stack of the photos he had taken of me on the beach. On top of the stack was the picture of me kissing Trevor. When I turned it over, I saw that John had drawn two faces on the back. The first had a frown. He'd drawn an "X" through that one. The second had an upturned smile with an arrow pointing to it.

I packed the photographs with my other souvenirs, which included two Fosters beer cans and a conch shell Trevor had salvaged from a dock. The conch shell smelled, even though we had left it on the patio wall to air out for a week, so I wrapped it tenderly in newspaper and plastic to keep it separated from everything else and tucked it in the suitcase with my clothes. I would treasure it all forever.

Chapter 15

The eighty-degree weather was gone, and the palm trees were gone, and the warm blue ocean was gone, and the Travellers' Rest was gone, and the little cottage at Harmony Acres was gone, and the cottage's patio where I sat with Trevor and Charles was gone, and the kitchen where we cooked and ate, and the bedroom where Trevor and I spent our nights and some afternoons were all gone. Most tragically, my dear friends were gone, even though I imagined them in the next room because that was where I had grown accustomed to them being over the past two weeks, and that was where I needed them to be. They were less than eight hours in the past. It was simply inconceivable that they were a year in the future and four thousand miles away from me now. That long stretch of time and distance felt like a tangible ache.

My apartment building was still where I had left it, dreary and dark at dusk. When Pansy and I got out of Karen's car, Karen waved and drove off, while Pansy pranced around my legs, happy to be home after perhaps wondering for the past two weeks if I was ever coming back.

My apartment was like a time capsule, with everything just as I had left it two weeks earlier—socks on the floor, dishes in the kitchen, unmade bed. It was a shrine to my anticipation prior to the trip. It was filled with my excitement, my daydreams, and my hopes as I had laid out my clothing, trying to decide what to bring. Some of the items I'd sorted through were still strewn on a chair, failed and disconsolate, frozen in sad disarray after having been rejected, even by me.

Savoring the last vestiges of those final moments before I'd left, I made my way through the two-and-a-half rooms. Here was my last cup of tea just before the cab came to fetch me and I gleefully ran out the door. The mug was sitting on the kitchen counter with a shriveled and dried tea bag stuck to the side of it. Here was the mail I'd collected the day I left, and left unopened on the kitchen table. There was an old newspaper on the floor beside the couch with a date that seemed a hundred years ago. My hairbrush was on the bathroom sink just as I had left it, with strands of my pre-Bahamian hair clinging to the bristles. I knew the clock radio had switched on every morning while I was gone because I hadn't bothered to turn off the alarm before I left. It had filled the lonely room with my favorite morning disc jockey, like the tree falling in the forest that no one is there to hear, every day for one hour at six-thirty in the morning before automatically switching off again.

It was like walking into a museum or a tomb, so many of my hopes were in evidence around me. It wasn't a sad place or reproachful place, as shrines to anticipation could be when you returned after experiencing a disappointment. But it was a testament to the passing of a moment, and the sobering realization that it was really over.

I wanted to go back in time to the hour when the tea in that mug was still hot and steaming, and my time with Trevor was still ahead of me, so I could relive and extend the moment. However, the apartment was also a memorial to the time before my relationship with Trevor had been tested. A part of me would not trade the present's knowledge with the past's uncertainty. I wasn't altogether unhappy to walk in on the past because I could tell it that everything would be all right.

I turned on my eleven-inch black-and-white television to bring some life into the room. My neighbor, an unemployed blind man who spent most of his day on a CB radio, came through the speaker, drowning out a Walt Disney movie where two smiling children now said, "Roger that, good buddy. Fuckin' A! Sounds like some real motherfucking good times! What's your twenty, man? Where y'all headed next?"

I threw my shoe at the TV set. Dust bunnies flew up as the shoe hit the floor.

My neighbor could do that for fourteen hours at a stretch—say nothing at all in the crudest, foulest language. A fluke in the sound waves, along with his proximity across the hall, turned my television into his loud speaker. I was privy to all his colorful one-sided CB radio discussions; my television did not project the voice of anyone he spoke to. It was a rare evening that I could watch a television program unassaulted.

In the apartment below me was Angelique, a four-hundred-pound woman who always wore stained muumuus and flip flops and whose gray bra straps always hung out of her sleeve and down to her sagging, dimpled elbows. She never left her apartment, though I sometimes caught a glimpse of her outside collecting her mail when her welfare check was due. She kept her trash piled five feet high on either side of a narrow pathway from the door into the living area, presumably because one never knew when one might need last month's garbage. I recognized her as another severely depressed person. She raised cockroaches, who liked to come visit me.

Down the hall was a trio of girls who may or may not be hookers or drug dealers. They were certainly popular with men, who visited them in a constant stream, beginning at dusk each evening.

I didn't speak to any of my neighbors because I felt it was prudent not to. I didn't know anyone, even to say hello in the hallway. And now I had come home to an apartment that was stuffy and cold with no one to greet me but Pansy.

Facing my apartment could trigger despair if I didn't immediately find something to look forward to. So I tried to focus my sights on a place four thousand miles away where Trevor lived, and looked ahead a year to Torc's next tour.

It didn't work; the stretch of time was too long. Instead, I focused on Trevor's first letter. When it came, I would focus on the next letter, and so on, living in an almost frozen state until I survived the year. My life was already suspended, waiting for some happy moment in the distance when Trevor returned to me.

I *felt* Trevor as if he were with me. He was a warm spot in the universe, always emotionally accessible in my mind, and even at this distance I could still sense him as if I were able to see his emotions passing over his face or listen to him tell me his thoughts. I could still feel his warmth. I felt no anxiety because my sense of him told me he was really, unequivocally mine and would come back to me.

I unpacked my little suitcase and lovingly unwrapped the conch shell. I sniffed it and smiled. It still smelled like the sea. It smelled like love and warmth and wonder. I placed it on a shelf between the two Fosters beer cans I'd saved from The Travellers' Rest.

I went to bed and imagined Trevor sleeping without me in his own bed. Did he miss me yet? Did he miss me as much as I missed him?

I thought of how I had successfully maneuvered my way through an entire two weeks at close quarters with a man, and managed to still love him. I thought of the fight we'd had, and how we'd made up. I thought of my rage, which had passed, and my mistakes, which Trevor had forgiven. I even thought of the way he held his silverware. Charles held it that way, too, as did John Collier and the rest. Somehow the irritation light had switched off when I was surrounded by people I truly cared about who all shared the same habits. That irritation was now spread and watered down to a mild, non-toxic level.

I fell asleep with hope because it all finally seemed possible.

I reached for him in the night and remembered, then started awake. I didn't care for being alone.

I arrived at work the next day with a suntan and tacked John Collier's picture of Trevor kissing me to the wall beside my desk. I then tried to readjust to my job. I sat down and looked at the work that awaited me, noting the things that had changed in my absence, and the things that were just as I had left them. It felt surreal to have to work again after two weeks on a beach, so shortly after having left to join the band on the road. My head was still in the Bahamas; my heart was still with Trevor.

I sighed when the phone rang. I kissed my finger and pressed it to Trevor's face in the photograph. I would write him a letter as soon as I got home from work. Then I reached over to answer my ringing phone.

My female coworkers filed into the building in clusters, each cluster timed exactly to the arrival of each successive Skokie Swift train. They called out pleasantries as they hung up their coats and settled in, asking me about my trip. The questions would stop when the envy and resentment kicked in, and their chins would lift with self-righteous disapproval if I were to bring up the subject. However, for now, they were curious enough to be interested in my photographs and stories.

Most of my coworkers were young and female, and all were pretty. I assume this was because the hiring manager was male. The unmarried ones were mostly all hard-drinking "party girls" who ranged in age from nineteen-year-old Denise to twenty-six-year-old Constance, and they hit the bars together at least once a week. They sometimes permitted me to join them when I tagged along with Angie.

The girls were a healthy mix of blonds, brunettes and redheads, petite and tall, plump and thin. The hiring manager seemed to have no particular preference. They all liked to dance and get raucous until the bars closed. They, like Angie, preferred New Town.

"When Trevor comes back into town, I'll take you backstage with me," I promised them all. Their disapproval melted. Suddenly, they found nothing inappropriate or wrong about my hanging around with rock bands, and they all made excited comments about Torc's next tour. I received an invitation to join them after work.

The beach, the band, Trevor, and Charles began to recede, and my real life took hold once again. By my fourth day home, I had sent Trevor two letters.

Chapter 16

During my first weekend home, Karen introduced me to the art of crashing backstage doors.

"Smile at the security guard but don't say anything. Just lean against the wall next to him. If he asks, you're waiting for your friend Debby."

I leaned against the wall next to the security guard and smiled. The security guard looked at me out of the corner of his eye, fiercely and suspiciously, and then stared straight ahead.

Karen remained a few feet away, gazing into the distance and gingerly holding a cigarette between two gloved fingers.

"You waiting for someone?" The security guard asked in a voice that was more pleasant than his expression might have suggested.

"Yeah," I said, smiling. "My friend Debby. She shouldn't be long." There was no Debby. I was following instructions. I bounced and shivered, as Karen had coached me earlier.

Three men with English accents walked up and flashed their passes. The guard let them through. They all looked at me as they walked through the door.

"A bit cold out here, isn't it?" one of them asked. He doubled back, said, "This one's with me," to the guard, fished a pass out of a pocket, and handed it to me.

Karen ran up immediately.

I smiled at the man. "I have a friend," I said. Karen smiled, too.

"Delighted," the man said, smiling back. He slipped a hand under each of our arms and led us in.

"I'm going to work now, but make yourselves at home," he instructed, then dashed off with the other roadies.

141

Karen hugged me. "You were brilliant."

It was a different famous band, in a different concert hall, with different music and different people milling about the stage, but it was essentially the same scene I had grown accustomed to. I noticed the same groupies that had been at the Torc concert. They struck the same lone postures in the stage area, but still congregated in friendly camaraderie in the bathroom.

"What's that about?" I asked Karen.

"Men don't go up to women in groups. It's too scary, so you never want to have three or more together. The best thing is to be alone. Men always come up to a woman who's alone."

"Would you rather be alone?"

"What, are you kidding? Gawd, no!" She laughed. "I'll just stand next to you all night long and collect your rejects. I'm not proud." Her goal of making it back to England was too important, she explained. One must press on as one can, even as Sloppy Seconds. And standing next to me was better than standing alone. Not only did all the men come up to say hello, she said, but I was good company.

She said I was good company. No one had ever told me that before. I couldn't stop smiling. That drew even more men over to us.

Men approached all evening, but I always demurred and explained that I had a boyfriend. They often then turned to Karen, who grinned at me.

Karen and I had not discussed in advance how I would get home. When Karen hooked up with a roadie toward the end of the evening, I sat on the floor in the hallway of the hotel and dozed with my back to the wall, waiting for my ride to finish up in there. It was tiresome, but this was an adventure and a learning experience. Next time, I would make other arrangements or bring cab fare. Rock and roll.

The next weekend, Karen stayed, and I left in a cab. I was already getting the hang of things, appreciating the free food, free beer, and free entertainment. I grew quite adept, and wrote about it to Trevor to tell him every detail.

I was buoyant for a few weeks, especially when Trevor's letters began to arrive. Then, the joy began to wear off, and I started to fully grasp the long stretch of waiting that reached out for months and months ahead of me. I wrote to Trevor constantly, every day. I took the high airmail postage to England from my grocery money and raced home from work every day to check the mailbox. But the depression had begun to settle in. I had some bad bouts of it.

Torc would not be touring the States again until next February. They were in the recording studio and should be wrapping it up in a few weeks. They would have an album out by Christmas, Trevor wrote. He would be taking a well-earned holiday shortly. Feeling pleased that I finally had a topic of conversation that seemed to interest them, I relayed this information to the girls at work.

More months passed. Other concerts followed. Those evenings pulled me out of my lethargy and propped me up artificially with adrenaline and excitement. They provided me with a meal I might otherwise would have had to do without. However, when there was a span of time between them, I tended to drop off the edge.

Chapter 17

"So, how was your week?" Dr. Silverman looked relaxed and tanned. He kept a large picture of himself standing on a sailboat on the wall behind his desk. He had been gone for two weeks, apparently to a place with a lot of sun.

"I had another thing happen this week." I was still angry, but embarrassment had crept in. Shame would shortly follow. "I got really mad again."

"Did you try what I suggested? You need to find something to divert yourself from your anger long enough to gain control of it."

"It didn't work." It never worked.

"Well, tell me what happened then."

"I was standing in the aisle on the bus. It was really crowded, and we were all pressed together." I took a deep breath and looked down. "This creep grabbed me."

"Where did he grab you?"

"My crotch."

"Did that frighten you?"

"No, it just made me mad. Only it was one of those times where I went off into one of my rages." I was speaking very softly, hanging my head slightly, intently picking at my cuticles.

"And?"

"And I grabbed the guy's crotch right back. Then I lifted his hand in the air and shouted, 'Excuse me, sir, but I found this on my crotch. Would you like it back?' Then I twisted his balls until he got tears in his eyes."

Dr. Silverman laughed.

I shot him a look. It wasn't funny.

"And what did he do?" Dr. Silverman cleared his throat and looked serious.

"He got off at the next corner, walking all bent over."

"That's it?"

"The other people laughed. Some of them clapped and whistled."

"And you're ashamed of yourself?"

"There are better ways to handle people than grabbing them by the balls and screaming at the top of my lungs." My eyes were tearing up. "I don't know what gets into me. I honestly don't."

"Describe a better way to handle a groper."

I didn't have an answer.

"You're hearing your grandmother again, telling you that nothing you ever do is right."

He began laughing again until he needed to wipe tears from his eyes. "I think you handled the situation perfectly. They teach exactly that sort of reaction in self-defense classes."

"But I was really angry. I was enraged. You know how I get when I'm enraged. And this time I got physical. I've *never* gotten physical before. Will it happen again? Will I totally lose control someday? Does it mean I could kill someone?"

"Doubtful," he answered. "I would bet you didn't *really* hurt him. You never hurt anyone, you just say things. And you say them to the very people who probably need to hear things that no one but you would ever tell them."

He didn't understand. By touching someone in anger, I had crossed a line, and it terrified me. Was I capable of doing something worse?

"So you're saying there's nothing wrong with me?" Why was I going hungry to pay him? My last meal had been yesterday's lunch, and I didn't get paid until tomorrow. I was getting by on saltines.

"I'm saying that you go a little over the top doing things that are actually appropriate for the situation. Then you get upset and ashamed of yourself because you didn't have the restraint to *not* do those arguably appropriate things, or because you didn't do those arguably appropriate things with a little less emphasis. But the end result is that people always seem to get your message."

He leaned toward me. "I hear all day long from people who are frustrated with themselves because they didn't have the nerve to say something, or can never, ever confront anyone about anything, or didn't think of the right thing to say until it was too late. You live their dream."

145

"But I confront people too often. Sometimes you're supposed to suck it in and smile." I tried to make him understand. "I don't have it in me to suck it in and smile, no matter what the situation is, or who I'm with. I always blow up and explode. People who aren't like me have better lives."

"Their lives probably aren't as good as you imagine. Granted, life threw you a rotten deal. I'm not saying your life is easy. I'm just saying—"

"You don't understand."

"What don't I understand?"

"Don't patronize me." I gave him my long stare.

He cleared his throat, and asked the question again, this time with a little less condescension and arrogance. "What don't I understand?"

"The issue is my rage. I cannot control my rage. I'm always, *always* angry. It doesn't matter if it's the right time or the wrong time. It doesn't matter if I should actually feel anger in a situation. Even a broken clock tells the correct time twice a day—did you ever hear that saying? The point is that I can't turn my anger on or off. I have no self-control. It takes over. It makes me overreact. It makes me say things I shouldn't say. It makes me yell at people I shouldn't yell at."

I started to weep. He handed me the box of tissues, but I brushed it away.

"Up until now I'd never hurt anyone, but this time I crossed that line." I cleared my throat and raised my hand so he wouldn't speak. "Maybe you're right, and I actually should have done it. I'd find it a lot funnier if there had been even a split second when I felt like I could just step away from him if I wanted to. I would be laughing, too, if I'd had the choice to either grab him by the balls or not."

Did he understand yet? How could I make him understand? "I didn't have any choice. I couldn't stop myself. I was literally seeing red and breathing through my teeth. That scares me. If I'd been just a little bit angrier, I might have actually pulled them off."

He looked at me as if he possessed wisdom he wouldn't share because I was so uncooperative.

I wiped my eyes. "When I was a kid, I had self-restraint. I always said and did the right thing. I never even spoke out of turn. Why did I know more about how to behave when I was a kid than I do now? I'm out of control, and I want to go back to being the way I was."

He wrote in his binder. I saw him repress a chuckle.

"Please help me."

Chapter 18

In August, the phone rang at two thirty on a Monday morning. I knew it was Trevor because nobody else called me in the middle of the night. I was instantly wide awake, vaulting into the kitchen to answer it.

He would be in town in September, he said. He was working the Jethro Tull tour so he could be with me again. When they ended the tour in Boston, he'd fly back to Chicago to stay with me before returning home to England for a few months. Would that be all right, him staying with me? Then he'd turn right around again and come back with Torc in February. He'd send me the finalized schedule as soon as he knew what it was, so I could plan my vacation around the tour.

He was coming! He was working for Jethro Tull! Squealing, I danced around the kitchen. This was the concert I'd been waiting for! This was the band that I loved! This would carry me through the entire next month! He would stay with me!

"Can I bring my girlfriends from work?"

"How many?"

"Between seven and nine, maybe…?"

"Fair enough. Tell them they're all more than welcome."

I was suddenly popular around the office, and the girls invited me to most of their nights out. I brought Angie with me now, instead of the other way around.

I knew which night the band was to arrive and where they were staying because Trevor had told me. I told Karen, who called Nikki, Linda, and Brenda, who told Charlotte, Patti, and Kim, and so on. This was how the groupie network operated. I was now officially plugged into it.

The day that the band arrived, Trevor called me at work from a pay

147

phone at the concert hall. He immediately had the phone wrested away by Keith, who was working the tour as well.

"I hear you have girlfriends."

"I do!"

"And that you'll be bringing them tonight?"

"I will!"

"Give it back, Keith." Trevor was suddenly on the line, while Keith was in the background protesting, "Bollocks!!"

I gave Trevor the names for the guest list, then wrote down his instructions and arranged to be at the backstage doors an hour before the concert. He had to return to work, so we said our goodbyes. I hung up and hugged myself.

"Only four more hours!"

We had planned this for days. We had all brought a change of clothing, our makeup, and curling irons to work. We got ready in the ladies lounge after the phones shut down. We traveled together by Skokie Swift, then by El train, and then by bus to the Chicago Stadium, where we gave our names and were simply waved in, moving smoothly past security with no resistance.

Keith spotted us first and bounded toward me with open arms.

"Holly!" he shouted, lifting me up and twirling me. Then he put me down and assessed my friends approvingly. I had produced a lineup of beautiful girls just for him. He grinned.

I whispered in his ear, "Remember, they aren't groupies, Keith. They've never been backstage before, so they're kind of naive. Be nice."

"I'm always nice," he answered distractedly, edging closer to Theresa. His taste evidently ran to petite, curly-haired redheads. "I'm Keith," he told her, lifting her hand to his lips and kissing it. "And you are…?"

Behind me, I heard, "Keith is a tosser. Be careful around him, ladies!" I froze for an instant, then turned and threw my arms around Trevor's neck. I burst into tears.

Keith kept the girls thoroughly entertained with beers and repartee while Trevor and I moved off to a corner to say hello, which mostly involved hugging each other, kissing and rubbing noses, and Trevor patting my back while I sobbed.

Keith caught my eye and lifted his thumb to me with a nod. My friends were a hit.

More roadies joined Keith and the girls. Two of these showed off by kicking a soccer ball around the backstage area while Denise and Angie clapped and shouted encouragement. They began doing elaborate elbow and knee tricks with the ball, which drew more cries of admiration from Constance, Vickie, and Geri. So engrossed were the boys at impressing these girls from a small insurance company in Skokie, Illinois, that they barely noticed the groupies, who were now filing in.

I knew none of these roadies, except for Keith and Trevor. It was odd to see them with this band, in the midst of these strangers.

"You'll see me on stage tonight," Trevor said with a tilt of his head and a wink. "I'm part of the act."

"Really?" I dropped my jaw with excitement, lifted my shoulders to my ears, and clapped my hands.

"I play the part of the hare."

Jethro Tull had an act to go along with their latest album, he explained. Jethro Tull always had an act, usually absurd and witty, and this time it involved a prancing large rabbit. Originally, one of the band members had worn the rabbit costume, pranced for a bit, and then peeled it off and gone on to perform. However, twice the zipper had stuck, leaving the band with a prancing large rabbit, but without the instrument normally played by the band member who was stuck inside the costume. The task had prudently been delegated to a roadie. Tonight it was Trevor.

As the roadies reluctantly put away the soccer ball, left the girls, and returned to work, Karen danced through the door with jazz hands, delighted to have found her name on the list. I linked arms with her, and we skipped to the food table to grab some beer.

The girls from work were making themselves very much at home, smiling seductively at everyone who glanced their way. They were injecting the backstage area with an entirely new, and somewhat pungent, ambiance. Ordinarily, the groupies—at least in Chicago—were self-contained and aloof. They always appeared cool and subdued, even elegant, and never made loud sounds or seemed smutty, whereas, the girls from the insurance company seemed prepared to advertise their availability by ripping off their shirts. Their laughter was strident, they hovered in clusters, and they drank to the point of unseemly incapacitation.

I worried that Trevor might be angry that I'd brought a group of raucous New Town barflies into his hallowed territory, even though the other roadies appeared to find them attractive. Trevor expected me to behave with impeccable decorum, as always, so I couldn't participate in their antics. I could only follow and anxiously watch.

When the concert began, Geri went out and climbed onto the sound stage with her beer, and danced for the soundman. She thought he was cute. He had to keep pulling himself back to his sound panel because his eyes kept wandering over to Geri's swaying buttocks off to his left. It didn't matter that *Thick as a Brick* wasn't remotely dance music; Geri found a beat.

Denise climbed onto the stage and quickly became dissatisfied with her seat on a speaker. She brazenly moved to a spot in the back, behind the drummer, and watched the performance over his shoulder, occasionally waving to the audience with both hands. When security pulled her away, she waited a few minutes and then went back again.

Angie staked out Denise's place on the speaker and stayed there for the rest of the evening, making me continually run to fetch beers for her so she wouldn't lose her spot.

Constance was indulging in some heavy petting with someone who didn't appear to be a roadie, and whose reason for being backstage was as yet undetermined. He had his hand down her pants.

Vickie and Theresa were in Ian Anderson's dressing room. They were jumping up and down on his couch in time to the music.

"Oh, crap," I said upon finding them there. "My ass is grass." Worse, I was missing the concert I'd waited so long for while I fretted over my coworkers' behavior.

I did, however, get to see Trevor prance onstage as the rabbit. I took pictures with his camera. When he returned to the backstage area, Keith took a picture of me hugging him in costume, then another of me wearing the rabbit head standing next to Trevor wearing the rest of the suit. In a later shot, Ian Anderson happened to be walking behind us, and stopped to flash a peace sign for the camera. I didn't know it had happened until I saw the picture, long afterward. I proudly tacked that photo up over my desk at work.

I stayed after the show and went with Trevor to the hotel. The next morning, I went to work from there, showing up late and forfeiting half a personal day. The following night I returned to the concert hall without the other girls, watched a really wonderful performance, and sank into the experience as if I had come home.

Chapter 19

On the last day of September, a Sunday, Trevor climbed out of his cab, walked into the entry hall of my building, and set his duffel bag on the floor. The instant I heard the bell ring, I flew out of the door with Pansy at my heels and pounded down the stairs to meet him. The concert tour was over, and Trevor had just flown into town to stay with me. His plan was to stay for several weeks, perhaps longer.

I had buffed and polished the apartment and was enormously proud of how tidy it looked. I had flowers on the kitchen table and some food in the refrigerator, which I planned to cook for him. I had recipes. I had a canister of English tea. I had given Pansy a bath.

He saw me through the glass entryway door and held out his arms. I threw the door open and ran into them, jumping up and throwing my legs around his waist and my arms around his neck. I burst into tears. Pansy leapt and barked.

Still hugging him around the waist with both arms, I walked him up the stairs and into my apartment.

"This is it!" I cried, wiping my eyes and grinning. "Welcome!"

Trevor put his bag down and looked around. "I like it, Holly. It's small, but big enough, isn't it? Very nice."

He kissed me, then moved toward the couch.

"I'm knackered. Can we just sit and visit for a bit?" He pulled off his crocheted sweater and threw it on the back of the couch, then sat down and kicked off his shoes.

I picked up the sweater under the pretense of hanging it in the closet. "You still have this sweater."

Trevor looked up absently and nodded. "Perfect for this time of year, isn't it?"

I looked at the sweater, noting Beth's carefully crocheted stitches, and frowned. Trevor apparently didn't catch the intent of my comment, or was deliberately choosing not to understand. I hung the sweater in the closet very slowly.

Then I brightened up. "Would you like some tea? I bought you some PG Tips."

"That would be lovely!" He smiled. "Have you anything to eat as well?"

He settled in and looked around with satisfaction, acquainting himself with Pansy while he rested. I turned on the kettle, then set some cheese and crackers on a plate and brought them out. When the water boiled, I poured us each a mug of tea and fixed Trevor's the way he liked it, with milk and sugar. I had purchased some milk especially for his tea.

Later, I presented him with a key to the apartment and took him out to show him around while we still had some daylight. Walking Pansy through the neighborhood, I pointed out the places with the best takeout if he wanted Greek, Italian, Mexican, Thai food, or pizza. I pointed out the stores and where to catch the bus downtown. I handed him a transit map, told him how much money he needed for bus fare, and explained the routes and transfers. Since I would be working the following day, Trevor planned to explore on his own and was very excited about it.

I took him inside a neighborhood tavern and grabbed a free Chicago Reader newspaper so he could look for things to do. He peered around, noting the dartboard, and the young people sitting at the bar. This would be his pub, he declared.

Then we returned to the apartment, where I pulled out the food I'd purchased, along with a recipe, and tried my hand at cooking for him. He stood behind me and coached. He helped me prepare the meat and potatoes, and he cleaned and chopped the vegetables. He also set the table and washed up afterward.

We fell into a routine almost immediately. Each morning, Trevor joined me for Pansy's walk, then escorted me to the bus stop and kissed me goodbye. I rode the bus to the Skokie Swift, swooping into my daily morning panic attack. He did whatever he wished for the entire day, bringing home bags of groceries and little treats for me, and the occasional bouquet of flowers. When I came home from work, he was waiting for me with dinner on the stove and the apartment tidied. On weekends, I did the cooking, with him instructing. He had the confidence of a television chef, chopping, stirring, sautéing and roasting, and gave me one tip that enabled me to be a competent cook from that point forward: "Your problem is that you lack self-assurance," he said. "Just use a little common sense, and you'll always find that good food plus good food equals good food." After that, I rarely had a failure.

When he was not at home, he left a backstage pass and a note with instructions to meet up with him, usually at the Aragon Ballroom, which was a thirty-minute bus ride away. Trevor always found roadies or rock stars he had worked with or made friends with over the years, so he had an inside contact for nearly every performance. On some evenings, he worked for a little extra money. I took that bus ride about three or four nights each week, seeing every big name that came through town. I even met some of the rock stars.

One evening after a concert we boarded the bus back to my apartment after visiting with the band backstage. I covered a yawn and gazed past Trevor out the window at the lights. Trevor was looking down at me with a kind of delighted wonderment. He placed his arm across my shoulders. He sighed happily, invigorated by the concert and meeting up with his friends.

"Everybody kept asking me who the beautiful girl was." He raised his eyebrows to demonstrate his pleasure and surprise. "I thought they meant Denise, but they meant *you!*" He was clearly pleased. "They all meant *you.*" He patted my hand, shifted his shoulders, and beamed with an expression of possessive self-satisfaction. "I never guessed everyone thought you were pretty. So of course, I told them that the beautiful girl was my own lovely lady."

I turned to him sharply with a half-frown and twisted smile, trying to decide whether I had just been insulted, and to what degree. I weighed my response carefully and allowed it to contain a small hint of a challenge.

"You had no idea anyone thought I was pretty?" I asked. "What have you always thought I looked like?" Out of the many questions that had sprung to mind in the last few seconds, those were the least confrontational. Was this a good thing or a bad one?

Trevor raised his eyebrows again. "Well, *I* always found you attractive. I just never suspected everyone else did."

I gasped, half-teasing, half not, and gave him a hard poke in the ribs with my elbow. Trevor looked bewildered, as though it hadn't occurred to him that I might take offense at a compliment. He noticed I was staring at him, awaiting explanation.

"I'm usually not attracted to the same women other men are attracted to, is all," he explained patiently. "I only know what I like, not what they like." He rubbed his side and took hold of my elbow to prevent another attack. "Well, I know they all like women who look like Marilyn Monroe, the way Denise does. I don't usually care for the type myself."

What type was he attracted to, specifically? I thought of that photo of Beth, the slightly plump, nondescript blond with the plain face. I thought about how Trevor had once chosen her, had been enough in love with her to want to marry her. I knew he hadn't chosen a plain woman because he couldn't attract a conventionally pretty one. In spite of the fact that he wasn't remotely handsome, Trevor somehow managed to make every woman he met become infatuated with him, including the gorgeous Denise and my surly grandmother. I knew he could have virtually any woman he wanted, at least in America where we were all taken in by his charm and his British accent. I knew he was with me because he loved me, and I also knew he still loved Beth. But Beth and I were nothing alike. I wanted to find a common denominator.

"You really never thought anyone else found me attractive?" This was new territory for me, and I was groping for an appropriate emotional response. Should I be hurt? Should I be angry? Should I laugh?

My looks had always been an impediment in developing friendships and relationships. I had had a limitless number of "meaningful conversations," believing I'd connected with a man on a deeper level, mind-to-mind, heart-to-heart. Then I'd learn he hadn't heard a thing I'd said, or was actually contemptuous of my opinions and had only pretended to show interest in the conversation in order to humor me while he tried to seduce me.

If I'd felt a friendship connection with a woman, I'd learn later that, during the entire conversation and no matter how nice I was, she'd primarily thought about what I looked like, and how much she hated me. I had never been valued for the things that were essentially *me*. Everyone reacted to and interacted with my face. Consequently, I had always worried that I was unlikable and had no real value.

Trevor frowned. "I definitely *know* there are men who are attracted to you." He looked at me defiantly as if he was possibly annoyed with the looks men gave me, or else he knew that someone specific found me attractive. "I just didn't realize everyone thought you were pretty."

"What attracted you to me when we first met?"

My beauty was the first thing, often the only thing, people mentioned when they described me. Whenever I had asked a man this question, his answer had been, "Your face. Your legs. Your eyes. Your figure." Nobody ever said, "You're funny. You're smart. You have a good heart. I like your ideas. I like talking to you. I just like being around you." I wanted to hear those things far more than I wanted to hear I was beautiful, but I rarely had. You could buy beauty from Maybelline, and eventually you lost it. If you had nothing beyond it, you were worthless. And I was becoming convinced I had nothing else.

Trevor looked as though he felt trapped by something he couldn't define. "Well, *you,* of course."

"The way I look?"

"Yes, that. I told you I always found you attractive."

"Anything else?"

"Your eyes."

Aha! "What about my eyes? Because they're pretty?"

"No." He paused. "I mean, they *are* pretty, but that's because you're behind them."

"What do you mean?"

Trevor seemed to be getting exasperated by the questioning. He felt it should all be obvious. Furthermore, discussing this was uncomfortable for him. "You were *in* there," he said. "There you *were.* I saw someone in there that I liked."

He was looking at me as if he had fully answered the question and thought I was perhaps a little dense for not understanding, or was merely pretending not to understand just to tease him. He looked cornered.

"You were very young, younger than I would have chosen, actually. But your eyes were old..." He thought about it for a moment, "Yes. That was it, I would say. You had old eyes."

"I have *old eyes.*" Horrified, I pulled a pocket mirror out of my purse and studied my eyes closely, touching the sides of my face. "Oh, my God."

"Yes, you do. That's how I knew you weren't just a shallow bit of teen crumpet with nothing to say, and why I didn't mind your age. I like a girl I can talk to."

He paused, and something like a wince or a shadow passed across his eyes. I wondered if he was thinking of Beth, who was two years older than he. Was he comparing us? Was I as good at conversation as Beth? How could I be? I thought hopelessly. She had a college education, and her age beat mine by seven years. The look passed, and I had his full attention once again.

"When you told me a little about yourself, I saw where all that came from." He squeezed my hand.

I looked at him and waited, nodding slightly for him to go on.

155

"It just seemed that you could be my friend and lover all at once. I just thought that perhaps we should be lovers." He said that with casual breeziness, and then abruptly turned the moment crass by raising and lowering his eyebrows suggestively and reaching under my arm to tweak my nipple. "And friends, of course," he added primly.

"You thought that *perhaps* we should be lovers?" I slapped his hand lightly and pushed it away. "*Perhaps?*"

"And friends," he reminded me. He smiled with teeth.

"But you didn't think I was pretty."

"What?" Trevor pulled back and looked at me with incredulity. "I thought you were *gorgeous*! I thought you were the most beautiful woman I had ever seen in my life! I loved you straight away—straight away, mind you, right here, right now, I *love* this woman, I *worship* this woman—and I couldn't get you out of your knickers fast enough to prove it." He growled and nibbled my ear.

"But if you thought I was beautiful, why would you think no one else would?"

"Because the women I find most attractive are not usually the ones other men fancy. It came as a surprise, that's all, that we were all in agreement about you." He smiled. He appeared pleased over his handling of the situation. He nodded, mutely declaring the conversation addressed, complete, and filed away.

"What else did you like about me? Anything?"

"Please, Holly." Trevor's face swiftly fell with disappointment that his escape had been so narrowly missed. He shifted uncomfortably, making short, exasperated grunts and grimaces to dramatize his unwillingness to participate any longer.

"No, tell me. I mean it."

He sighed, and then grew reflective. He spoke slowly. "You seemed strong enough, but a little lost and adrift. Something about you made me want to take your hand and hold it. Pat it like so." He demonstrated.

Most men wanted to take my breasts and grab them, as Trevor had done earlier.

"And then do what? Take care of me?" My voice rose in pitch at the suggestion, and I stiffened a little.

"No. It seemed as though you didn't want to be taken care of, which I liked." He thought for a moment. "Well... I would say that you didn't *want* to be taken care of, but you *needed* to be, actually. That combination always tugs at me a bit." He gave me a quick look, realizing too late that he had said the wrong thing and couldn't take it back.

I pushed some air out of my nose in a snort. "I am totally independent," I said defensively, crossing my arms over my chest and turning slightly away from him. I was totally independent. I was. Had I not been self-supporting and living on my own for three years?

"I know that, my darling."

"It's true," I insisted. "I am."

"Exactly so."

"You don't think I can take care of myself!"

He kissed my cheek. "No, I hope you need me. That's all."

Trevor looked out the window thoughtfully for a moment.

"I suppose you manage without me," he said quietly. Then he turned back to me, and added, "But you didn't seem quite as lost after the first time I held you. I thought that might mean I was good for you."

He fingered the handrail on the top of the seatback in front of him and looked out the window. "Would you say that I'm good for you?" He asked the question casually, but the way he said it made me forget that I was a little angry with him.

"Yes," I answered, reaching over to loosely take his hand with both of mine. "Yeah, I would definitely say so." Trevor was the most important person in my life. His love for me, and my love for him, was literally keeping me alive.

Trevor smiled, his face revealing more relief than he had probably intended.

"Right, then. Because you're good for me as well." He patted my hands and settled comfortably back into his seat. We rode in silence for another mile until Trevor reached up to pull the cord to stop the bus at our corner.

"Up, now." He nudged me. "Off we go. We left already." I rousted myself from my seat and stumbled to the rear exit as the bus came to a squealing stop. I pushed the doors open and stepped onto the curb.

We walked toward my apartment through the dark, still in silence. I looked down and thought for a moment, then looked up again. "If I were ugly, would you still love me?"

"What kind of question is that?" Trevor sounded helplessly exasperated. "I could never find you ugly." We turned up the sidewalk to the entrance of my building. He opened the door for me and followed me up the stairs; he pinched my bottom once on the way.

Taking off my coat, I persisted. "But say I got into an accident. Say I'm suddenly ugly. What then?" I threw the coat across the back of a chair and reached down to pick up Pansy, who was frantically wagging her entire body. Trevor took my coat and shook it out, then carefully hung it on a hanger in the closet. He twisted himself out of his crocheted sweater and kicked off his boots.

"You would still be my beautiful lady," he said, putting his sweater on a hanger beside my coat. He reached down and grabbed his boots to place them neatly by the door. He gathered up my shoes, which I had just kicked off, and walked them to the bedroom closet.

He was not one to placate or flatter, and I knew it. He was telling me the truth. I took a moment to digest it. Still trying to sort out the issue in my head, I followed him into the kitchen with Pansy at my heels. I tried to think of a question with an answer that would definitively settle the matter for me.

"Have we anything to eat? I'm famished." He turned on the kettle for tea.

Trevor could see from my face that I hadn't shifted my focus to the topic of food. He sighed in defeat.

"Well, right then." He blew air between his lips and didn't wait for the next question. Offering a challenge of his own, he countered, "Right then, I have one for you. If *I* were suddenly ugly, wouldn't you still love *me*?"

I considered Trevor's face. I reached out and ran my finger over one of his protruding ears. I touched the side of his cheek, pausing to finger an acne scar, then brushed my fingertips over thin lips covering crooked teeth and down to that receding chin. I reached up to smooth a wayward wisp of fine, unkempt, colicky hair. I looked into those small brown eyes peering out at me over that large beak of a nose, and grinned.

"Well, yeah. I guess I probably would," I said, giggling. I covered his face with the palm of my hand and gently, teasingly pushed. Trevor grabbed my hand and lightly nibbled my fingertips.

"There you have it. Love is love." Having finally settled the matter, Trevor kissed me lightly on the lips. Then he turned his back to me, and leaned into the refrigerator to study the cold cuts.

I had no further questions. I beamed.

On off nights, Trevor preferred Lincoln Avenue, where he settled in for a blissful evening of live blues, idolizing the artists, and whistling and applauding the loudest of anyone in the audience after every song. He begged for photographs and autographs, collecting them like treasures.

Whenever he called me at work, I had to wait while every one of the girls in the department chatted with him before the last one finally transferred the call to me. He was everyone's darling, and they all had crushes on him. He often accompanied me when they invited me to the bars, and he eventually got to know most of them quite well. He frequently allowed me to invite them to shows, but often insisted they remain in the audience and not go backstage. I didn't argue.

Even though things outwardly seemed perfect, trouble loomed. During the weeks he stayed with me, I developed a hypersensitivity to all of his habits and mannerisms and could only barely suppress my rage over his having invaded my space. I counted the days to his departure in November and suffered through five weeks of irritation, resentment and anger. I deliberately misread him and took offense, looking for some basis for the irritation. I did this knowing I loved him. I was enraged, knowing full well it was my illness and not anything he had done, but I was unable to manage my feelings and enjoy my time with him. My nerves were constantly assaulted and frayed, and my only relief was solitude.

This was why I could never have a roommate. I simply could not have anyone in my sphere for any period of time, even Trevor.

Nevertheless, I managed to hide all of this from him. I screamed at him in my mind, but was very civil and self-contained when I spoke aloud. I thought daggers at him, and smiled. I made love to him tenderly, wanting nothing more than to sleep alone, and awoke to his kisses, wishing I could brush them away. I held onto my self-control by counting the days until his departure, telling myself this wouldn't be forever, and I would have my apartment and my life back shortly.

Then when he left, I was bereft and lost. I missed him and agonized over when I could see him again. I sank into a deep depression and clung to Trevor in letters I wrote three or four times a week.

Chapter 20

"Hey. I just got *All Torc'd Up*." That was the album they had just released, and Karen was calling to tell me she had a copy. "Got a minute? You need to hear this."

Karen held the phone up to her stereo speaker and played a song that for Torc was uncharacteristically soft, sad, and melodious. I couldn't make out the lyrics Angus was singing.

"It's pretty, but I don't understand the words."

"Then I shall read them to you. It's called *Beyond My Reach*. Music and lyrics by *John Collier*." She said that with a slight emphasis, and then cleared her throat.

> *Molly danced along the sand for me,*
> *A dark and graceful sprite.*
> *As I photographed her running toward the sea,*
> *She turned and smiled.*
> *Through the lens I watched her pirouette,*
> *A dark-plumed bird in flight,*
> *Her body haloed by the sun in silhouette,*
> *I was beguiled.*

As Karen read, I began to feel weightless and lightheaded. More stanzas detailed the singer's yearning and the girl's beauty. He described her eyes, her hair, her body, and the way she moved. He sighed and longed for her, but couldn't have her because she was his best friend's lover. Then Karen read the chorus:

Down on the beach, she said
She'd made a promise to be true.
Beyond my reach, she said,
And there was nothing I could do.
The joyful dancer cloaked in mournful black
Is lover to my friend.
My luck is cursed.
He found her first.
Still I love my Molly, love her to the end.
I will love my lovely Molly to the end.

I didn't immediately react or respond.

"Are you still there?" Karen asked.

"Yeah. Wow."

"This is some pretty heavy shit, Holly."

"Yeah. Oh, my God."

"I'm not surprised he wrote it, are you? I'm just surprised he made Torc record it, instead of selling it to someone like Bread or Donny Osmond."

"Oh, my God. Trevor knows about this song." I covered my mouth with my hand and closed my eyes.

"It really took some balls for John to do this. I thought they were friends."

"Oh, my God." I felt queasy.

"I thought he'd get over you. Didn't you?" She whistled through her teeth, and then laughed.

I hadn't mentioned to Karen that John seemed to be attracted to me, so I was taken aback and bewildered over how she knew.

"John?"

"No, Angus," Karen scoffed. "Of *course*, John. *God.*"

"What are you talking about?"

Karen gasped. "Are you serious?"

I got defensive. "Yes! What are you talking about?"

Karen began to laugh. "He's got it really bad for you."

"He's just a little attracted to me, is all."

"Oh, my God. Holly. That's it? He's 'a little attracted' to you? That's what you see? You've never noticed those little hearts popping out of his eyeballs whenever he looks at you? Listen to the song!"

"No. Come on." I blew air through my teeth derisively. "Since when?"

"Oh, Holly, honey." Karen's voice turned maternal. "You are so dense. Since that first day on the bus when you blew him off. That must have been what did it. He wants what he can't have."

Was that what John had meant, when he talked to me about "witches?" That he only wanted what he couldn't have? That didn't seem quite right, in retrospect, but I was in shock and couldn't recall exactly what he'd said.

"He was staring at you the whole week we were on tour with them. It was a hot topic of conversation behind your back. I participated," she admitted without shame. "You really never noticed it?"

I didn't answer. In my life, men were wallpaper, and they were almost always attracted to me. I couldn't allow most of it to register because I couldn't function if I felt constantly stalked, hunted, studied, and watched. I was dense in self-defense.

I shared with Karen some vague and incomplete bits and pieces of what happened in the Bahamas on the beach that day. I described it dismissively, as if it were of no consequence.

"It's all taken care of. He shouldn't bother me anymore. I mean, listen to the song, right?"

"Too bad you finally get immortalized, but they don't spell your name right. That part kind of sucks."

I bought the album because this was an emergency that warranted the expense. I played the track on my old record player and pulled out the album insert to read the lyrics. Over the next few days, I played the song and read the lyrics again and again. I never sang along. Then, finally, I put the album away and vowed to never touch it again.

I wondered what Trevor thought about it. I never brought it up and neither did he, nor did either of us ever mention the photo collage on the inside of the album jacket, all color photos of the band in session or in concert, with one black-and-white photo of me pulling up the sides of my shorts as I waded through the waves, head cocked, laughing, with my hair blowing sideways in the Bahamian trade winds. This was why I'd received a legal document months earlier from Chester, their manager, asking me to sign a release for the photograph. I'd signed it without question because I was flattered and proud. I thought it was exciting and fun, and I trusted them. When I babbled about it in a letter to Trevor, I had no idea the photo would be on an album with that particular song. It stung.

The song made it to number nine on the charts. I heard it on the radio all the time and never told anyone it had been written about me. People would only hate me that much more, if they even believed me. Whenever anyone asked me about it after talking to Karen or seeing my picture in the album insert, I shrugged and changed the subject, wanting to cover my face and squirm away.

John was cool toward me when I joined them on tour. He smiled and winked, but then brushed quickly past me whenever we met backstage or at the hotel. He never had time for a chat and never sought me out for a brief exchange of news or hellos. He never joined us on the bus. We never spoke because I was just a roadie's girlfriend, and he was a world-famous rock star who traveled in a Lear jet with models and actresses, and occasionally deigned to nod toward me out of pity or condescension when we passed each other. It hurt my feelings a little, but I was relieved at the same time.

Still, there was always a flicker in his eyes, and probably in mine as well, when we saw each other. A song and one splendid hour on a beach always hung between us, frozen in suspension.

Chapter 21

I joined the 1974 "Torc It Tighter" tour in Phoenix in February. Trevor flew me there because I had decided on the West Coast for my vacation. We traveled from Phoenix to Los Angeles, then to Las Vegas, then over to San Francisco, and up to Portland, Oregon, Seattle, Washington, and finally to Vancouver, British Columbia. I flew home from there after spending ten days on the road and two nights each in Los Angeles and San Francisco. Our days off were in Las Vegas and Seattle, and we wandered around each city with Charles. I lost thirteen dollars in the slot machines in Las Vegas, and Trevor won twenty-three. We all went to the Space Needle together in Seattle and had lunch there.

There were some new faces in the group, but most of the old roadies were back, so I had returned home to family. We still had Virgil driving the bus, but Wayne had been replaced with Pete. Butch was gone, replaced by Joe. Liam was gone, replaced by Dennis.

Angus Adkins was enamored of the New York Dolls and David Bowie, and he now wore eye makeup and lipstick onstage. His suspiciously blonder hair was feathered and teased to a height and width he'd never previously achieved. His platform shoes were encrusted with glitter, his satin pants were skin tight, and he wore a rakish scarf at his throat. His satin shirt was open to the waist.

Geoff had gotten a perm and was sporting an Afro. John Collier had shaved his sideburns and mustache and was wearing his hair short. Lucas was now wearing a fedora to cover his receding hairline.

It was different this time because I shifted back into irritation. I spent most of my time with Cherise and Barb, the other girls traveling with the band, avoiding Trevor on the bus whenever I could. I cherished the time I spent away from him and suffered through his affectionate hugs and kisses with smiles I didn't feel. When I was near him, I was nervous and felt dread, waiting for him to do something that would trigger another neurotic reaction. And yet, I loved him. I needed him. I wanted to be with him. I wanted more than anything to enjoy him as much as he deserved and to relish the time I spent with him. I just couldn't stand being with anyone so constantly at close quarters.

In Vancouver, I sobbed and cried when he put me on the plane. I couldn't bear to part and felt I would die without him.

I flew home and waited anxiously for Torc to make their way across country and meet up with me in Chicago in two weeks. Then, after they finished the tour, Trevor would again return to live with me, this time for three months, before flying back to England. I counted the days. I planned the meals. I collected the recipes. I thought of things to show him and places we should see together. I endured near-collapse in the days leading up to his arrival and broke down in tears when he finally came to my door.

He stayed, and he meticulously paid his share of rent, did his own laundry, and bought groceries, but I couldn't stand having him around. I couldn't stand it. He was always pleasant and helpful, but even that infuriated me because I couldn't blame him for anything when I was irritable. I simply could *not* abide having a roommate. I had to experience soul-crushing loneliness because I couldn't be with anyone, even Trevor, for very long.

Then I took him to a special exhibit at the Art Institute. Trevor, bored, insisted we leave before I had seen everything. He found nothing about it to enjoy. I could only barely contain my outrage. When we arrived home, I stopped myself from hurling his knapsack at him and tossing him out. I closed the door to my bedroom, with him on the other side, and fumed.

Nevertheless, I learned to hide my feelings, and Trevor seemed not to notice my nearly uncontrollable irritation over everything he did. I began to vent my frustration elsewhere, snapping at people when I was actually angry at Trevor for always being around at times when I needed solitude and sleep, or when I needed time to process things and write in my journal without someone pointing out a story in the newspaper or interrupting my train of thought with small talk. I could hold my peace in Trevor's presence when I really wanted to scream at him and send him on his way, but my hold was tenuous. Had I not known he was leaving, I would have erupted.

The four thousand miles seemed like heaven to me, with Trevor on the other side of the Atlantic. Writing letters and keeping a distance seemed like the best possible relationship.

Wound tightly and verging on an explosion, I snapped at Geri at work for cracking her gum, and then felt badly about it afterward. I went to her contritely and tried to explain that things irritate me and get out of my control. It was a problem I was in therapy for. It had nothing to do with her. Would she forgive me? I tried to explain that I couldn't help it, that I don't mean it, and I apologized.

My apology triggered a sense of self-righteous indignation in Geri. I had exposed my weakness to her, and she pounced on it.

"If you *know* you're this way," she said smugly and pointedly, "then why don't you just stop?" She gave me a pursed, accusatory look and refused my apology. She cracked her gum. She crossed her arms over her chest and looked away.

The rage was always simmering beneath the surface. I had contritely bared my soul, yet she refused my apology. I had done what I could, all I knew to do, and she was unwilling to meet me halfway. Her response was insensitive, ungracious, and mean. She never considered me as someone with a problem I was fighting every day with every ounce of my strength, even when I explained that to her, nor did she accept that I essentially meant well, and that my apology was the best I could do to make things right.

The rage spiked in me. The black blood coursed through me. There was no stopping me now.

I wanted her to feel the same insult she'd dealt me. Maybe then she'd understand what an insult it had been, and how cruel and out of line she was. Sometimes knowledge comes in painful bursts, so I administered one to her.

Geri had a problem with her weight. She had gained twenty pounds within the last year.

"If you know you're fat," I said coolly, "then why aren't you thin? It's the same thing."

It *was* the same thing. We are all subject to impulses, reflexes, and needs that we can't always rein in. Her sanctimonious criticisms were rooted in ignorance, so I couldn't have explained her behavior to her without making it personal and making her *feel* it.

Geri's jaw dropped, and she gasped. "You bitch!" she hissed. "It's totally different for me. You can *choose* how to act. You don't *have* to be this way."

"You can choose what to eat, and how much. You can choose to exercise." I narrowed my eyes. "I'm thin, you're not. Should I condemn *you* the way you're condemning *me*? Hmm?" I glared.

"It's totally different," she said indignantly, nonchalantly opening a manila folder to obscure a bag of potato chips lying on her desk. "I have a slow metabolism." She glared back. Her expression was so vicious it looked twisted and grotesque.

"Of course." My sarcasm hit the target.

Geri gasped again. "I don't feel sorry for you. Why should I? You think you're so much better than everyone else, and you're vain and spoiled. Everything has always been so *easy* for you! You're used to having everything handed to you." Her face twisted even further. "You make me sick. You make *everybody* sick. You really do." She paused, and then added triumphantly, "Nobody really likes you. *Nobody*."

I'd heard all that before from dozens of girls, dozens of times, with the words varying only slightly. Consequently, I didn't flinch because nothing anyone ever said to me surprised me or pushed me off-balance anymore. I held my ground. I shrugged and gave her my El train stare.

"The only thing 'different' is that you're on the receiving end of it this time. How do *you* like it? How does it feel?" Frustrated, I stared at her and curled my lip. She obviously wasn't going to draw any parallels or gain any insight from our exchange. That being the case, I had nothing further to say and went back to my desk. Later, I would berate myself over having quarreled with her. I should have shown more restraint. But for now, I fumed.

At a loss for retorts, Geri huffed, stood up, and stormed away to complain about me to the other girls. I was certain she deliberately relayed the conversation inaccurately and slanted it in favor of herself. She didn't speak to me for days. The other girls formed a circle around her, against me. I was shut out, except for Angie, who cheerfully shrugged, and said, "Geri's a bitch."

My exclusion from the group was almost welcome. It was a relief to go to concerts without having to make arrangements for the other girls. However, when they missed the Peter Frampton concert and overheard Angie and me talking about it, they rethought their position, relented, and forgave me.

How did people do this? How did people endure other people? Why was humanity not insane from its proximity to other humanity? I wondered this as I watched Trevor sit in my chair and read the paper. It was *my* chair. It was *my* paper! It was *my* apartment. How *dare* he infringe on *my* space?

And yet, I needed him. I was dependent upon him for companionship and conversation, and for keeping me above water. I needed his affection and his constant reinforcement. I needed him because I loved him with my whole heart. While he was there, I was rarely depressed; the issue was primarily the irritability and rage I had to swallow and hide from him.

I survived weeks, and then months, of Trevor. I grew used to hating having him there and learned to capture moments of solitude by closing the bedroom door and telling him I was reading and didn't want to be disturbed.

But it was so lonely without him. I knew that, too. When he wasn't around, I had no one to eat with, and I couldn't share stories and jokes. I had no one to tell me what he thought about this or that. I had no one telling me he loved me. I had no one to love.

Still, I asked questions in my mind of Trevor that my grandmother might have asked of me: Why did you buy Chinese when I wanted pizza? Why didn't you cook? Why did you cook this when I didn't want it? Why are you so friendly with strangers? Why weren't you friendly with that waiter? Why don't you clean up? Why did you clean up so that I couldn't find what I was looking for? Why are you still here? How can you leave me and go back to England? *Why are you still here* when I can't stand to be around you?

Then he went away, and I picked up where I'd left off, alone, desperate for him to return, lonely, depressed and sad. I wrote to him several times a week.

In 1975, Trevor made arrangements to spend two months with me and then meet up with the tour afterward, when it began in Los Angeles. He arrived in March. We had a routine, and we fell into it as if he had never left. He courted my grandmother and kissed her cheek, and made much of the meals she fed us when we went to her apartment for dinner every other Sunday. If he answered the phone when she called, he asked her how she was feeling, sympathized with her over her sad life, and winked at me while I rolled my eyes. Grandma adored him and always made him chocolate cake. She talked to him far longer than she ever talked to me.

"I have to hand it to you," I'd once said admiringly after he'd hung up from a chummy conversation with Grandma.

"Be kind," he'd answered. "All of her sisters got named after flowers, but she was named after a nut. That grieves her. It's all quite sad."

He rekindled his friendships with the girls at work, reacquainted himself with the people at his favorite tavern, bought books at his favorite used bookstore, took buses around the city while I was at work, and left me backstage passes for the bands that came through town. He filled the refrigerator with groceries and surprised me with flowers. He walked Pansy and kissed me goodbye as I boarded the bus each morning. He kept the apartment tidy and always hung Beth's crocheted sweater carefully in the closet after once catching me dropkicking it when I found it thrown over a chair.

"I wish you didn't wear that sweater," I'd said softly.

"Why?" He'd asked, bewildered. "It's a lovely sweater."

"I don't like it." I said, pouting a little.

"Don't be silly," he replied. "I have nothing else for in-between weather." Then he repeated, "It's a *lovely* sweater."

Even my irritation had become part of my routine. I could never have a happy life, so I settled for half-a-happy-life when Trevor was around. No matter how I lived, I would need to sacrifice something crucial, and I had begun to accept this.

One day, Trevor was sitting on the couch when I came home from work. He was staring at the television, which was off.

"How did the move go?" I asked, closing the door behind me. Pansy ran up and jumped on my legs. I scratched her neck. Angie had taken the day off to move and had asked Trevor if he could help. He'd agreed.

His head shot around. He was furious.

"She had only three cardboard boxes and nothing packed. She expected me to pack her things, carry them across the alley to her new flat, unpack them, and then repeat, over and over. Both of these flats are in the bleeding attic, so there were stairs to climb as well. It was effing horrendous. It was an effing disaster. I left her midway into it and told her to find some other silly plonker to move her things. I won't."

"Aw, geez." I winced. "I'm really sorry." I should never have volunteered him, knowing he was too sweet to say no. I should have known Angie would find some way to make the whole thing unendurable. Three boxes. She could be so ditzy.

"Don't you be sorry," he snapped. "You did nothing wrong, nothing at all. Don't you *dare* apologize for her," he fumed indignantly, turning away from me.

"Wow." I put my purse down on the table and kicked off my shoes. Then I sat beside Trevor on the couch and pulled his head into my lap. I massaged his neck and shoulders.

"Keep her away from me," he said angrily. "I don't care for her at all. And if I were you, I'd find another friend. You're far too good for her." He

169

murmured "Hmmm" and smiled as I continued rubbing. He frowned again. "She's bollocks, that Angie. Complete bollocks. You're far too good."

Then he pulled away from me and stood up. He paced to the kitchen and back. "Three boxes. What kind of silly bollocks is that? Expecting me to pack her bloody things in that foul, smelly flat with those cats." He made a face. "Those bleeding, filthy cats. I *hate* cats."

"What do you want for dinner?"

"I felt dirty when I left. Bloody hell, that stench! That filthy cat stench! I came home straight away and took a shower. Scrubbed myself raw to get the stench off. Everything in her flat felt sticky."

He demonstrated his revulsion with a grimace and a lolling tongue, and by shaking his hands in the air as if he were covered with bugs. He stopped.

"Gyros then, if that's what you'd like as well," he muttered distractedly. "I could do with a gyro, but anything is fine with me."

"Angie's apartment is really gross. I warned you, though."

"I had no idea what you meant. You couldn't be serious, I thought."

He paced to the kitchen again, and then turned.

"I won't go back there. You can't make me go back. I won't help her anymore. Tell her I said to not even ask me." He pointed his finger at me for emphasis.

"Sure," I said consolingly. "She won't though. She can take a hint. So, let's have gyros, okay?"

He turned away again.

"You don't make things harder for people when they're helping you. You do everything you can to make things *easier* for them. Otherwise you're a bleeding ingrate. You have everything packed and ready to go. You don't make them pack and unpack for you and carry three bleeding boxes back and forth, back and forth, stumbling over filthy cats and kicking over their bollocking cat box.

"I did that, you know. Knocked over the bloody cat box because I couldn't see it over the bleeding boxes I was carrying. Cat turds and litter grits all over the kitchen. Stepped in it and got it all over my effing shoes. It was completely disgusting. Everything about the day disgusted me. I am thoroughly disgusted by today. *Thoroughly* disgusted."

He stopped and reached for his wallet. He looked inside, fingered some bills, then absently said, "I'll go for it and be back directly." He grabbed his crocheted sweater from the closet and pulled it on, turned and yanked the door open, pushed through it, and slammed it behind himself.

"Wow, Pansy," I said. "I've never seen him this pissed off before."

Pansy looked up at me and wagged her tail.

Trevor returned a little sheepishly twenty minutes later, sorry for his earlier outburst, carrying a fragrant bagful of dripping gyro sandwiches. I followed him into the kitchen, where he set the sandwiches on the kitchen counter.

"I didn't even kiss you hello," he said. He cupped my face in his hands and kissed me.

"Hello," he said into my lips.

"Hello," I said.

He let go of me and pulled some plates from the cupboard.

"No more talk of Angie," he said. "Not one word."

We ate at the table with cucumber sauce dripping down our arms and chins.

"You have to be really brave to eat this in public," I remarked. "I would never eat it in public. I love it, though."

"I've developed a taste for it myself," Trevor remarked, licking his wrist. "I'll miss Nilo's. I'll need to look for a place in Sussex when I finally get back. But what I'll miss the most is Italian beef. You absolutely cannot find it anywhere else in the world but here." He chewed thoughtfully and swallowed. "I need to have some before I leave on Friday. Let's do that tomorrow."

I nodded and looked down at my sandwich. I stopped chewing. I'd lost track of time, and Trevor had just caught me up. He needed to fly to Los Angeles and pick up the tour *this* Friday morning, not some Friday weeks away in the distant future.

"We have three full days left. I thought we might do something special before I go. What would you like to do?"

Still looking down, I shrugged. Then, two tears fell into my lap. Trevor saw them and laughed.

"Holly! I daresay you're sorry to see me go!" He leaned over and wiped my cheek with his thumb.

I shrugged again.

"I should think you'd be glad to be rid of me," Trevor said, chidingly.

I shook my head and looked down. My lower lip trembled. I knew I would spend the next three days in mourning, depressed because he was leaving. I wouldn't want to do anything special because I'd spoil it with tears. I just wanted to keep him here to myself for as long as I had him.

171

"I haven't left yet, my darling. I'm still here for three more days," Trevor said gently. "The tour comes through here in three weeks, and you'll be flying out to meet me in six."

"I know." I shrugged. I would fly out to meet him in Miami, but that would just be for a weekend. I'd used up my vacation time when my sick days ran out this year after I'd slipped on the ice and sprained my wrist and ankle. I had spent days at home, and days going to the doctor, and then had caught something in my chest that kept me in bed for a week. My grandmother had come by to cook, do my laundry, and walk Pansy until I was able to do it myself.

My shoulders had begun to heave. I didn't want him to think I was clingy or immature, but I couldn't keep myself from crying. I felt as if my heart was being ripped out. None of the irritations of the past few weeks mattered. None of the fury mattered. None of my desperation to get him out of my apartment and out from underfoot seemed real anymore.

I burst into tears, and sat there shaking and sobbing like a little girl. I wanted to scream, "Don't leave me!" But I didn't scream. I merely sobbed. However, I *thought*, "Don't leave me."

Trevor put down his sandwich. "Oh, Holly." He got up and came over to me, bent down, put his arms around me from behind, and pressed his cheek against mine. "What's this? What's all this?" He nudged me off the chair, then sat down and pulled me onto his lap.

"I'll miss you," I sobbed.

"I can't stay here. You know I can't. I have to go. It's my job."

"I know."

He sighed. "You won't come with me? Have you any holiday time left at all?"

"Not anymore." I certainly couldn't quit or take unpaid leave because I had rent to pay. Even after two years, certain that Trevor loved me, I wouldn't risk my independence. I shook my head. "I can't."

"You know I would take you, if you came. I'm not happy to leave you, you know. I'm not at all happy to be leaving you."

"I'll be fine." I took in a deep breath and sighed. "It's just so silly. I don't know why I always cry like this. It's just silly."

Trevor pressed his lips to my ear.

"I'm sorry. I *am*."

"Nothing to be sorry for. I love you, too," he murmured, squeezing me in a hug before gently pushing me off his lap. "Sunset Boulevard is playing at the Rogers. Shall we go see it?"

The Rogers Theatre played old movies for one dollar admission. Trevor and I went there occasionally.

"Sure," I said, wiping my eyes and grinning.

"Finish your sandwich. It starts in thirty minutes."

On the following night, I came home to find Trevor flipping through a packet of photographs he had just picked up from the pharmacy. He had developed two rolls of film containing pictures of me, the concerts we'd gone to, and his friends at those concerts. There were pictures he'd taken in the city during his daily explorations and a picture of Pansy.

He handed me the pictures he'd already looked through, and then continued to sort through the rest of them.

There he was, smiling down at me from the stage at the Aragon Ballroom with one arm across the shoulder of his friend Clive, who worked for whichever band had been playing there that night. I no longer recalled who or when from all of those Aragon concert nights.

There he was, standing by the buffet table backstage for Bachman Turner Overdrive and Pete Seeger. Thin Lizzie had played backup that night, and the lead singer, Phil Lynott, was standing beside him talking to Denise. I'd have to bring this one to work and show her. Trevor had invited the girls from work backstage for this show, and there was a group shot of all of us.

There Trevor was at the Wise Fools Pub, standing drunk, deliriously happy, and awestruck beside a very cordial Howlin' Wolf, whom we had gone to hear one Saturday night.

And there was me. I was staring at the camera with a look of smoldering hatred, sharply asking, "What?" as Trevor surprised me to snap my picture. "Look at me, Holly, darling!" was all he'd said to trigger that reaction.

I studied the picture with welling eyes.

"That's a lovely shot of you," Trevor commented approvingly.

I looked up. "You like this picture?" I blinked back the sudden tears.

"Of course. Don't you?"

I didn't answer.

"Look at this one," Trevor chuckled, passing me another photograph. I took it, but didn't look at it. I was still studying the photograph of me, completely sobered and sorry, completely regretful for all I'd thought and felt during the weeks Trevor had been staying with me.

I surreptitiously tucked the picture into a back pocket. Trevor wouldn't miss this one, whereas I would need it to remind myself. I held the other pictures and stared off into space, rousing myself as Trevor pointed to a picture and laughed. I smiled distractedly, then handed him the photographs and excused myself.

I went into the bathroom and leaned on the sink. I slipped the picture out of my pocket and stared at it. God bless him. He didn't even see. He didn't even see it… yet. How long could I keep this up?

I took the picture to work with me in the morning. Perhaps I saw more in it than anyone else would see because I knew what I'd been thinking at the time it was taken. Would anyone else know?

I had barely removed my coat before I handed the photograph to Angie without saying anything. She looked at it and laughed.

"Oh, my God! Who took this?" she said. "Someone you hate. No wait. It was your grandmother, wasn't it? You're so funny! I can always tell."

"Yeah." I smiled stiffly and took the picture back, then carefully put it into my purse. I placed my hands on my desk and leaned into them as if I were going to stand up, but instead sat perfectly still, frozen in that position until the phone rang and startled me into thinking about my job.

As we headed into the final hours of Trevor's stay, nothing he did bothered me. I reacted to none of the things that had enraged me in the preceding weeks. I felt no irritations, no resentment, no anger. I had the patience I might have had, had he told me he had only three days to live. Regret and sorrow had replaced fury. I was gentler and sweeter and took nothing for granted. I truly loved him. I was so sorry.

Trevor good-naturedly relinquished one last trip to the Halsted and Lincoln Avenue blues bars and stayed home with me. I held his hand tightly as we watched television. I wordlessly took off my shoe and hurled it when my blind neighbor with the CB radio preempted the programming to say, "Yeah, it's a motherfucker all right, good buddy. Fuckin' A!"

"This is ghastly," Trevor remarked. "I cannot believe the police do nothing." He walked over and switched off the television.

"They said it's a problem for the FAA or the FCC. One of them. I forget. But the police won't help."

"When I come back, I'll figure out what to do," Trevor promised. "We shouldn't have to live this way."

Chapter 22

"**T**his week it was my grandmother. I was her one phone call from jail, and I had to go pick her up so I could bring her money." I was sinking into my chair, my chin on my chest, defeated.

"But you don't drive." Dr. Silverman observed.

"Why, yes, thank you. I know that. I had to take the El. We left jail on the El together. The happy pair of us."

"And she was in jail because…?"

"She spoke to someone on the bus."

"And she said…?"

"She started spewing about the Jews. She likes to prowl cemeteries looking for people she knows. It's her hobby because, if everybody else dies first, she wins. So she's on her way to this cemetery in Evanston to see who's there that she knows, when she strikes up a conversation with the person next to her, and starts spewing. She starts spewing about the Jews."

I paused meaningfully. "It was on the Broadway bus, by Devon."

Dr. Silverman nodded.

"Do you have a mental picture of my grandmother spewing about the Jews in a bus at Broadway and Devon?" I leaned forward, met his eyes, and tapped my forehead with my forefinger.

He nodded again. The corner of his mouth began to twitch.

"So… can you guess what happened next?"

"There was a Jew—"

"There was a *shit* load of Jews," I spat. "And a fistfight broke out between them and my sixty-three-year-old grandmother. She has a black eye, and someone pressed charges."

"Who started the fight?"

175

"Them, of course. That's what my grandmother swears. They're all after her."

"But you think...?"

"I told her to never, *ever* speak to strangers. Never. No good could ever come of it."

"So how do you feel about all this?" Dr. Silverman wiped his hand over his mouth to cover a smile, but the smile was still in his eyes.

"I feel like she raised me. I feel like I inherited her genes. I feel like I needed a better role model."

I picked at the upholstery on the arm of my chair. "I feel like I'm terrified that I'll be just like her when I get older." I looked up. "I'm scared of that every day."

I burst into tears, too upset to even take the tissues he passed to me, and rubbed my eyes with the heel of my hand.

I was angry enough to strangle someone. Trying to regain control, I pick-pick-picked at the upholstery on the chair. Breaking a thread, I pulled it, played with it, twisted it, and dug my fingernail into it. Given enough time, I could unravel the entire chair.

"Why didn't anyone help me to grow up to be a normal person?" I turned to him in fury, accusing. "What's wrong with me that they all just left me with her, knowing what she's like? Why didn't they ever come to see me? Huh? Or call? They never even called to say hello. They all just left me with her to live or die."

I grunted and slammed my fist on the arm of the chair. "What's wrong with me that nobody cared? What is wrong with me that I'm not worth caring about?"

He didn't answer, waiting for me to vent a little more.

I glanced at the clock and noticed my time was nearly up. Rather than hear him tell me to leave, I stood and walked out without looking at him or saying goodbye.

Chapter 23

The dates on the 1975 tour schedule were all crossed off, all past. All cities had been spent and abandoned. The spotlights were all darkened, and the stages were all empty or serving some other band.

Somewhere on Interstate 80 in Pennsylvania, the Heil Sound equipment truck was rumbling westward toward Marissa, Illinois. Meanwhile, the tour bus was several states away, heading back toward the Wild West Productions rental company in Dallas, Texas, winding and rolling through the Smoky Mountains past breathtaking vistas, charming waterfalls, and a short stretch of road lined with red lights that quickly filled the rearview mirror, then disappeared. I knew that Virgil was jacked up on amphetamines, unblinkingly focused on the road, drinking coffee from a thermos, peeing into a coffee can, and flinging it out the window rather than stopping. That was how he drove—single-mindedly—when tours were over. I knew that because it seemed as though I knew everything about everyone, after two years.

I also knew that the atmosphere at the hotel in New York City was elated, with roadies winding down in preparation for the weeks of languid free time stretching out ahead of them. Last minute demonstrations of loud camaraderie were no doubt being exchanged with phone numbers and addresses. Last minute back-slappings, goadings, and insults were being bantered about. Like soldiers at the end of a war, they no doubt spoke with focused intensity about cities and hometown girlfriends, and of favorite local foods and local haunts that were now only hours away, scattered across England. They were recapping the more memorable moments of the tour, the people they had met, the landmarks they had seen, climbed, or photographed, drawing comparisons and arguing about the best and worst concert performances, the best and worst hotels, the best and worst food, the best and worst groupies, the funniest, the best, and the worst experiences. They drank—I knew that with certainty—as they told their stories. I was sure they laughed at the same volume, and with the same level of boisterous misbehavior, they'd demonstrated at the beginning of the tour when they were fresh and eager to get started. The tone would only be different now because it carried a whiff of finality and a dash of sadness.

The newer members of the road crew always believed they would never forget. Every experience was unique and memorable, and every other person on the team was a friend for life. Some of these newer roadies were probably choked with nostalgia fueled by alcohol and were exchanging maudlin reminiscences with men whose responses ranged from equally emotional to indifferently amused. I knew that two or three of these newer ones still had girls they hadn't dismissed in an earlier city as unnecessary encumbrances; there always were one or two girls remaining at the end.

For the road veterans like Trevor, this tour would soon be indistinguishable from past and future tours, and past and future years; these stories would soon coalesce and meld into a confusing, formless blur of other stories and other tours, as would the faces of some of the roadies and lovers they would never see again. Their goodbyes were always more cheerful and detached, and the girls they still had with them were less apt to hear promises; they would be even less apt to receive a letter or a phone call in the months ahead.

It was Rock and Roll. You experienced, you left, you didn't look back, and you didn't regret. You only paused to remember briefly, you rarely spent time to reflect, and it was only during the last few hours before the final parting that there was any underlying poignancy. It would quickly pass. You moved on. After two years I knew the drill by heart.

Trevor called to tell me that Torc's concert performances throughout the tour had been executed with wildly varying degrees of musical artistry and competence, an issue that was of less concern to Trevor and the crew than it was to the band and the record company, but which impacted them nonetheless. They had heard the rumors, but had just learned from Rob with certainty that the band was breaking up, and that this tour was its last. The proceeds from the ticket sales were being tallied in an office in London by suited accountants. The figures were then examined by unsmiling executives who were equally grim over sales of the latest album and the failure of any song to reach the Top Forty on the charts on either side of the Atlantic. In a series of meetings, they had opted to drop the recording contract. Consequently, the band had decided to split.

Angus Adkins's wife Terri and his manager Chester had persuaded him to admit himself into an alcohol rehabilitation facility. Angus had celebrated his impending sobriety by shutting himself in his five-star penthouse hotel suite with an Asian hooker and a case of Jack Daniels, refusing all calls. He didn't appear to check into the facility as scheduled. Prospects for his recovery were still uncertain.

Chester learned of Angus' four-day bender from newspaper headlines. Shortly afterward, he received notification of a pending lawsuit from the hotel citing damages of $19,651.37. In his own defense, Angus said to a newspaper reporter, "Who knew a fucking hotel room was worth that bloody much?" The reporter quoted him in the New York Times with three dots in place of the word "fucking." The tabloids published photographs of Angus with the hooker, who wore a halter top, denim mini-skirt, and thigh-high patent leather platform boots. The story made it to the Chicago Tribune, and consequently into my scrapbook.

Chester accepted a job with another band, one that would eventually make him a very, very wealthy man. Meanwhile, Terri filed for divorce. Angus's girlfriend Petra flew back to London, then on to Paris with another married lead singer, whom she had met at a party in Los Angeles, and who had brighter prospects than Angus, as well as a limitless supply of cocaine. Geoffrey was negotiating with another recording company to cut a solo album. John and Lucas were leaving to form another band. The hooker was back on the streets.

The Bahamian compound with its four little cottages on the stretch of private beach was up for sale and had received a bid from a developer who was considering it as a possible investment in a brilliant new concept: timeshare condos.

What would this all mean for our relationship? I didn't want to think about it. Surely Trevor would find another gig, and surely he would come back, but the uncertainty frightened me. My letters to Trevor became increasingly anxious. I wrote and told him about that one piece of coffeecake in the back of my refrigerator, left from when he'd stayed with me. He might never come back again to buy more, so I couldn't eat it, and I couldn't throw it away...

He wrote back. "Eat the cake, my darling. I'll be back to buy you some more." But would he really?

Then several weeks went by, and I didn't hear from him at all. I kept writing letters, mailing them, and waiting for a response. I went numb from fright sometimes, worrying that it was over.

Chapter 24

I was wearing my bathrobe when the phone rang. I had just gotten out of the shower, set my hair in rollers, and settled on the couch with a book. I hopped up and ran into the kitchen. "Hello?"

"Holly! Holly, my love! How are you, gorgeous? I've missed you, my beautiful darling."

"Oh, my God! Oh, my God!" I hugged myself. "Oh, my God, Trevor. I just got your letter! Where are you calling from?"

"In front of the Rogers Theatre. I'm at a pay phone."

"What?" It didn't register. "No really. Where are you? In the States or in England?"

"I'm at a pay phone on the corner in front of the Rogers Theatre. One minute…" There was silence while he apparently stuck his head out of the phone booth to look up. "That old Frank Zappa movie is playing. *200 Motels*. Shall we see it?"

I was in shock, trying to make sense of what he was saying. How on earth did he know that *200 Motels* was playing at the Rogers?

Then it hit me. At that same moment, it also hit me that I was in my bathrobe, that my hair was in rollers, and that the apartment was filthy. "Oh, my God." What was I going to do? He was practically right outside my door! "Oh, my God, Trevor. Why didn't you give me a little warning that you were coming?"

"I wanted to surprise you. I should have told you but… I wanted to surprise you…" His voice trailed off.

He was practically right outside my door! I nearly squealed.

"My hair is in rollers. It isn't even dry yet. I'm in my robe," I gasped. "The apartment is a pigsty! Aw, geez. It's gross in here. It's bad, I swear. I

181

really don't want you to see it." I began moving dishes into the sink while I spoke. "You must be hungry."

I checked the refrigerator and slammed it shut. I only had mustard, a small jar of mayonnaise, and an old, stale piece of coffeecake.

"I have no food; I can't even feed you. If I'd known you were coming, I'd have gone to the store. I'd have cleaned up this mess. Why didn't you tell me you were coming?" I clicked my tongue, cheerfully exasperated. "We can have a pizza delivered, I suppose. Are you hungry? Oh, my *God*. I'm not wearing any makeup! I look like a witch. Can you at least give me five minutes to get the rollers out of my hair? No, never mind, don't do that. Come here now. Get here *right now*. Just keep your eyes closed and don't look at me or the apartment. Hang up and come *now. Hang up!*"

I slammed down the phone and ran to pick up some dirty clothes from the bedroom floor. Then I ran toward the kitchen, stopping to open the door to the hallway a crack. I had no time to do the kitchen… my hair! My hair! I ran back to the living room and began clawing at the rollers, pulling them out and dropping them into a pile on the coffee table.

Pansy's squeal told me Trevor was in the hallway. She had been standing watch in the doorway, then barked and bolted out the door. Trevor's face appeared in the doorway, and he was holding her.

"Well, come in!" I called, bouncing slightly with excitement, tossing another roller onto the pile, and pulling at the next one. "You don't see me doing this," I ordered sternly. "Close your eyes."

Trevor stared at me and stepped into the apartment reverently, as if he were approaching the altar of a church. He placed the dog and his bag on the floor. Pansy, deliriously happy, yipped and clawed at his legs while barking.

I grinned, then ran to hug him with rollers still dangling.

He walked over. grabbed me, and lifted me up, then put me down and gave me a long, hard kiss. He closed his eyes and pulled my head to his chest.

"I'm home," he whispered, kissing the top of my head and reaching into my robe. He fingered the small of my back and slipped his fingers under the elastic of my panties, the only thing I was wearing under the robe.

He gently pried himself away and took a step back to look around.

"I'm home!" he cried in a loud excited voice. He touched the lamp, the couch, and the television. Turning on light switches, he did a quick tour of the apartment looking into each of the two and a half rooms, plus the bathroom, touching things he recognized, stopping at the window to celebrate the uninspired, colorless view. I followed, gasping with dismay and humiliation, begging him to not go in there, to not look at this or that, scooping up clothes from the floor, wiping dust from furniture with the palm of my hand, grabbing coffee mugs off the desk, and racing to the kitchen sink.

Trevor saw a cockroach climbing the wall. He took off his shoe and smacked it with the heel. "The lovely Angelique is still hoarding her garbage then, is she?" He turned to me and grinned. "Of course she is. And we're out of Black Flag again."

I grimaced and looked around the messy apartment helplessly. I was embarrassed. Then I recovered and started asking questions.

"How long can you stay? How long have you known you were coming? What band are you with? Why didn't you *tell* me?"

"Let me just take it all in for a moment," he answered, smiling and looking around. Then he burst out with it, telling me about his new job, and how he had kept it a secret so he could surprise me.

He scraped the roach onto the edge of the trashcan and threw the shoe toward the couch. He took off his other shoe and hurled it. Then he turned and kissed me.

"It's very good to be back." He then began to tell me how he had persuaded the bus driver to make a detour down Clark Street. He described how, when they'd approached my corner, he'd shouted, "Let me off!" The other roadies had banged on the windows and shouted at him, as it pulled away, "Leaving me to my fate with you," he teased.

Pansy had jumped and chased him throughout his tour of the apartment and was now writhing on her back in leg-kicking ecstasy. Trevor squatted and rubbed her stomach.

"My beautiful baby girl," he cooed. "Did you miss me?" The dog scrambled up and excitedly licked his face. He hugged her, and the two of them rolled together on the floor at my feet while I watched and laughed, pulling the rest of the rollers out of my hair. When I reached up to pull out the last roller at the very back of my head, my tie loosened, and my robe fell open.

Trevor looked up at me standing in front of him with my open robe and froze. I self-consciously tried to wrap the robe around myself again, but he stopped me. He reached over and grabbed the edge of the robe. He pulled. I let it slip off and knelt down on the floor beside him.

"Pansy, go. You go," Trevor ordered. The dog looked startled, then ran under a chair.

"You stay," he said, pulling me down, rolling over onto me, kissing me, and slipping his hand between my legs. "I've missed you."

"I've missed you, too."

"Do you love me?" Trevor kissed my neck, then moved his lips down to my chest.

"Yes, I love you. Of *course,* I love you."

"How much?" He playfully licked, then sucked my nipple. "How much?"

I gasped as he nibbled softly.

"How much do I love you?" I giggled. "Hmmm. In dollars or pounds? In kilometers or miles? In liters or gallons? On the left side of the road or the right?"

"Tell me." His tongue moved down and flicked lightly over my belly. "Tell me now, you vixen, or I go no further south."

"I love you more than anyone on earth."

"Do you mean it?" He peeled back my panties. His lips now rested on my pubic area. "Or are you merely saying that in order to get me to service you with my tongue?"

"Yes, I mean it." I ran my fingers down the side of his face. Then my face briefly convulsed for a moment. I felt as if I were about to burst into tears. "You know I do. You're my family. You and Pansy."

"Thank you. I feel the same about you," he said quietly, reaching up to touch my face, studying it. Then he moved down and burrowed into me with his tongue. He looked up, peering over my stomach.

"Did you really miss me? Are you really glad to see me?"

Feeling every kind of emotion, I nodded. "I hate it when you're gone," I said softly.

"We must do something about that," he murmured. "Yes, we must." His hands and kisses moved back up my body, barely touching me. He shifted himself up, sitting lightly on my pelvis with his knees pressing up against my hips, his hands flat on the floor beside my ears. He sank on top of me, then saw Pansy watching.

"We can't do this in front of the baby," he whispered. Then to Pansy, he said, "I am taking your Mummy to the bedroom where I intend to do naughty, naughty things with her all night long."

He rose and took my hand to pull me to my feet. "Come with me."

Once upright, I threw my arms around his neck and pressed my face into his chest. I began to sob.

"What, Holly? Be happy!"

Trevor cooed as if to a baby, kissing my eyes and rocking me in his arms. "I'm here now. I'm here."

"I *am* happy." I wiped my eyes, but still wasn't finished crying. "But it's like a roller coaster. When you come, I have to brace myself for when you leave. The whole time you're here, that's all I'm doing. I barely get used to you, then you're gone, and I have to work myself into a place where I can deal with you leaving, and then get through the rest of the year alone. The next thing I know, you're here again… and I have to brace myself *again* because you're leaving."

I sobbed again, wiped my nose, and summed it all up: "I try not to cry, but I can't stop it."

Trevor took my hands, led me to the couch, and sat down beside me. He gently pushed my hair back from my face, then took both of my hands again.

"Would you like me not to leave?"

I shrugged. I could only have half a life. It was hell when he stayed and hell when he left.

"I'm really okay with everything. Seriously. This is what you do, and I know that. I just miss you, and I cry." I sighed. "Just ignore me."

Trevor shifted to one knee on the floor in front of me. He lifted my hands to his lips and lightly kissed them.

I looked at him. My eyes widened. My fingers stiffened. I began to panic.

He seemed a little puzzled by my expression, but he apparently couldn't stop the momentum of the moment. *Please stop*, I silently prayed. He carried on.

"How would you like your own house with a garden and all the flowers you want? It can be either here or in England, wherever you like."

I prayed again for him to stop. I looked around the room—anywhere but at his sweet and earnest face.

"I want to be your family and keep you safe. I want to take care of you, always."

I might have confronted him about his choice of words, but this was not the time for that. This was the time for me to run away. *Please stop. Please*, I thought.

"I'll send you to school. That's what you want more than anything, isn't it? I'll see that you get your degree. Would you like that? And I won't ever leave you again. When I have to travel, I'll take you with me, and we'll travel together."

He wouldn't stop. It was coming. *Help. Help me.*

"I want to be your husband, Holly. I want to have babies with you…" He pressed my hands to his lips again, then held them to his chest. "… and fight with you over the bills, and sleep with you and wake up with you. I love you, and I want to spend my life with you."

I edged away. I looked away.

"Holly, will you marry me?" He confidently waited for my answer.

"No." I didn't elaborate, and I didn't soften it. I let it hang in the air like a stench.

Trevor knelt frozen, staring past me. He let go of my hands.

"Right," he said, running his hand down his chin and then across the back of his neck. "Right, then."

If he asked me why, would I tell him? Probably not. I stayed silent, and he didn't ask.

He stood up, looking dazed. "Right, then. All right."

He walked to the kitchen, opened the refrigerator, and stuck his head inside. He emerged with a contorted face, but he quickly regained control. He stood straight again and shut the refrigerator door.

I studied him, dried-eyed but somber and watchful. "We can order a pizza," I suggested quietly.

"Right!" Trevor answered brightly. "A pizza."

"You're hungry?"

Trevor shook his head and smiled stiffly. "Not at all. No, thank you." He walked to the living room window and hid his face in the drape.

"Do you want me to make some tea?"

"Wonderful! Yes!" Trevor pulled his face out of the drape and gave me that same stiff smile. "Tea would be lovely. Very good. Thank you. Yes." Then he turned back to look down at the street.

I slipped into my robe and went to the kitchen to fill the kettle and put it on the stove. I walked over behind him and put my arms around his waist. Trevor absently patted my hand. I pressed my cheek to his back. "Let's leave things the way they are. Please?"

Trevor pulled away and went into the kitchen.

"The water is nearly boiling," he said with feigned cheerfulness, bustling about, whistling, getting mugs and spoons, pulling sugar and coffee creamer down from the shelf. He had already looked in the refrigerator and knew I had no milk. All I had was a piece of coffeecake I couldn't eat and couldn't throw away.

"Nothing like a good cup of tea," he called as the kettle began to whistle.

He didn't utter a word of complaint about the powdered coffee creamer, I noticed.

He poured boiling water into the two mugs. "Nothing like a good civilized cup of tea, I always say." He flashed a tight smile; he might have been saying "cheese." He stirred his tea and took a sip. "I'm just passing through, actually. One show tomorrow night, and we go on to Madison afterward." He tossed me a calculatedly indifferent glance. I sensed the anger and confusion beneath it.

I nodded.

"But I can leave tonight if you'd rather." There was a subtle tinge of hostility in his voice.

I gasped and thought, *No, don't leave me!* I could do nothing at all to fix this, and he was about to leave me alone with it.

"You don't want to leave, do you? You aren't leaving, are you? You just *got* here." I started to cry again.

"No tears, Holly." His tone was sharp, irritated, impatient, and disdainful. It was aloof and indifferent. "Enough of that. No more tears, please."

I was startled into frozen silence. I looked at him, frightened.

He seemed unmoved and affronted, as if he were asking, "How dare you cry?" Yet he seemed shaken and on the verge of tears himself. Perhaps he was thinking, "How dare you cry in front of me when I cannot cry in front of you?"

"No, I just... *please,* don't go." Tears streamed down my cheeks. "Please don't do this to me, just pop in like this and then leave. I can't—"

I was going to beg, and he could see it.

"I need to find a pub," he said abruptly, cutting me short.

"Can I come with?"

"No, thank you," he replied. "I'd rather go alone."

I wiped my eyes, but said nothing.

"Well." He picked up his bag, paused for a second, then put it down again and went to the door. He turned the knob and opened the door. "I'll be back later. I still have a key." Then he slipped out and was gone.

Two hours later, Trevor tiptoed in, quieted the dog, and stood in my bedroom undressing in the dark while I silently watched from the bed. He left his clothing on the floor, got into bed, and wrapped his arms around me. I returned his hug with a tight one, kissing his face and lips.

He kissed me a little roughly, then made love to me almost violently, something he had never done before. It was painful, but I deserved pain so I didn't protest. I let him grunt and grimace until he was spent, then I rolled over, covered my face, and wept.

In the morning I didn't know what to say or how to face him. I slid out of bed and pattered softly to the bathroom, pulling my pink robe from its hook behind the door and putting it on, hugging myself as I walked back. I hesitated when I reached the bed, waiting for some sign from Trevor that I was still welcome.

He had been wordlessly watching me, but he sighed as I stood before him. He held out his arms. "Good morning, my beautiful darling."

I crawled into his arms and buried my face in his neck while he absently fingered my hair

I had to go to work. Trevor would enjoy a leisurely morning, then would lock up and head to the concert hall that afternoon. It seemed much as it had been on those mornings over those weeks and months when Trevor stayed with me and had visited with, or done an occasional day's work for, the various English bands that had come through town. I would come home, find a backstage pass on the kitchen table, and would meet him there for the concert that night. That was our life. For the moment, everything seemed just as it had been.

Trevor made no mention of the marriage proposal and didn't act any differently from before when we arose. He snuggled up behind me when I put the kettle on the stove, wrapped his arms around me, kissed my neck. I made the toast. He made the tea, muttering about the vile manner in which coffee creamer turned perfectly good tea into toxic bilgewater, but using it anyway, making a face. He took Pansy for a quick walk while I showered. When I climbed out of the shower, he was waiting for me. He picked me up wet and squealing and threw me onto the bed for a quick morning roll, this time sweetly, tenderly, and gently, gasping and murmuring, "I love you," throughout and afterward. Then he contentedly sprawled on his side and watched me dress for work, wolf-whistling as I slipped into my underwear.

We held hands on the walk to the bus stop. He waited for my bus to come, kissed me goodbye as I climbed on, then returned to my apartment to pass the time until he needed to leave for the concert hall.

I didn't expect to find him there when I returned home. But when I ran to the kitchen table and picked up his note, my heart sank, and I felt cold. There were no instructions and no backstage pass. "Must go it alone tonight," the note read. "Hope you don't mind. I'll call if I'm coming back. If not, take care. Love, T."

He didn't specify if he meant if he was coming back "tonight"... or "ever."

Chapter 25

On the night Trevor left me, the roadie he was rooming with, Noel, took Karen's friend Robin with him to the room. Trevor apparently knew Noel from his school days, and the two were good friends. Consequently, they spoke to each other in confidence when they thought Robin was asleep.

"Trevor was pretty upset, I guess. He wonders if you and John Collier may have a thing going," Karen said. "Robin says he called it 'that festering love song,' and he called John a 'snooty arse.' John apparently never said anything, and never apologized, and kind of avoids him. I guess they haven't really spoken since the album came out, so who knows if they'll ever be friends again?"

"Oh, my God," I moaned. "Oh, God." It just kept getting worse and worse.

"He said the song was 'John Collier's *Layla.*'" *Layla* was the song Eric Clapton wrote to George Harrison's wife, Pattie Boyd, declaring his love for her. "I still can't figure out why the band recorded it. It seems like such a mean thing to do."

"There's nothing going on between us. There never was. Trevor knows that." I felt like a criminal, coming between John and Trevor, and then turning Trevor down. But there was nothing at all that I could say or do without making everything worse.

"I know, honey. Trevor has to blame someone, right? He's just licking his wounds." She paused. "Why did you turn him down?" she asked. "I know it's none of my business…"

"I don't know," I told her. But I did.

First one letter came, and then another. Trevor described the tour and the cities he visited, and shared gossip with me about the band, the wives, the girlfriends, the groupies and the roadies as he traveled around the country. In July, they flew to Europe where, for the sake of saving postage, letters became short notes on postcards that always ended with "Love, T." In late September, the tour would continue to Japan and then Australia. Trevor mentioned Australia in passing on a postcard from Rome, conversationally, as if it were merely one more interesting stop as he traveled the world.

He hadn't seen Beth in four years and hadn't communicated with her in two, since the onset of his relationship with me. I had no doubt that he had written to her recently, telling her he was coming to Sydney, and I had no doubt that the Sydney concert was consuming much of his thoughts. As unlikely as it seemed, my intuition told me that she was still waiting for him and hadn't married or moved on. I began to plan my life as though it were a fact, that Trevor was going back to her and severing ties with me.

I knew when I told Trevor no that it was the end of us, and I had been mourning the relationship ever since. I could have continued on indefinitely the way we were, but I suspected he wouldn't allow it. If I didn't marry him, he would leave me. Afterward, I knew I was right because of his reaction when I turned him down, and the fact that he'd left so abruptly with just a note rather than a proper goodbye.

He wouldn't give me a second chance. I didn't deserve a second chance because my answer would be the same were he to ask me a second time.

Did I regret my decision? No. It wasn't a choice. Was I jealous of Beth? No, I'd never perceived Beth as a threat, and I'd never resented her. She'd had him first, and for a longer period of time. The Girlfriend Code demanded that I respect that, and her.

Now I really needed her. I was holding my breath in a way, entrusting the most important person in my life to someone I had never met without any proof beyond my intuition that she was still even there for him or that he would go to her. Strangest of all, this was how I drew solace, reminding myself that I was sending him to her instead of merely sending him away.

I sent letters to Trevor's parents' house, never knowing if they reached him on the road, or how long it took for him to get them. But I sent fewer letters than I used to, bracing myself as July became August, and August turned to September. I kept my letters light and funny.

In September, I didn't write to him at all, but I thought a good deal about Sydney, Australia.

I went to fewer concerts with Karen, preferring to stay at home and sleep. She and Angie began to call me, concerned, to try and rouse me out of my lethargy and entice me into going out with them.

At work I began turning down invitations to go with the girls to the bars.

"What's with her?" Constance asked Angie from across the aisle. I had declined the last four invitations.

"She's depressed," Angie replied. "It isn't a good time."

"What does *she* have to be depressed about? *Nothing.* What a spoiled brat."

"I'm right here, Denise. I can hear you. Go to hell." I glared at her.

"*Sorry!*" Denise replied good-naturedly. "Touchy, aren't we?" Her phone rang, and she answered it.

"There's no such thing as depression," Vickie contributed, knowingly. "It's just self-pity. You'll never see *me* getting depressed. The trick is to just think yourself happy."

"Think yourself happy. That's all? Just think yourself happy?"

"That's right," she said. "I was depressed once, and I just thought myself happy. Gone in an hour. Just like that. I just think happy thoughts."

"Wow." Ignorance abounded. I could pick a fight over it, but I was too depressed. I stood up to go to the ladies lounge, where I intended to hide in one of the stalls.

"I don't feel sorry for you," Vickie continued as I walked away. "You're just fishing for pity to get attention. You haven't been worshipped enough today, is my guess." She snorted, and Geri giggled. "Nobody's going to fall for it."

September turned to October, the tour ended, and the next postcard arrived from England. Trevor made no mention of Australia or Beth, but he did tell me he and Charles had both been hired for the upcoming '76 Paul McCartney and Wings tour. He would see me the following spring, he promised. "Love, T."

Throughout the winter, his letters arrived with touching regularity. They were less frequent than before, one each month instead of one each week, but the tone never changed, and he always signed them with "love."

I wasn't fooled. For the first time since I'd met him, I began actively looking for another boyfriend. It was imperative that I find one soon to cushion the final breakup at the end of May, when the Wings Over America tour reached Chicago. I wouldn't find a boyfriend, of course. Or I would, and it wouldn't last. My relationships, except for Trevor, had never lasted more than a month, or at the most, two. I couldn't seem to go more than a few weeks with anyone, so I doubted I would have that cushion when the time came.

Nobody I met throughout those months was right. I needed a relationship that was simple, uncomplicated, and didn't require analysis and examination, but which kept me interested and kept my spirits up. It must be with a man who made no emotional demands, but would be there for me and didn't mind that I wouldn't be there for him. That criterion was impossible to fill. I inspected, evaluated, and dismissed dozens and dozens of men during those months, feeling increasingly frantic.

"What reason do you have to believe that you know what he's thinking?" Dr. Silverman challenged. "From the sound of things, nothing's really changed, and you're panicking for no reason." He tapped his lips with the eraser end of his pencil. "You may just be fabricating everything out of fear because you know he went to Australia in the fall."

"No, that's not it. I feel him."

"And that's how you know these things?" He raised an eyebrow.

I nodded.

"Do you think that's rational?" When I gave him a look of exasperated longsuffering, he asked, "Would you call it, say, telepathy?"

He had little patience with telepathy and had expressed this on several occasions. Anything he couldn't explain was rooted in psychosis.

I shrugged and gave him a steady look that fell just short of a glare. "Maybe it's just what happens when you love someone," I told him a little snappishly.

This was not a good day for me, and I had been edging toward rage for hours, obsessing over all the things that made me angry and all the things people had done to me, hating everyone. In fact, the stress of my deteriorating relationship with Trevor, the uncertainty, the fear, and the sorrow were wearing me down. I was experiencing real problems. I had always been shy and had always been socially wary and uncertain. Now I had become withdrawn, and during the past few months, I had turned increasingly defensive, mean, confrontational, and even paranoid at work. I probably wouldn't be fired, at least not yet, but my supervisor had already had a discussion with me. "Your personality doesn't wear well," he'd told me. "You're difficult to be around. Work on it."

At the same time, I had recently pulled myself out of isolation and was now having wilder and wilder drunken escapades in the bars with Angie. I was still sleeping through my weekends but began binge drinking on work nights, acting out and letting off steam, commencing the evening as the life of the party, only to end it in sudden uncontrollable tears. Angie always cheerfully mopped me up and stuck me in a cab with a hug and a five-dollar bill. I swung from one extreme to the other, oftentimes in the same hour. The next morning, I always went to work with a violent hangover, nursing it in the ladies lounge, unable to focus when I sat at my desk to work.

I was frequently landing in the beds of strange men, sometimes meeting them in bars and sometimes at concerts, waking up and feeling alternately repulsed and angry, or frantic that someone might leave me before I could furiously hurl him out of my life. I wasn't nearly as promiscuous as Angie and wasn't even as bad as most of the women in the New Town bars, but I was bad enough. For me, anyway. It was a sad, sad winter.

Now, at my Tuesday session, I was still weak from the hangover I had awakened with that morning, and was red-eyed from inadequate sleep.

I believed I was about to lose my anchor, and I was afraid I would spin into oblivion, as I did during my panic attacks, once Trevor was really gone. I could still sense him though, and was clinging to that for as long as I could. It was what I had left. My sense of Trevor told me that I didn't have long.

I would fight Dr. Silverman whenever he dared to question it. His expression was one of patronizing patience. He was going to permit me to explain it all to him without further comment, but he would not be persuaded. I was certain the notes he took would not contain any indication that he believed me or thought my sense of Trevor was real.

"It's not mysterious. You tune into someone, and then you know how it is with him." I was defensive and challenging. My hands were in fists.

He looked up from his notes with a pleasant but carefully guarded expression and studied me as if *this* was the part of me that was crazy: feeling connected to Trevor. I wondered briefly what was wrong with him or missing, that he had never experienced it himself. It was like trying to explain the color red to someone who was colorblind and accusing you of lying about it. I sighed.

"It's not like I can read his mind or anything. I don't know what he's thinking or doing. I never said *that*. It's like a hum in the background. When he's focused on me, I sense it. If he pulls away, I sense that, too. It's like knowing when someone comes into the room or leaves it, even though you aren't paying attention to them."

194

I can't explain it to this person, I thought, irritated and indignant. This was basic human stuff he should already know, and it was too hard to put into words. I gave him a tight-lipped, superior look. He looked back, studying me, seeming thoughtfully alert.

"I just trust it. It's no big mystical deal or anything. Humans were equipped with this kind of radar since creation. Radar is how we communicated before language. Look it up."

I regarded him argumentatively. Where's *yours*? I thought. Radar *this*. I was shooting mental thunderbolts at him while I fidgeted in my chair. I wanted to scream or break things—his things. My nostrils flared. I didn't blink. One wrong word and I'd fly at him. Once again, I was only marginally in control and about to lose it.

He acknowledged my bloodshot eyes and my challenging, accusatory, condescending tone with one raised eyebrow, but he didn't comment. He did, however, recognize what was angering me. He obligingly adjusted his own condescension to a lower frequency.

"Well then, do you *feel* that he's stopped loving you?"

I noted his more respectful, less patronizing, tone. My fury lessened somewhat, but my suspicion deepened that he was only being placating because he was secretly contemptuous of me. I continued to watch him through narrowed eyes, waiting for him to insult me so I could attack. It was like entering the Hate Phase with a soon-to-be-ex-boyfriend.

This may in fact be my imagination, that I'm feeling Trevor, I thought. However, I lead a very painful, lonely life, and I sometimes need very, very badly to feel connected to another human being. Don't you dare roll your eyes at me and trivialize me until you've experienced this loneliness of mine and this illness of mine, which you never, ever cure no matter how much I sacrifice to pay for your supposed expertise. Don't you dare dismiss the accuracy of the knowledge I obtain through my methods of sensing the people I love, while you continue to fail me. In fact, I thought, edging even closer to rage, it is your professional failure that cost me this relationship.

As I inwardly churned, he waited for me to respond, then finally repeated the question: Did I think that Trevor had stopped loving me?

It was difficult for me to counter the rage and respond objectively, but I thought about Trevor. The love was still there. He was still there for me like a steady heartbeat. I shook my head. "He still loves me. I think he probably always will."

"So why are you worried? What do you think is happening with him?" He was again pretending to believe me when he really didn't.

I glared at him. I hated people who were deceitful, and I hated people who were smug. He was both. I hated him.

He liked to cross his legs like a woman, toe pointed, then hold his pencil in both hands, while stretching his arms out so his wrists rested on his knee. He did this. It irritated me. I gritted my teeth in outrage that he was assaulting me with his appallingly irritating gestures and mannerisms.

He also liked to peer at me intently down his nose, with a serious mouth. He did that as well, and considered my psychosis as he waited for me to provide him with more substantiating evidence of it.

God, I hated him. I had frequently considered switching shrinks, but I didn't want to have to repeat this process, bringing a new one up to speed after spending a fortune on this one. Plus, it would mean I'd be paying two of them because I still owed this one almost nine hundred dollars and would be running up a similar tab somewhere else. My budget wouldn't stretch that far. Furthermore, this one accepted my monthly dribbles of payment without comment and never pestered me to pay off my ever-increasing balance. I could stop altogether, dump him, but it was too big of a risk. I had to have someone to talk to, just in case, even if I got nothing at all in return for my money. I was stuck with this man whom I hated.

Still, I was so tired of talking about my life. I was so tired of everything. I wanted to shriek and rip the wallpaper off the walls. He *made* me feel that way. It was all his fault for being so irritating and so lacking in insight.

I didn't shriek and rip the wallpaper. Instead, I chewed my cuticles and swung my crossed leg back and forth wildly to relieve the pressure in my spine. I felt as if I had an electric current shooting up my back. My skull felt tight as well, as if it were too small for my brain. I twisted in my chair and twirled my hair. I shifted my weight from one side to the other and glared at him. I made exasperated gasps. I scowled and thought death rays at him. *God,* I hated him!

I uncrossed my leg and slammed both feet to the floor in an angry stomp.

"Would you *please* stop *doing* that?!" I yelled, half-standing, pounding my fists on the arms of my chair as I leaned forward. "Jesus *Christ!*"

He looked at me, startled and perplexed.

"Sitting that way. You make me crazy." I curled my lip and gestured with a limp hand as if I were brushing away a fly. I settled back down and turned my head away.

As soon as I'd spoken, it was as though I'd been punctured, and the pressure in my skull was released. The shame set in within seconds, if not instantaneously. I understood that I was rude and cruel. I understood that I was crazy and wrong. I knew better than to scream at people for crossing their legs and would never have done it if every nerve ending hadn't been charged and my head about to explode from pent-up fury and irritation.

Dr. Silverman readjusted his sitting position. "Is this all right?" he asked. He seemed genuinely interested in doing whatever he needed to do to appease me. That was sad, I thought. I felt sorry for him for caring about what I thought when I was so crazy and worthless. On the other hand, if he'd said that to make me feel doubly demeaned and remorseful and unbelievably mortified, he'd succeeded. Should I hate him for that as well?

I looked at him, then covered my face with my hands and nodded. I removed my hands and looked down, ashamed. I was such a bitch and such a burden to everyone. People couldn't even sit right for me. I postponed my hatred for another time and welcomed the shame.

Out of humiliation, I wouldn't apologize, but I would try to sweetly cooperate. It was easier to be cooperative, now that I'd had my outburst. I was always a bit more compliant after an outburst, and I hated him a little less as well.

Later, I would agonize over my behavior. For weeks, I would berate myself mercilessly out of shame. I always did. I was always haunted and obsessive for ridiculously long periods of time over large things and small. My entire life was one long merciless examination of my failings. Each episode was another defeat and provided evidence that I had no more control today than I'd had the day I started fighting this... whatever *this* was. Each defeat affected me the way justifiable grief affected someone else, because my defeats defined my worth.

I sighed and avoided his eyes. "I'm sorry, what did you ask me?" Perhaps that quick "I'm sorry" would suffice as my apology.

"I asked you why you were so worried, and what you thought was happening with Trevor."

"Right. He's..." Actually confronting the question, I realized my sense of things was vague. I had to think about what I sensed and assign it a tangible description. It took me a minute, and then I found the words. "He's shifting focus."

That was what I sensed. I was no longer directly in his sights. It was more as though I was still within his range, but off to one side. Trevor's hum was getting almost imperceptibly, yet unmistakably, weaker and farther away.

"He's moving on. I have to let him go." I stared at a corner of the ceiling and was caught off-guard by a sob. I controlled it by waving a hand in front of my face to dismiss the tears.

"Does he say this in his letters?"

I shook my head and lowered my hand, putting it in my lap. I looked down.

"No. Everything's pretty much the same. Neither one of us ever mentioned the marriage proposal again. Not even once."

I regained control, looked up, and gave a rueful half-smile, as if the situation was somewhat humorous.

"Can you write and tell him how you feel? Can you patch things up with him?"

"There's nothing to patch up. It's not like he's angry. He's just pulling away. I have to let go of him now." I could probably put things back together with Trevor. I imagined there might be a way, but even attempting it would be hurtful and selfish. I would disrupt whatever he'd been doing in the past few months to adjust and move on. I would tear him in two for no reason because nothing would be fixed or changed.

He was safe and secure now. Beth had waited for him for years. She still loved him and finally had him back, I believed, so any interference from me would completely break her heart, and for no good reason because Trevor and I would still be confronted with the same problems. There would still be only one solution, and this was it. My choices were to either do it now with pain and limit it to Trevor and myself, or do it later with pain multiplied tenfold, and pull Beth into the wreckage.

The sob I'd been fighting caught me. I knew exactly what this felt like now. "It feels like I gave my child up for adoption. The papers are signed." I buried my face in my lap, cradling my head with my arms until the session was over, and the doctor sent me on my way.

Chapter 26

In late March I began seeing a man I had met in a New Town bar. He was gorgeous, French, and spoke very little English, all of which suited me. Philippe was a 25-year-old chemical engineer, tall, dark and stunningly, shockingly, freakishly handsome: a geek in a Greek god suit. He drew as many stares as I did and seemed as relieved to have me to ward off the advances of women as I was to have him to ward off the advances of men. Finally, I had found and identified my new boyfriend.

We fell in with each other immediately and spent most of our free time together, both on weekends and during the week. A portion of that time consisted of his taking me to French restaurants and feeding me. He kept feeding me! I liked that very much and was pleased to watch myself gain seven pounds. My ribs were softening, and my collarbone wasn't as pronounced. All my waistbands were tight, but my bust was a little larger, and I felt better than I had in quite a while.

I got my long hair cut short, completely changing my look the way women often do as a symbolic gesture after a divorce. At one of the concerts we'd gone to during Trevor's last visit, Supertramp had a bevy of beautiful dark-haired girls with them, all with the same sleek mushroom haircut. I wanted to look like the pretty girls who had been with Supertramp. Everyone was wearing the Wedge this year, like the figure skater Dorothy Hamill, but this variation was different and adorable, and I wanted it because it made me look French. I was moving on, too.

Philippe was good for me. Weeks went by, and I showed no evidence of depression, despite the ticking clock and the fact it was May. Even my energy level was high. I didn't catch myself dragging through the day, and when I was home alone I could stay awake until ten, instead of crawling into bed hungry and exhausted at seven thirty. On typical weekends, I'd always slept for twelve to fourteen hours a night, often until afternoon, even if I hadn't gone out the night before, unless I had plans that forced me out of bed. With Philippe, I was up at dawn, showered and dressed, ready and eager to do whatever he'd planned.

I had been the same way each time Trevor was in town. What that meant, I believed, was that I needed a relationship to feel good, even though I could never sustain one for long. I never drew the connection between being in relationships and regularly eating healthy food.

As the relationship progressed, I enjoyed our time together immensely. Philippe didn't surreptitiously eye other women when we were together. He was perhaps as glutted and deadened by attention from the opposite sex as I was. He didn't exhibit any signs that he was seeing anyone another than me. He had every opportunity to troll around the city and steep himself in gleeful debauchery with droves of willing women, or men, had he been so inclined, but was content to patter barefoot around his apartment most evenings in t-shirts and sweatpants while reading science journals or industry texts in French, or cuddling with me in front of the television. I brought over a supply of my own books and studied while he did. Pansy came with me. My toiletries were in his medicine cabinet, and Pansy's food bowl was in his kitchen. I had clothing hanging in his closet.

Each week he made a tape in French and shipped it off to his family in lieu of letters. He sometimes put the microphone to my mouth and told me to speak so they could "meet" me, and he let me listen to the tapes they sent him in return, although I couldn't understand much. I was trying though; I had begun taking French lessons in the basement of a Parisian woman who advertised in the Chicago Reader and charged five dollars a class. I practiced my pronunciation on him. We even discussed flying together to his home in Paris for a short trip, and I applied for a passport.

He caused me no angst and no concern because I felt no connection to him as I had with Trevor. My usually crippling and intense fears of abandonment were quiet, perhaps because he didn't really matter to me, and I was emotionally detached from him. We had no deep discussions about anything. I had no idea if we even shared the same philosophy of life, and no way of immediately finding out. But he was perfect for me. The skies had opened up and dropped him into my lap. It was all fun because he was fun.

"If this is bad, wouldn't it suck to be famous? God, I'd hate it," I remarked, spearing a piece of duck à l'orange from his plate and popping it into my mouth. I closed my eyes and moaned. Duck. Duck is good. I would order it next time.

What prompted the remark was a woman who had earlier slipped Philippe a matchbook with her phone number on it, over my head, in fact, as I leaned down to reach for my purse under my chair. He had held it up to show me. Then, in an exaggerated mime, he had pretended to put it into his jacket pocket while raising and lowering his eyebrows. He laughed when I put my fists on my hips and pretended to be angry, then shook his head and threw it on the tray when our waiter returned with the main course.

He'd crossed his arms over his chest and grinned smugly and triumphantly. With this incident, he'd gotten even with me for an incident earlier in the evening when he had returned from the bathroom to find a man asking me for my phone number. My new suitor had looked up. The beautiful Philippe was standing just a little too close to him, leaning into him with exaggerated friendliness, smiling broadly and wickedly, holding an over-eager hand an inch from the man's nose, offering to shake.

The man had looked at Philippe and blinked. He refused his hand, and then wordlessly slinked away with his eyes down, walking in short, unsteady steps, psychologically beaten to what appeared to be a bloody pulp. Philippe had frowned and wagged his finger at me, then leaned over to kiss me. He'd laughed.

I was about to suggest that we keep score.

"Suck?" He asked me this with his puzzled look of, "*Je ne parle pas l'anglais.*" ("I don't speak English.")

"*Sucer,*" I'd answered helpfully. I'd been dutifully studying useful French words and phrases, both in class and out. "All these people in your face all the time, wanting you or wanting something *from* you. If you're famous, there's no way of knowing who really likes you, or who's just using you."

I was thinking of my experiences with Torc and their groupies and hangers-on. I remembered John Collier's description of what it was like to not know which of those hangers-on he could trust, and how he said he pulled himself into a shell out of self-defense. I'd never wished myself into the world of the famous any closer than Trevor took me.

"It's bad enough to just be you and me, you know?"

He nodded in agreement, smiling thoughtfully, apparently mulling over the downside of fame and pushy fans, but I couldn't guess the degree to which he was following my train of thought. He had nothing to add.

"I hate being harassed, don't you? Being famous would really be *manger la merde*. Did I say that right?" It was a phrase Philippe had taught me that meant "someone or something you dislike." I'd only learn later that his translation was imprecise, and that the phrase actually meant "eat shit."

Philippe perked up and showed renewed interest in the conversation. "*Oui!*" He grinned and kissed the air while lightly clapping his hands. He wrinkled his beautiful nose and leaned over to run his hand down my cheek.

"*Je t'adore*," he purred, spooning another bite of duck into my mouth.

It was beginning to look as though Philippe would carry me safely past Trevor, who was due in a mere three weeks.

Chapter 27

"**W**here do you find all these foreigners?" my grandmother asked accusingly. The fact that she adored Trevor was beside the point.

"Drunk in a bar," I answered, sullenly flipping through a magazine in her living room during my biweekly Sunday visit. I had learned long ago that it didn't matter what I said because talking to Grandma was like talking to the radio.

I'd brought Philippe with me this time. I had warned him and tried to persuade him that he really, *really* didn't want to come. He'd insisted that he really did, and now no doubt deeply regretted that he hadn't listened to me.

Philippe was in the bathroom, affording Grandma the opportunity to find fault with him behind his back. She refused to grill him with impertinent and insulting questions because his accent disturbed her too much. It also prevented her from imagining they had hatreds in common so she could share with him a moving story about her lifelong persecution at the hands of the blacks, the Jews, her sisters, or the Mercy nuns. Clearly, they had nothing in common, and clearly this made him the enemy. Without the sturdy certainty of language, she must draw conclusions about him on her own. She did not solicit his input. His alien French-ness spoke for itself.

"He looks sneaky," she told me in a stage whisper, frowning, just as we heard the toilet flush. Grandma shut her lips tight with knowing indignation as his footsteps drew closer.

"Don't you dare call him a 'frog' or I'll hit you," I warned.

Grandma was well-versed in all the derogatory terms for any culture, race, religion or ethnic group, and she used them.

"So help me, God, I'll whack you so hard your head'll spin," I hissed. I was using one of her favorite threats, and relaying it to her in a perfect imitation of herself. "I'll whack you to hell and back. I mean it." I did mean it. Of all the frail old ladies in the world, she was the one I could hit.

"What are these?" She ignored my remark, reached toward the coffee table, and fingered Philippe's Gitanes with suspicious affront.

"Try one," I suggested, turning to open a window. "It'll rock your world."

Philippe walked in. "Holly, she say zay stink to high hay-ven," he said conversationally, winking at me.

I had met him, not by smiling and flirting—which seemed to repel him or frighten him away, I later observed—but by nudging him in the ribs and impishly remarking that the smoke from his French cigarettes was rank and disgusting. "You stink to high heaven," I'd said. I'd handed him a Marlboro he'd watched me pilfer from a pack sitting unattended on the bar, and somehow he'd found me charming. In retrospect, it made sense. I later learned that Philippe was 90% imp himself and was seeking a partner in crime.

Grandma gingerly picked up the pack. Her face exaggeratingly expressed her disapproval. Nevertheless, she shrugged and took a cigarette. She lit it, puffed, mulled over its qualities, and then quickly snubbed it out.

"I like *American* cigarettes," she said pointedly, disapprovingly, glaring at Philippe.

Philippe pursed his lips in a tight "O" at the insult. He said nothing, but raised his eyebrows and rolled his eyes in a cheerful, but characteristically wicked, expression. He shrugged and made noises and hand gestures of greatly exaggerated, insincere apology. He caught my eye with a guilty expression and laughed.

Grandma looked on with haughty superiority, aghast that he should find her distaste for him and his cigarettes amusing, instead of hanging his head in shame.

I gathered my things to quickly leave before Grandma gathered her thoughts, such as they were. Then I hurried Philippe out the door.

"Why can't you date an American?" she asked later on the phone. "Why do you always have to date these sneaky foreigners who probably all have syphilis of the brain?" She paused. "*You* know how they are in Europe," she hissed. Then returning to a normal tone of voice, she continued, "I can't even understand what this one is saying." I heard her take a drag from her American cigarette. "He could be saying *anything* to you. *You* don't know."

"How in hell do you get syphilis of the brain? Do you get infected through the nose or the ear?"

"If you aren't careful, if you're crazy enough to fornicate with all these crazy foreigners, you're going to get it, too," she warned ominously. "And don't swear. All those years of me teaching you not to swear. I wasted all those years on you and your filthy mouth. Do I get any thanks? No. I get foul language."

"The word 'hell' isn't foul language; it's geography," I'd retorted. "Hell is the name of the place I hope you move to after you die in a really bad nursing home." Anything at all triggered her abuse, so I was about to hang up on her.

"Oooph. Show some respect for your elders who raised you when nobody else wanted you, you sassy brat," she'd snapped back. "You had nobody in the world but me, and I took you in and fed you because nobody else would. Nobody." She clicked her tongue. "That's because they all had sense enough to see that you were crazy. That's why your father never wanted you. That's why *nobody* ever wanted you. You ought to be locked up in a lunatic asylum because you're so crazy, just like your mother. I should have you locked up. I should have had *her* locked up—"

At that, I did hang up, without saying goodbye. Then I skipped my next biweekly Sunday visit until she called me, sweetly trying to lure me back with pot roast. I resumed my sullen visits without Philippe, who made no further effort to accompany me.

Philippe turned out to be a wonderful diversion. We discovered polka bars and spent at least one evening a week on a crowded, smoky, dance floor as we bounced to the strains of tubas and accordions and sang along to, *In Heaven There is No Beer*. On other nights, we experimented with different restaurants and explored the city's nightlife, or appeared together as a confirmed, off-limits couple in the New Town bars, where we danced, or talked and laughed with our tavern acquaintances.

I had never had so much fun with a man so consistently. We had no deep, probing conversations and each event-filled date kept me buoyant and hopeful that perhaps I wasn't going to take a nosedive and crash into another depression. I always had something to look forward to. One date after another kept rising closer to the top of my "Best date in my life" list, pushing our earlier dates further and further down on the list, and pushing the other men I'd dated off the list entirely… except Trevor, who would always remain at the very top. And in a few weeks, the amusement parks would be opening. Philippe was definitely an amusement park kind of a boyfriend, and I couldn't wait.

Best yet: I was seven weeks into a relationship, and I had done nothing to sabotage it. I hadn't become depressed, I hadn't burst into tears in a bad drunk and blabbered to him incoherently, and I hadn't flipped into a hostile, paranoid, accusatory mood and shocked him with narrowed eyes and seething, vicious remarks. He didn't get on my nerves, and I hadn't panicked in terror that he was about to abandon me. I hadn't had even one of my typical psychological meltdowns I'd always had with men I'd dated before, but which I had managed, with enormous effort, to restrain and hide from Trevor. Philippe seemed perfectly content to continue to hang around with me, which suggested that I might be cured, but I doubted it.

Cured or not, I thought I might survive the Paul McCartney and Wings tour. I had only one week to go…

Within that final week before Trevor and the concert tour were due to arrive, my gorgeous French boyfriend slept with Angie. It was Angie who confessed, describing an evening when Philippe had called to break our date with the excuse that he was caught entertaining a friend visiting from France.

"I was the friend," Angie said. "I ran into him at the Roadhouse during happy hour, and we got a little drunk…"

This was a serious, unforgivable, Girlfriend Code violation, and I couldn't overlook it. Nevertheless, her shuddering grief was touchingly disproportionate to my sense of loss over Philippe. She was usually cavalier and thoughtless about her sexual exploits. I'd never seen her look so conscience-stricken and remorseful. She forced an armload of her clothes on me as a peace offering while she sniffled, hung her head, wiped her eyes, and apologized.

I was stunned and hurt and betrayed—I would never have done this to a girlfriend, not ever—but I forced myself back into the familiarity of disappointed cynicism. I didn't hold a grudge: Philippe was one of the most beautiful men I'd ever met, and he had that wonderful French accent. I had watched women who seemed willing to take him under our table in a restaurant, right in front of me. I couldn't help but notice that every woman who saw him stared after him, then critically assessed me with a slightly curled lip and eyes filled with hatred. By dating him, I had been asking for trouble and, quite frankly, had expected it. Angie simply brought me back down to earth.

Note to self: Never date a pretty man.

The important thing was that Angie was essentially good-hearted, and I knew it. Besides, gorgeous French boyfriends were far easier to replace and of far less long-term value than girlfriends. I couldn't realistically have expected the relationship to last more than a few weeks anyway because none of my relationships, except for the one with Trevor, ever had.

I accepted Angie's apology and took the clothes. They didn't fit. Rather than give them back, I passed them along to somebody else.

Then I confronted Philippe, who lied about the night he had spent with Angie in heavily-accented, poorly articulated, panicky English interspersed with French. Not only was he a cheat, but he was a liar as well, in two languages. I would have probably forgiven him if he'd told me the truth and apologized. I knew Angie and knew that Philippe was most likely not the one who had initiated the incident. But he lied about it, both on the night it happened and afterward, and I could never forgive a lie. Lies, particularly when someone was caught red-handed, were an insult to my intelligence.

I effortlessly slipped into the Hate Phase and made no effort to coax myself out of it. How could I replace Trevor with someone like Philippe? I could not. I had raised my standards and would never compromise them.

His English was limited, but Philippe understood, "Don't call me anymore." Except that he still called me. I hung up the phone. He then had his English-speaking co-workers call me from his office and try to mediate with me on his behalf. "Hi, I'm (Jean, Doug, Chris, Jim, Beverly), a friend of Philippe's. He's really sorry, Holly. He's really, really sorry. The poor guy's going crazy here. Would you *please* see him or talk to him? Please?"

I told them all to tell Philippe to please stop all this and just leave me alone. "Tell him '*manger la merde*,'" I said to Beverly, the last one to call.

Philippe, listening on the extension, broke in with, "*Non, mon chéri!*"

"Did I say that right?" I asked sarcastically. Then I slammed down the phone. I couldn't deal with drama, lies, or frantic promises I was reasonably certain he would break. There were only days to go, and I was now consumed with seeing Trevor. That was all that concerned me right now.

"If it's any consolation to you at all," Karen told me over the phone a few days after his last phone call, "Philippe hates Angie's guts. We ran into him last night at the Fat Black Pussycat, and he started screaming at her in French, waving his arms and everything. He didn't care who heard him. Then he walked out. I don't know what he said, but it wasn't nice. Then she just went home, so the evening was a total bust."

I sniffed in disgust.

207

"You know what I think?" She changed her mind and caught herself. "Never mind. It's crazy."

"What?"

"Nothing," Karen said sharply.

"You can't do that. You can't start to tell me something, and then stop like that."

"It's crazy though. It's nothing." I heard her take a drag on her cigarette.

"Now you *have* to tell me."

Karen sighed again, this time uncomfortably. She spoke, but hesitantly and with pauses between the words.

"It's... just this thing... I saw her do... *once*. It's nothing."

"What?" I twisted the phone cord and listened.

Karen spoke quickly, as if she wanted to race to get all the words out before she changed her mind.

"She looked at you one time when you didn't see. It was this look. She had this look on her face."

"She hates me, right? She hates me. That's what this is all about." Tricked again. I had been tricked again into thinking I had a friend. How many years? Three. I'd been fooled for three years. I bit a cuticle and spit it out.

"*No!* No, that's not it. It was a different kind of look." Karen wrestled with herself while I twisted the phone cord. Then she continued, "She was looking at you... I don't know. She was looking at you like she had a crush on you or something."

"What?"

"It was probably just my imagination. It was nothing..." Karen cleared her throat and laughed a little.

I didn't breathe for a minute while the words sunk in.

"No," I finally said. "If it was only one time, there was probably a guy behind me, and she was looking at him—"

"Or twice." Karen broke in emphatically, with meaning. "Maybe twice."

"*Two* guys..."

I was shaking my head and hitting it with my fist. Then I turned and banged my head rhythmically against the wall.

Karen paused, then finally burst out with it. "It's all the time, Holly! They've got a pool going at Flanagan's, betting on whether or not she'll get you into bed. I wanted to tell you that for a long time, but I couldn't bring myself to do it."

"People are placing *bets*?"

How naïve and stupid was I? I wondered. How did I miss this? I was officially a pathetic loser with no self-respect. I hadn't even recognized that my friend was only my friend because she wanted to have sex with me. Even girls were like men where I was concerned.

I started thinking back to the times she'd answered her door naked, or stripped down to change her clothes in front of me, or the time she threw her panties in my face... the way she always pressed her breasts up against my arm when she leaned over to tell me something... How stupid was I? Oh, my God... I was going to die of shame and embarrassment. How did I not see this? How did I go for three years and not figure this out, believing I had a friend... believing she was my friend because she *liked* me?

"Angie sleeps with about five or six different guys a week. She likes *men*."

"Didn't that ever strike you as a little over the top? What's she trying to prove? Do you ever see her go out with the same guy twice? No. Maybe she thinks she'll hit the one who finally scratches the itch, but he's not out there." Karen stopped herself. "I should never have said anything."

"No. You can't unsay all this. You said it."

"I just had this theory, is all."

"What theory?" After a lengthy pause, I snapped at her. "Tell me!"

"Okay." I heard her light another cigarette. "When you sleep with your friend's boyfriend, you lose both the guy and your friend, and they both hate you. Or the friend does, at least. You're absolutely guaranteed to lose your friend. If you keep the guy, you now have a boyfriend you know cheats on his girlfriend, so he'll probably do it to you." She paused. "Are you still there?"

"Yeah. I'm here."

"So on top of all this, you have to live with the knowledge that you're a horrible person because you did this to your friend. So what are you thinking, really, when you do it?" She paused to give me an opportunity to reply, but I stayed silent. "I'm trying to put myself into Angie's head. Philippe is really cute, but the rest of us had it under control, right? And there are hundreds of other guys. Angie finds them everywhere, every day. It isn't like she's desperate. Plus she doesn't go after people's boyfriends. Have you ever known her to do that?" I had to admit, I hadn't. "So this was something else."

209

"Angie has a serious problem with self-restraint. Have you never noticed?" I asked.

"Does she? Hmm?" Karen asked pointedly. "I personally think she wanted to sleep with *your* boyfriend. *Holly's* boyfriend."

"Yes, I know that," I snapped bitterly.

"I kept seeing her look at you that way, and it got me to thinking, is all. He was the closest thing to you that she could get. I just thought that she might have slept with Philippe because she couldn't have you." Karen let me have a moment to think about it. "So do you get it?" Karen paused, but I didn't answer her so she continued. "She wasn't doing your boyfriend. She was having sex with *you*. By proxy. She was using Philippe to do it because you kept ignoring her signals."

I slid to the floor and still said nothing.

I heard her click her tongue with regret and take in a deep breath. Having voiced her opinion, Karen was anxiously trying to summon it back. "It's just stupid. I'm sorry."

My hands started to shake as I gathered my thoughts. After a few moments of silence, I finally spoke. "If that were true, she would have slept with Trevor, too, don't you think?" I scoffed, but I was suddenly frightened. "And that's impossible. He would never sleep with Angie in a million years. He hates her."

"I know. I'm just really stupid. It was just this twisted, brainless theory of mine. You know me. I'm just an idiot."

"Trevor would never. Not ever."

"Absolutely. He just wouldn't. Not ever. Not even if he liked her. *I* know that, and *you* know that." Karen paused. "Why does Trevor hate Angie so much? When exactly did it start?"

I thought back. "He helped her move, and she made him pack her stuff, too. She only had three boxes, so he had to keep running back and forth, up and down three flights of stairs, packing and unpacking. He thinks she's an idiot." As I spoke, I began to realize that Trevor's hatred was a little extreme, considering the circumstances.

"He helped her move, but you weren't there, right? Were they alone?"

"Well, yeah, but he didn't stay. He left in the middle of it." It wasn't like Trevor to let someone down in the middle of a job he'd promised to do.

"Hmmm." Karen didn't say anything more.

"Do you think she slept with him?" My voice was soft, plaintive, and a little shaky. I was so confused…

210

"No! Never!" Karen said with conviction and reassurance. "He would never sleep with Angie in a million years. Not ever."

"I know it. He would never—God! Oh, my God!" I folded over, and twisting the phone chord around my neck, pressed my chest into my lap. "Oh, my God!"

"I know I'm wrong. I'm totally wrong. I should never have said anything."

"Karen?" I sat up again. My eyes were welling up.

"What?"

I choked back a sob. "Tell me the truth. Do you want to have sex with me, too? Is that why you're friends with me?" My voice slid into a squeak.

Karen snorted. "Gawd no! Not unless you suddenly become English and grow a dick!" she shouted and laughed. Then she caught herself and spoke gently, "No, honey, no. I don't want to have sex with you. I'm just your friend."

"Really?"

"Really and truly."

"Thank you," I said. And then I burst into tears.

I put Angie out of my mind as much as possible, avoided her as much as possible, and demurred several times when she tried to make plans with me. I had too much to deal with. All my preparation to sail through Trevor's visit had been sabotaged, and I was left dealing with shock and trauma I couldn't possibly have anticipated. It was all because of Angie. I no longer had a friend. Soon I would no longer have Trevor, and I'd have very little to fall back on... I tried to grasp it all, but couldn't. I had to sink into it slowly, bit by bit, but had no time for slowly sinking.

I no longer had a boyfriend. I missed Philippe as much as I hated him, and I frequently thought about calling him, but I knew I never would. There was no point in going back to him because I'd never be able to see him the same way again.

Primarily, though, I didn't call Philippe because the incident made me realize it was actually better that I be alone when Trevor came. I didn't know how I was going to react, and I couldn't have explained what I was going through to a new boyfriend, particularly one who didn't understand English very well. I also had a feeling that when the tour left town, I would be more in the mood for days in bed, un-showered and staring, than for polkas, tubas and beer.

Chapter 28

"**H**ave you ever considered that you might be very rigid? I hear you being judgmental about everyone else's conduct, and I see you being almost puritanical when it comes to your own behavior. You see things in black and white so much of the time." Dr. Silverman had listened to my description of the Philippe fiasco and was questioning my decision to sever ties with both Angie and Philippe.

"This 'Code' you always talk about. Is it really necessary? There are so many variations to human nature. People make mistakes. Can you try to imagine yourself being more tolerant of other people, and less strict in your own actions? I sometimes think you carry that 'Code' around with you like a ball and chain."

I stared at him and tears welled up in my eyes. I felt as if he were attacking and judging me.

"If you try being a little easier on other people, you might find yourself feeling more forgiving toward yourself."

I felt cornered and defensive. I felt threatened. "I *have* to do it this way. I can control just this one thing. Being good is a *choice*. I just choose and follow through."

"I see. Go on."

"But I can't control whether or not to be nice. I'd like to be a nice person, but I can't because things just always get away from me. People get on my nerves, and I snap at them, or I pick fights with them, or I hate them because my brain is going zzzzztttt. I have no control over any of that that."

He nodded and jotted something down in his notes.

I was picking at my cuticles again. "My grandmother never taught me the rules, so I had to figure them out myself. Grandma always told me I was bad, and I'm going to hell. I'm just trying to be good. The Code helps me figure out how. So do my lists." I was getting deeply unnerved and upset, for some reason. This conversation was triggering something far deeper than I'd ever probed before. I burst into tears. Then it spilled.

"I'm just trying to be a good girl because I can't be a nice one," I sobbed. "I just want to be a good girl." I choked and pressed the edge of my sleeve into my eyes. I felt like I was four years old again. I rubbed the back of my hand under my nose. I wrapped my arms around myself and shook. My teeth were chattering.

For the first time in the years I had been seeing him, Dr. Silverman seemed to really connect with me. I saw what appeared to be compassion in his eyes, and I noticed his lips parting slightly. It was as though he finally understood me, and I had touched him somehow. He nodded without saying anything.

"Maybe if I'm a really good girl, they'll want me." I barely whispered it. Where had that come from? Why was I so upset? Then, in my head, I heard my mother saying, "Always be a good girl" and knew I'd hit the source. I smeared the tears off my cheeks with my hands, ignoring the box of tissues on the table. Then I looked down into my lap.

"Holly, you *are* good. You were *always* good. Your grandmother lied to you. Don't listen."

His voice didn't sound like a shrink's voice. It sounded like a hug. It sounded like a caring father's voice, and it hit me somehow, deep down. "You're a wonderful girl. I'd be very proud if you were my daughter."

For the first time I almost believed someone could be proud of me. I looked up. "Really?" I asked.

"Yeah," he said, and handed me the box of tissues. I accepted a tissue and wiped my eyes.

Chapter 29

The dinners stopped, my extra pounds would soon drop off, and I felt myself begin to slip into depression again. So now there were none, and I had no safety net.

There was no hope, Trevor had written, of me going backstage for this concert. Absolutely no one was permitted back there. "I'll try to get you a pair of tickets," he wrote. "I may not be able to get them, so no promises, but I'll do my best. Just be forewarned that it doesn't look good."

There were still no promises, no phone calls, and no tickets a week before the tour reached Chicago. Nevertheless, I held a drawing at work to determine who would accompany me to the concert, which had sold out less than two hours after tickets went on sale weeks earlier. The winner was Denise, who climbed up onto her desk strewing paperclips like confetti and screaming with her arms outstretched.

Finally the call came on Sunday. When I heard Trevor's voice, I burst into tears.

Trevor instructed me to meet him that evening at a bar called Bananas on Sheridan Road, where the band would be hosting a party at midnight. I was to come alone and tell no one about this party, he warned me. No one. It was private.

It seemed absurd that I should be an invited guest to a private party hosted by Paul McCartney and Wings. What does one wear to a party hosted by Paul McCartney and Wings? It was merely a rhetorical question because I would attend wearing black. No one would notice my shoes in a crowded, darkened nightclub, so the scuffed platform sandals I chose were fine. Everything was fine because a Paul McCartney party was so surreal and abstract that nothing about it actually mattered in a literal sense. No one would even see me at a party hosted by Paul McCartney because all eyes would be on him. I could wear a clown suit, and I would be perfectly fine. Realizing this, I felt reassured and confident as I chose between outfits that were all several years old. I pulled on a black leotard and a pair of black slacks and tied a scarf around my neck, then went by bus to the nightclub.

Bananas was crammed with people in every stage of jittery excitement. Secrecy must not have really been mandatory, or else the Bananas Sunday-after-midnight regulars had all shown up unaware and were now calling friends who arrived in a steady stream. This was *not* a private party; it was a bar packed full. The hum was high but steady, and the crowd was concentrated near the door, which clearly indicated Paul McCartney was not in the building. The rest of the band had arrived, however, and were socializing with the people throughout the club or playing foosball with fans in the back. People stared around themselves in search of rock stars and hovered near the front, waiting for Paul McCartney's entrance with unabashed excitement. No one even pretended to be coolly indifferent.

I couldn't find Trevor. Hardly looking anywhere else except to quickly glance around the room at times to make certain I hadn't missed him, I watched the door. I ordered a drink and continued to stare at the door, taut with excitement because Trevor was coming and praying I wouldn't cry.

An hour and two drinks later, neither Paul McCartney nor Trevor had arrived. I began to panic. I scanned the room more carefully and urgently than before. I studied the crowd slowly and lingeringly, making certain I didn't miss anyone. I finally noticed two eyes staring at me, boring holes into me from the shadows behind a column in a booth against the far wall. They were Trevor's.

I gasped, pushed my way through the crowd, hurled myself into the booth, flung my arms around his neck and kissed him. He buried his face in my hair and didn't come up for air for an unusually long time. He didn't even say hello.

"How long have you been here?" I asked, scolding, linking my arm through his and leaning against him. He clearly had seen me. Why had he not come up to me?

"I've been here for a while." His voice was quiet. "I saw you come in."

His eyes were different. I didn't need an explanation, and I was not going to cry. I was too frightened to cry anyway.

215

"Why didn't you come get me?" Oh, my God. I covered my mouth with my hand. He had squandered an hour I could have spent with him. Time was running out, and he had robbed me of an hour... I felt the tears welling up, but pushed them back.

He looked down at his glass and shrugged, then looked back over at me with that odd expression. "I wanted to watch you for a bit," he said simply. He gave me a very slight smile that lasted only an instant before he looked away. He fingered his beer glass and stared into it.

I squeezed his arm. He patted my hand. I took his hand in both of mine, entwined all of my fingers through his, and pulled it onto my lap for safekeeping. He said nothing, but looked up at me in a few moments with that intent, searching look before turning away again.

"You're so quiet." I brushed a wisp of hair off his face and kissed his cheek. He was going to make me cry, and I was determined not to. "Aren't you happy to see me?"

He started to say something, then replaced the words with a tight smile and a shrug. He nodded. He looked back into his beer.

"I cut my hair," I offered conversationally.

Trevor obligingly looked at my hair and reached up to touch it, letting his fingers follow the line of my hair as it used to be, not as it was.

"It's my Supertramp Girlfriend Mushroom Cut. Now I look just like Supertramp's girlfriends. Don't you think?"

Trevor chuckled a little but didn't say anything.

"Do you like it?"

"It's very elegant," he said, quietly stroking it, adjusting the memory in his hand to its new length. Abruptly, he dropped the hand and took a final swallow from his glass. "Come on, then. Let's have a look around." He motioned for me to get up, and slid out of the booth after me.

"Is Paul McCartney really coming?"

"No. His little girls needed to be put to bed, didn't they? He isn't much for parties like this anyway. The rest of the band are here, though." He pointed them out to me. "That should be enough to keep the panting hordes from rioting."

He took my hand and led me over to what was normally the dance floor. It was now a roped-off area that separated the press, the photographers, the band, and its entourage from the local bar-going riff-raff. It was guarded by bouncers and uniformed security, who glanced at Trevor's pass and waved us through.

"Then why does everyone think he's coming?"

"Because there's always a chance that he will." Trevor gave a wry grin. "But he won't."

Trevor picked up two paper plates from the end of a buffet table and peered at the picked-over leavings, which included the usual cold-cuts, stale cocktail rye bread squares spilling out of torn cellophane packaging, raw vegetables turning limp on a round cardboard tray, and cheese cubes beginning to dry and turn dark. Some beers floated in melted ice in a metal tub on the floor. He grabbed two and handed me one.

"Are you hungry?"

I nodded. He loaded both plates with uninspired-looking food, while I looked behind me at the people pressing up against the ropes. One of these was holding up twenty dollars, now thirty, now forty to a security guard in hopes of being allowed inside; he wasn't. These people all watched the lucky two or three dozen of us enviously and studied us intently, wondering who we were and why we were important enough to warrant admission into the most hallowed square footage in the building. Some of them must have wondered if my old and sadly-worn outfit was somehow an odd form of *chic*. The clown costume theory hadn't worked for me on this occasion. Cameras flashed.

Trevor and I sat side-by-side in metal folding chairs at a long aluminum table covered with a torn tissue tablecloth that was damp from spills. We chewed in silence, on display for the staring people pressing up against the ropes. He looked over at me, smiled, and made an effort to behave normally.

"Eat your vegetables, Holly. There's my good girl."

He touched my lips with a carrot slice and popped it into my mouth. Then he patted my mouth with a paper napkin and wrinkled his nose at me. I hugged him around the waist. He grinned, pulled me toward him with an arm around my neck, and kissed the top of my head.

A photographer seated on the other side of the table was surreptitiously shooting pictures of us, perhaps mistaking us for people of importance and prestige as we gnawed our little squares of rye bread, recording our time together with photographs I would yearn for but would never, ever see.

Charles wandered over looking uncharacteristically outgoing, even almost giddy, with a very beautiful, American redhead on his arm. He held up his girlfriend's hand to show me her engagement ring and introduce her to me.

"Pamela's agreed to take me on," Charles said, clearly overjoyed. His girlfriend beamed and pressed up against him coquettishly.

"Isn't she lovely?" Trevor asked. "Lucky man, our Charles. He's a very lucky man."

"I'm really happy for you. Congratulations," I told the couple, looking from one to the other, smiling.

Gratified, pleased, and proud, Charles and his beautiful fiancée wandered off to hold up the hand with the ring and tell somebody else.

Trevor studied Charles and Pamela as they meandered through the roped-in area from one cluster of people to the next, ringed hand held aloft and glinting. His eyes followed them thoughtfully for several minutes. I watched him watching them, and said nothing. Then Trevor looked back at me with a face that was expressionless and unreadable.

"Well, then. Dinner was lovely."

"And glamorous."

"Very glamorous, indeed. May I escort you home?"

The bus ride was relatively short. Holding hands, we took the familiar walk up my street, went up the stairs and through the hallway together as we'd always done, and greeted Pansy who seemed in danger of a seizure, she was so excited to see Trevor again.

We made tea and took our mugs to my bed where we sat together, our backs to the wall, leaning into each other shoulder-to-shoulder. Trevor seemed to be studying everything in the room intently, as though he wanted to sear it into his memory. He nervously fingered his mug.

We spoke about virtually nothing. I had questions about Paul McCartney and the tour—Trevor now had the most exciting job in the world—but each time I asked anything, Trevor shrugged and said, "They're just another group of rock stars. It's just another gig. It's not that different." Or, "I don't commiserate with them, really. I do my job, and they do theirs."

There were long silences between efforts at conversation, and I did most of the talking. I asked questions that he answered with one or two words before he drifted into preoccupied silence once again.

So I told him a little about what I'd been up to, leaving out any reference to gorgeous French boyfriends with whom my friend Angie was sleeping. He looked distracted and withdrawn, but tried to appear interested in the day-to-day goings-on in my apartment building and neighborhood, and at my job, chuckling or expressing sympathy when it was appropriate.

Finally, he interrupted me mid-story as I described an incident at work. He squeezed my arm and cleared his throat.

"Holly... I'm getting married." He whispered it quickly and softly. His eyes wouldn't quite meet mine.

There it was. He had said it. I stiffened and looked down at my hands but didn't cry because I couldn't. Fear and trepidation had frozen the tears all evening. Now those tears were replaced by shock I had thoroughly prepared myself for, for months, but still had not expected to this degree. It took my breath away.

"To Beth?" I asked quietly, still looking down. My voice and my hands shook just a little.

"Yes. She's in England now, staying with my parents. We're marrying at the end of the tour."

Staying with his parents in England? How odd, I thought. Why wasn't she with him, like Pamela was with Charles?

Then I understood. Beth was in England because of me. Trevor had created a Beth-free space so that he could break the news in person and say goodbye. It was respectful, chivalrous, and sensitive, very much like Trevor. He also would not want Beth to actually see him interacting with me, and thereby unquestioningly know how he felt about me and possibly be haunted by it. He was being chivalrous and sensitive to her as well.

Had I been Beth, though, I would have been worried, knowing he was with me again. Did she not realize how much he loved me? Then I thought, of course she knew, because Trevor would have told her. So why was she allowing him to see me like this? If I had been her, I would have felt threatened and frantic.

No, on second thought, I would not. I would trust Trevor beyond reason. He did not take his commitments lightly, nor did he take love and honor lightly. He was as loyal as they came. Had I been Beth, I would have freely given him this because it would crucify him to have to break the news to me brutally, with a fiancée watching or waiting nearby. He could not have endured hurting me—hurting her as well—more than he had to.

Was that what Beth had done? Freely given him this? My intuition told me that she had. If so, it reassured me that she understood him and loved him, and that he really would be fine with her. Without me. I owed both Trevor and Beth my gratitude for this.

219

Beth must be readying herself for the flight that would carry her to the next city on the tour, where she would join Trevor, holding up a ringed hand and moving with him from one cluster of people to the next. No doubt she and Trevor would be together permanently by the end of the week. I knew this, but I didn't ask him to confirm their plans. Asking anything about his life now seemed… improper, somehow, like prying. Suddenly, my dearest and most cherished friend's personal life was none of my business.

"Then Beth was still waiting for you. I knew she would be."

He looked over at me with a puzzled frown and cocked his head.

"I'm all right," I said in a soft, soothing, steady, reassuring voice that contained no self-pity or reproach. I was so proud of myself for letting him go without a scene; I was offering him a clean break and not making him feel guilty or think that I was trying to pull him away from Beth. I squeezed his hand tightly. "I'm okay. I *am*. I'm going to be fine. And you're going to be happy."

He looked away. Then he looked back.

"I think it turned out for the best. I think you're doing the right thing." My voice trailed away. I looked down again, biting my lip, tightly holding my hands around my mug. The tea in the mug rippled slightly.

Then I shrugged. It was a shrug relinquishing my control over the situation. I was acknowledging that I had always been in the Number Two spot and couldn't ever have changed that. However, in retrospect, sorting through things I didn't quite notice at the time because I was preoccupied with trying to remain controlled, I wondered if Trevor interpreted the shrug differently.

He stared, bewildered and confused. He seemed introspective and even a little upset. His lips parted slightly, but he said nothing.

Trevor continued to stare at me, then started to say something, but stopped. The look in his eyes was helpless and angry, even wild for an instant. He pressed the heel of his hand to his temple and turned away. Then he ran his fingers and thumb down over his eyes and took in a long breath.

He asked, "Do you?" in a biting way that did not invite a reply. If I hadn't known him better, I might have thought he was being sarcastic.

"Yeah," I whispered.

His look was intense and probing, and it was masking something—I couldn't quite read it. Then the expression softened as he nodded and smiled, just a little ruefully, widening his eyes for a second as if he were processing something unexpected. We sat in silence again for a few minutes, staring into our mugs. It was Trevor who spoke first.

"I want us to make love." His voice wasn't passionate; it was flat and emotionless, and a little distant.

"I can't. You're getting married."

"*Please*," he said more forcefully, with a tinge of pleading.

I sat and thought for a moment. "Would you rather be with her or with me?"

He didn't hesitate. "With her."

I took a sharp intake of breath. It took me a moment to move past the sting of hearing it and to fully absorb what he had just said. At first I was hurt, realizing I had no right to be. Then I nodded, feeling a curiously calming sense of relief. He wanted to be with her, not me. I had finally done something right.

As for Trevor, he had just knowingly or unknowingly given me a gift. Whether he said them out of simple honesty, out of his strong code of loyalty, out of insightful kindness or spiteful unkindness, he had, with those two words, just absolved me of all doubt, uncertainty, guilt, and regret for the entire rest of my life.

Now I was overcome by a feeling of mind-numbing desolation. My sadness was only for me, though, and I was used to being sad. Trevor, I knew, would be fine. I pulled my knees into my chest and wrapped my arms around them in the closest approximation of the fetal position that one could assume while sitting upright on a bed.

"I can't. Not even to say goodbye. It's too much."

I buried my face in my knees and arms. I couldn't make love to him. He wanted to be with her, not me, so making love to him would be like a death. Even if he'd said he wanted me more, he was Beth's, not mine, and I supposed that he always had been. But still, I didn't cry. Grief had once again taken me beyond tears.

He pressed his fingers to his eyelids for just a second, then nodded and placed his mug on the nightstand. He gently pried my mug from my hand and placed it there as well. He turned off the lamp. He spoke without resentment or bitterness into the darkness: "Fair enough, then."

We lay together, fully clothed, side-by-side, and did not make love. We also did not sleep for hours. I knew from his breathing that he was awake, stifling sobs. I lay dry-eyed in his arms as he shuddered and gasped, and could do nothing but mourn while the pain and loss washed over me in waves.

We each suffered alone. There was nothing either of us could do to comfort the other because we were respectfully pretending we thought the other was asleep. Any acknowledgement of the other's pain would be unwelcome and intrusive. Toward dawn, we both slept for a short time, exhausted.

When the alarm went off, we silently replayed our old morning routine, sipping cups of tea and taking turns in the shower. We spoke little as we walked Pansy around the block together.

Later, we walked to the corner and hugged tightly as my bus pulled up to the curb. Then we let go.

"I'll call you later to let you know if I was able to get tickets," he said.

I smiled and nodded, then climbed the steps to the bus that headed north to the Howard station, where I would catch the Skokie Swift. The door slid shut behind me.

Trevor ran across the street to the stop for the bus that headed downtown, where he would meet up with the other roadies at the Sheraton Hotel and ride together with them to the Stadium tonight. As the light changed and my bus pulled away, I turned my head to look at him through the window, standing at the bus stop with his hands in his pockets, his shoulders slumped, and his chin pointed upward, eyes closed. Then I lost sight of him.

True to his word, he called later that day to tell me he'd gotten me two tickets for Wednesday's performance. It was a quick conversation; he had only stolen a minute to call from a payphone backstage. He said a hurried goodbye and hung up.

Wednesday's concert was the final performance of three. From Monday until then, I worked days while Trevor worked nights. There was no reason for him to come home to me, and no reason for him to call, so we wouldn't see each other or speak again until the concert. I moved through the days mechanically and on little sleep—insomnia had replaced oversleeping—trying to wade through my emotional banquet and make sense of what I felt, feeling almost ashamed of my thrill at having tickets and getting to see Paul McCartney. It was odd to be looking forward to the last time I would ever see Trevor. When the concert was over, the full impact was going to hit me, I knew. I repeatedly dealt with the dread by pushing it out of my mind. Then it would come back again, mostly to awaken me with a jolt in the middle of the night.

I didn't know what to bring Trevor to say, "Goodbye," and "Thank you." If I gave him a gift, he would discard it or give it away out of loyalty to Beth. I thought of a box of candy or a bottle of wine, but there was no nearby store that I knew of that sold candy gift boxes, and security would never let me past the door with a bottle. There was, however, a florist. I bought a bouquet of daisies wrapped in yellow paper and carried it with me to the concert hall.

Denise and I stood in front of the Stadium will-call window while the crowd jostled and pressed into lines around us.

"Holly Salvino," I told the woman behind the window, wincing in anticipation of disappointing seats in the upper balcony. She reached into a drawer and pulled out an envelope with my name written on it in Trevor's handwriting. She slid it through the window.

"Oh, my God," Denise and I said in unison. I grabbed the envelope and tore it open.

"Where are our seats?" Denise squealed into my ear. "Open it! Where are they?"

I stared at the tickets. "Tenth row middle. He got us tenth row middle."

"Holy shit," Denise breathed, awestruck. She jumped up and spun around. "Wow!" She grabbed my arm again and pulled me through the door.

"He paid in blood for these tickets," I moaned as she dragged me through the crowd. "I love him so much."

"I love him, too," Denise agreed. "God knows."

We found our seats. As Denise settled into hers, she looked around with a haughty half-smile, scanning the crowd behind her to see if anyone happened to notice her sitting in a tenth-row-middle seat at a Paul McCartney and Wings concert. I carried Trevor's daisies to the side of the stage and waved a roadie over. He went backstage to fetch Trevor, who appeared in seconds.

"Hi," I said, handing him the bouquet. He looked at it quizzically. What on earth would he do with flowers? But then, what on earth would he do with anything I could have given him now?

He accepted the bouquet with a nod.

"Thank you for everything." Did he understand the degree to which I meant that, and all that it encompassed?

"It's quite all right," he said, darting an anxious glance over his shoulder. He had to go. "My pleasure. Really."

Then, a look I recognized crossed his face: He'd left already. I was his past, and he wouldn't look back again. He was feet forward, pointing toward Beth. The door was closing on me even as I stood there.

223

"Duty calls," he said. "Take care of yourself and be good." With a quick salute, he backed away. "Rock and roll!" he called out. Then he turned and disappeared.

I saw Trevor's daisies again. Paul McCartney carried them onto the stage—they were clearly recognizable by the bright yellow paper—then gallantly presented them to Linda McCartney, who placed them on her piano where they remained throughout the show. At the end of the evening, Linda stood up and raised the bouquet aloft. With a swoop and a shout, she hurled it up and into the audience.

I covered my mouth with my hands. How amazing! This was a once-in-a-lifetime thing I couldn't let pass, I thought. If I could say it before the flowers landed, it would all come true.

"Please let Trevor be happy," I whispered quickly. I had made the sacrifice. I needed it to be *for* something.

The audience had been on its feet during most of the show. At some point, we had climbed onto our seats, trying to see around girls sitting atop shoulders in front of us. Deafening screams and cheering rang in my ears as laser lights swirled above me on the ceiling, and the bouquet soared over the crowd in a high arc. It fell toward dozens of reaching, flailing arms.

I shouted into the noise as an afterthought: "And me, too! Me, too!"

I said it in time.

Epilogue

July 25, 1978

Dear Trevor,

I hope everything is going well with you. I know it is. I know everything is wonderful because Karen just called and told me she ran into someone at a concert the other day who said you were in Australia, and that your wife had a baby… boy? Or girl? The person she talked to wasn't sure about any of the details. I am so thrilled and excited for you, but I wish I'd gotten more information.

Congratulations! You'll be such a wonderful daddy, Trevor. Your baby is so lucky! All the blessings and happiness in the world!

She said that Charles and his wife *also* had a baby! Does he still tour? Have you seen each other? Who is he working for these days? It's funny to imagine the two of you with baby carriages!

Karen is fine, still the same, though I don't see her as much since I stopped going to concerts. She's going back to England in October. She's got her fingers crossed that it will stick this time.

Angie got another job and so did I, so we pretty much lost touch since the last time I talked to you.

I moved to a better apartment. No lovely Angelique, and no CB radios. There are no cockroaches, either. It's really nice.

Pansy died two weeks ago. I've been crying ever since. I even sleep with her collar. Isn't that stupid? I don't know why I do these things. I'm still crying, as you can see. It's all over this letter. She was my closest family, so I haven't been taking it very well. I had to tell you though because nobody else would understand.

Well, that's about all. I just thought I would tell you I'd heard about the baby and how *very* happy I am for you.

Love, Holly

August 11, 1980

Dear Trevor,

I couldn't believe it when Torc went on a comeback tour! (Didn't they just break up?) Oh, my God! So I had to go to the concert last night and see if I could talk to somebody who knew what you were up to these days.

Our dear Angus. His new girlfriend half-carried him off the stage. I raised my beer to him when he passed, and he kind of squinted at me, but he didn't say hello. I'm sorry to say his voice is pretty much gone. He wasn't hitting the notes, and twice his voice just plain cracked. He was also looking pretty ragged, and his color wasn't good. My guess is that he isn't very healthy. I'm kind of worried about him. I know I laugh at him, but I really do love him. (You know that, right?)

I cornered Lucas, and he remembered me and was really nice. We hung out in the dressing room for a little bit, talking about you and Charles. He's totally hopeless with details though. He said you had two more children, but had no idea when, or whether they were boys or girls, much less their names. He thought they were twins but wasn't sure. Then he was pretty sure they were twins. Then he wasn't. He said Nancy would know, but she was home with the kids and hadn't come on the tour. I wanted to whack him for not knowing. He did say you were still in Australia and doing... something, but he couldn't remember what. I hope you're doing well, whatever it is!

John Collier remembered me too. We went out for a late dinner and caught up.

All that was missing was you and Charles.

Love, Holly

April 26, 1986

Dear Trevor,

It's your birthday!!! Just so you know, I think of you every single year on April 26 and send you happy birthday thoughts. Can you really be 37???? (Can I really be 32????) Happy birthday, and all the best to you!

I'm sure the news reached you that we got married two years ago. It all just kind of happened, and here we are.

Being married is still a little weird for me. I never could see myself actually married, but I'm okay. Really good, in fact. It turns out I handle being married pretty well. I was terrified for no reason.

John is a session musician now and writing songs for other bands because he doesn't want to tour anymore. He says he's getting too old for it (and so am I!). He's quite a homebody, actually. He built a darkroom, which he loves, and develops all the pictures we take. Mostly baby pictures these days. That's one of his favorite things to do. He's teaching me photography, and I'm really getting into it!

I was thinking that maybe I'd finally go to school, now that we're so staid and settled. It's tough to study with a baby, though, so I may have to wait for that. For now, I'm just taking non-credit classes in art. It's very fun! John helps me a lot and often joins me, painting. We have a room with two easels and a very beautiful view, so we paint dueling landscapes. (Sometimes mine is better, and sometimes his is, but he always says that mine is.) We have a huge house, and my plan is to eventually cover every wall with our artwork and his photographs!

We had the baby last year. He's the most gorgeous thing you've ever seen (aside from your own children – I know now that you have two boys and a girl!). He's walking now, so I'm certain he's a genius. John is over the moon with being a father. That's the main reason he mostly stays at home. He wants to change diapers (I mean "nappies") and be on the receiving end of hurled strained carrots and green beans and experience everything.

Karen lives in London, not far away, so we get to visit! She's married now. He's not in the music business at all, but he's perfect for her, and she's so happy! They have a daughter, Daphne.

John and I took a drive to Sussex the other day – "a retrospective tour," he called it. He still worries about what you think of us being married. It doesn't matter that you were already married when we first got together, and it doesn't matter that John and I have been together for far longer than you and I ever were. We both had a serious crisis over you at the start of our relationship because we knew you'd hear about us through the grapevine, and we didn't know how you might take it. You know how sensitive John is about everything, and how much he values his friends, so he went through a great deal of angst and self-reproach. He's as bad as I am about that.

He wrote to you right away so he could tell you before you heard it from someone else. Did you get that letter? Or any of the others? We never knew because you never answered. But he kept trying. Each time you didn't answer, it made it worse for him and threw him into an introspective funk. We both have had residual guilt and sorrow for the past six years because we need your blessing and your friendship. We do.

The thing is, we knew immediately that we couldn't be with anyone else, and we couldn't be apart, so not being together was never an option for us. I know how that probably sounds to you, and I'm biting my lip while I write it, but I'm just explaining what happened. I wouldn't go on tour with him at first – I had no vacation time; it wasn't practical – but after getting three consecutive five-hour post-concert phone calls that lasted till 4 or 5 a.m., beginning with one only hours after he left me, I agreed to fly to him, and I finished out the tour. Afterward he helped me pack up my apartment, and he took me to England. We've been together ever since.

I need you to know that I quit my job to follow him. That's how serious it was, and how certain I was that we were supposed to be together. I'm telling you this because we both need for you to understand that we didn't come together lightly, at your expense. There was never anything between us before 1980. My ending up with him was not a reflection of my feelings for you. He did not choose me because he is a disloyal friend, or to take a stab at you.

We came together because we had to, and we did it long after you had married and moved on. Our being together was apparently all in the scheme of things, because everything happened the way it had to in order for John to identify me as his "one." If life hadn't happened just exactly the way it did, he would never have given me a second glance. He can tell you a story about witches sometime that will explain it all. And I immediately knew and understood that he was right.

Anyway, last week he took me to Sussex and gave me the Grand Tour of his youth. He showed me the house he grew up in, and yours as well, the house that I'd sent hundreds of letters to. He showed me where you all hung out as teenagers, your school, and the field where you all played soccer (I mean football.). He talked and talked. Being back there opened the floodgates, and he didn't stop talking until he was hoarse and exhausted and completely drained.

The song, "Beyond My Reach" has always haunted him. He wonders if you never wrote back to him on account of it. He says he doesn't blame you. He never intended to record it, but Chester decided they had to replace a track on the album, and when he was poking through John's sheet music, he found that song. He picked it because he wanted to see if they could widen their market to a different type of audience by releasing it as a single. Angus and Geoff sided with Chester because they thought the whole thing was really, really funny. John argued (pleaded, really) but he was outnumbered. John never knew how to broach the subject with you to apologize. He said that afterward he was so humiliated that he couldn't look either one of us in the eye, much less talk to you about it.

No one was ever supposed to know about that song. John writes music the way I used to keep a diary, and the song was a private diary entry. After I moved in with him, he showed me a folder of "Molly" songs he'd written around that time. He'd left the folder out, and Chester found it.

I remember thinking he was snubbing me after "All Torc'd Up" was released, because of the way he acted. Did you, too? That's not what it was, though. He was mortified.

He takes full responsibility for the photo in the album insert, though. He just wanted it there because Angus stole his song. He's sorry about that, too.

The day was very intense for him, as if he were purging demons. At times he almost wept. But afterward he seemed very calm and serene, as if he'd gotten it all out. It was so good for him, and I was so relieved and happy. He was finally able to find his peace with you. I only hope you can find your peace with us as well.

He loves you so much, and he misses you so much. You have no idea. Whether you like it or not, or even see it that way, we're still your family and will think of you as our family too, forever. Really.

Love, Holly

229

May 16, 1989

Dear Trevor,

Just a note about Angus dying. I'm not surprised it was his liver, damn him. They're playing Torc all over the radio today as a tribute. It made me sad, and also made me think of you and the rest of the crew. I'm just so sad... We both are. John broke down and cried when he got the call. He's getting ready to fly to the funeral without me. I don't like traveling when I'm pregnant and this far along, so I'm staying home and sending loving thoughts in the direction of Angus... wherever he may be.

My grandmother died last year as well. We'd been back for visits at least twice a year or more, but she had a sudden stroke, and we weren't there when she passed. The weirdest part is how hard it was. It's almost harder to lose someone you had a bad relationship with than it is to lose someone you had a good relationship with. You have regrets, you know? You just can't put them to rest. I was so far away, and she was totally alone. It was more difficult for me than I would have expected. Thank God for John and Karen.

On the bright side, we're expecting the baby in June. Sonogram says it's a girl!!

Love, Holly

August 2, 1995

Dear Trevor,

We just got back from Sussex where we visited John's Aunt Ruby, who hasn't seen the children in a while. We don't make it out that way very often. It brought you to mind because John can't go back there without reminiscing about the two of you.

We have two children now. The oldest is a boy, 10 years old. Our second is a girl we named Claire, breaking my family's tradition of naming girls after various forms of vegetation. I'm trying to break lots of family traditions – that's kind of my life goal. Wish me luck. She's six, and she wants to be a veterinarian. Our son is learning violin, and he's very good. He wants to be a musician when he grows up, like his dad, who has a bass guitar ready and waiting for him. He begins his lessons shortly. John is very proud and excited!

Karen is still in London and doing well. It's so wonderful having her nearby! I wouldn't be nearly as happy without her here.

We bought a computer last year, and we're all fighting over it. We may even get another one! Do you have one yet? Isn't it all amazing? I just love it. I'm getting addicted to chat rooms and e-mail and online shopping. Yay!!

Love, Holly

November 30, 2006

Dear Trevor,

So how do you like getting a big manila envelope filled with 30 years' worth of letters all at once? I used to write letters to you out of habit whenever I wanted to share something with you, and then not mail them. I kept them all these years. Anyway, today I decided to finally send the letters to you. John has your last address in Australia, but I decided to send them to the house I'd always mailed my letters to, because I know you won't ever get them there. To be certain, I plugged your parents' address into an Internet address search and found someone else lives there now.

I'm leaving it all to the Fates, whether or not you receive this, and I'm not putting a return address on it because a very small part of me—say, 2.5 % of me—hopes these letters can still be forwarded. That part of me would be crushed if the envelope was returned.

The rest of me doesn't want to find out that you *did* get them because the rest of me knows how stupid and self-indulgent it would be to actually try to contact you to unburden myself. I know you could find us easily enough. I also know you never chose to in the last 26 years and never answered any of John's letters. Point taken. Nevertheless, I'm still pressing ahead, but I wanted to make certain before I mailed this that the coast was totally clear. If you receive it through some fluke, I am humbly sorry, but it is not my fault. Die, 2.5 percent girl!

I have a crazy reason for all this. I'm mailing all these letters because I had a dream about you last night. Then, as I was still having the dream, the clock radio switched on, and they were playing Van Morrison's "Brown Eyed Girl." That combination of dream and song completely unraveled me. It was like getting hit with a stun gun, and I'm still reeling from it. The universe really had it in for me today, I gather. Unbelievable. You hadn't crossed my mind for a long time until last night, but I woke up from the dream "feeling" you just like I did when I knew you.

In my dream, you were rereading all of my old letters, and you asked me, "Did you ever really love me?" The dream felt real, and you sounded anguished, as if it mattered to you a whole lot and you really didn't know. All day, ever since, I've had this "Trevor hangover," sensing and feeling you the way I did when we were together. It feels as though there's only a membrane separating us, and if I squinted hard enough in the right direction I could see you. My subconscious dredged up feelings I've had on ice for decades and made me worry that you never knew.

So now I'm mailing off letters that will never reach you because I'm hoping the same universe that sent me that dream and that song will let this message vibrate upward from the bottom of the dead-letter pile and reach you in a return dream. Or something. The bizarre way I've been feeling today, that makes perfect sense.

Yes, I did love you. I'm writing now, 30 years later, in response to your question in my dream, whether you ever see this or not, to tell you that I loved you very, very much. I still do. I have to. You're part of my heart.

I never told you how proud I am that you once asked me to marry you. From the moment I laid eyes on you, I thought seriously about marrying you and studied it the entire time we knew each other. I'd made a decision about us quite a while before you proposed, so I didn't have to think before giving you my answer: No. There was no question.

I know I handled things badly. My only excuse is that you caught me totally off-guard, and I panicked. Once I'd blurted it out, I couldn't soften it without telling you more than I wanted you to know at the time. Now my subconscious is catching up to me after 30 years, sending me reproaches in the form of a dream where I had to see and feel how much I hurt you. It's my fault, and I am deeply sorry if you've believed for all these years that I didn't love you.

I am so very sorry. Even if it doesn't matter to you at all after all this time, I need to say it: I am so sorry.

Did you have any inkling of how ill I was? I think I hid it from you pretty well. But, just three weeks before we met, I called a neighborhood dealer and asked him for a couple of dozen barbiturates. He'd known me since grade school and knew I didn't do drugs, so he came over without the pills and sat with me for hours, talking me out of killing myself. If I'd called anyone else, you and I would never have met.

That was the girl you wanted to marry. I am here to say that it is pure evil to commit suicide on the people who love you. After that, I vowed I wouldn't ever do it. I hung on tight, and that incident was as close as I ever came. But despair is a really tough enemy, and I came so close that time that I never felt entirely safe. That was how my mother went, if you remember. All it takes is for your resolve to slip just a little bit for just a little while, and poof! It's over, and you've destroyed everyone else, along with yourself. I couldn't promise you or myself that I wouldn't do it to you.

You also never saw the rages, the irritability, the mood swings, and the hostility. I could hold it in for short periods of time, long enough for you to get back on your bus and leave, but it got trickier to hide when you were around full time. I really believed, and it's probably true, that my only option was to have a relationship with you through the mail, and only be with you for short visits. That meant I couldn't marry you no matter how much I loved you, even if not marrying you meant losing you, and I knew it would.

I kept seeing you spending your life as my "keeper," following after me, trying to get me out of bed during my depressions, cleaning up embarrassing social messes, and explaining away my behavior to the band and to other people who were shocked or angry. I could always hear you in my head, fretting over what "the boys" thought of me. I couldn't tell you any of this because you would have been a hero and married me anyway, only to be really, really sorry later on. Or, you would have rejected me when you had a clear picture of the problems I was dealing with because I put your career at risk. Either way, I was scared.

I would have been the wife you couldn't take anywhere and didn't want to go home to. You'd recover from losing me, I knew that, but you might never have recovered from keeping me. So I didn't say anything and let you go.

Now, at 53, I know I had an obligation to tell you everything and let you make an informed decision. But put yourself into the head of a twenty-one-year-old girl who's emotionally ill and ashamed of it, and please try to understand. I made the decision for you because I wanted to do the right thing for someone I loved very much.

I didn't know it was fixable. Nobody did, back then. The depression turned out to be caused in part by malnutrition. I kept buying books to find the cause of it and paying a shrink to treat my depression instead of buying food. There's irony for you. Then I read about a study in Norway where they learned that some people can't process Vitamin B properly, so they're chronically deficient, even if they eat right. That deficiency triggers depression unless they take supplements. So, if you start out chronically deficient, and then don't eat at all, it's deadly. It turns out I have that condition, so I'm pretty certain my mother had it too. That may have been what killed her.

That's not all. Finally, years after I knew you, I was diagnosed with Borderline Personality Disorder. It's something that can happen if you're hyper-emotional and extremely sensitive, or if you're abused, neglected, or have some sort of trauma in childhood, which unfortunately I did. It's like a fracture, in a way. That was what caused the rages and the irritability and the rest of it. That condition can also make you suicidal. It doesn't respond to medication, but it usually improves on its own somewhat as you get older. I didn't know that when I was twenty-one.

Once they'd defined it as a condition, and I finally had a diagnosis, a therapist showed me how to manage it. I'm fixed—really—and in amazingly good shape. But back then, nobody really knew much about it, or what was wrong, or what to do with me.

I wouldn't marry John for four years because of it. I gave him a slew of "No's." He would wait a while and then ask again. "I may be deferred, but I will not be deterred," he always said. It got to be kind of a joke between us. By the time I was 30, it had gotten milder, especially because I was eating properly, so I wasn't afraid anymore. Plus, we'd already been tested, living and touring together for years, and we always moved past the bumps. We were still really good together and getting better.

You should have seen him when I finally said, "Yes," and let him put that ring on my finger. He'd already made up his mind before morning, after we met up again at the comeback concert in 1980. He slipped out and bought a diamond ring while I was still asleep. He needed help from the hotel concierge because the stores weren't even open yet, but he prevailed and found a ring, and I woke up to a marriage proposal.

I said no, but this time I explained why. I told him what he could expect with me and asked him if he was still willing to try. He said yes. I asked him if he was sure about that. He said yes. I told him a long distance relationship was all we could realistically ever have. He said no, absolutely not, that we'd work through it. He wore me down and had me with him in days, in a state of "pre-engagement." I made him wait years in that state, so he stashed the ring away on a shelf, pulled it out occasionally to ask again, then put it back. I told him it was for his own good.

He's put up with a lot from me over the years. He's a good man, our John.

The important thing is this: When you have this condition and it's untreated, it's as devastating to the people you're close to as it is to you. I understood that without being told. John got the milder end of it because I was so much older and had figured out some coping strategies, but it was still pretty bad for him sometimes in those early years.

You, however, knew me when it was at its peak, so it would have been far worse. It wouldn't be necessary for me to let you go if we'd been born later and met now, but I made the right decision for us in 1975. I spared you years of grief, and I spared myself the despair, frustration, and guilt of being a burden to you, and failing at marriage because of what I was and couldn't help.

But even that wasn't the whole story.

I always knew that you loved Beth and that she loved you. I also know you loved me. I never questioned that. After we met, you got rid of every piece of jewelry and every stitch of clothing from every woman you'd ever received a gift from. I knew you had boundaries you'd never cross, like remaining emotionally attached to someone when you were seriously involved with someone else. Those presents represented emotional attachments to you, and you severed all of them for me.

The big tip-off was that crocheted sweater Beth made for you. You never gave up that sweater, not even when I asked you to, and for that reason, I knew that you loved her a little bit more than me. I was realistic. I saw the sweater every time you came, so every time you came, I knew you hadn't picked me, not really. If you hadn't kept wearing it, I would probably have made you take your chances with me despite everything. There's no telling what kind of disaster it all would have led to. The sweater saved you.

The way I saw it, you and she stood a much better chance than you and I did, so I always knew I'd done the right thing. If you'd married me, you not only would have had to settle for your second choice, but marriage to me would have been a nasty surprise.

I would have had to *be* the second choice and the nasty surprise. That's almost worse. And it isn't that I didn't trust you, but sometimes love is conditional in ways you can't predict until you're actually faced with those conditions. Sometimes it dies, and sometimes it turns bitter and ugly. I had no control over what I was experiencing and no control over how you might feel about it or react to it in the long term, especially after I'd had

235

years to wear you down. Even you have your limits.

Everything happened the way it was supposed to. I always knew on account of that sweater that I was only borrowing you for a little while and that I'd eventually have to give you back to her.

I also knew that if you had found something in her to love for so many years, then she was someone I could entrust you to. I would trust anyone you love who loves you, and I knew she'd take better care of you than I could. I believed in my heart that she would. I still believe in my heart that she did, and that you have had a good life and been happy all this time. That's what I wanted for you, but I knew I couldn't give it to you myself.

I hope you understand and can forgive me.

My love – *OUR* love – forever and always,

Holly

Made in the USA
Lexington, KY
03 February 2013